MARKED *fur* MURDER

DIXIE LYLE

St. Martin's Paperbacks

This is a work of fiction. All of the characters, organizations, and events portrayed in this novel are either products of the author's imagination or are used fictitiously.

MARKED FUR MURDER

Copyright © 2015 by Dixie Lyle.

For information address St. Martin's Press, 175 Fifth Avenue, New York, NY 10010.

5550 7213

ISBN: 978-1-250-03109-9

4/15

Printed in the United States of America

St. Martin's Paperbacks edition / April 2015

St. Martin's Paperbacks are published by St. Martin's Press, 175 Fifth Avenue, New York, NY 10010.

10 9 8 7 6 5 4 3 2 1

CHAPTER ONE

You can't kill a Thunderbird with lightning.

That's what I desperately wanted to tell the investigating detective, a square-shouldered black man with a neatly trimmed beard at odds with his tangle of dreadlocks. His name was Officer Forrester, he was a new hire for the Hartville Police Force, and he was currently questioning me—Deidre Foxtrot Lancaster—as part of a homicide investigation.

It shouldn't even have needed to be stated. It should have been glaringly obvious that a supernatural being descended from an ancient Indian tribe of weather spirits—spirits that tossed around thunderbolts like they were baseballs—would sneer at a few hundred volts of house current.

But that was in my world, a decidedly weird place stocked with ghost pets, reincarnated cats, telepathic canines, and the occasional animal deity. Lieutenant Forrester's day-to-day existence was no doubt a bit more mundane; the only Thunderbirds he dealt with were the kind either involved in fender-benders or reported stolen.

Forrester and I were not hunched over a scarred wooden

table in a windowless, locked room for our interrogation, either; no, we were seated in a large, comfortable space lit by a wall made of glass, both of us sunk into oversized beanbag chairs of neon orange and pink. ZZ was redecorating again.

"Sorry about the chairs," I said for the third time. I don't normally repeat myself, but I was kind of in shock. "My boss doesn't just embrace change, she kisses it. With tongue."

<Oh, for God's sake. Quit apologizing—it makes you look guilty as hell.>

That rough, raspy voice was Tango. She was the black-and-white tuxedo cat currently curled up and purring in my lap. She and I could communicate just by thinking—

[Don't be absurd, Tango. He's obviously a professional, and as such will shortly eliminate Foxtrot as a suspect.]

—and those deep, cultured tones belonged to Whiskey, the dog lying at my feet. He was an Australian cattle dog (though his accent was British), sometimes known as a blue heeler, and looked a little like two dogs smushed together: His chest and legs resembled those of a golden retriever, while his upper half was speckled black, white, and gray. One of his eyes was blue and the other one was brown, which added to the effect.

He was also—technically—dead. Looked, smelled, and felt like an ordinary dog, but actually made of ectoplasm. That's what allowed him to shift his shape into any other breed of dog, of any size or shape. He could communicate with me telepathically, too.

Get that look off your face. I am *not* crazy.

My *life,* however . . . that's pretty much nuts. Aside from the ghost dog and the reincarnated cat (did I forget to mention that part? Life number seven, in case you were wondering), there was also what I did for a living. And the non-living, I guess.

Officer Forrester and I were in the sitting room of the

Zoransky mansion, situated on the Zoransky estate, which abuts one of the largest pet cemeteries in the continental United States. The estate was home to my boss, Zelda Zoransky, her son, Oscar, and a private zoo that cares for animals who need it. I was ZZ's administrative assistant, which meant I handled not only all the day-to-day details of the estate but also the minutiae of ZZ's hobbies and interests, which were legion.

Oh, and I looked after the graveyard, too.

Not the grounds themselves—that was done by a sixties survivor named Cooper—but all the animal souls within. And by "look after," I mean protect from danger. The Great Crossroads was a mystical nexus where dead pets could leave their respective afterlives via one grave and hop, swim, trot, or crawl to the human one via another. It was sometimes called the Rainbow Bridge, but there was no actual bridge involved—just a constant swarm of the furry, scaly, or feathered formerly-alive on their way to visit the humans who loved them in this life and now love them in another. Love, it turns out, beats death.

None of which had much to do with my conversation with Officer Forrester, though. That was mostly about the body in the swimming pool.

Forrester finished writing something down on his notepad, looked up, and smiled. "All right, I think I've got everything I need about the deceased and how the body was discovered. I'd like to ask you a few questions about the people currently staying in the house. You said Ms. Zoransky is hosting a saloon?"

I nodded, then knocked back a huge gulp of Irish breakfast tea from my Three Investigators mug. "Salon. It's an old Victorian tradition—get a bunch of interesting personalities together to engage in lively discussion. ZZ invites all sorts of people to stay here, where they can eat and drink and generally indulge themselves. The amenities of the estate are provided free of charge, the only rule being that everyone has to show up for supper. She likes a nice mix of politics, popular entertainers, and science, usually."

"So I wasn't imagining things—that really *was* Keene?"

I nodded. "Our semi-resident rock star, yeah. He likes it here, comes back a lot. He's always an interesting dinner guest, so ZZ's given him a standing invitation." I sounded fine—calm and in control—but that was more out of sheer habit than anything else. When I'm in crisis mode, you could blow up a car fifty feet away and I'd have noted the make and model before all the wreckage had hit the ground. It has nothing to do with being brave, just years of training.

But that wasn't how I felt. Inside, I was screaming.

"Who else?" Forrester asked.

"Let's see. Teresa Firstcharger. She's an aboriginal rights activist. She contacted ZZ and asked if she could attend."

"Is that usual? People asking to attend?"

"Sure. Her salons are very popular. But the main reason ZZ said yes was because Teresa had some influential friends vouch for her. She's a rock star in the activist world, gets a lot of celebrities to endorse her cause. Johnny Depp is one of her supporters. But she has kind of a reputation, too."

Forrester tapped his pen against his knee. "What sort of reputation?"

"Well, she rubs elbows with a lot of rich and famous people. And some people claim she's *all* elbows."

"Any truth to that?"

I shrugged. "Some. Unfortunately, one of her elbowees was also one of our guests. Who was here with his wife."

"Things got ugly?"

"Things got deadly. You saw what we fished out of the pool." It was a glib and heartless thing to say, but I'm one of those people who use humor to deal with pain. Right then, I was doing my best to put a wall of bad jokes topped with razor-sharp wit around my feelings so I could keep functioning; on the other side of that wall was a whole lot of hurt. From the look on Forrester's face, I'm guessing he'd encountered this kind of reaction before.

"Uh-huh," he said. "So was there some sort of confrontation?"

"You could say that. The Metcalfes were talking in the lounge when Teresa arrived. She walked right up and—well, she was very blunt. Told him he could do better and she should get lost. I thought there was going to be a fist-fight."

"How did Mr. Metcalfe take it?"

"He was embarrassed and angry. His wife was . . . just angry."

"All right. Who else is a guest?"

"Let's see. Have you heard of Theodora Bonkle?"

"I'm afraid not."

"She's an author. Writes mysteries and children's books; I'm a fan, and so is ZZ. Theodora's an interesting person in her own right, too."

Forrester glanced at his pad, scribbled something down. "Oh? How so?"

"Well, the fact that she used to be a he is hardly worth mentioning when compared with the rest of her life. Theodora suffers from schizophrenia, which led to her being hospitalized at one point. She was placed on medication to help control her hallucinations, which worked—but as it turned out, the drugs blunted her creativity so much she couldn't write. She mounted a legal challenge to be taken off them for specific periods of time, and won."

Forrester frowned. "So the court agreed it's her right to be crazy?"

"Only now and then. And yes, this is one of the thens."

"Okay . . . anybody else?"

"Dr. Efram Fimsby. He's an exotic meteorologist, an expert on unusual weather patterns. Climate change is one of ZZ's current obsessions, so he's here to talk about global warming and storm systems and things like that. Like Theodora, it's his first time here. Oh, and Rustam Gorshkov. He's an animal psychic."

Forrester raised his eyebrows. "He reads animals' minds?"

<Nobody reads a mind, Einstein,> Tango remarked. <A brain isn't a book.>

[And if it were,] Whiskey added, [yours would undoubtedly be a softcover. You do understand the inherent pointlessness in telling someone they can't read your mind by making a telepathic comment they can't hear?]

Tango yawned and stretched, extending one paw as far as she could and stretching her toes so the claws popped out. <I was being ironic.>

"That's what Mr. Gorshkov claims," I said. "But it's a little more complicated than that. See, he has a dog that paints."

"A dog that paints."

"Yes. He says it's a collaboration—he stands a short distance away and concentrates, and the dog paints what he tells her to."

"Oooookay . . ."

I tried for another gulp of tea, but it was empty. I set the mug down on the floor, regretfully. "And that's about it. I've already given you a list of the household staff, and who was here last night."

He nodded. "Yes, thank you. You're very organized. There's one more thing before you go, though."

I knew what he was going to ask, of course.

<Here it comes.>

[If he didn't ask, it would mean he was incompetent.]

Forrester looked up from his notes and made eye contact with me. "What exactly was your relationship with the victim?"

"We weren't close. In fact, we hadn't known each other for very long."

"But her brother works here."

"Yes. I know him . . . quite a bit better."

Forrester's eyes softened. "How's he holding up?"

"Ben's sister is dead," I said. "He's not doing that well."

The victim's name was Anna Metcalfe. Ben Montain, her brother, was ZZ's head chef—and my boyfriend.

He was also a Thunderbird. So was his sister.

This wasn't the estate's first murder investigation, but it wasn't a common enough occurrence that I'd evolved a routine to deal with it. Yet. I was already making lists in my head for the next one, though:

1. Compose schedule for questioning of staff.
2. Line up possible replacement in case of incarceration or death of staff member.
3. Update résumé in case of murder of employer.
4. Find less stressful line of work.

But I very much doubted anyone on the staff had killed Anna. One of the guests, though—that was another matter.

When Forrester had left, I took Whiskey downstairs while Tango elected to nap. He trotted beside me, his nails making little clicking noises on the polished hardwood. [So. A Thunderbird, killed by electricity. Doesn't seem possible, does it?]

"Not in the least. I need to talk to Ben—" At that moment I heard the air-conditioning die. I notice little details like that, because little details like that make up my whole life—not just noticing them, but being responsible for them. And the air-conditioning should definitely have been on, since it was a hot and sunny day. I groaned and pulled out my cell phone.

As it turned out, it wasn't just the air-conditioning that had died, it was the power for the whole house. And when I went to look at the fuse box in the basement, I found out why—all the breakers had been tripped. I reset them, studied the equipment for a moment, then headed upstairs for the kitchen.

Which is where Whiskey and I found Ben, of course. He wore a crisp white apron and a look of embarrassment on his face. "Foxtrot. There's something you should probably know—"

"We just had a surge that knocked out the power. Did you notice?"

"Well, yeah—"

"Of course, the fancy new equipment ZZ just had installed told me where the surge came from."

The embarrassment on his face deepened. He's got a good face, all rugged lines and planes that show traces of his Native American heritage, though most people miss that due to the blond hair. Anyway, it's a good face, even when embarrassed. "So, yeah, about that—"

"It came from this kitchen," I said. "And on an entirely unrelated note, what's that?" I pointed.

"It's an electric hand mixer."

"It's not in very good shape."

"That's because I kind of—took it apart."

"That explains all the exposed wiring. Not so sure about that weird smell, though. Sort of like burning insulation, or maybe melting plastic? With just a touch of ozone."

His expression had gone from embarrassed to abashed to downright sheepish. "Just stop, okay? I was doing an experiment."

"Let me guess. Said experiment involved exposing a

known Thunderbird to house current in order to see if it would *kill* him?"

"It didn't."

"I can see that. But that doesn't mean it wasn't excessively stupid."

He shook his head. "I'm sorry if I fried anything. But this proves exactly what I told you: There's no way Anna was electrocuted. A hundred and twenty volts didn't even tickle, Foxtrot. So how could it have killed her?"

"I don't know, Ben." Anna had been found floating face-down in the swimming pool, with a plugged-in electric hair dryer in the water next to the edge. Official cause of death hadn't been announced yet, but the medical examiner's opinion was that it was a case of electric shock drowning, something that usually only occurred around marinas. Docked boats connected to a power source on land formed a large, floating electrical grid; if that grid wasn't 100 percent secure, voltage could leak into the surrounding water. Anyone swimming into one of these electrified zones would find their muscles paralyzed, leading quickly to drowning.

Unless, of course, they were supernaturally immune to the effects of electricity.

"Anna wasn't electrocuted, she drowned," I said. "Which means that the hair dryer was tossed in after the fact to make her death look like something it wasn't. What we don't know is who did it or why."

[But we shall find out, Ben. I promise you.]

Ben glanced down at Whiskey and nodded. "Thanks. That means a lot."

Ben and I are the only two around here who know about Whiskey and Tango's true nature, and we try to keep it that way. Both Anna and Ben only recently learned about their Thunderbird heritage, and this was the first time they'd seen each other since Anna discovered what she was, told Ben, then bolted for another continent—Australia, to be exact. She was worried that her newfound powers would spiral out of control, causing hurricanes or tornadoes or worse, and the remoteness of the outback was the best short-term solution she could come up with. Ben could have done the same, but he decided to stay put and deal with it.

Her worries proved unfounded. Australia wasn't racked by unexpected storms, and Ben—after a bumpy start, and some help from yours truly—got his own abilities under control fairly quickly.

This was supposed to be a triumphant reunion. It hadn't turned out that way.

Oscar walked into the kitchen. Oscar Zoransky is ZZ's son, a man in his middle thirties who carries himself like an aristocrat, believes alcohol to be one of the major food groups, and has the ethics of a man always trying to invent a better snake oil. Oscar never met a scheme he didn't immediately buy a drink, take out for dinner, and wake up naked in a Vegas hotel with. He dresses well, is almost as clever as he thinks he is, and sounds a lot like Higgins from *Magnum, PI.*

"Ah," he said. "My condolences on the passing of your sister, chef. Foxtrot, if I might have a moment of your time?"

Ben waved a silent good-bye and vanished into his office. I did my best not to sigh. "What is it, Oscar?"

"It's the accommodations for Kaci and Rustam. They simply won't do."

"What's wrong now?"

"The bedroom you put them in isn't suitable. The view is too bland."

"Mr. Gorshkov objects to the view?"

Oscar shook his head. "No, Kaci does. She informed Rustam that it wasn't stimulating enough for one of her artistic temperament."

The sigh I was trying to suppress made another escape attempt, which I narrowly foiled. "Fine, I'll have them moved to a suite in the west wing, overlooking the gardens. Will that be satisfactory?"

Oscar raised his eyebrows. "I shall inquire forthwith. And really, Foxtrot, don't take that tone with me. We all put up with your canine companion without complaining; the least you can do is show a little professional courtesy to a fellow enthusiast."

[Fellow enthusiast? I'm a dog, not a model railroad.]

I reached down and scratched behind Whiskey's ears. "Pay no attention to the man, Whiskey. We enjoy you, we don't 'put up' with you."

<Speak for yourself, Toots.> Tango strolled up, yawning. I wasn't quite sure how she'd gotten into the kitchen, but cats have their ways. <One dog in the house is bad enough. Two verges on abuse.>

Oscar reached down and stroked Tango. She butted against his legs, purring. "A pity Rustam couldn't have found a talented feline, instead. I've always been more of a cat person."

<Tell him that's redundant. Not liking cats automatically disqualifies you from personhood.>

[Whereas liking them qualifies you for sainthood.]

<What's your point?>

[Saints are used to suffering. And being kind to the insane.]

Oscar straightened up. "Thank you, Foxtrot. I'll inform Rustam." He nodded and strolled out of the kitchen.

I went in search of Shondra, ZZ's head of security, and found her in her office, studying video footage on the bank of monitors across from her desk. Shondra was ex-military, short and lithe and lethal, dressed in plain black pants and a blue dress shirt with creases sharp enough to shave with. She flicked a glance my way when I entered, and motioned for me to sit down with the mug of coffee she held.

"Find anything?" I asked. Whiskey sat down at my feet.

"Only that no one entered or left the estate last night between ten PM and seven AM. There's no cameras out by the pool, of course."

"What do you think happened?"

Shondra scowled. "Someone died. That's all I know."

"But?"

"But who uses a hair dryer out by the pool? There wasn't even an outlet close enough—she had to plug in an extension cord. Where did she even find one?"

"There was one in the cabana. We keep it there in case we need to run power out to the pool."

"But not *in* the pool."

"Not usually, no."

"You think she was suicidal?"

I blinked. "I barely knew her. But nothing Ben's told me would indicate that."

"I doubt it, too. If people want to electrocute themselves, they use a bathtub. Nice and private. Nobody throws an electrical appliance into a pool and then dives in after it."

"So you think someone killed her?"

Shondra didn't reply at first, just gave me a hard stare. It's pretty much the only stare she has, and I'm used to it. After a moment she said, "I think it's a definite possibility."

"So do I. Especially after the fight she had with her husband."

"I wasn't there, but I hear it was epic."

"That it was. Firstcharger is a real piece of work. She does a lot of good for her community, but I've met bulldozers that were more sensitive to other people's feelings."

"You think she'd kill to get what she wanted?"

I frowned. "I don't know. It doesn't seem very likely, does it? Picking a public fight like that beforehand?"

"Murders aren't always elaborately planned, Foxtrot. Usually they happen in the heat of the moment and everything afterward is a desperate attempt to hide the evidence."

She had a point. Murder was most often a poorly thought-out impulse with an obvious perpetrator—unfortunately, none of *those* murderers seemed to know about this place. We attracted the kind who killed with an esoteric poison derived from ground-up tapeworms delivered via blowgun while disguised as a shrub.

[You forgot the part where they escape in their flying submarine.]

Sorry. Thinking too loud again?

[Perhaps a tad.]

"How's ZZ taking this?" Shondra asked.

"I don't know. She's in her room and asked not to be disturbed. But if I had to hazard a guess, I'd say not well."

Which bothered me a lot. ZZ was like a force of nature herself; she could be as unpredictable as a tornado, as relentless as a hurricane, or as brilliantly cheerful as a sunny day. Anger, grief, or a steely resolve to get to the bottom of things were all reactions I'd expect. Hiding in her room was not.

"She'll probably be down for dinner," I said. "She never misses those."

"What about Ben? How's he?"

"Shaken up but soldiering on. I told him he could take some time off if he needed it, but refused. Needs to cook to take his mind off it, he says."

Shondra gave me a knowing look. "I hear that."

"Yeah. The more you do, the less you have to think. It can be therapeutic, give you time to process below the surface."

"As long as you don't overdo it. When my mom died, my dad started working seventy-hour weeks. Worked so hard at avoiding the grief he almost ran himself right into a grave next to her. Keep an eye on Ben, okay?"

"I will."

I told her I'd talk to her later, and Whiskey and I continued our rounds. Next up was Dr. Efram Fimsby, the meteorologist from Australia. I found him in the library, looking through one of ZZ's art books, a collection of photographs from the turn of the century.

Fimsby was a tall man in his fifties, with a round belly and a scruffy white beard. He wore a tattered brown sweater that looked like he'd mugged a scarecrow at pitchfork-point, and brown corduroy trousers. He looked up when Whiskey and I walked in and smiled. "Hello, Foxtrot! Just enjoying your esteemed employer's literary treasure trove. Eclectic, to say the least."

"True. I doubt many people have a signed copy of Madonna's *Sex* book and a first edition of *Origin of Species*. Or at least not shelved together."

He chuckled. "Well, they both ultimately deal with the same subject, don't they? Mating, and the inevitable consequences thereof. Evolution, in all her terrible glory."

"I don't think I've ever heard it put quite that way before," I said. "But I think Ms. Ciccone would approve. Or possibly make it into a music video."

"Yes, that seems likely. What can I do for you, Foxtrot?"

"I was just wondering if you'd spoken to the police yet. Lieutenant Forrester said he planned on talking to everyone, but I wasn't sure if he'd gotten to you."

"Oh, yes, the detective. He did, in fact. Turns out I was the last one to see her alive, actually."

I hadn't known that. "Really? When did you speak to her?"

"Last night, up in my room. She came to me for advice

about a rather sensitive matter." He hesitated, looking solemn. "So sensitive I was forced to lie to the police. I told them I only talked to her briefly in the corridor, when she was on her way to the pool."

[Ah. *Now* we're getting somewhere.]

"What did she ask your advice about, Dr. Fimsby?"

"Her circumstances, Foxtrot. She'd recently undergone a rather significant change in her life, and was now worried about the consequences. So much so she thought someone might try to do her harm."

"And now she's dead. I understand you trying to protect her privacy, but—"

"It's not her I'm trying to protect, Foxtrot. It's her brother. You see, I'm worried that whoever killed her will try to kill him, too."

CHAPTER TWO

I stared at Fimsby for a second before replying. "And what," I said carefully, "makes you think she was murdered?"

"Because they shared a secret, Foxtrot. One I'm afraid I can't reveal. But Anna told me about you and Ben, which is why I'm telling you this now. You need to convince him that he's in danger."

"Wait. This is all too murky and mysterious for me. Why would Anna even confide in you in the first place?"

"We didn't meet here by chance, Foxtrot. Did you know she'd recently been to Australia? She contacted me there, asked me some very odd questions. I helped her, as best I could, and she convinced me to come here to meet with her brother, as well."

"But—ZZ was the one who invited you."

Fimsby looked uncomfortable. "We enlisted her aid as a ruse. She disliked lying to you, but we persuaded her it was in everyone's best interest. I'm sure she feels terrible, now."

"I'm sure she does. She's retreated to her bedroom and won't talk to anyone."

"Not even you?"

"I haven't tried yet. When ZZ says she wants to be alone, she means it."

While true enough, that had more to do with respecting my boss's wishes than any physical limitations. If it was important enough, I could reach ZZ by just pounding on her door and yelling—but it would take a dire emergency for me to resort to those measures, and this was hardly that.

But whether or not to bother ZZ was the least of my problems.

[Foxtrot. Do you think it's possible Fimsby is aware that Anna and Ben are Thunderbirds?]

I don't know, Whiskey. Fimsby's a specialist in exotic weather patterns. He's from Australia. When Anna's abilities first manifested, she ran for the biggest, emptiest place she could think of, the Australian outback. And Fimsby said she'd come to him for advice on an unusual problem . . .

[But that doesn't mean he *knows.* And even if he does, he doesn't know that you know.]

I know. Which means that admitting I know is a big no-no, in case what he knows isn't what I think he knows. You know?

[Is it just me, or has that word lost all meaning?]

"While I understand the need to respect Anna's privacy," I said, "we're discussing this while she's on the way to the coroner. If it's true that Ben's life is also in danger, then I think you need to be a little more forthcoming."

I gave him my best Shondra-stare, locking eyes and projecting resolve. He stared back, his features composed but stern.

[Don't back down, Foxtrot. Think fierce thoughts—that's the key to winning a staredown.]

I did my best. I thought about Vikings rushing into battle waving their swords in the air. I thought about Zulus charging into the fray with their spears held aloft. I thought about Maori warriors making menacing faces as they bellowed at their foes.

The last one was a mistake, though. Maoris think sticking their tongues out makes them look scary, and they cover their faces with intricate tattoos that in my overstressed imagination looked more like the face of a dad who had fallen asleep in the presence of a toddler with a Magic Marker. Totally ruined my staredown mojo.

"I wish that I could," Fimsby said at last. "But it's not my place. I promised Anna I would tell no one, and I must honor that promise even in light of her death. If you knew the secret, you would understand."

He paused. I waited. After a moment, he continued. "Please, just tell Ben what I've told you. I don't want to approach him directly."

"Why not?"

"We are not the only ones involved, Foxtrot. Discretion is called for."

[He smells of fear. Whatever he's talking about, he's genuinely afraid.]

Whiskey, the nose that always knows. "I'll let him know."

"Thank you. And Foxtrot—tell him I'm sorry for his loss. The death of a sibling is always devastating."

I nodded. "Excuse me. We'll talk more later."

"Certainly."

Whiskey and I left.

As soon as we were out of earshot, I said, "He doesn't know I know."

[Are you sure?]

"Yes. That long pause? He was hoping I'd admit I was in the loop. I did my best to seem clueless instead. Think he bought it?"

[I can smell fear, not satisfaction, so I have no idea. However, you do feign innocence quite convincingly.]

"Thanks. I'll call on you as a character witness at my trial, okay?"

[And why would you be on trial?]

I looked down at him, opened my eyes as wide as they could go, and blinked once. "Golly, mister. I have no idea. I really, really, don't."

[I'll send you a cake with a file in it. It's your only hope.]

"Didn't know dogs could bake."

[We can't. You're doomed.]

We were on our way to talk to Ben—mysterious warnings about murder and family secrets tend to jump right to the top of my to-do list—when we were interrupted by a very distinctive noise: a rhythmic grunting. Were this coming from the gym, the zoo, or even one of the bedrooms, I would have ignored it—but the sound was emanating from the breakfast nook just off the front hall. I poked my head in to see what was making it, and found Miss Theodora Bonkle.

Miss, not Ms., by her own insistence. Approximate age, mid-forties. Dressed in a peasant frock, sturdy walking shoes, and a loose-fitting white blouse. Brown, frizzy hair pulled back in a sensible bun. A wide, rugged face wearing a tad too much makeup and thick, tortoiseshell glasses.

Muscular, tattooed arms, currently pumping iron.

She was sitting on a wooden kitchen chair, brow furrowed in concentration, one manicured hand hefting a shiny silver barbell up and down. It was a bit incongruous, like finding Popeye in drag.

She noticed me and smiled, perspiration running down her face. "Oh! Hello, dear. I was just getting in a few reps before indulging in a cup of tea. Would you care to join me?"

"In the tea, sure. You know we have a fully equipped gym, don't you?"

Theodora put down the barbell, picked up a napkin, and dabbed at her face. "Oh, I know, dear. But lifting weights helps me think; it oxygenates the blood, giving brain cells that extra little boost·they sometimes need. Add a little caffeine, and *voilà*! A recipe for inspiration."

"Sounds good to me," I said. I sat down, noting that Theodora already had two cups and a teapot in a cozy on the table before her. "Are you expecting company?"

"Not exactly." She had a slightly breathy, soft voice that seemed to be from another century. "Considering the parameters of this gathering, I figured that anyone who happened by was fair game. I find that the only thing better at stimulating creativity than tea and exercise is a good conversation."

I laughed and sat down. "Well, I'm glad to see you're embracing the spirit of the event."

Whiskey stayed on his feet, his head cocked as he studied Theodora. "Hello, sweetie," Theodora said. She put out her hand, and Whiskey sniffed it. "How are you? Some of my friends aren't fond of dogs, but I certainly am."

[Hmmm. She smells of rabbit.]

She probably owns one. In fact, Theodora Bonkle owned at least one, though not in the physical sense; one of her more famous creations was a character named Doc Wabbit, a trickster who spent as much time getting into trouble as he did solving mysteries. His partner was a kind and gentle soul named Very British Bear, who rescued DW as often as he needed rescuing himself. They were the heroes of a series of children's books called *We Solve Everything!* where they had grand adventures while answering some of life's Big Questions: Where do lost socks go? Why do people have to take baths? What makes air invisible?

But those weren't the only books Theodora wrote. Oh, no.

She also wrote mysteries, under the name T. B. Kloben.

They starred an investigator named Killian, a man with a dark past that is never fully explained. He seems to be seeking redemption for terrible things he's done, though what those things are is only hinted at. None of the people he helps know him—in fact, most of them don't want his help, at least at first. Killian's approach is to look for trouble, insert himself into a situation he doesn't understand, and refuse to go away until he's made things better. He doesn't care if people like him, he doesn't care about consequences, he doesn't care about rules. The one certainty he carries with him is that there is *always* something good to be accomplished, as long as you stick it out to the bitter end. He always does.

The first book was called *The Meddler,* and to date had sold two million copies. He was a classic example of an unlikable character you wound up rooting for anyway; a movie was currently in development, with Dwayne Johnson rumored to be taking on the lead role.

I loved both series, even though I didn't have kids. I was the one who'd introduced ZZ to the books, and she was the one who told me to invite Theodora to a salon—despite Miss Bonkle's ongoing psychiatric problems.

"How are you settling in?" I asked, pouring myself a cup of tea. What I really wanted to know, of course, was exactly how crazy she was at the moment—not that I could ask that.

"I'm fine, thank you for asking. However, Very British Bear has a question."

The smile froze on my face. I could actually feel little icicles forming on my cheekbones.

"Yes?" I managed.

"He wants to know if you really have a honey badger here. Doc's been telling him that honey badgers eat anything that's overly sweet, and Very's a bit worried."

I studied her face. Whiskey studied her face.

[She can't be serious.]

I think she's serious.

[She's pulling your leg.]

If so, feel free to start calling me Hoppy. "We do have a honey badger in the menagerie. But we keep it securely locked up, so Very has nothing to worry about."

Theodora nodded. "Well, I'll try to reassure him, but he tends to take Doc at his word. God knows why." She rolled her eyes.

And then there was a pause.

It wasn't one of those pauses where both people just happen to fall silent at the same time because neither of them knows what to say. It wasn't one of those pauses that occur because one person has just dropped a conversational bombshell and the other person doesn't know how to respond. No, it was an *expectant* pause; the kind that seems to last nine months and gets more and more uncomfortable as it grows. The kind that eventually gives birth to a response that's more blurt than reply.

"Well," I said weakly. "Both of them are . . . short."

Theodora raised one plucked eyebrow. "Short?"

"And . . . furry."

[And imaginary.]

My smile was now so firmly fixed you couldn't have gotten it off my face with a crowbar, though I desperately wished someone would try. A nice blow to the head—at the moment, that sounded heavenly. I kept waiting for Theodora to give me a wink, a grin, anything to let me know she was kidding.

"Short and furry," she mused. "I suppose that's true. Can't be easy, going through this world being their size and species. Bears get a certain amount of respect, but rabbits? It's no wonder Doc acts the way he does."

[Also, there's the whole non-existence problem. By which I mean they don't exist.]

"Then it's a good thing they have each other. And you," I said.

[They don't have anything, Foxtrot. They're fictional. One's null, the other void. They have neither pulse, breath, nor voice. The state of their reality isn't. If they had a family crest, it would be a zero rampant on a field of nothing. When their names are announced at roll call, only silence ensues. Their glasses are half empty and half gone. They are, to put it simply, *not*.]

Have you been watching Monty Python reruns late at night again?

[You know I despise television. But John Cleese *is* a genius.]

"I wish I could stay and chat more," I said. "But I have some rather urgent business with our chef. If you'll excuse me?"

"Yes, of course." She nodded graciously and smiled. She didn't seem crazy at all, except maybe in a Norman-Bates's–mother sort of way. Who was, you know, actually Norman Bates in a dress. After he'd killed his mother.

Norman Bates didn't have forearms like a stevedore, though.

"He said *what*?" Ben asked me. We were in the kitchen, Ben chopping vegetables for dinner.

"That Anna came to him for advice. That he knows a great big secret about Anna and you but won't tell me what it is. That ZZ and he and Anna arranged this get-together, and that you're in danger."

Ben gestured with his knife. "But—that sounds like he knows about me and Anna being Thunderbirds! And ZZ, too!"

"Not necessarily. He was very cagey when I talked to him, which means he might have done the same thing with ZZ. I'm not sure how much he actually knows."

"He's a weather expert, Trot. I don't think Anna went to him for fashion tips."

"Granted. But let's not overplay our hand here. He's being really careful, and so should we. If someone killed Anna, that someone could very well be after you, too."

"Let them try," Ben said grimly. "They killed my sister. I'm going to make them *pay*."

At that very instant there was a menacing rumble of thunder. It wasn't a coincidence, ironic or otherwise—and I didn't have to look any farther than Ben's eyes to find the lightning that went with it. "Hold on there, cloud cowboy. I know you're angry, but keep in mind *what* you are, too; lose your temper and somebody else might pay the price. Somebody like every person on the eastern seaboard."

"All right, all right. Point taken."

"No, *I'm* the one taking point. As in, I'll find out who did this, and why. Then, if you still want to introduce them to the business end of a tornado, I'll understand. But there's two very important things I want you to keep in mind: One, we don't know for sure this is related to you and Anna being Thunderbirds; and two . . ."

"What?"

"Two is that we've both learned there are some very scary things out there in the universe. And birds—even Thunderbirds—aren't always at the top of the food chain."

That tamped down his anger a little. He knew exactly what I was talking about. "Yeah, okay. But there are two things *you* should keep in mind: First of all, it's really goddamn unlikely some big, scary supernatural being would bother throwing a hair dryer into a swimming pool to cover up a murder."

He paused. I waited.

"What's the second thing?"

He scowled at me. "I don't have one. Really thought

something would come to me by the time I was finished with thing one, but no go."

I tried not to smile. He was angry and hurting and had every right to be, but he was also downright adorable. "Take it easy, sweetie. Whoever or whatever is to blame, I'll find out what's going on. I promise."

"I know you will. Just be careful."

"I will, don't worry. You should, too—and you can start by staying away from Fimsby. Whatever he knows, he's being cautious for a reason. It might seem like confronting him and demanding he talk is the way to go, but it's really not. What if *he's* the killer? Maybe this is just a way to draw you out, make you expose yourself."

Ben considered this. He put the knife down on the counter, carefully. "Huh. But you said he knew about Anna and me—"

"I said he knew *something* about Anna and you. He didn't specify, and I got the feeling he was fishing for information. Don't get all worked up and jump right into his net, all right?"

He gave me a grudging nod. "Fine. I'll avoid him. What if he approaches me?"

"Play dumb. Plead the Fifth. You know nothing, see nothing, hear nothing, and besides, you were home watching TV. Got it?"

"Jawohl, mein fraulein."

"Was that a *Hogan's Heroes* joke?"

"Don't judge me. I watch *Barney Miller* and *The Mary Tyler Moore Show,* too."

"Y'know, I think I'm going to pretend I'm dating a time traveler, as opposed to a senior citizen."

"What can I say? I have a soft spot for the classics. When you said I was home watching TV, you were right."

I sighed. "We really need to get out more, don't we?"

"Who has the time? If we didn't work together, we'd never see each other."

I smiled. "Then it's a good thing we work together, isn't it?"

He smiled back, then pulled me in for a kiss. He was a great kisser.

But sadly, I had to focus on the aforementioned work. I regretfully ended our smooch and patted him on the chest. "I gotta go, Weatherman. Me and ZZ need to talk."

"All right, all right. But can't you come up with a better nickname? Weatherman makes me sound like I wear plaid sports coats and make lame jokes."

"Thunder Boy?"

"Better, but no."

"Stormy Bear?"

"Worse."

"Thor Lips, Mighty Wielder of the Mystic Tongue Hammer?"

He made a face. "Forget I brought it up. Go do your thing."

"See you later, Thor Lips."

Then it was time to pay my boss a visit.

Zelda Zoransky had led an interesting life. She was born into money, but came of age in the sixties; that, plus a rebellious, curious, and intelligent nature led to her embracing the counterculture and rejecting her family's more traditional values. She spent decades traveling the world and exploring whatever caught her fancy, and when her parents died—leaving her, the sole heir, all their money—she finally decided to settle down. She moved back into the Zoransky mansion, spruced the place up, and built a zoo on the grounds. She'd been filling it with animals who needed help for quite a while now, but a single cause wasn't enough for ZZ; her globe-trotting era might be behind her, but these days the Internet can bring the world to you. And if you've got a few hundred million in your back pocket, it can bring all sorts of other things—and people—to your doorstep, too.

Which is why she needed me. I was the one who handled the logistics side of things, the one who lined up the experts, bought the equipment, ordered the supplies. This meant not only that ZZ and I spent a lot of time together, but also that I had to know and understand how she thought. Some of her hobbies were ephemeral, some were not. My ZZ-ometer wasn't a precision instrument, but it could gauge the level of her interest: Momentary Whim was at the bottom, while Growing Obsession was at the top. Everything in between was a constantly shifting landscape of intrigue and consideration, and the key to navigating it lay in understanding the woman who was continually renovating the whole place. I thought I did.

But it wasn't like her to keep things from me.

Whiskey and I stopped in front of her bedroom door, my hand raised to knock. Raised, and apparently stuck in that position. Maybe the door was radiating some kind of invisible force-field. Sure, that was it.

[Do you want me to wait outside?]

"What? Why would I want that?"

[A confrontation with the leader of the pack is always difficult. I will understand if you need to do this alone.]

I smiled. Even though he sounds like a barrel-chested butler from a century ago, Whiskey is still a dog. "It's not that big a deal. I'm fine, really."

[Then why aren't you knocking?]

"Um. No reason. Just refining my plan of action, that's all."

[I see. One knock, or two? A light rap, or something firmer? Weighty decisions, indeed.]

"Sarcasm is not support."

[Would it help if I accompanied you and growled menacingly in the background?]

"No." I paused. "But you could do that stare you do—you know, when I'm eating something really greasy and forget to offer you some? Sort of accusatory and disappointed at the same time."

[Done. Now either knock or run away—the anticipation is unbearable.]

I knocked.

"I'm busy, Foxtrot," said ZZ from inside.

"How'd you know it was me?"

"You're the only one who bothers me when I tell everyone I want to be left alone."

"Yes I am. Can we have this conversation face-to-face, please? Or is it easier to be rude to me when the door is closed?"

"Kind of." She sounded a little guilty, so I just waited. After a moment, the door unlocked and swung open.

ZZ was in her sixties, with curly, orange hair—that she refused to call red—slowly going gray. She was currently wearing purple satin pajamas and oversized bright-green slippers made to resemble three-eyed aliens trying to eat her feet. She stared at me defiantly, then turned and stalked back inside. Whiskey and I followed.

ZZ threw herself back onto the enormous, circular bed like a recalcitrant toddler. I resisted the urge to cross my arms and threaten her with a time-out.

"Very well, Foxtrot," ZZ sighed. "What current emergency is beyond your entirely remarkable abilities?"

"It's about Anna."

Her face didn't so much fall as plummet. "Ah. Whatever Ben needs, Foxtrot. Time off, funeral expenses, anything. Please, just take care of it."

"I am. But there's something I need your help with."

"What?"

"Understanding why you lied to me about Efram Fimsby."

Her eyes widened. ZZ was, by nature, honest; she was used to getting her own way by simply asking for things as opposed to being manipulative. Besides, lying took a lot of time and energy that she'd prefer to spend on other pastimes. "I'm not sure what you mean by that, Foxtrot."

"Yes, you are. You invited him here because he asked you to, and it has something to do with a big secret Anna was keeping. I just talked to Fimsby and that's what he told me."

She glanced away, then back at me. "Oh. Well, then. I'm sorry, but—they swore me to secrecy, Foxtrot. Anna was very insistent. I had no choice."

I frowned. "You're not really helping with the whole understanding thing, ZZ. Why all the secrecy? What was Anna hiding? Why couldn't she tell her own brother, at least?"

"I—I can't say, Foxtrot. She told me it was important Fimsby attend the salon, and that it had to appear I invited him on my own. I wasn't supposed to let Ben or anyone else know Fimsby and Anna were acquainted."

[That would seem to agree with what Mr. Fimsby said to you.]

Yes, but it doesn't tell me anything new. "But *why*, ZZ? Why would you agree to do that?"

Now she just looked miserable. "I wish I could tell you, Foxtrot, I truly do. But I can't. Please, just accept that and trust me."

Damn. Whiskey was right, confrontations with your pack leader were hard. I couldn't exactly command my boss to 'fess up—though I could work the guilt angle mercilessly. "You know best, boss. It's not like I expect you to trust me or anything."

I could practically see that one strike home. "I *can't*, Foxtrot. It would just burden you."

"Hey," I said gently. I sat down beside her on the bed. "It's okay to burden me. I have strong shoulders, remember? That's why you hired me."

She gave me a troubled look, then nodded slowly. "I suppose that's true. All right, then."

She took a deep breath and composed herself. "There wasn't just one secret, Foxtrot. There were two. And one of them has to do with *me*."

CHAPTER THREE

I stared at ZZ. "You? In what way?"

"In a blackmail sort of way, Foxtrot." She paused, and then said, "Well, perhaps *blackmail* is too strong a word. Maybe graymail. Let's just say that Anna knew something about me that I didn't want other people to know, and she threatened to spill the beans if I didn't invite Fimsby."

Now *that* was unsettling. Normally ZZ didn't care what other people thought of her, or what she did or said. She was famous for it. More than one guest has picked their jaw up off the floor after ZZ delivered one of her colorful opinions over the salad course—and if there's anything she hates more than keeping her views to herself, it's being pressured to do something she doesn't want to. So what could possibly accomplish both at the same time?

"You're not going to tell me what it is, are you?" I asked.

"No, dear. But it may come out eventually anyway, and if that happens you'll understand why I kept it from you."

[Foxtrot. You're getting distracted by a secondary scent. Focus on the main trail, please.]

"Okay, so you were a gun-running NyQuil addict that ran a Smurf cult in another life. *What was Anna's secret?*"

She stared at me. I stared at her. I'm pretty sure Whiskey was staring, too, but I was too busy to notice who at.

After a moment ZZ blinked and said, "I don't know."

"What?"

"I don't. She said she was in trouble, and that Ben might be, too, but she couldn't give me any specifics. Naturally, that wasn't enough for me, so I refused. Which is when—"

"—she waved the graymail in your face, right." I snorted. "Do you have any idea how *exasperating* this is?"

"I'm sorry, dear."

"I deal in facts, ZZ. Schedules, bills of lading, contracts. I am severely allergic to the vague, and so far every wispy, insubstantial non-fact in this affair is making me feel like sneezing my head off."

"I *am* sorry, dear."

"A secret is one thing. A secret that's hiding another secret is something else. And when half the number of people who knew the original secret are now *dead,* that's something else *entirely.*"

"Well put, dear." She waited, then added, "Are you all right now, or would you like me to apologize again?"

"I'm fine, just frustrated."

[Ask her to apologize again. It couldn't hurt.]

"What did Fimsby say to you?" ZZ asked.

"That Anna contacted him while she was in Australia and asked him some very odd questions—and no, he wouldn't go into detail about that, either. He seems sure Anna's death wasn't an accident, and that Ben may be next. He was just as tight-lipped with me as Anna was with you, and wouldn't even approach Ben directly. He seems to feel we're being watched."

"Does Ben know any of this?"

"As much as you do. I talked to him first."

ZZ frowned. "And he had no idea what was going on, either?"

"No. Whatever Anna discovered, she didn't talk to him about it. The only one who seems to know what's actually going on is Fimsby, and he doesn't seem inclined to share."

"Then we'll just have to convince him otherwise, won't we?"

That was the ZZ I was used to. "We will. But I don't think we're gonna accomplish that in here, unless your plan is to invite him to a slumber party and weasel the information out of him while we braid his hair."

"Not really practical, is it? No, I think we need another approach. Problem is, I don't know how to proceed."

"Fimsby obviously has an agenda. If he won't share it with us, we need to find out all we can on our own. Forewarned is forearmed, and you know me: I prefer five- or sixwarned if possible."

"And how do you plan to attain this level of preparation when Fimsby won't talk?"

I grinned. "Leave that to me, boss. Research is my middle name, remember?"

[I thought your middle name was Foxtrot.]

"So here's the plan: Leave Fimsby alone. He's no doubt expecting either you or Ben to talk to him, so keeping our distance will throw him off balance."

ZZ nodded, but she looked unsure. "And then?"

"I'll do some more digging, figure out what's actually going on and what Fimsby's agenda is. *Then* we can talk to him and not be totally in the dark."

"That's your plan? Digging and figuring?"

"Pretty much."

She sighed, but it was one of relief. "Well, you excel at both. I'm so sorry I kept this from you, Foxtrot. I didn't want to—it felt like keeping a secret from myself, actually."

"Aw, boss. You say the nicest things. But I understand, believe it or not. Everybody has secrets."

[Indeed.]

And then I left, taking my telepathic ghost dog with me.

I like to read. I used to read a lot more, when I was younger—but then I chose a career that swallows my time the way a hippo swallows cantaloupes (in case you've never seen a hippo eat cantaloupes, it's like watching a steam shovel gobble bowling balls. Yeah, not really that great a metaphor, which is why I went with the whole hippo thing in the first place), so these days I don't get to just kick back with a novel very often.

But when I do read, I like mysteries. I like how many different kinds there are: hard-boiled, police procedurals, cozies. There are mysteries that center on particular places, or cultures, or professions. There are even mysteries about people who own cats—though *own* isn't really accurate when describing one's relationship to a cat.

My cat used to curl up in my lap when I read. That was back when I'd probably be deeply enraptured by a dog-eared (sorry, Tango) Agatha Christie paperback; now I'm more likely to be eyeball-deep in research at a workstation, and my childhood pet is long dead.

Which apparently hasn't changed *her* routine at all.

<*You're doing this ALL WRONG,*> she said for the umpteenth time, trying to get comfortable on my lap. <*What's the matter with you? It's sitting, for Bast's sake. You used to be really good at it.*>

I gave up trying to work the keyboard and give Tango a comfortable spot to sprawl at the same time. "I used to be a limber tween with a hammock, an overstuffed armchair, and a pillow fort. Currently I have to make do with an overpriced office chair designed to keep my back straight. Sorry if that inconveniences you."

<Oh, it does. There's no room between your belly and the edge of the desk. Plus, your thighs have gotten all bony.>

I glared down at her. "Bony? You know how many hours with a ThighMaster I put in to get those things in shape?"

<Well, you can stop, now. You need ice cream—lots and lots of ice cream.>

"How did I have you for all those years without realizing you're made of pure evil?"

[If you were a dog, you'd have figured it out much sooner.] Whiskey was relaxing on my office couch, which I let him get away with because ectoplasmic fur doesn't really shed. [Probably before birth.]

<Mmmmm. Ice cream . . .>

"Stop. I'm trying to do research, here. I don't have time for—for—"

<Chocolate raspberry swirl?>

"Stop."

<Double fudge rocky road?>

"Cut it out."

<Mocha cheesecake with chunky mouse bits?>

"I'm serious—wait, what?"

<Mmmm. Catnipstachio with a ribbon of pureed sparrow . . .>

"Are you drooling on my skirt?"

[Fortunately, evil diluted by gluttony tends to be less worrisome for the general public. Though not for the local population of songbirds and small rodents.]

<I'm gonna go get a snack.>

[Our amazement knows no bounds.]

Tango jumped off my lap and trotted out the door of my office. Whiskey and I watched her go.

[And how is your research coming along?]

I leaned back and stretched. "Unsuccessfully. I know a little more about Fimsby, but not much. He's a meteorologist

who studies unusual weather patterns. He's chased tornadoes in the Southwest, braved monsoons in Asia, and studied blizzards in Alaska. Could be a really useful person for
a newly fledged Thunderbird to know, actually."

[Which is, no doubt, why Anna went to him in the first
place.]

I frowned, studying the screen. "And apparently trusted
him enough to enlist his help. But what kind of help? What
sort of trouble was she in?"

[When one animal is threatened by another, it's almost
always for one of two reasons.]

"Which are?"

[Either the other animal is competing with the first for
the same resources, or it's attempting to turn said animal
into a resource. Usually by eating it.]

I sighed and swiveled my chair away from the computer.
"Unfortunately, there's not a lot of research to be done on
Thunderbirds. Native American weather spirits, can take on
human form, used as messengers to the gods. And a tribe of
them apparently settled on Vancouver Island in Canada
quite a while ago and interbred with the locals. Humans, I
mean, not birds."

[Perhaps we need a more immediate source. There *is* a
Native American presently on the grounds.]

"Firstcharger? Well, yeah, but how am I supposed to
start that conversation? *Hey, mind if I ask you about a few
Native myths? I'm sure you must be an expert on the subject, what with being a genuine Indian and all.* It would
be like strolling up to Shondra and quizzing her about
Zulu marriage rites."

[Humans are so touchy about their cultures. We canines
have a saying: No matter how high it is off the ground, it
still smells the same.]

"Please tell me that doesn't refer to what I think it does."

[Granted, like many sayings it's not literally true. I mean, they *do* all smell different—otherwise, why bother sniffing them? The point is, whether you're talking about a Great Dane or a dachshund, their hindquarters—]

"Yes, yes, I get it. Everybody's butt is equal in the great butt-sniffing go-around that is life. Maybe if human beings all used that as a universal method of greeting things would be a lot more equal, but we don't. We have all these protocols and prejudices and social conventions, and I can't risk alienating one of ZZ's guests by saying the wrong thing to her. Besides, Thunderbirds are part of a coastal tradition; with a name like Firstcharger she's probably descended from a Plains tribe."

[A bit odd her being here in the first place, though.]

"I suppose. Still, no odder than Theodora."

[That's an entirely different sort of odd. Less coincidental and more . . .]

"Schizophrenic."

[Exactly.]

"I'll talk to Firstcharger eventually, but I think I'll skip the supernatural stuff. She's a suspect because she slept with Anna's husband, not because of her race."

[I don't know why humans are so touchy about their breed, either. A terrier doesn't get upset when you assume he's fond of rats.]

"You know, sometimes I'm really, really glad I'm the only one that can hear you talk." I got to my feet. "Come on. I've found out all I'm going to about Thunderbirds on the 'Net. Time to go converse with actual people."

We headed downstairs and then outside. I was looking for two guests in particular, and thought I knew where I'd find them.

They weren't in the gardens, though, or the menagerie. Caroline, our resident vet, said they'd been there but left a short while ago. Then she told me where they were going.

The cemetery.

The Zoransky estate abuts one of the largest animal graveyards in the United States, housing upward of fifty thousand former pets ranging from mice to thoroughbreds. It's also a mystic nexus, kind of a Grand Central Station of beasty souls; a place where animals can leave their respective afterlives and enter a human one, in order to visit those they loved—and still do.

Most people are completely unaware of this. They think of the cemetery as a final resting place for their pet—or, as I used to, as just a resting place. It's quiet and pretty and there are benches; in fact, not too long ago it was my favorite spot for a tea break and some peaceful meditation.

Now, not so much.

Other people still take advantage of its bucolic charms, though, and those often include our guests. Keene enjoys strolling among the headstones and reading the epitaphs for inspiration, while others prefer to take pictures. Annie Leibovitz got some spectacular shots of Lady Gaga riding a marble horse here.

And some people like to paint. Though in this case, *people* means "Border collie."

Whiskey and I found them over by Davy's Grave, of course. It's a nice setting, surrounded by tall trees, with a number of benches. Davy was the first resident of the graveyard, way back at the end of the nineteenth century, and as such his grave has been afforded special status over the years. I've never actually seen Davy in the ectoplasmic flesh myself, but not every dog likes to roam. He might be content in doggy heaven, or may have moved back in with his former (and long-since-deceased) owner.

Anyway, the current dog occupying the space was Kaci, a sprightly brown-and-white Border collie. She sat gripping a rubber bone tightly between her jaws, the bone lashed crosswise to a short artist's brush. She stared intently at the canine-height easel before her, which held a square white canvas about two feet across. The canvas showed a few bold strokes in black, but I wasn't sure what they were supposed to be. Several small cans of paint were lined up neatly in a row beside Kaci.

On one of the benches, around ten feet away, were two men. One of them was stout, with an elegant gray goatee and mustache: Rustam Gorshkov. He wore an expensive topcoat, pin-striped trousers, and square-toed boots; his hands rested on the head of an elaborately carved cane upright between his knees, and his eyes were closed. The expression on his face was one of deep concentration.

The other man, sitting beside him and staring at him with rapt interest, was Oscar. Oscar wore a wide-brimmed white Panama hat, khaki shorts, and a pale-green silk shirt. He looked a little strange to me for a second, and then I realized it was because he didn't have a drink in his hand.

Whiskey, of course, was focused on Kaci. Dead or not, he was still a dog, and as such had dog concerns. And to dogs, with their deeply ingrained sense of pack structure, the most important thing upon meeting another canine was to immediately establish exactly what their relative social positions were. I've wondered what it would be like if people meeting each other for the first time ranked each other with the same obsessive precision:

ELDERLY BANKER: Hello. I drive a Mercedes, I own five homes, and my wife is thirty years younger than I am.

YOUNG LAWYER: Hello. I'm a junior partner in a large firm. A number of professional gangsters owe me favors. I have a large penis.

Yeah, I know. But it'll take those two all evening, half a bottle of scotch, and several anecdotes to impart that information, whereas dogs do pretty much the same thing in under thirty seconds without saying a word.

Whiskey approached Kaci carefully, his head slightly lowered. They were approximately the same size, which is always the first factor that comes into play. A large dog will sometimes ignore a much smaller one; a small one will never do the same for a dog that's significantly bigger.

Kaci knew he was there. I saw her eyes flicker toward him, and she gave an almost imperceptible whine. Other than that, though, she didn't move.

"Focus, Kaci, *focus*," Gorshkov rumbled. His eyes stayed closed.

Oscar gave me an irritated glance. "Foxtrot, please. Can't you see she's working?"

I could have called Whiskey back, of course. But I was curious to see how Kaci reacted to him. *Ignore me,* I thought loudly. "Whiskey, get back here!"

Whiskey sniffed the place dogs always sniff first. Kaci stayed perfectly still. It went on for what I thought was a little too long. *C'mon, Sherlock. Unless she's smuggling the Crown Jewels up there, I think you've done just about all the investigating that's required.*

[Ah, yes. Almost done. Just give me a minute . . .]

Seconds ticked by. *Okay, seriously. That's enough.*

[Hmmm. Yes, yes, absolutely.]

"Whiskey!"

He shot me a furtive look, then trotted back with an innocent expression on his doggy face. His voice, however, held some embarrassment. [I'm so sorry. Certain instincts simply won't be denied.]

I don't have to remind you that you're dead, do I? I'm not even sure what suffix to attach here. Necrovoyeurbestialisomething.

[Please. The only breach of protocol was when you called me back before she could reciprocate. *That* was rude.]

I suppose by canine standards, it was. "Sorry," I said, though not to Kaci. "How's today's masterpiece coming?"

"It is not, I am afraid," said Gorshkov. His eyes were open now, and he was staring at Kaci with a disapproving look on his face. She, in turn, was studying Whiskey intently. Green paint dripped from the end of her brush and onto the ground. "Her concentration, it is broken. We must take a break and refocus. Excuse us." He got up abruptly and limped over to Kaci. He spoke a word in Russian, and she dropped the paintbrush into his hand.

Well, that wasn't the effect I was trying to produce. "I'm sorry," I repeated. "I'll take Whiskey back to the house. It won't happen again."

"No, no," said Gorshkov. "Is all right. The inspiration, it was not coming anyway. We were about to take break. Really, is fine." He began to put lids back on the paint cans.

Oscar's glare could have blistered said paint off the side of a house. "Really, Foxtrot. You're supposed to assist our guests, not hinder them."

Gorshkov straightened up. "Oscar. You must learn first lesson of art. Creative urge have no master, or mistress. Blaming Foxtrot *or* her nice dog like blaming car wash for making the rain."

Oscar's look softened. "Very well. I don't suppose there's any way to make the rain come back?"

Gorshkov shrugged and went back to putting lids on cans. "We wait, we have a little walk, we try again. Maybe have lunch first."

Oscar sighed. "Yes, of course. One can't hurry art, can one."

Gorshkov finished what he was doing and snapped a short lead to Kaci's collar. He spoke another word in Russian and she trotted off with him—but not without more than a few backward glances at Whiskey.

Good luck, Kaci, I thought at her. She didn't react, but

then it wasn't like I'd asked her a direct question. Or maybe she only understood Russian.

I sat down next to Oscar. "I really am sorry—though I'm also still a little skeptical about the whole Leonardo da Doggy thing."

Oscar favored me with a tolerant sigh. "Oh, Foxtrot— *you*, of all people? I thought you'd embrace the notion of an artistic animal, since you're always extolling the virtues of your own hairy companion."

"Whiskey's smart, but I don't claim he can paint my portrait. Intelligence and creativity are two different things."

[I'm afraid I have to agree. Dogs tend to think more like engineers than artists.]

Oscar shook his head, but he wasn't arguing with Whiskey—he couldn't hear him, after all. "No, but neither does one preclude the other. Human beings can be clever *or* creative, and animals can, at the very least, be clever; doesn't that suggest they might be able to manifest the other talent, as well?"

"I'll grant you that," I said. "It's not the possibility that Kaci's actually creating art that I have a problem with. It's what you said before that, about humans being clever *or* creative. Some humans even manage being both at the same time."

The faintest trace of a smile bobbed to the surface of his face. "Ah. You doubt not our guest's capabilities, but their sincerity."

"Convince me otherwise, Oscar."

He chuckled. "I, Foxtrot? And why would I know anything about Mr. Gorshkov's possibly deceitful conduct?"

"For the same reason sharks study lawyers. Professional curiosity."

He conceded the point with a graceful nod. "Very well. If this is a scam, it's a good one. I've watched him closely while Kaci paints, and have been unable to detect any way he might be influencing her actions other than what he claims—with his mind. He does not speak, or even move. Kaci seems to consider various brushstrokes, depending on what she's painting, and that varies widely. It's not simply a question of rote learning, which I understand a Border collie is quite capable of; she appears to actually be concentrating on the object in front of her, and doing her best to capture it."

"Mmmm. If that's the case, then how exactly is this a collaboration?"

Oscar shrugged. "That part is much murkier. Gorshkov goes on about artistic synergy and how Kaci is actually tapping into the artistic area of his own brain, but it's all very metaphysical and ill defined. Then again, this is art, not science; one can't always expect a simple and concise explanation in such matters."

[In my experience, one can rarely expect such an explanation from Oscar in general.]

"True," I replied. "So very, very true . . . so. Is she any good?"

Oscar smiled. "Have you ever heard of Miracle Mike?"

"Wasn't that a movie about male strippers?"

"He was a chicken destined for the roasting pan in 1945. However, the aim of the axman was a trifle off, and his blow only took off the top of the cockerel's head as opposed to severing it cleanly. Any chicken will demonstrate the ability to run around—for a few moments, anyway—immediately after having his head chopped off, but Mike did them one better: He not only ran around, he refused to fall down."

"Wait. Are you saying this chicken had his head chopped off and *lived*?"

"Indeed. Apparently enough of his brainstem was left to keep autonomic functions going. The wound healed, in time, and his owner discovered it was possible to feed him by the simple expedient of dropping food down the hole on the top of his neck. Mike survived for another eighteen months."

I eyed him warily. "This sounds like the setup for an elaborate punch line."

"I have no punch line to offer you, but I do have a point. This chicken could not dance, or perform magic tricks, or do anything of note other than breathe. But he became quite famous, Foxtrot; Mike the Headless Chicken toured the country, and people paid money to see him. At the height of his popularity, he earned four and a half thousand dollars a month and was featured in both *Time* and *Life* magazines."

He paused. "Kaci is a dog who paints. The quality of her artwork hardly matters, does it? The point is, her work was created by a canine, a species that has yet to master the most rudimentary forms of self-expression. That alone means whatever she produces is sure to be valuable—and become even more so."

I suddenly saw his point. "Oh, for—you see this as an *investment opportunity*?"

He sniffed. "And what's wrong with investing in art? If it weren't for the patronage of the wealthy, many famous artists would never have produced their most stunning works."

"Sure. But the value of an artist's work always goes up after they die—and the life expectancy of a Border collie is considerably shorter than your average paint-stained wretch laboring in a studio."

"Twelve years, on average. But up to seventeen, in healthy specimens."

"And Kaci is how old?"

"Four," said Oscar. "Meaning I can expect a sizable return on my investment in somewhere from eight to thirteen years. Barring unforeseen accidents or sudden illness, of course."

[I'm guessing he could recite a list of medical ailments Border collies are prone to from memory.]

No doubt. "So you're convinced they're the real deal?"

"My dear Foxtrot—again, you miss the point. Reality, in this case, is much like art: entirely subjective. It doesn't matter whether or not Kaci's creations are 'real'; what matters is whether or not other people perceive them as such. I believe they will. And I believe they'll back that perception with cold, hard cash."

Oscar got to his feet, tipped his hat to me, and ambled off in the direction of his new four-legged venture. I glanced down at mine. "Well?" I asked. "What's the verdict? Could you pick up any telepathic chatter between Gorshkov and his protégée?"

[No, but that's hardly unusual. Communication between you and me is based on the fact that you can communicate with animal spirits, and I am one. I can't "speak" to Kaci with my mind, any more than you can do the same to Oscar. I could, however, ask her directly.]

The last statement was projected with such elaborate casualness that he might as well have just painted his intentions on a billboard and set it on fire. "Fine, Romeo. Just don't bother her while she's working, all right? You've already gotten me in trouble once."

[I shall be the soul of discretion.]

"You'll be the soul of discretion later. Right now we have to—"

That was as far as I got. I was interrupted by the abrupt appearance of a herd of cats, sprinting at top speed across the crest of the nearest hill and straight toward us.

A herd of cats was unusual enough. But these felines were all deceased, as well.

And apparently being chased.

CHAPTER FOUR

The first thing I always notice about ghosts—other than Whiskey, that is—is how colorful they are. Whites and oranges and yellows shine like neon; grays look silver; even browns and blacks somehow take on a brilliant sheen. I can see how the phrase *the Rainbow Bridge* caught on when talking about the place where animals cross over, though at the moment the bounding cats I was watching flowing over the top of the hill resembled a river of multicolored light more than a bridge.

[Good Lord,] Whiskey said. It was all he had time for, and then the wave of cats was flowing around and past us. A few even leapt right through me, though they avoided doing that to Whiskey.

And then I saw what they were apparently fleeing from. Theodora Bonkle charged into sight, pausing at the top of the hill to look around frantically. I had no idea what she could be searching for; she couldn't possibly see the same cats I just had.

Could she?

She spotted Whiskey and me and waved. "Foxtrot! Did you see them?"

I frowned at her as she hurried down the hill to join us. "See who?"

"The cats! Apparently, there were quite a few of them."

That stopped me for a second. "Apparently?"

"Well, I didn't see them myself. But Very British Bear did, and he's quite reliable. Well, perhaps *reliable* isn't the right word, but he never lies."

I knew certain people were sensitive to the presence of ghosts, but it had never occurred to me that a figment of someone's imagination might be one of them. "Haven't seen a living soul since Oscar left," I said, quite truthfully. "What, exactly were these cats doing?"

Theodora squinted at me suspiciously, much as if I were hiding a herd of spectral cats behind my back. "Following me, at first. It started when I was examining a headstone, and progressed until there was quite a mob at my heels. Or so Very British Bear says."

"You said at first. Did things . . . go wrong?"

[Really, Foxtrot. It's hardly kind to encourage the delusions of the mentally ill.]

Quiet, this is interesting. And we saw those cats, too.

"I believe it was more in the nature of a misunderstanding. Despite my companions being able to see them, the cats remained entirely unaware of either VBB or Doc Wabbit. Infuriated Doc to no end, I can tell you; he hates to be ignored. I don't know where he gets those sticks of dynamite, but thank goodness they never seem to have much effect. Beyond scaring Very, of course."

"Of course."

"I counseled patience. While neither Doc nor Very had ever reported seeing a ghost before, I was quite sure that must be the case—we were in a graveyard, after all. But as we traveled from grave to grave, accumulating feline spirits as we went, I felt sure that something odd was going on."

[How *ever* did she arrive at that conclusion?]

"The cats were ignoring Very and Doc, so they must have been following me. *Ipso facto.* And there was only one reason I could see for them to be following me: the marbles."

"The what now?"

"Oh, I'm sorry—did I fail to mention that? I found a marble on the grave of a cat named Happy. Being curious by nature, I picked it up, studied it, then returned it to whence it came. Before too long, though, I saw another one. This one had been placed on the plot of a cat named Felix. Intrigued, I began to look for others, and soon found half a dozen more. It was about then that Very told me we had acquired an entourage."

[Of course she had. All it takes to captivate a cat's attention is a shiny object. More than one and they're practically hypnotized.]

"Okay," I said. "So what did you do then?"

"Well, I knew something was up. I decided to test my hypothesis by visiting a grave that did not have a marble upon it, and asked Very if we had subsequently been joined by another apparition. He reported that we had not."

[How terribly scientific. It's fortunate she has such trustworthy hallucinations to gather data from.]

Now I understand why dogs don't get irony. You've all had yours replaced with a gland that produces sarcasm instead.

"So," continued Theodora, "having verified the causative link, I decided to pursue the matter in a more direct way by establishing a dialogue. Considering the various barriers to communication—species, invisibility, death, a natural tendency toward aloofness—I thought a more dramatic approach was needed. Calling up the names on the headstones from memory, I pointed a finger in the general direction of the feline crowd and declaimed, 'Happy! Felix! Snuggles! Milo! Sailor! Parker! Claudius! Pickly Pete! I know you're there!'"

She paused. "In hindsight, perhaps that was a bit much."

"Did it get results?"

"Oh, yes. They bolted, and we gave chase. I thought perhaps they might lead me toward an answer—or at least further information—but I'm afraid they simply outpaced me." She looked crestfallen.

I wished I could help her, but my position as Guardian of the Great Crossroads came with one strict rule: Keep my mouth shut. Confirming the existence of ghost cats would be a definite no-no . . . but maybe I could assist in another way. "You know who a good person to talk to about this would be? Cooper, the groundskeeper for the graveyard. If anyone knows what's going on with those marbles, he would."

She brightened immediately. "What a splendid idea! Could you arrange an introduction?"

"Sure. He's got a little cottage just over that rise. Follow me."

As we walked, I told her a little about the graveyard's resident caretaker. "Coop's an old hippie. I get the feeling ZZ gave him this job out of a sense of obligation—she and Cooper go way back, though I've never been able to pry any details out of either of them. Maybe you'll have more luck."

We arrived at the cottage, a small, neatly kept white bungalow. Cooper answered the door at the first knock, a steaming cup of coffee in one hand. He was tall and skinny, with a long face and a graying ponytail that stuck out from under a battered straw hat that seemed to be permanently attached to his head. He flashed me a grin from under his bushy gray mustache and said, "Foxtrot! Good mornin', hello, and *namaste*!"

"Back atcha, Coop. Someone I'd like you to meet—Cooper, this is Theodora. She's a guest at the estate and wondered if she could ask you a few questions about the graveyard. That okay with you?"

He stepped back and motioned us in. An old Rolling Stones T-shirt hung from his lanky frame, and scuffed cowboy boots peeked out from the cuffs of his worn blue jeans. "Come on in," he said. "I just put on a fresh pot of coffee, if you're in the mood."

"That would be lovely," Theodora said.

The interior of the cottage was a little weird.

Cooper had a love of all things mystical. He wasn't particularly discerning about which flavor, either; new-age crystals threw rainbow sparkles over crimson-fanged, six-armed statues of Indian goddesses; Native American carvings hung on the walls over bookshelves crammed with lore ranging from the pagan to the metaphysical. One of his lamps had a cow skull for a base. The furniture was old and worn but comfortable, and there was a huge throw rug covering the floor inlaid with a psychedelic mandala. "Make yourself at home," Cooper said, and went to grab us some mugs.

We settled in, Theodora at one end of the couch, me in an armchair, and Whiskey at my feet. [Always such interesting scents in this house. Stirs the memories.]

Oh? You spent time at an incense factory?

[No, as a drug-sniffing dog.]

Well, I did say Coop was an old hippie.

"What an enchanting place," Theodora said in her soft, breathy voice. She peered through her glasses at a skull adorned with a red candle on the coffee table. "It practically *bleeds* inspiration."

Cooper came back with a mug of coffee and handed it to Theodora. "Black, right?"

She took it from him and raised her eyebrows. "Why, yes. How did you know?"

Cooper sat down next to her on the couch. "Oh, I just kind of have a feel for those things. Generally get the coffee one right. Foxtrot, I put some water on for your tea."

"That one has nothing to do with ESP," I said. "Coop knows my habits."

Cooper chuckled. "Guess I do. Know the boneyard, too. It's got its own habits, believe me."

"I'm sure it does," Theodora said, taking a delicate sip. "Have you been here long, Mr. Cooper?"

"Going on twenty years, give or take. Doesn't seem that long to me, but for some of the critters buried here it was their whole lifetime, birth to grave. I try to keep that in mind."

Theodora nodded. "It would give one a certain perspective, wouldn't it? And perspective is *so* important . . . what's that, Very?" Theodora fixed her eyes on a spot at her feet, bent over slightly, and listened for a moment. "No, no, no. You don't take perspective in a pill, Very. You're thinking of a *prescription.*"

I glanced over at Cooper. His eyes flicked from Theodora's face to the spot she was gazing at and back again, but he didn't look fazed in the slightest.

"Well now," said Cooper. "Might you be talking to Very British Bear, Miss Bonkle?"

"Why yes, Mr. Cooper. Would you like an introduction?"

"I'd be honored, Miss Bonkle. Is Doc Wabbit around, too?"

"I'm afraid he disappeared into your bedroom as soon as you let us in; he's terribly curious. But he'll be back once he's finished rooting about—ah, here he is. Doc, say hello to Mr. Cooper."

Theodora's eyes seemed to be fixed on a spot to the right

of the couch; Cooper looked in the same general direction, leaned forward, and said, "Hiya, Doc."

Whiskey whined and looked anxious. [But there's nothing there!]

Take it easy. Obviously Cooper's a fan of her work, too. He's just being polite.

But I wasn't so sure. Knowing Cooper, he probably believed in the existence of Theodora's imaginary friends in some metaphysical way. And who was I to say he was wrong? Just because I could see ghosts didn't mean I could see *everything*, after all. In my experience, the world always turned out to be much weirder than I thought it was—and I lived in a pretty weird world.

"Doc says *Hiya* right back," said Theodora. "And Very says, *How do you do*?"

"I do just fine," said Cooper. "Welcome to my place. Make yourself at home, but be careful of the snake."

"Snake?" I said. "You have a snake?" I glanced around nervously. Most animals I'm fine around, but a six-foot-long python was another matter.

"I'm not rightly sure," Cooper replied. "Guess I should explain. See, I came into the living room last night, and I heard this strange sorta noise. Like a *ssshh-clack, sssshh-clack, ssshh-clack*. Then I looked over at the bookcase, and there was this enormous tube on top of it. Thick as a telephone pole. And it was moving, sliding down the side of the bookcase. The noise was the sound it was making as its belly rubbed against that little edge there, where the veneer is loose? That little strip was getting pulled back and then snapping forward again."

"Wait. You *found* a snake in your living room?" I asked. "One as big around as a telephone pole?"

"Pretty much. First thing I thought was *Wow, I wonder how long it is?* So I started to follow it, you know, with my eyes. It went down the bookcase, and around the coffee table, then into the kitchen and out to the garage, over the fire truck—"

"Cooper. You don't have a garage. Or a fire truck."

He gave me a long-suffering look. "Well, of course not, Foxtrot. But you know how dreams are."

"This was a dream?" I asked.

Cooper nodded. "Didn't I mention that part? But it wasn't just *any* dream. I could tell."

"How so?" Theodora asked.

"Well, I'd taken some peyote before I went to bed. Peyote dreams are always something special."

[Indeed. I can't wait for the appearance of the flaming dwarf dressed as his mother.]

"I understand your concern now," Theodora said with a firm nod of her head. "This creature in your dreaming vision was not of this realm but another. Perhaps even the one that both Doc and Very inhabit."

Cooper gave her a nod of acknowledgment. I kept my mouth shut.

"A valid concern," Theodora said. "In fact, Doc, Very and I had an encounter with a group of ghostly cats this very morning, which they could perceive and I could not. Which brings us to the reason for our visit."

Theodora told Cooper the same story she told me. "And so you see why we've come to you. Can you perhaps shed any light on these events?"

Cooper leaned back, sipped his coffee, and considered the question. "Well, now. People leave all sorts of things on the graves here other than flowers: chew toys, leashes, blankets, hamster wheels. But usually people just come to visit one grave and leave something personal. I've noticed those marbles myself; they've been appearing over the past year or so, but I've never seen the person leaving them. At first I thought it might be a kid who left a few here and there while his parents were paying their respects to a family pet, but I wasn't sure, so I left 'em where they were. Then, when more and more showed up, I thought maybe it was a crow or something leaving them. Always on cat graves, too."

"Ah, so now we have a time line," said Theodora. "The past year. But who? And why?"

"Too bad we can't just ask the ghosts," said Cooper.

[Consider yourself lucky you can't. Talking to cats is always an option of last resort.]

"Very wants to know about the snake," Theodora said. "He's a little worried."

"Well, it just kept on going forever, near as I could tell. I followed the thing out into some kind of desert, and it just never ended. Seemed like I'd been walking the length of it for hours when I finally woke up. It was beautiful, too."

"Beautiful?" Theodora said.

"Yeah. It was all these different colors, each one of 'em really brilliant. Like a living rainbow."

That got my attention. Cooper's dreams have proven prophetic before, and ghost animals all have that vivid, brightly colored appearance—even the ones that are black or brown. Maybe this "living rainbow" was more like an unliving one. "And that was it?" I prompted. "Nothing else happened?"

Cooper scratched his chin and thought about it. "Nope. But it felt important."

Theodora frowned. "Well, this is most interesting. Marbles, of course, come in many colors, too—as do, I suppose, cats. There's a mystery here, of that I'm sure. I should have known this would happen."

"What do you mean?" I asked.

"I'm in the research phase for my next Meddler novel. It seems as if every time that happens, a mystery pops up and demands to be solved."

She saw the look on my face and hastily said, "Of course, there's also the much more serious crime that occurred at the mansion—but I try to leave those to the police. I'm not Miss Marple, after all."

"A new Meddler book?" said Cooper. "That's good news. What's it about?"

"I'm not entirely sure yet. A murder, of course. Possibly something having to do with animals, though I'm leaning more toward birds than snakes."

That got my attention, though I tried to hide my reaction. Even though Theodora didn't know it, a bird had already died—a Thunderbird. Or maybe she knew more than she was letting on . . .

"Mr. Cooper," said Theodora, "would you mind terribly if I called upon your expertise in this matter of the marbles? I find that a little amateur sleuthing is just the thing to get me in the right frame of mind for fictional crimes."

"I'll do whatever I can to help, ma'am."

"Excellent. I believe the first matter at hand is to document the graves themselves, and their occupants. That I can do on my own—yes, Doc, you and Very can help—and once I'm done we'll put our heads together and try to make sense of this thing."

Cooper grinned. "Sounds like a good time to me."

I got to my feet, and Whiskey sprang up beside me. "Well, then—I'll leave you to your investigation. If you need anything to help you along, just let me know."

"Thank you, Foxtrot," said Theodora, rising as well. "And you, Mr. Cooper. We'll talk again soon."

"Looking forward to it," said Cooper. "I'll show you out."

When Cooper had closed the door behind us, Theodora and I parted ways, her back to examine grave sites, me and Whiskey back to the house. I wished her—and her two compatriots—good luck.

When she was out of sight, I turned to Whiskey and said, "Rainbow snakes and dead cats? What do you think?"

[It's tempting to dismiss them as the offspring of chemical imbalances. But the ghost cats were real enough, and Cooper's description of the snake was suggestive of an animal spirit. The overlappings of certain realms are well documented—dreams, insanity, and the afterlife are not that far apart in certain ways.]

"Ways you can't talk about, right?"

[Not in any detail, I'm afraid. But remember, the Great Crossroads acts as a psychic amplifier; naturally sensitive people will find their perceptions heightened while here. For someone like Cooper, who actually lives on the grounds, it may even be a cumulative effect.]

"And Miss Bonkle?"

[It could be amplifying certain mental effects in her, as well. Not all of them positive.]

Terrific. That's all I needed, one of ZZ's guests having a full mental breakdown. Well, I'd dealt with that sort of thing before—not here, but at other points in my varied and hectic career.

I used to work for this guy named Damon Inferno. Lead singer of a death-metal band called Slotterhaus that had a number one single in the UK a gazillion years ago, followed by several increasingly forgettable albums and a steady decline in album sales. Unlike some groups that would have imploded beneath the morale-crushing reality of dwindling paychecks and venues, the Slotterhaus gang refused to let their fifteen minutes of fame come to an end, keeping that minute hand at fourteen-and-a-half through sheer, bloody-minded determination and grim tunnel-vision. They lived on the road and played every hole-in-the-wall bar, club, or hall that would have them. They were like zombie dinosaurs: mindless, dead, nothing left but old bones . . . but still shambling through the night, hungry for the flesh of the living. Lacking any real brain themselves, they decided to hire one. They picked me.

Working for Slotterhaus was my first real job. I guess I'll always owe them for that, but I think me being young, cute, and willing to work for cheap had more to do with them hiring me than any actual qualifications. That, and the fact that I had two unbreakable conditions to working for them: first, that they had to pay me; and second, that I wouldn't sleep with any of them. They didn't have a lot of respect for women—or authority, or common sense, or themselves, for that matter—but they'd give it to you if you insisted firmly enough. I did.

Damon may not have ever attained the status of a true star—more like a piece of space junk falling out of orbit in a brief blaze of light—but he was still something of a legend in certain circles. Okay, so one of those circles was his own bandmates and the other was mostly people who were dead or in rehab, but there was still a community who spoke of Damon's exploits in tones of hushed awe. And by *hushed awe* I mean whoops of stoned, drunken laughter.

They'd tell the story about Damon, the aquarium, and the tank of laughing gas. Or Damon and the seventeen strippers. Or Damon, the hot tub, and the distillery—that one has a deranged plumber in it, or at least one so high on cocaine he was arrested naked on top of a city bus.

Taken together, they formed a mythology of the epically wasted. But when I thought about Damon, none of those stories was the one that came to mind.

I thought about the time I found him hiding under his own bed.

It took me two hours to coax him out. He was convinced that his whole life was an elaborate practical joke conducted by a conspiracy of every person he'd ever known, and that they were about to reveal the punch line: He'd never been a success. Nobody had ever bought any of his albums, or played them on the radio. Every groupie he'd ever slept with had been paid to do so, and his friends were all actors.

He was completely, absolutely sure about all of this. His demeanor alternated between coldly lucid—he would list "facts" to support his case that almost made sense, or were at least hard to disprove—and bouts of hysterical weeping.

I'm not proud of how I finally got him out: I produced a bottle of gin and offered to have a drink with him, something I'd never done before. One drink turned into several—for him, anyway—and he finally calmed down and came back to himself. We never talked about it again, and two months later I was working for someone else.

It wasn't until he'd crawled out from under the bed that I saw he had a knife in his hand.

It was one of those wooden-handled, serrated-blade models you get when you order a steak from room service. Made for sawing through meat. A good choice if you wanted to hack through your own wrists . . . but there was a moment when he got to his feet, clutching that knife in his hand, when I was sure he was going to use it on me. When the madness was still in his eyes, and even he didn't know what he was going to do next. I remember that look well. It wasn't hostile or fearful or manic. It was just disconnected, like watching a car whose driver has vanished and is now drifting out of its own lane and toward oncoming traffic.

Had I just seen that same look on Theodora Bonkle's face?

CHAPTER FIVE

<Ghost cats?> Tango asked. She was eating at her bowl in the mansion's kitchen while I waited for Ben to finish receiving a grocery order at the back door.

Yep. Tearing along as if being chased by a muscular transgender mystery author and her two imaginary friends, I replied.

Whiskey, nosing around for scraps on the floor, glanced my way. [Yes. It was extremely odd.]

<I'll say. Who doesn't love the imaginary friends of muscular transgender mystery authors? Who, I ask?>

[Cats, apparently.]

"At least dead ones," I said out loud.

"Dead what?" asked Ben, walking up with a crate of produce in his arms. He set it down on the stainless steel of the table and started pulling leafy green things out of it.

"Cats," I answered. I gave Ben a condensed version of the story while he unpacked groceries. ". . . and that's how I spent the last hour."

Ben frowned. "I thought you were looking for Anna's killer."

"I am. But accomplishing anything around here is

always like juggling and reciting Shakespeare from memory while trying to run an obstacle course."

His frown softened. "I'm sorry. I know how much you have to deal with. But this is my sister we're talking about."

I went to him, put my arms around his waist. "Hey. I understand. This is important to me, too. I promise you, we'll get to the bottom of this. Just try to be patient, all right? And remember that you have a crack team of supernatural sleuths on the case?"

He looked into my eyes. No lightning crackling there right now, just a deep, rich brown. Like staring at chocolate, really. In more ways than one.

"Okay," he said softly. "I trust you. You're the most capable person I know."

<Ahem>.

Those luscious brown eyes rolled upward. "Sorry, Tango. Didn't mean to imply you weren't just as capable. Or not a person."

<Just as capable? Please. I'm more capable than anyone within a hundred yards. I'm so capable I should be wearing a cape.>

[Yes, very clever. If wordplay were a benchmark of competence you'd surely be the envy of us all. Sadly, deeds tend to count for more than words.]

<Depends on the word, you otiose fopdoodle.>

[I beg your pardon?]

<Go on, beg away. It's the quiddity of being a groak, after all.>

[The use of esoteric terminology does little to refute my statement.]

<So says the dirhinous teratosis.>

"Okay," I said loudly, "that's enough of that. We have a killer to catch, and we're not going to do it by calling each other names." I paused. "What the hell is a groak, anyway?"

<Somebody who hangs around the dinner table hoping to be fed.>

"There's an actual word for that?" Ben said. He gently broke my embrace and stepped over to one of the fridges.

<There's a word for everything, my ephetic gossoon. Which means "skeptical lad," by the way.>

[Fascinating. Your grasp of utterly useless knowledge is both impressive and extensive. Now can we get down to work, please?]

<Certainly, you nugatory alliaphage.>

"That's not exactly fair," said Ben. He pulled a pan full of chops out of the fridge and carried it over to the table. "I've never known Whiskey to eat garlic."

"Is that what *nugatory* means?" I asked.

"No, *alliaphage.*" He picked up a knife and started trimming fat off the chops. "It's a word I learned when I became a chef."

Tango licked one paw. *<Okay, you got me. I couldn't think of the term for "deceased humper of random objects.">*

[Still highly inaccurate. Despite my post-living state, I have no romantic intentions toward the inanimate.]

<Aha! So you admit you liked to get amorous with furniture when you were still breathing!>

Whiskey gave Tango a pitying look. [I yearn for the creation of feline psychoanalysis, so you can finally get the help you desperately need.]

"Oh?" I said. "Is that the *only* thing you're yearning for?"

[I don't understand what you're referring to.]

<I do. Those long, soulful looks in her direction, the hopeful panting when she glances your way . . . you've got it bad, pal.>

Whiskey stared at me accusingly. [You told her.]

"Who, me? What, you think when two females get

together all they talk about is who's crushing on who? I think I'm offended."

<*Me, too.*>

[That statement would carry more weight if being offended weren't how cats spent a third of their time. The other two-thirds they're asleep.]

<*Nobody had to tell me anything, Ty-D-Bol breath. You're pining so hard you smell like a Christmas tree. And Ty-D-Bol. The pine-scented kind. See what I did there?*>

[I'm not pining.]

<*How does that work, anyway? I mean, you're made of ectoplasm. You don't even have to eat.*>

"Oh, he eats, all right," said Ben. He tossed a scrap of fat from the chops he was trimming in Whiskey's direction; Whiskey snatched it out of the air in one quick chomp.

[Thank you. While it's true I don't need to consume food, I can ingest the occasional morsel for pleasure or to help heal from injuries. As you well know.]

<*Yeah, yeah, I know you can take stuff in. But it's one-way, right? You and your "superior spiritual digestion." Nothing comes out the other end?*>

[Not as such.]

<*Nothing? Nothing at all?*>

[I fail to see where this is going.]

"Not me," Ben said. "Wish I did, though."

<*Look, I'm not denying you have the equipment, even if it is made of ectoplasm. But what good is a gun if you don't have the bullets? You're not just firing blanks, pal— you're pulling the trigger on an empty chamber. No bang for your buck, if you get my drift.*>

Whiskey tried to sit a little straighter, which in some breeds would convey an increased sense of dignity. As a blue heeler, though, it just made him look perkier. [This conversation is both inappropriate and absurd. First of all, I am not "crushing" on anyone. Second of all, to reduce the emotion of love to a series of crude repetitive actions is to disrespect the profound, eternal force that underlies everything we do as Guardians of the Great Crossroads.]

He paused, gazing at us solemnly.

"Yeah, he's got it pretty bad," I said.

<Real shame he can't do much about it. In a crude repetitive way, I mean.>

"Oh, I'm sure he feels that's all beneath him."

<Or at least it was.>

"Speaking as a fellow male," said Ben, "can we knock off the teasing? It's not exactly fair."

<Fair? There's nothing fair about sex, Ben. There's the yelling and the neck biting and the searing pain, and all of us just have to put up with it.>

There was a moment of silence.

"Um," I said. "That's an interesting view of the process, Tango."

<Actually, I kind of enjoy it. But I could do without the spikes, let me tell you.>

"Spikes?"

Ben sighed. "Spikes," he said. "Don't ask me how I know this, but a male cat's anatomy has certain features you might not expect it to. Considering what its purpose is and where it goes."

<You know, it's not even the spikes, so much. It's more the fact that they point backward.>

"Can we talk about something else, please?" I said. "I'm wincing so hard I think I may have sprained something."

<Sounds painful. Not as painful as the spikes, though.>

"Tango, please," said Ben. "I think we're all wincing now."

<Why? Is there something wrong with your spikes?>

"Ben doesn't *have* spikes," I said.

<Really? Well, that explains a lot . . . did he have them removed? I always thought that's what they meant when

a male cat got "fixed," but all that happens is he loses in-terest in sex. You call that fixing something? Leave the sex drive alone and get rid of the spikes—that's a decent re-pair job.>

"Okay, I think it's time to take this show on the road," I said.

"Please do," said Ben. He gave me a quick kiss.

"C'mon, troops," I sighed, and exited the kitchen with Whiskey at my heels and Tango padding along a few steps behind.

While it might seem strange to be trailed by both a dog and a cat, people will accept the most unusual behavior from animals by simply filing it under *that's so cute!* in their own brains. After a while, that particular file gets renamed *ordinary stuff I see every day,* and then it be-comes more or less invisible.

That's how it works for the staff, anyway; the guests never stop marveling at it. Which can sometimes be use-ful, which is why I wanted both of them with me at the moment.

I found Hayden Metcalfe in the study. When I first met him my initial impression was of a tall, distinguished gentleman who dressed impeccably and looked at the world with a sort of amused disdain. The man I saw now, slumped in a wingback armchair and staring at the ashes in the fireplace, bore little resemblance. He was unshaven, his graying hair disheveled, dressed in the same track suit and running shoes he'd been wearing when he got the news early this morning. From the half-empty bottle of Napo-leon Brandy beside him, it seemed he'd decided to try run-ning without leaving his seat. Well, it worked for Damon Inferno—for a while, anyway. Hayden gave me no more than a cursory glance when I sat down opposite him, Whiskey dropping down to lie at my feet. Tango stalked to a corner of the room and curled up on an ottoman.

Sometimes I felt like the clerk in a mask store. Most of the people I've worked for have spent their entire lives constructing a facade—from their outward appearance to how they behave in public, there are layers and layers of carefully crafted personas that they wear to deal with others. But I get to see them when they take those masks off; I get to see them when they switch from one to another, or even advise them on which one they should wear. Sometimes the experience is touching, sometimes it's disappointing, often it's disturbing. One of the reasons I like working for ZZ so much is that her masks are designed to reveal, not conceal.

Hayden's mask had slipped right off his face. Gone was the casual composure, the easy smile, the confident gaze. What had replaced it was shock, disbelief, and anger; the grief he was keeping at bay with the booze, but the others he couldn't shake.

"Mr. Metcalfe?" I said. "Hayden?"

He blinked once, slowly, then looked at me again. "Yes?" he said. His voice was hoarse and unsure.

"How are you holding up?"

"How am I holding up?" He stared at me blearily and then lifted his glass and shifted his gaze to it. "Three sheets to the wind, my dear. Working on number four."

Well, at least he could still talk. "I'm terribly sorry for your loss. Anything that I or ZZ can do, just ask."

He took a gulp of his drink before answering. "Can you bring my wife back?" he said. "Can you go back in time and convince her that going for a late-night swim by herself was a bad idea? Failing that, can you locate the inventor of the hair dryer and throttle them in their damn crib?"

"Are you sure she was by herself?"

"What? Of course she was. I wasn't with her. Who else would have been?" His glare was more befuddled than angry.

"I don't know—maybe one of the other guests? What time did she go down to the pool?"

"She left our room around eleven."

"Kind of late for a swim. Was it a habit of hers?"

He looked away. "No. We'd been arguing, which I'm sure comes as no surprise. She left as much to get away from me as anything."

"Don't blame yourself," I said.

<*Unless you're guilty. Then go ahead.*>

"I can never sleep after a fight with my boyfriend," I said. "I always wind up going for a long walk to straighten things out in my head. And, you know, reargue the points I didn't make in the first place."

"Yes, well," he said, staring into his glass. "There didn't seem to be anything else to say. I thought maybe in the morning things would be better, so I just went to bed. But I was wrong, wasn't I?" He drained his glass. "Things weren't better at all. They were just . . . over."

[So he was alone. No alibi.]

If he's telling the truth, I pointed out silently. "That was quite the . . . *disagreement* you had with Teresa First-charger."

His reply was almost a snarl. "Disagreement? That's one way to put it. The unbelievable *nerve* of that woman . . . saying those things right to Anna's face."

"Then they weren't true?" I kept my voice neutral.

He glanced at me sharply. "That's beside the point. Shoving Anna's face in it like that, in front of complete strangers—the woman has no class, no class at all."

I refrained from pointing out that having an affair in the first place didn't show much class, either. So did Whiskey and Tango, but then animals don't always have the same view of monogamy that humans do.

"Anything that happened between Teresa and myself was a private matter," he continued. His posture changed, his shoulders pulling back and his head coming up as he tried to express his offended dignity with his body. "Doesn't she know how that sort of thing looks . . . what that . . . *appearances,* you know . . ."

And then something happened.

His body rebelled. All that manufactured outrage ran into the high brandy content in his bloodstream and they fought it out. Normally, the outrage would have won; it was used to dealing with brandy, after all.

But this time the booze had an ally, a great hulking brute named grief. It pounded that outrage flat with one thump of its fist; Hayden's shoulders slumped and his face crumpled. "Oh, hell," he said. "What does it matter now? Who cares what's proper, or how things appear? She's gone. Just *gone.*"

His voice was different, too. It was puzzled and sad and very, very weary. "I tried to be a good husband. I wasn't, but I tried. I don't know if that counts for anything or not."

I didn't say anything. Often, pain bleeds honesty, and anything I might say would just stanch the flow.

"It was exhausting, being married to Anna. Having to say the right things, meet the right people, act the right way. She chose me, you know. She could have married anyone, but she chose me. I used to think it was for love, but that was naive. No, with Anna it was always about control. The golden rule."

"The golden rule?"

He gave me a bitter smile. "The one who has the gold makes the rules. She had the money, you see. I had the proper upbringing, but my family suffered some extreme reversals in the financial crash. She more or less rescued me; Lord knows I wasn't ready to fend for myself."

[She adopted him?]

<That's one way to put it. Slapped a collar around his neck is another.>

"That must have been difficult for you," I said.

He poured himself another drink. "*Emasculating* is the word you're looking for. And yes, it was. But the funny thing is, I wasn't even aware of it until I met Teresa. She was the one who made me see the bars on my cage. No matter what you might think of me for cheating, I didn't go looking for it. I thought I was happy."

"But you weren't?"

"No. I wasn't. I was *comfortable,* you see. Not the same thing." He gestured at me with his drink, a little amber liquid sloshing out. "Happiness is . . . *wilder.* Unpredictable. Or that's how Teresa made me feel, anyway. Maybe it was just a case of the grass being greener on the other side of the bed."

No money of his own, and a mistress who brought out his wild side. Hayden was looking more and more like my prime suspect, though Teresa Firstcharger wasn't exactly off the list, either. "Were you and Anna going to split up?"

He stared into the distance with haunted eyes. "I don't know," he whispered. "It's not what I wanted, no matter how things might look. I told Teresa we were through."

"Oh? What happened to happiness?"

He took another quick drink and looked away. "Sometimes comfort has to be enough," he said quietly. "Or maybe it's just that the fear wins. That's the way Teresa sees it, anyway; she thinks I'm a coward. I've lost both of them now."

Maybe, I thought. *It's surprising how fast forgiveness shows up on the heels of a fat inheritance.*

<Or maybe she was never mad at him in the first place.>
[Indeed.]

Pain tends to give people tunnel-vision—all they see is what's right in front of them, and what's sitting there is their own suffering—but Hayden surprised me. "How's Ben doing?" he asked.

"He's angry."

He nodded. "So am I. I'm just not sure at whom, or why."

"Try Efram Fimsby."

He frowned. "Fimsby? Why?"

"Because he's the reason you and Anna are here. Anna met him in Australia, and they cooked up this get-together between them. Any idea why?"

Some not-very-nice things I should point out right about now: questioning someone who's been drinking gives you an advantage. Questioning a drunk who's emotionally vulnerable gives you a bigger one. Hitting an emotionally vulnerable drunk between the eyes with a surprise revelation is like shooting fish in a teacup.

Boom.

His eyes widened in shock. If he was faking it, he was awfully good. "What? But—I thought this was one of your employer's salons—"

"Yeah, no. ZZ was in on it, but Ben wasn't. It had to do with all three of them, though—Anna, Ben, and Fimsby. Fimsby won't tell me anything, Ben doesn't know, and Anna's dead. *What was the reason, Hayden?*"

"I—I don't know. She didn't tell me everything. She started acting strangely just before her trip to Australia."

"Strange in what way?"

"Nervous, distracted. Odd mood swings." He hesitated, thinking. "She seemed very sensitive to the weather. She'd cry when it rained, and stop when it was over. I was worried she was having some sort of breakdown. But she seemed better after she came back. You're saying she was hiding something?"

I knew the reason for Anna's behavior, of course: She'd just discovered she was a Thunderbird, descended from a line of ancient, god-like beings who could control the weather. But I couldn't tell Hayden that, and it wasn't the secret I was after anyway.

But sometimes, when you pounded on a door long enough, you got results. Not necessarily the ones you wanted—it might just be someone opening a window and yelling at you to go away—but results just the same.

I saw the look that crossed his face, though he tried to hide it. "You say Ben is part of this," he said. "And ZZ."

"Yes. Though Ben's just as much in the dark as I am, and ZZ—well, let's just say ZZ is being dragged into this very reluctantly and leave it at that."

"Leave it? When it seems she was instrumental in arranging this whole thing? No. No, I don't think I will." He put down his glass with the exaggerated care of the inebriated, and lurched to his feet. "I will have words with the woman, by God. Yes, I will."

I got up, too. "Hold on. Words about what? What are you talking about?"

He glared down at me, but I didn't back off. "I'm talking about the *secret*. The one Anna knew and Ben didn't. The one ZZ doesn't want to talk about. I should have known—appearances, just like I said. Everybody's so concerned with bloody *appearances*."

He tried to step past me, but I was both quicker and completely sober. I stayed in his face like a dance partner who's forgotten how to go backward. "*What* secret, Hayden? If this involves Ben, I deserve to know. Maybe you and Anna kept secrets from each other, but we don't."

That stopped him like a slap to the face. I hated playing the your-wife-is-dead-but-my-boyfriend-isn't card—hell, I wasn't even sure it was really a card, or just a piece of cardboard with some crayon squiggles on it—but I was desperate. Also a little worried Mr. Brandy might steamroll right over me if I didn't get him to shift into neutral.

"Very well," he said. His breath was combustible. "I suppose you have that right. You know, of course, the story of how Ben came to work for ZZ."

I did. ZZ had found Ben slinging hash in a hole-in-the-wall diner off the interstate, and after sampling one of his omelets hired him as her personal chef.

What ZZ was unaware of was that Ben wasn't quite the diamond-in-the-rough that he appeared to be. In fact, he'd grown up just as privileged as ZZ, was classically trained as a chef, and had been running his own restaurant only six months prior—right up until he'd had a fight with his father (also a chef) over creative differences and had quit in anger. He'd taken the diner job not out of desperation, but simply to prove to himself that he was his own man and could make it without his father's help.

"Sure," I said. "So what?"

Hayden fixed his bleary, red-rimmed eyes on mine. "So it's a lie, Foxtrot. A total, complete lie."

CHAPTER SIX

"What do you mean?" I said to Hayden. "Are you trying to tell me that never happened? That Ben made it all up?"

Hayden swayed slightly on his feet, but his voice was steady. "No, Foxtrot. *That* part of the story is entirely true. It's how it came about that's false. I'm surprised you didn't figure that out for yourself."

"Figure *what* out?"

"That the wealthy all know each other. Look at all the different kinds of guests ZZ gets. Know what they all have in common? Lots and lots of money. When you're rich, the whole world's your private club."

"That's not true," I said. "ZZ has plenty of guests that aren't rich. Scientists, activists—"

"Oh, you can invite anyone you want to *visit* your little clubhouse. But only the members get to enjoy all the privileges. Only the members do *favors* for each other."

That wasn't exactly true, either—but the meaning behind those words was. And *that* truth was suddenly, horribly obvious.

I sank back down onto my chair. "ZZ wasn't in that diner by accident. She knew exactly who Ben was."

"Of course she did. Did you really think the Montains would let their only son slave away in a greasy spoon? Not that they cared about his welfare—they were just thinking about appearances. About how his actions—his *status*— would reflect on them."

<So what? He went from sleeping in a crappy place to a much nicer one. What's it matter how it happened?> Despite their stubborn pride, cats can be very pragmatic when it comes to their own comfort.

[It's a matter of honor, Tango. He thought he earned his rightful place in the pack, and he didn't.] Dogs, on the other paw, while normally very practical, have a keen understanding of social protocols.

"So that's what she couldn't tell me," I said. "She said I'd understand if I knew. And I guess I do."

"Do you?" Hayden seemed to abruptly remember he no longer had a drink in his hand, and set about correcting that. "I'm not so sure. It's a very odd thing, to be a kept man in our society. Makes you question your own worth. Your own ability. I've been one for so long I'm not sure what I'm going to do now that I'm on my own."

Whatever you want, I thought. *Maybe you'll just find another strong woman to tell you what to do. Maybe you already have.*

But I wasn't entirely unsympathetic. I'm used to dealing with big egos in both sexes, and I know how fragile the male one can be. Hayden may have gone into his marriage with his eyes open, but Ben was blissfully unaware he was being manipulated. He'd set out to prove he could make it on his own, and the fact that the exact opposite was true would be like a punch in the face. Or maybe lower down.

Hayden, having poured himself another shot and drained it, then demonstrated the kind of immediate, impulsive decision making that alcohol loves to fuel. "He has to know," he declared. "He must be *told*."

He lurched forward, glass still in hand, his intentions a lot clearer than his thinking. I leapt to my feet to try to block him, but he was already past me. I grabbed his arm and tugged, trying to slow him down. "Wait! What about Fimsby?"

He staggered to a halt. "Fimsby? What's Fimsby got to do with this?"

"Exactly. What does Fimsby have to do with this? He's an Australian meteorologist. Think about it."

His brow furrowed as he did. "That makes no sense."

It did, but only if you knew what I knew. "I *know*. And until we figure out how he fits into all of this, it would be *extremely* unwise to just charge in, hurling accusations. I mean, an *Australian meteorologist*. Think of the ramifications!"

I saw him trying. Just as I'd hoped, it was a baffling enough statement to send his brandy-soaked brain into a self-defeating whirl. He found his way back to his chair and sat down without prompting, muttering, "Hmmm. Yes, that could be . . . huh."

I doubted he'd come to any coherent conclusions, but after all his talk about male disempowerment I very much doubted he'd admit that—not to me, anyway. At the moment I was the living embodiment of his resentment: a hypercompetent woman in charge of just about everything.

"Look," I said. "Until we have a little more information, let's just keep this to ourselves, all right? And if anyone's going to tell Ben, it's going to be me."

He studied me for a moment before replying. When he did, he sounded much more sober—and sadder. "I wanted to spare you that. He'll hate you for it."

"No, he won't," I said.

But I wasn't so sure.

*   *   *

When Hayden had promised me he wouldn't confess what he knew to Ben or ZZ, I went to have a little chat with my boss.

[Foxtrot?]

"Yes?"

[You're walking in a very peculiar way.]

<Yeah, I noticed that, too. Shoulders back, arms swinging, head up. Moving quickly, but not running. I think it's called striding.>

[You forgot to mention the steely gaze.]

<I did? My mistake. Steely, very steely. And then there's the overall sense that she's a train.>

[A train?]

<A train. You know, charging ahead in a straight line, hard to stop, going to cause massive damage when she reaches the end of the line . . .>

[Oh, you mean a *runaway* train. Yes, I see it now.]

"I am not a runaway," I said grimly. "I am in perfect control. When I reach my destination, I will come to a complete and graceful stop. And *then* I will cause massive damage."

[Ah. So more like a train loaded with high explosives, then.]

<I was gonna go with a train full of rabid badgers. More poetic.>

[Do you really think so?]

"I am not going to get drawn into a discussion of the poetic qualities of badgers, rabid or otherwise. I am going to talk to ZZ. About. *Things.*"

<That's really not a good idea, Toots. Not in the state you're in.>

"What state would that be, Tango? You're good with words. Am I in a state of displeasure? Anger? Incandescent white-hot fury?"

<How about gonna-lose-her-job-in-the-next-ten-minutes-if-she-doesn't-cool-offitive?>

[Offitive?]

<Grammar. Had to stick a modifying suffix in there somewhere.>

I strode up the stairs. "I'm not going to get fired. I'm just going to ask her a few questions."

[And once she answers them, you'll resign. Your sense of honor and fair play will demand it.]

"That's not going to happen." I reached the top of the stairs and headed down the hall toward ZZ's office.

<Right. How many former jobs have you quit?>

"A few," I admitted.

[And how often was it over a matter of principle?]

I hesitated. "Maybe once or twice."

<How many?>

"Okay, every time. But I always had a very good reason."

[And perhaps you do this time, as well. But you *can't* quit, Foxtrot. Not this time. You have a greater responsibility to keep in mind: the safekeeping of the Great Crossroads.]

<Yeah. Me and the mutt might be able to pull off living in a graveyard, but you're gonna attract attention if you start sleeping in a mausoleum.>

That stopped me. Which was a good thing, because I was honestly a little overwrought. Which in turn was weird, because overwrought is an emotion I don't generally do. I'm good at keeping my head in a crisis; even when I've had people loudly threatening to remove it with a rusty knife—true story—it's stayed firmly in place and kept functioning.

But this wasn't about me. It was about Ben.

He was my first serious relationship in a long time. And during that long time, I'd apparently been storing up all sorts of feelings just in case I needed them later, which is exactly the sort of delayed emotional response I'm also terrifically good at.

I leaned up against the wall of the corridor and got my breathing under control. "Ooookay," I said quietly. "This is ridiculous. I'm acting like a high school bully just beat up my boyfriend."

[Perhaps a better analogy would be a teacher who betrayed a fellow student's trust, but with the best intentions.]

I thought about that. "You're right. You're right. ZZ's a good person. All she did was give a complete stranger a good job and then consistently compliment him on how well he's doing. What could be wrong with that?"

<Sure, that's the right way to look at—uh, you're striding again.>

"What could be wrong with that?" I repeated, yanking the door to ZZ's office open. "I don't know. Let's go ask her."

ZZ looked up from her desk. "Ask me what, dear?"

<Don't do it, Toots.>

[Foxtrot, I beg of you to reconsider—]

Relax, both of you. I'm all right. "You know that thing you couldn't tell me? Somebody else did."

She met my eyes calmly and didn't seem at all bothered by their steeliness. "Are you bluffing, Foxtrot?"

"What? No. I know about Ben, and the real reason you hired him."

Her gaze dropped. "I'm sorry, but I had to check. You're an excellent bluffer."

"Yeah, my poker face is legendary. But apparently, some people can pull that sort of thing off for *years*."

She nodded but didn't wince. "I suppose I deserved that. Would you like an explanation, or would you prefer to keep using me for target practice?"

I shook my head. "No, that's all I got. But I'm not exactly happy."

"I know. Please, come in and close the door. I'll explain as best I can."

I walked into the room, Whiskey at my heels. Tango

stayed out of sight, back in the hall. *<Best if I hang back, Toots. I've got my reputation to think of.>*

I pulled up a chair and sat down. Whiskey sprawled casually at my feet, panting, but I knew he was alertly listening to every word. "All right, I'm listening."

ZZ leaned back in her chair. "Growing up, you had a cat—Tango. You loved her so much you named the stray Ben adopted after her. Right?"

[If only she knew . . .]

"Right," I said.

"Well, I didn't have any pets. My father didn't believe in them. No matter how much I begged and pleaded, he wouldn't let me have anything—no cat, no dog, not even a hamster. I guess maybe that's why I went a little overboard with the concept when I got older."

"No, no, not at all. Lots of people have their own zoo." She chuckled. "At the time, I thought my father was being heartless. But that wasn't it; in fact, it was my heart he was worried about. The death of a pet is often the first real experience with loss a child has, and it's always traumatic. Having the graveyard right next door emphasized the harshness of that reality. My father wanted to protect me from that; a misguided notion, but ultimately a caring one. He did, however, allow me to have riding lessons. I don't think he really understand just how deeply a little girl can fall in love with a horse."

I did, though. "What was her name?"

"His. His name was Zephyr. He was a four-year-old pinto Saddlebred, and for a while he was my best friend. I only rode twice a week, but I looked forward to those times like nothing else. I was eleven years old.

"But then we had the accident.

"I was out riding him one day, and I took him off-trail. Not very far, but far enough. I don't even remember why; there was something I wanted to look at, a flower or a tree or something. Anyway, the footing wasn't good, and he stumbled. He limped back to the stable, but I wasn't worried. It didn't seem that bad."

"But you were wrong?"

"Yes and no. It was an incomplete fracture, which in a human being isn't serious at all. But a horse's physiology is very different from someone with two legs; they weigh a lot more and the limbs that support them are highly specialized, complex tools. When one of them breaks down, the consequences are far reaching.

"The fracture was in the lower leg, which made it worse. A horse has fewer blood vessels there, which means an injury will heal slower."

"I'm not going to like where this is going, am I?"

"Bear with me, Foxtrot. You're right, the news wasn't good. The owner of the stable said Zephyr would have to go away for a while. Then my father, as much as he dreaded telling me, confirmed my worst fears. Zephyr would have to be euthanized."

She paused, then smiled. "I wanted him buried here, of course. Father refused. He wanted the whole thing over with, didn't want a constant reminder of his daughter's heartbreak that close. I carried on for days, completely inconsolable. Eventually they took me to a therapist, who helped me get over it. It took almost a year."

"I'm not seeing how this is relevant."

"You will. You see, the man who owned the stable was a friend of my mother, not my father. He was rich, too. But unlike my father, he was a romantic—he believed in miracles, I suppose. And a year to the day after Zephyr's accident, he gave me one."

"A new horse? Zephyr's offspring, maybe?"

ZZ's smile widened. "No, Foxtrot. Zephyr himself."

"But I thought—"

"So did I. But when Mr. Montain told me Zephyr had

to go away for a while, that's exactly what he meant. My father was sure the horse would be put down, and he didn't want to get my hopes up; better to have them euthanized, too, and get it over with." Her smile faded. "It's just the sort of man he was. Not really surprising we didn't get along."

"Montain? So the owner of the stable—"

"Was Ben's grandfather. A sweet man, who decided to spend an inordinate amount of money on healing a little girl's heart. Do you have any idea how difficult it is to get a horse's leg to heal properly? Even today, it rarely succeeds. There's some hope for prosthetics, but nobody's managed it yet. It's the weight of the animal itself they can't solve. You can't put that kind of pressure on the injury, and if you try to redistribute it to the other legs it causes a condition known as laminitis. Even slings under the body don't work properly—you get bedsores and problems with breathing. It takes a great deal of persistence, expertise, and luck to do what he did. That, and the willingness to spend lots of money. I don't know exactly how much Phillip Montain spent rehabilitating that horse, but it was several times what the animal was worth. In terms of money, anyway."

I wasn't feeling quite as outraged anymore. "That must have been quite the reunion."

ZZ's eyes gleamed with tears, but it was her smile that really shone. "Oh, Foxtrot. Even now, that memory can make my day. How many people get to have someone they loved given back after death has taken them away?"

[I know at least one. Though the story isn't nearly as touching when the one returning is a cat.]

Oh, crap. My anger was getting harder and harder to hold on to. "I think I might know what that feels like."

"Then you'll understand how much I owe Phillip Montain. He was the one who asked me to take Ben in, not Ben's father. And I couldn't say no."

I sat there, not saying anything. ZZ waited.

[Foxtrot? What are you going to do?]

I don't know. Let me think.

I wanted to be angry. I wanted to be *righteously* angry, playing the role of avenging heroine in this little drama. But I couldn't, because there was no villain to point an accusing finger at. There was just a worried grandfather who wanted to fix things for someone he loved, and a grateful woman trying to repay a miracle. How could you be angry at any of that?

"Okay, I get it," I said at last. "But it's still a lie. One that's going to hurt Ben a whole lot when he finds out."

"Then maybe he shouldn't find out." She looked at me steadily, not tiptoeing around the issue.

"So you want me lie to my boyfriend?"

ZZ sighed. "No. If he asks you, you should tell him the truth. But if he doesn't ask, then you shouldn't tell him."

"How is that any different?"

Now her smile was sad. "It's all about who's willing to carry the pain, Foxtrot. Telling him will get rid of your guilt, but it'll hurt him. Keeping quiet means you hurt instead. And you'll hurt a whole lot more if he ever finds out you knew and didn't tell him."

"But what about the *truth*? Don't you think he has a *right* to know?"

"Yes, he probably does. But protecting the people you love isn't always about doing the right thing. Sometimes it's about doing what you have to."

"Yeah. I guess it is."

ZZ opened her mouth, then closed it again. When she spoke, her voice was firm. "Whatever you decide is up to you. I'm not going to tell you what to do, and I'm not going to hold your decision against you—*whatever* it is. You understand?"

"I do." I got to my feet. "I have to think about this. Whatever I decide, I'll let you know first. That's only fair."

"Thank you, Foxtrot. You know that I trust your judgment, dear; sometimes even more than my own."

That made me grin. "Yeah, but then you go ahead and do whatever you want anyway."

"True. But at least you slow me down."

I nodded good-bye silently, and left. There didn't seem to be anything else to say.

Not to her, anyway.

I didn't have a lot of time to mull things over, though. In my job, that was usually the case; you needed to deal with more than one problem at a time.

My next problem walked up to me as soon as I stepped out the front door. I was hoping for a quiet walk in the gardens, but no such luck—I was going to have to deal with a visibly upset Germanic chauffeur, instead.

Victor was ZZ's driver. He was tall, stern looking, sharp featured, and stern. Today that sternness had been cranked up a little higher, courtesy of what he held in his hands: one of Kaci's paintings.

"Ms. Lancaster," he said stiffly. "I do not wish to disrupt your day, but I must register a complaint."

Uh-oh. Victor wouldn't complain if someone set him on fire. He might demand a fire extinguisher in a cold, formal tone of voice, but there would be no complaining.

"About?" I asked.

"This." He thrust the painting at me like a prosecuting attorney confronting a witness with damning evidence. "It is *inexcusable*."

I squinted at it. "No, I think it's a butterfly. Or a bird."

[Really? I would have said an orchid.]

"That is beside the point," he said, glaring at me in a way that suggested the point was not only very, very sharp but about to be plunged into my chest. "It is my responsibility to operate and maintain Ms. Zoransky's vehicles. I cannot do

this if they are continually being misused and maltreated."
He continued to glare at me from over the top edge of the
butterfly-bird-orchid painting, which had been executed in a
vivid scarlet. It felt a bit like being studied by a vulture over
the remains of a bloody corpse.

"And how, exactly are they being misused and maltreated?" I asked him.

"By *Mister* Zoransky. He's using the Rolls-Royce as if
it were a pickup truck." Victor was practically quivering
in indignation. "Filling the trunk and even the backseat
with canvases. And some of them aren't even dry yet!"

I nodded. "Okay, Victor. I'll have a word with Oscar.
I'm sure we can arrange a more suitable means of trans-
portation for the paintings. I'll have one of the rental
agencies drop off a van, okay?"

He nodded sharply. "Thank you. I will return this to
the garage." He wheeled about and retreated, holding the
painting like he intended to shoot someone with it if they
tried to stop him.

[I'm not a huge fan of art, but I know what I like,] Whiskey said as we continued on our way. [That painting was
exceptional.]

"Oh, absolutely. But an exceptional what? A bug? A
flower? The rare and elusive Rorschach bird?"

[I sense a certain amount of sarcasm.]

"You sense correctly. Anyway, if you like her paintings
so much, why not tell the artist?"

[I'm not sure that would be proper.]

I rolled my eyes. "Please. If you can't even tell her you
like her art, how are you ever going to tell her you like *her*?"

[I'm not. I mean, I don't. That is, I am not going to because I do not. Ahem.]

"Oh, *ahem* yourself. For a detective dog with a keen
nose, you sure can be clueless. Come on, Romeo—time to
step up."

[I must say I'm finding your remarks highly inappropriate.]

"Oh, am I being a little intrusive? Unlike you, who sees nothing wrong with commenting on changes in my menstrual cycle?"

[I simply noticed you'd introduced more asparagus into your diet recently. Really, it was obvious to anyone with a nose.]

"And your interest in Kaci is obvious to anyone with eyes. Or is there some sort of rule against fraternization with the living?"

[No, of course not. But honestly, how could I—]

And that's when we were interrupted by Teresa Firstcharger.

"I think you've avoided me long enough," she said, stepping directly in front of me. Whiskey and I were walking down one of the garden paths, flanked on either side by towering green bushes; Firstcharger must have been standing behind one, though there didn't seem to be room.

She wore a brown leather jacket over a black T-shirt printed with a Native American art design—one that looked oddly familiar—black jeans, and cowboy boots. Her long black hair was held back with turquoise-inlaid silver clips. She was tall and slender and strikingly attractive, her cheekbones high and sharp, her eyes dark with long lashes. She wore little to no makeup, and she didn't need any.

"Uh, hello," I said. "Ms. Firstcharger. I'm sorry, were you trying to reach me? I thought I'd given all the guests my cell number—"

"And hello to you, too, Whiskey," she said, ignoring me and looking down. "You look as surprised to see me as Foxtrot is. Your nose letting you down?"

[I assure you, madame, that my nose is functioning perfectly. You were simply downwind of me.]

"I suppose I was. How lucky for me the wind seems to be on my side."

It took me a second to realize what had just happened.

Teresa wasn't talking to me.

She was talking to Whiskey.

CHAPTER SEVEN

Teresa Firstcharger grinned at the expression on my face.
"I'm sorry," she said. "Did I interrupt a private conversation?"

I looked down at Whiskey, who was staring at First-charger as intently as a sheepdog at a recalcitrant ewe. I looked back at Firstcharger, who had her arms crossed and a lazy smile on her face.

"No, I—wait. What?" I said cleverly.

"Nicely put. How about you, pup?"

Whiskey said nothing. His gaze was so steady you could have balanced an egg on it.

Firstcharger laughed. "Nothing to say? What's the matter, Tango got your tongue?"

I tried again. "Wait. I . . . No. What?"

"I can see I'll have to hold up this conversation all by myself. All right, then. You're investigating Anna's murder. She and I had a very public confrontation the night before. I was one of the very first people the police talked to, but you haven't. Why not?"

Okay, third time's the charm. Except she kept lobbing bombshells at me and I hadn't even been able to dodge, let alone react intelligently. "What makes you think Anna was murdered?" Okay, that's better.

"Maybe I have animal spies of my own," she said. "A little bird could have told me. Or a fish."

"There aren't any fish in the swimming pool," I said. Ooh, good one, Foxtrot. Tango would have mocked me for a good five minutes if I'd said something like that to her.

Firstcharger let it pass, as apparently she had bigger fish to mock. "Are you afraid of me?"

"Should I be?"

"Depends on how smart you are. I thought you were fairly bright, but maybe I was wrong."

I felt a surge of anger. Dammit, this woman was playing me like a . . . fish. Or a violin. Or a violin made out of a fish. *Get it together, Foxtrot.* "All right, Teresa. Where *were* you when Anna died?"

"Alone in my room. Asleep." The amusement in her voice was a challenge.

I accepted. "Guess you didn't do it, then. Not that I ever thought you did."

"Oh? Why not?"

"Too obvious. Nobody planning a murder starts a public fight with the victim hours beforehand, unless they're extremely stupid. You're not."

She nodded graciously. "True. Even so—"

I cut her off. "But you *can* converse with my dog. Not a lot of people know that trick, and one of them is a Thunderbird. Just like you, right?"

For the first time, she looked at me with respect on her face. "So I wasn't wrong about your intelligence. Good. That'll make things more interesting."

It may have taken me a few minutes to get up to speed, but my brain seemed to have finally kicked in. "That's what you meant when you said the wind was on your side. You're controlling it. And since you know Anna was murdered, you must have known what she was, too."

"And what her brother still is. For now, anyway."

"What do you mean?"

"Someone killed one of us, Foxtrot. Two more are still here. You think the killer's going to stop?"

[No one else is going to die.]

Firstcharger looked back at Whiskey. "Found your voice, did you? Good—I was beginning to think I'd offended you."

[I wasn't offended, merely cautious. Why are you here, Thunderbird?]

"Just like a dog. Straight to the point. Sadly, I'm not that transparent. You'll learn why I'm here soon enough."

Whiskey growled. I knew how he felt. [Be advised that this place is under our protection. Any attempt to cause trouble will be dealt with harshly.]

She snorted. "Yes, I'm sure you've pissed on every available fence post to mark your territory. But I'm more than just a dead canine who dug his way out of a grave, or a cat who can talk to spirits. I'm the messenger of the gods, the voice of lightning and the heartbeat of thunder. If blood still pumped through your veins, I could freeze it solid or make it boil. You don't frighten me, little ghost dog."

"Then you're not as smart as you think you are," I said.

"No? We'll see. Good-bye, Foxtrot. I'm looking forward to chatting with you at dinner." She stepped past me and sauntered away.

We watched her go until she was out of sight. Neither Whiskey nor I said a thing for a moment.

Then Whiskey sighed. [I believe the situation just became somewhat more complicated.]

"You think?"

Another Thunderbird. It seemed so obvious now, but I'd never even considered the idea before. Maybe it was subconscious political correctness, or maybe it was just that my mind really wanted all this supernatural craziness to stay contained within my own little group.

But that was the thing about craziness: It didn't want to be contained. It wanted to sprawl, and flail, and generally be as inconvenient as possible. Until little old me came along and wrestled it back into the corral.

[Really? You're making *cowboy* references?]

Um, sorry. I'm a little rattled.

We'd continued on our walk, heading toward the zoo. I was still reeling, trying to figure out my next move; I should really talk to Ben, but after what ZZ had revealed to me I found myself dreading the idea. If I didn't tell Ben ZZ's secret right away, I'd be lying by omission—but if I did tell him, it would add more chaos to an already turbulent mix. Then again, I really *had* to tell him about Teresa Firstcharger . . .

Argh.

[Excuse me?]

"Argh. It's a universal human term loosely translating to 'I'm overwhelmed and frustrated, somebody make this stop.'"

[I see. Comparable to a good whine, then.]

"Yeah, pretty much."

We got to the zoo. I nodded hello at Oswald, our resident ostrich and escape expert. He gave me that idiotic look ostriches do so well, which is really just intended to make you forget they're descended from giant, meat-eating dinosaurs. Then he usually tries to eat your cell phone. If that doesn't work he makes a mad dash for the exit; if it does, he disables the GPS tracking and *then* makes a mad dash for the exit. Idiotic, yet cunning.

Which is when I saw Caroline hurrying toward me, looking worried. Caroline's our vet, in charge of a wide variety of exotic animals. Just seeing the expression on her face reminded me that *Argh* also acted as a universal beacon, drawing even more trouble your way. It was the wounded wildebeest of epithets.

"Foxtrot," Caroline said. "Do you have a minute?"

"Sure," I said. I did my best to say it in a cheerful, positive way, instead of the surly mutter it wanted to be. "What's up?"

"More like what's out."

"Oh, no. It can't be Oswald—I just saw him."

"No, not Oswald. That's just it—it's not one of ours."

I frowned. "It's not one of our what?"

"Snakes."

My eyes widened. "Snakes? What sort of snakes?"

"Well, snake, actually. Singular, not plural. I've been getting calls from people who claim they've seen some kind of python on the grounds."

"Please tell me they're talking about John Cleese or Eric Idle. Even Terry Jones."

She shook her head. "No, this is probably closer to Burmese than Monty. Big, multicolored, and apparently very fast. It vanishes whenever someone tries to get a closer look."

"That's . . . pretty weird." And there was no way I was going to make it even weirder by bringing up Cooper's dream.

Caroline sighed, brushing an errant wisp of blond hair back from her forehead. "Not as weird as you might think. Snakes, especially the big constrictors, are exactly the kind of pet attractive to people who shouldn't be pet owners in the first place."

"True. I blame Alice Cooper. Or possibly the Bible."

"The thing is, they live a long time, they never stop growing, and they could give Oswald escape lessons. If they don't manage to free themselves, sometimes their owners just let them go and hope they survive on their own."

I crossed my arms. "And I'm guessing that usually doesn't go too well."

"Not for the local ecology. There are nine particular species of snake that cause the most trouble. They grow up fast, travel long distances, and have lots of little snake babies while chowing down on the local population of wildlife: birds, rodents, amphibians, anything they can catch. They can adapt to a wide range of climates and they don't mind cities."

I frowned. "How wide a range of climates?"

"About a third of the country. Florida already has thousands of them. And those nine species include the heaviest and longest snakes in the world. The reticulated python can grow to over twenty feet in length, and the green anaconda can mass over two hundred pounds. It's a big problem."

Now even Whiskey was glancing around nervously. "Two hundred pounds?" I said. "That's big enough to swallow . . ."

"A person, yes. Attacks on humans are rare, but they do occur. The bigger threat is to the ecosystem. In Guam, an invasive reptile called the brown tree snake devastated the local fauna in just forty years: half the bats and lizards gone, and ten out of twelve native avian species completely wiped out."

"That's horrifying. What kind of snake are we talking about here? One of the enormous ones?"

She shrugged. "I don't know. The coloration reminds me of a Boelen's python, but they don't get much bigger than ten feet in length—and the reports I've been getting are of something much larger. Of course, people always tend to exaggerate these things."

I had a sudden thought that made me shudder. "Any chance one could get indoors?"

"It's possible, but unlikely. They tend to avoid people, for the most part."

She gave me a quick rundown on where the thing had been sighted—several times just outside the graveyard, and once in a tree on the edge of the estate. "Pythons are quite good at climbing," Caroline added.

"Thanks," I said. "I'll make sure to point that out to all our guests on the second floor."

I assured her I'd look into it, and she thanked me and hurried off. "Want to make sure all my animals are accounted for," she said over her shoulder.

I looked down at Whiskey when she was gone. "I guess I should do the same. Though something tells me even a giant snake wouldn't give you that much trouble."

[An ordinary one, no. But this one sounds far from mundane.]

"Maybe it isn't real. The graveyard acts as a psychic amplifier, right? Could Cooper be broadcasting his dreams?"

[An intriguing idea—but Cooper's been the groundskeeper for years, has he not?]

"True. Why now? And if his dreams *were* being beamed around the neighborhood, I'd expect a lot more sightings of giant skeletons in top hats smoking doobies as opposed to rainbowy snakes." I sighed. "Another thing to look into. You sure you can't morph into a version of me? Dual Foxtrots would sure come in handy."

[I'm sure they would. But as you are a most singular creature, replicating you would prove impossible in any case.]

I grinned. "Why, thank you, Whiskey. Despite your duplication abilities, you're quite the singular creature yourself. Shall we continue along our way in hopes of new adventures, or simply wait here for them to spring upon us?"

[I sense I'm being mocked.]

I laughed. "No, not at all. I love how you talk. Just thought I'd give it a try myself."

[I see. In the future?]

"Yes?"

[Please refrain.]

"You got it, Toots."

[That's hardly better.]

The one nice thing about being overwhelmed by things you have to do is that it makes it easier to put off hard decisions. And by *nice,* I mean "attractive yet very bad for you."

"Hello, love," Keene said. He was sprawled on a lounger in the middle of the lawn wearing a gold lamé Speedo and sunglasses. His drink had an umbrella in it.

I frowned at him. "Did you know there's an umbrella in your drink?"

"Ah. I was wondering where that had gotten to. Drat, now the handle's all wet."

"Also, you're drinking out of a fishbowl."

"Of course I am. The umbrella wouldn't fit in anything else."

Whiskey lay down at my feet with a resigned look on his face. *What do you think you're doing?* I thought at him.

[Getting comfortable. You and Keene tend to go on a bit.]

"Hello, Whiskey," Keene said cheerfully. "You know, I really love that one-brown-eye/one-blue-eye thing. Been considering doing it myself for my next tour. What do you think?"

[Hmm. Not really your style.]

"Yeah, you're right. Bit too Marilyn Manson for me. But I could rock an early Bowie look."

Keene can't actually talk with Whiskey telepathically like I do. But he's one of those people very attuned to animals in general, and his side of their pretend conversations is often eerily accurate.

"Awfully glad I ran into you, Your Foxiness. Or you ran into me. Or trotted into me, I suppose."

"I thought you were going to stop calling me that."

His grin was wide and bright as a sail on a sunny day. "What, Your Foxiness? But it's a *title*. We Brits are big on titles. Anyway, it beats the alternative I came up with."

"Which would be?"

"I refuse to say. It's filthy and disgusting and you deserve better."

"Tell me or I'll have the maid short-sheet your bed."

He chuckled. "You would, wouldn't you? But really, I can't. Though I could give you a hint and have you work it out for yourself."

"And how's that better than just telling me?"

"Plausible deniability, love. Plausible *deniability*."

I shook my head, but I was smiling. "Okay, hint away."

"Try to imagine your nickname as said by Elmer Fudd."

I did, and understood immediately. He giggled maniacally at the look on my face. "Now, now—before you go planning my murder, I should tell you that I've divulged that particular phrase to no one. Take it to my grave, I will."

"That's not exactly a sterling reason to keep you alive."

He appeared to consider this while sucking on the straw jutting from his fishbowl. "Ah. Perhaps you're right. I shall have to take steps to ensure my safety. Explicit instructions in my will, coded messages in a safety deposit box, legal counsel sworn to secrecy. If you're going to kill me, you'd better do it before teatime—I'll have it all locked down by then."

"By then you'll be on your third fishbowl and will have forgotten your own middle name."

"Good point. Maybe I should put that in the coded message as well. Important to be prepared."

"Is that a new tattoo?"

"I'm flattered you noticed. Yes, I had it done by this chap in Amsterdam. Brilliant artist, does all my stuff. You like it?"

I squinted. "Um. I'm not sure. It's definitely . . . unique. Never seen an angel doing that before."

"It came to me in a dream. Or possibly a stupor. Hard to tell the two of them apart, sometimes."

"Not for me. I can always tell when you're in a stupor. Speaking of which—what were you up to last night?"

"Oh, the usual. Working on some new material in the study, mostly. Was going to go for a dip in the pool but decided against it. Now I wished I had." His smile shrank. "Poor woman. If there'd been someone else there, maybe she'd still be alive."

There was, I thought to myself. *But who?*

I heard a meow from the bushes beside the front door, and Tango emerged a second later. "Hello, kitty," Keene said. "I'd offer you a lap, but I'm covered in sunscreen."

<Hey, Toots.> Tango strolled up casually, then sat and started grooming herself. *<What's new?>*

[Let's see. ZZ explained why she lied to Ben and Foxtrot has agreed to inform her before telling Ben. There may or may not be a giant snake loose on the grounds. Teresa Firstcharger claims she's also a Thunderbird, and can communicate with us the same way Ben does. Also, Mr. Keene has acquired a new tattoo.]

<Wait. Say that last part again?>

[Teresa Firstcharger is a Thunderbird—]

<No, no. The part about the snake.>

[Giant snake, actually. Some sort of escaped python.]

"You're staring," Keene said.

I blinked. "Am I? Sorry." Sometimes I tended to zone out a little when listening to Whiskey and Tango's voices in my head, and when that happened my eyes fixed on a single point. In this case, it was Keene's abdomen—which was in pretty good shape for a guy who spent his days lying around sipping from booze-filled fishbowls.

"Don't apologize on my account," Keene said. "I quite

like it when you stare at me, Foxtrot. Here, look what I can make the angel do."

<Giant python? Please tell me you're kidding.>

[No, I'm quite in earnest. Possibly an anaconda.]

"No, really, you don't have to—huh. That's interesting."

"Isn't it? Looks like she's really playing that accordion."

<Details! Where was this giant python seen?>

"Sticking out of my trousers," Keene said. "That was my first choice for location. But that really only works if the angel's playing a trombone."

[In a bush, I believe.]

Tango glanced back at where she'd just come from. <Bush? Which bush?>

"Not *your* bush," I said.

"Whose bush?" Keene asked.

[Oh, dear. Now you've done it.]

"Nobody's," I said quickly. "I was just thinking out loud."

"About your bush?" He raised his eyebrows.

"No! Forget about my bush." I realized what I'd just said and tried to change the subject. "What was that about your trombone?"

"I didn't get a trombone. I went with the accordion, see?"

<I hate pythons. Horrible way to die. They just squeeze and squeeze and squeeze—>

"Accordion, right. Don't they call that a squeezebox?"

[I can't believe you just said that.]

"I believe they do," Keene said. "Are you trying to tell me something, Your Foxiness?"

"Absolutely not," I said. "I have to go."

And then I ran away, while attempting to look casual instead of panicked. Whiskey followed me, and after a moment so did Tango.

[Well, that was disturbing.]

<I'll say. What's the plan to deal with this python problem?>

"We don't even know if there *is* a python," I said under my breath. "And even if there is, I have more urgent things to deal with."

<More urgent than two hundred pounds of crushing death? I don't think so.>

[*Hypothetical* crushing death. Though there's nothing hypothetical about *Foxtrot's* crush.]

<I thought dogs didn't do wordplay.>

[Stating the obvious isn't wordplay.]

"There is nothing obvious about my crush!"

Silence. I could almost hear crickets chirping inside the quiet shocked emptiness of my skull.

<Uh-huh. Anyway, about that snake—>

[Yes, of course. The snake.]

<You're the one with the superpowered nose. Can you smell it? Is it nearby?>

[Oh, it's practically right next to us. The giant snake we're not supposed to talk about.]

The hair on Tango's back stood up. *<What? Where?>*

"Nowhere," I said. "Cut it out, Whiskey—you're terrible at metaphors. There's no elephant in the room *or* giant snake in the pants. I do *not* have a crush on Keene."

<Yeah, right. Just so we're clear—now there isn't *a snake?>*

[That's still uncertain.]

Tango darted ahead, then turned and glared at both of us. *<Then let's stop talking about who wants to yowl in the moonlight with whom and get our priorities straight. THERE'S A GIANT DAMN SNAKE OUT THERE!>*

I stopped and sighed. "Okay, okay. You're concerned, I get that. But there's a lot going on right now, Tango. Tell you what—why don't you do some investigating on your own and report back? Ask around the graveyard and the zoo, see if any of the ghosts or animals have spotted the thing?"

Tango considered this. *<I suppose I could do that. But if I see one scale—just one—I'm outta there.>*

She scampered off, steering well clear of the bushes. Whiskey and I watched her go, and I had a sudden pang of guilt. "She'll be all right, won't she?"

[Don't worry about Tango. Any snake that tries to eat her will suffer her wrath.] He paused, then added [And mine.]

I smiled. For all their jabs at each other, each of my partners cared deeply about the other. Any telepathic cry from Tango would produce an enraged ectoplasmic dog in the time it took him to sprint from here to there. And having seen some of the breeds Whiskey could transform into, I doubted there was a snake alive he couldn't face down.

Of course, that was assuming the snake was alive in the first place . . .

CHAPTER EIGHT

I knew I had to tell Ben about Firstcharger, but I didn't know if I should do the same for Fimsby. He hadn't even admitted he knew Anna and Ben were Thunderbirds, so telling him Teresa was one too didn't make much sense. But if Ben was in danger from whoever killed Anna, then so was Teresa.

Unless she *was* the danger, of course.

Sometimes when you don't know what to do, a little fresh air and exercise can clear your head. Well, I'd been out and about all morning and things had only gotten worse. Time to try the opposite approach—I was going to hole up with some tea and my computer. When in doubt, do research.

I hadn't had much luck learning about Thunderbirds online, but maybe I'd do better checking out Teresa Firstcharger herself. A little digging turned up a history that seemed to confirm what she'd told me: While her family name was indeed from a Great Plains tribe—the Blackfoot Confederacy—her maiden name was Hwitsum and she was a member of the Cowichan tribe. The same one that the Thunderbirds supposedly married into when they gave up being weather spirits and took on human form.

She'd been active in First Nation politics since she was a teenager, beginning with her local tribal council; she'd spent a few years agitating for reform in the reservation where she'd grown up, then developed bigger ambitions and started to travel.

She'd met her first husband at a powwow in Washington State. He was a mover and shaker in the aboriginal rights movement, and catapulted her onto the US federal stage. Her marriage hadn't lasted, but she'd kept the name and the political connections that went with it. Her interests seemed to lie mainly in ecology—no surprise there, considering her heritage—but she wasn't above attaching herself to higher-profile issues if it would get her some press. There were numerous photos of her with celebrities ranging from real estate moguls to movie stars, and in every one of them she was dressed like she'd been born on the red carpet. She was glamorous and ambitious and obviously very smart. Even without the ability to call up typhoons at whim, she was a major player.

I'd known some of this before I started—I research all of ZZ's guests before they arrive—but I hadn't really grasped just who Teresa Firstcharger was. I'd mentally slotted her in with ZZ's activist friends, most of whom were well-meaning enviromentalists with idealistic goals but little real clout. She was a different creature entirely; her modus operandi seemed to be to find an opportune climate, zero in on the most prominent alpha male and then roll over him like a hurricane.

I shook my head. "I could never do that," I muttered. "Not in a million years."

Whiskey lifted his head from the carpet. [Do what?]

"Chew through relationships like they were potato chips. I understand ambition, but *using* people the way Firstcharger does? No way."

[Using people is the inevitable result of ambition, is it not?]

"Depends on how you're using them. Making friends, trading favors, manipulating events? Sure. But romance is a different game, as far as I'm concerned. Sleeping with someone for political advantage is just wrong."

[Humans have such convoluted mating rituals.]

I leaned back in my chair. "I guess. We're convoluted beings. Must be a lot simpler, being a dog."

[Oh, yes. I remember it well; everything was much less complicated. Pleasures were simple, emotions were pure. For the most part.]

I frowned. "But not anymore. Now you use words like *convoluted* in everyday conversation with a member of another species. I guess death comes with an automatic upgrade in intelligence?"

[You know I can't talk about certain things, Foxtrot.]

"Yeah, yeah." I'd run into this before with my supernatural partners, and while I grudgingly understood, it still annoyed me. If there's one thing I can't stand, it's being out of the loop. I love the loop. I live in the loop. I keep a toothbrush, a change of clothes, and a spare cell phone charger in the loop. "So tell me, Romeo, what's a canine romance like? Simple and pure sounds pretty good to me."

He sat up and regarded me solemnly. [It begins with a scent. A musk, interlaced with a thousand delicate variations of chemical beauty that makes human perfume seem as heavy and solid as a ball-peen hammer. It tells me more about her than mere words ever could, for there is no possibility of deception. It is her soul, filigreed upon the wind.

[I approach. I circle. We communicate with body language, a subtle dance that speaks of desire and expectation, of loneliness and need. Eyes flicker, posture shifts, there is an invitation and a challenge. I respond with my own signals, letting her know me as best I can; not of my desire—that much is understood from the very beginning—but of my status, my fierceness, my own longing and need. When we finally merge, there is as much gratitude and sympathy for our mutual plight as there is an overwhelming sense of destiny and joy. Our connection at that moment is complete and total, our most fervent hope not for pleasure but that our union produces offspring, our genes locked together in an embrace that will outlast both of us.]

I stared at him. He looked back, calmly.

"What happened to simple?" I finally managed.

[I did say, "for the most part."]

"I guess you did. I'm sorry, Whiskey; I've been ribbing you about your crush on Kaci without really thinking about what I was saying. That was inconsiderate and rude. I apologize."

[There's no need, Foxtrot. There are consequences to dwelling on the material plane, even as an ectoplasmic being. Having certain memories stirred up by particular . . . *scents* is simply one of them. It's hardly your fault.]

"No, but I should be more sensitive. It must be strange, to go from being a living animal to an ectoplasmic one. You can eat but don't excrete, you can change your shape and size . . . and apparently you're a lot smarter than when you were alive."

[Control over my bodily functions, increased ability and intelligence—not that different from a stage you humans go through. I believe you call it "adulthood."]

Well, he had me there. Small children and dogs did share a number of qualities beyond cuteness—though what it really made me wonder about was what human beings turned into when they died. Did we get a similar upgrade, or were those options only for animals?

I knew better than to ask, though. Instead, I said, "Let's see if I can make it up to you."

[And how do you propose to do that?]

"Hey, I'm a professional facilitator. And to facilitate any project, the first step is always to know what you're getting into. In this case, I'm guessing there's not a lot I can find out about Border collies you don't already know, so let's tackle this from another angle: Kaci's owner."

I straightened up and started tapping keys. "I wasn't able to find out much about him on my initial research run, but we have more information now. I had a little chat with him when he first arrived, and he told me the estate reminded him of a park in Kiev where he grew up. Let's see . . ."

[And what do you hope to find out?]

"Maybe he intends to breed her. You can pull off a passable Border collie, right?"

[Surely you're not intending what I think you are.]

"Why not? All we need to do is establish your artistic bona fides and you're a shoo-in. The real question is, what branch of the arts are you best suited for?"

[Foxtrot. I am not wooing Kaci by posing as a fellow artistic canine.]

"Quiet, I'm working. We need to convince Rustam you two are the perfect match, which means figuring out what he likes other than painting—uh-oh."

[Other than the inherent dishonesty in such a maneuver, there's also the simple fact that my position doesn't allow me to draw attention to—did you just say "uh-oh"?]

"I did. I tried searching for *Rustam Gorshkov*, *Kiev*, and *art*."

[What did you find?]

"Nothing on Gorshkov. But there's a story here about a Rustam Groshenko who was involved in dealing forged paintings. And there's a photo."

I turned the monitor so Whiskey could see. He did me

one better, transforming into a small poodle and leaping onto my lap. He peered at the screen intently.

[Hmmm. It might be him, but it's difficult to say. And the similarity in names could be a coincidence.]

"True. But con artists often change their last name and keep the first—easier to keep track of that way." I studied the picture. "It gets worse. He disappeared when he was out on bail, and he had connections to the Russian mob. If this is him, he's not a nice guy. At all."

[Which, ultimately, doesn't matter. I can't conduct a romance with Kaci, Foxtrot. It simply . . . wouldn't be practical.]

I shrugged. "Since when is love practical? Usually it's impractical, inconvenient, and aggravating. But that doesn't mean it isn't worthwhile."

[Very astute. Might I remind you that she's among the living and I am not?]

I grinned at him. "Love beats death, Whiskey. Remember?"

He gave me a long-suffering poodle look and jumped off my lap. [I know, I know. But the question of the moment is what beats nosy, interfering partners of another species . . .]

I have a standing invitation to attend dinner at the house, but I chose not to that evening. I went home at five, taking Whiskey with me, and ate there. There was too much going on among too many people, and the thought of facing all of them across the table seemed exhausting. Besides, I had to prepare for my own evening—I had plans. Not quite the same plans as I'd had before the day unfolded, but plans all the same.

Ben showed up around seven. He had a helper who spelled him on certain evenings, like tonight: date night. Sometimes we stayed at his place—he had his own cottage on the grounds—but I wanted to get away from the estate for a while. Also, if I was going to break bad news to my boyfriend, I wanted the home-field advantage.

But he hadn't come alone.

<Hey, Toots. What's for dinner?> Tango scooted past my legs as soon as I opened the door.

Ben sighed and stepped in after her. "She insisted on coming along. Says she has big news."

"It can wait," I said. I threw my arms around him and kissed him. Hard.

Okay, here's the part where I explain all the strategic advantages of showering him with affection before delivering my own unwelcome news, and exactly how I'm going to tell him to minimize any possible ugly scene.

Except I'm not.

If I was dealing with him at work, sure. I do that kind of finessing all the time, though rarely with household staff. But I wasn't at work; I was at home, he was my boyfriend, and under those circumstances I do my best to turn that part of my brain off. I'm not always successful, but I try.

As usual, Whiskey pretended he wasn't there and Tango interrupted us far too soon. *<Hey! Enough with the lip-lock. Disgusting habit, anyway.>*

Shut up. Busy.

<Hey, did I tell you about that mouse I dismembered today? It was epic. I totally ripped off—>

"Aaaaaand we're done." I pulled away from Ben, but not too far. "Sorry. Tango's in my head, and she's not playing fair."

"Yeah, I heard that, too. Okay, T-cat. What can't wait?"

<Dogs, usually. They're terrible at it. Me, I can wait all day if I have to.>

"Your *news*, Tango," I prompted. "Tell us your news."

<Oh, right. Let me get comfortable, first. Lap?>

I surrendered to the inevitable and sat down on the couch.

Ben waited until Tango sprang up and settled in, then sat down next to me. Whiskey trotted over nonchalantly and dropped to the ground at my feet. I took a second to just appreciate it; being loved is one thing, but having the ones who love you snuggled up against your body is something else.

<Okay. I spent the afternoon stalking the serpent.>

"Serpent?" Ben said.

"Oh, I think I forgot to mention that," I said. "There may or may not be a giant, multicolored snake roaming the grounds." I told him about Cooper's dream and the calls Caroline was getting. "Tango said she'd follow up, see if any of the animals—deceased or otherwise—had encountered the thing."

<Yeah. You want to let me tell the story, or do you have your own spellbinding version you want to share?>

"Sorry. Take it away."

<So, I began at the zoo. I could only talk to the animals who were awake, but you have to start somewhere. I questioned a warthog, a cockatoo, a pair of pygmy marmosets, and a turtle. I concentrated on small animals first, because I figured they'd be the most aware of an impending threat. Plus, they're easier to intimidate.>

"A warthog is small?" Ben asked.

<Not really, but he's nervous. Was initially sold as a Vietnamese potbellied pig and pampered like a baby. His owner got rid of him when he wouldn't stop growing. Waste of good bacon, if you ask me.>

"Sadly, no one ever will," I said. "You might want to be a little nicer to Perky. He outweighs you by a factor of ten and has a mean pair of tusks."

Tango yawned. <Big deal. That's like strapping a pair of butcher knives to a little old lady. Perky's scared of his own shadow—he's got the personality of a neurotic poodle. Or is that last part redundant?>

[I've known a few poodles who would disagree with that assessment,] Whiskey said. [But only a few.]

"Did any of the animals see anything?" I asked.

<Nah. Well, Perky thought he might have, but it turned out to be a garden hose. He wouldn't go near it.>

[And did you, perchance, happen to talk to any of the *actual* snakes in the menagerie?]

<They were all asleep. Didn't want to bother them.>

[Indeed.]

<What's that supposed to mean?>

[That you never went within twenty yards of the snake habitat.]

<Why should I? I could hear them snoring from twenty-five.>

[Yes, of course. Snakes are notoriously loud creatures, especially in their sleep.]

<How would you know? Ghosts don't sleep. And knowing that, I headed over to the graveyard, where I figured I'd have a better chance of someone seeing something. Of course, most of the spirits there are just passing through, so finding someone to question is kinda difficult. I had to go to the prowlers.>

The prowlers were animal spirits not ready to go on to their respective afterlives; they hung around the Great Crossroads the way transients hang around a bus station, attracted to the activity but not really part of it. Some of them were confused, and occasionally they could be hostile.

"Who'd you talk to?" I asked. "Topsy?"

<No, she makes me uncomfortable.>

"Why, because she's an elephant?" Ben asked.

<No, because she's an electric *elephant*. All that supernatural voltage makes my fur stand on end.> Topsy had died of electrocution over a hundred years ago.

"Understandable," I said. "So who, then?"

<Two-Notch. I relate better to fellow carnivores, anyway.>

Two-Notch is—was—a shark. She thinks the Great Crossroads is a huge aquarium, and won't venture past its boundaries. "How'd that go?"

<She claimed to have seen the thing. In the ditch by the side of the road, just past the fence—of course, she thought it was slithering around on the other side of a glass wall. Two-Notch isn't what you'd call a reliable witness.>

I stroked Tango's silky back. "You believe her?"

<I believe she saw something. Whether or not it was a giant snake is a lot harder to know. But according to her it was really, really long.>

"How about the coloration?" I asked.

<Sharks don't see in color, so she didn't know. Did I mention how long it was?>

[Yes, but you failed to say how long.]

<Longer than Two-Notch's attention span. As in, she saw the head, but got bored and swam away before the tail came into sight.>

I sighed, scritching behind Tango's ears. "Which might be saying more about a dead shark's ability to concentrate than anything else."

<I don't know, Toots. Most of what I know about fish has to do with how they taste, but sharks aren't exactly known as being flighty. Which makes them swimmy, I guess. Which also doesn't seem right, so forget I brought it up.>

[An action I take following most of your pronouncements.]

"So what's the verdict?" Ben asked. "What is this giant snake? Real, imaginary, or other?"

<It could be a ghost. Sometimes they're visible to psychically sensitive people. And other ghosts can see them, of course.>

"So, maybe another prowler," I said. "Drawn by the

Great Crossroads like the others. And who knows how long it's been traveling? A big snake like that probably doesn't move that fast."

<You'd be surprised. And then you'd be dinner.>

[Not if it's among the formerly living, Tango. Physical appetites tend to perish along with the corporeal form.]

<Yeah? That's not what I hear, you old horndog—>

"Let's lay off the romantic slurs," I interjected. "At least for tonight, okay?"

"Yeah, it doesn't exactly help set the mood," Ben added.

<Mood? There's a mood? Nobody told me about a mood.>

"I *tried*," Ben said under his breath. "But noooo, you had to tag along . . ."

<Cats do not "tag along." Cats grace you with their presence, if you meet our standards.>

Whiskey got to his feet. [Come on, Tango. The two-legged ones want some privacy.]

<But I'm comfortable.> She demonstrated by stretching out to her full length and closing her eyes. I rolled mine—as nice as it is to be trapped under a boneless cat, I had other plans.

"You can be comfortable somewhere else," I said firmly. "And I don't mean under my bedroom window, either. Telepathic eavesdropping is *extremely* rude."

"Not to mention unsettling," Ben muttered.

<Oh, all right. Like I really want to hang around and listen to those kinds of noises, anyway.> She did that cat thing where she went from completely inert to full speed ahead with no transition time, like a kernel of corn popping off my lap.

"Ow! Watch the claws!"

She sauntered over to the door, where Whiskey was already waiting patiently. I got up and opened it for them. "Couple of hours, okay?"

[Certainly. Nothing like catching up on the neighborhood news. I wonder if the schnauzer down the block is over that urinary tract infection yet.]

"Yeah, keep me updated on that. I'm all aquiver."

<Don't wait up.> They slipped out into the night, and I closed the door gratefully behind them. Well, semigratefully.

I sat back down beside Ben. He smiled at me, then saw the look on my face. "Uh-oh. What's wrong?"

"There's something you need to know. I talked to Teresa Firstcharger today. She claimed she was a Thunderbird."

Ben's eyes widened. "What?"

"Yes. And she could hear Whiskey's thoughts." I told him about the conversation I'd had with her. "She knew about you and Anna, and she's convinced that the killer is going to strike again."

Ben was on his feet now, pacing while he tried to process what I'd just told him. "You're sure she's a Thunderbird?"

"Well, I didn't ask her to prove it—"

"Why not?"

"What was I supposed to do, tell her to whip up a tornado? She said she was manipulating the wind to keep Whiskey from smelling her, and that seemed to be true." Even to me, it sounded like a weak excuse. "She had me on the ropes, okay? She more or less ambushed me while Whiskey and I were out for a walk."

He whirled around and stared at me. "Did she threaten you?"

"No. She was just very . . . forceful."

"What does she want?"

"I don't know," I admitted. "She wouldn't tell me. She was all cryptic and ominous and in my face, and then she left."

"Huh. Another Thunderbird." The expression on his

face was hard to read; thoughtful, yes—but what was he thinking? "I never really believed there were others out there. I considered the idea, but it just didn't seem real." He shook his head. "If she is what she claims to be. Maybe she can just read animals' minds—seems like there's a lot of that going around."

I hadn't mentioned Teresa's parting comment about looking forward to talking to me at dinner, and I wasn't about to. I'd told myself ZZ's dinners last for hours and I couldn't call off my date with Ben, but I knew the real reason: She'd intimidated me. Me, steadfast Foxtrot, able to stand up to blustering CEOs and brain-damaged rock stars without flinching, avoiding a possible confrontation with another woman. Okay, a supernaturally powerful woman, but still.

"Whatever she is, she seems to know what's going on," I said. "And so does Fimsby. Too bad neither of them want to tell us about it."

"Anna went to Australia to get her Thunderbird powers under control. She went to Fimsby for help. They must have discovered something that threatened not just her, but all Thunderbirds." He rubbed his temples in frustration. "But I talked to her earlier that day. She didn't say a thing! And why wouldn't she just call me once she'd found out about the—whatever-it-is?"

"You're right—this doesn't make sense. On any level. But since there are two people who have a lot more information than we do, we obviously have to convince them to share some of that information with us. Tomorrow, we go on the offensive."

He nodded, slowly. "Good idea. You tackle Fimsby, I'll talk to Teresa. That makes the most sense, right?"

I hesitated. "Sure. One Thunderbird to another. Just be careful, okay? She's kind of . . . intense."

He sat back down beside me. "I can handle intense. You've never seen me and my father really get into it."

His father. That reminded me of the deal ZZ had made with Ben's grandfather, and I didn't want to think about that. I couldn't tell him right now, I just couldn't. "Not that kind of intense. What I meant was she's a man-eater. She'll go all sexy and feminine-wily on you, I guarantee it."

He flashed that country-boy grin of his, the one that made it hard to believe he'd grown up in a place a lot like the Zoransky estate. "Why, Foxtrot—is that a trace of insecurity I hear? I can't believe it."

"What, it surprises you that I'm not perfect?"

"No, you have plenty of flaws—"

I punched him in the shoulder.

"Ow. I just find it hard to believe that insecurity is one of them."

I snuggled a little close. "Well, you haven't talked to her. She has a very commanding presence, plus you and she are two of a kind. That's a little scary."

"Think of it as an early-warning system. If she and I do hook up, we won't be able to keep it secret; the weather'll go crazy for a hundred miles around."

"Only a hundred? You must be getting old."

He put his arms around me, pulled me in closer. "Nah, just holding back. I only pull out the really impressive stuff on special occasions."

We kissed. It went on for a while, until I heard a rumble of thunder, which made me giggle. "Cut it out, Zeus. You're going to worry my neighbors."

Ben pulled back, the look on his face suddenly worried. "That wasn't me."

"So? Thunder is a natural occurrance, you know."

Now he was on his feet. "This isn't."

He strode over to the window and stopped, looking out. "I can feel it. Like the sky is a giant harp and someone just plucked one of the strings."

He held up one hand, his fingers wide, and brushed

the air gently. "Where are you?" he murmured. "And what are you doing now?"

He closed his eyes, concentrating. I knew who it must be, and what she must be doing. Isn't it great when you're on a date and your boyfriend gets a text from another woman?

And then it began to snow.

Big, fluffy white flakes, drifting slowly out of the summer sky, down through the cones of streetlight. For a second I was sure a volcano must have erupted somewhere, and these were ashes I was looking at. But no; they dissolved into dots of wetness the instant they touched down on the still-warm pavement.

"Hah!" Ben said. "Oh, *that's* good. I see how you did that . . ."

He wasn't talking to me, of course. And his eyes were still closed.

"Um, Ben? I know this is exciting and all, but you think maybe you can convince your new friend to shut down the snowflakes before she drives the local weather forecasters into multiple breakdowns?"

He was moving his hand now, like he was conducting an invisible orchestra. "Don't worry, it's not like that. Totally harmless. This isn't an attack, it's a demonstration."

"More like an invitation," I muttered under my breath. "Ooh, baby, you just make me *melt* . . ."

"Huh?" Ben said, and then he made this really strange noise, kind of a crash-tinkle-*chunk* sort of noise.

And then he crumpled to the ground, and I saw the arrow sticking out of his chest.

CHAPTER NINE

My reaction was pretty much instantaneous.

I leapt off the couch and caught him before he hit the floor. He's not a small guy, but adrenaline gives you strength; I'm no cop or fireman or paramedic, but I've had to deal with more than a few emergencies in my time. I've developed the kind of reflexes that make me jump toward the disaster instead of away from it.

"What the hell?" Ben said. He sounded more surprised than wounded, which is often the case. I've seen sudden injuries produce not just shock but denial, like the roadie who got his finger torn off in a rigging accident insisting his hand was fine. I had to get him to count his own digits three times before he'd agree to go to the hospital.

"You've been shot with an arrow," I said. It was jutting from his upper breastbone, closer to his shoulder than his belly. Definitely missed the heart, and didn't seem to be bleeding too profusely. "It doesn't look life threatening. Don't move and try to stay calm. I'm calling nine-one-one."

"Stay calm? I just got shot with an arrow!"

I already had my phone out and held to my ear. At the same time I was explaining things to the nice lady on the other end of the line, I was shouting in my head as loudly as I could for Whiskey and Tango to hightail it back to the house. I didn't know whether or not they could hear me; if we'd been near the amplifying effect of the graveyard they would have, but I'd specifically told them to get out of braincasting range.

Ben's skin had gotten very pale. He reached up to the arrow, but didn't touch it. "An arrow," he muttered. "Who shoots people with an arrow?"

"Someone trying to be stealthy. Hold on, the ambulance is on its way."

"I'm okay," he said, and tried to sit up. He got about half-way before he made a sound somewhere between a grunt and a scream and sank back down. "We have to be ready," he gasped. "In case they try again."

"Relax. The cavalry is on its way. But I very much doubt if Rambo is still out there—this was a coward's attack. Whoever did it is long gone."

"They better be," he growled. "If the next person through that door isn't wearing fur or a uniform, they're getting the wrong end of a thunderbolt rammed down their throat."

"Take it easy. The last thing we need is for you to lose control and flood the county. Was it her?"

He looked confused for a second. "Who?"

"Teresa Firstcharger. The woman you were just playing a duet with."

"I—I don't know *who* that was. I mean, I think it was another Thunderbird, but I don't know for sure. That was all new to me."

"That little demonstration was intended to draw you out, Ben. And once it did, you got shot. With an *arrow*."

"Yeah. I guess I did."

I could hear sirens now, getting louder. "Could you at least tell if the other weatherperson was nearby?"

"No. They might have been miles away, or across the street. Sorry."

Then the paramedics showed up. While they were getting Ben into the ambulance, the police arrived. And while I was talking to them, my two furry partners finally put in an appearance.

Whiskey came at a dead run, his nose having told him something was wrong long before his eyes. Tango wasn't far behind. Whiskey skidded to a stop at my feet and whined anxiously as I knelt down and reassured him. [Foxtrot! What happened?]

Ben was shot with an arrow. He's okay, but I need you to search the area and see if you pick up any familiar scents. The arrow came in through the front window, so start across the street.

[Are you all right?]

I'm fine. Go!

Tango trotted up as Whiskey took off, looking much more casual but sounding just as stressed inside my head. <Ben was shot? Who did it? What happened? Tell me everything!>

Just hang on. I have to talk to the cops first.

"Your dog is going to be okay?" Officer Forrester said. His black dreadlocks looked even more out of place against the blue of a police uniform. "He seems a little spooked."

I did my best not to smile. "He's just a little high-strung. I'm kind of surprised to see you out on patrol, though—aren't you a detective?"

"Hartville isn't big enough to support a full-time detective. Mostly I'm in a radio car—though if you keep this up I'll be full-time plainclothes in a week. An electrocution *and* a shooting, Foxtrot? With a bow and arrow, no less?"

"It's pretty weird, I know. But ZZ attracts a weird crowd; sometimes that leads to—well—"

"Weirdness?"

"You can't be in here, kitty," one of the ambulance attendants said. "Come on, shoo."

<Ben! Are you all right? Why is there a stick in you? I'm coming along!>

"Hey, kitty," Ben said. The painkillers they'd given him had started working; his voice was slow and peaceful. "M'okay. Look, I had a cat toy permanently installed in m'chest. C'mon, get the feathers. Get th' feathers."

<Maybe later. Are you all right?> She meowed pitifully, then hissed as a paramedic tried to grab her.

"M'fine. Why's everybuddy askin' me that? Hey, you wanna see a trick?" he asked the paramedic. "Betcha ten bucks I can make it snow in here."

"I'll get her," I said quickly. I stepped over and scooped Tango up, then whispered to Ben, "And you—behave, okay? Leave the nice weather *alone!*"

He muttered something incomprehensible and passed out.

"He'll be okay," said the paramedic, a young blond guy with a bushy mustache. "Doesn't look like the arrow hit any major arteries."

I kept Tango in my arms; I could feel how upset she was as well as hear it. "Take good care of him," I said. "His boss will cover any and all expenses."

The paramedic nodded and shut the door. The ambulance sped off.

"Tell me exactly what happened," Officer Forrester said.

So I did. I left out the part about Ben's duet and just said we were looking out the window at the strange weather when the arrow smashed through the glass and into Ben's chest.

"Yeah, the weather," Forrester said. "That was odd. Almost as odd as getting shot with an arrow while standing at a window." He was studying me intently, but apparently he couldn't bring himself to actually say out loud what he was thinking.

He asked me a few more questions, but there wasn't much to tell. Forrester went across the street to see if he could figure out where the arrow had been fired from, by which time Whiskey had already finished investigating the area. [No luck, I'm afraid. It must have been fired from a vehicle that then drove off. Impossible to track.]

Whiskey, Tango, and I went back into the house. The pool of blood on the floor was bigger than I'd thought it would be, and just looking at it made me a little dizzy. I went in to the kitchen, put on some hot water for tea, then got some paper towels.

I didn't cry as I mopped up my boyfriend's blood. Not because I'm tough, but because I was too busy thinking. Thinking and planning. I'm good at those things.

And I was very, very angry.

[What are we going to do?] Whiskey asked as I worked.

<*We're going to find whoever hurt Ben and rip their throat out,*> Tango spat.

I didn't say a word. I just scrubbed harder.

[Foxtrot?]

"Tango's got the right idea," I said grimly. "But her approach is all wrong. This isn't a one-on-one fight."

<*No, it's a three-on-one fight.*>

"It's not a fight at all, Tango. If it were, we'd lose." I gathered up all the blood-soaked towels and began stuffing them into a plastic bag. "No. When my kind sets out to kill something bigger and stronger than we are, we use a different term. Like I said, this isn't a fight."

I tied the top of the bag into a tight plastic knot, then marched into the kitchen and dropped it into the garbage can. "This is now a *hunt*."

* * *

Whenever possible, prepare.

I have many mantras, but that one's the most important. Even though I often have to improvise on the fly, what
gives me the ability to do so is having as many resources
on hand to call on as possible. I'd carry a fully loaded back-
pack at all times if I could get away with it, but I made do
with less tangible but just-as-vital assets and tried to keep
them close by at all times.

I made some phone calls. I got in my car and visited a
friend. I told Whiskey and Tango what I had in mind. I
checked in at the hospital. I *prepared*.

And then I went back home and went to bed.

Soldiers sleep whenever they can, because they never
know when they'll get the chance again. It might seem like
the last thing you'd be ready to do on the eve of battle, but
it made good sense. It was a good allocation of available
resources.

That didn't mean it was easy.

Tango had no problem going to sleep, of course; she
just curled up on my hip and was snoring away in seconds.
Whiskey, on the other hand, was on guard duty downstairs.
He didn't need sleep.

I lay awake in the dark, thinking. I was used to dealing
with problems, not going to war. Strangely enough, it
didn't seem all that hard—just a different set of problems
to solve, really.

The anger helped.

In the morning I stuck to my routine. I showered, had
breakfast, walked Whiskey. Then all three of us got into
the car and drove to the hospital, where I was told Ben was
doing fine but asleep. They'd removed the arrow last night
and it was now in possession of the police.

"It wasn't actually an arrow," the doctor who did the pro-
cedure told me. "It was a crossbow bolt. They're shorter,

but the device that launches them can be very powerful. If it hadn't hit his breastbone it would have punched right through the other side."

I thanked him and told him I'd be back later. Then I drove to work.

My first order of business was to reassure everyone that Ben was going to be fine. I'd already lined up a replacement chef for the next few days, and Ben's doctor had assured me Ben would be out of the hospital soon.

The last person I talked to was Shondra, ZZ's head of security. She wasn't happy, and as soon as her office door closed behind us she let me know.

"What the hell happened, Foxtrot?" From her tone of voice you'd think I was the one who'd skewered our cook.

I chose my next words very carefully. "Something crazy. Something random. My best guess is teenagers from the city, out in the 'burbs and looking for trouble."

"So they shoot someone with an arrow?"

I shrugged. "Don't ask me to explain it. Sure, New York is tourist-friendly again, but all the dangerous lunatics had to go somewhere."

"That sounded like an explanation. Not a very good one, though."

"You have something better?"

She had her hands behind her back and her feet slightly spread, a military posture she sometimes dropped into out of habit. "Two members of the same family killed or injured within twenty-four hours? *Random* isn't the word that comes to mind."

"Maybe not. That's why I had a talk with security at the hospital."

"Good. You have any idea who would want to hurt him or his sister?"

I did, but I couldn't explain that to Shondra. In fact, I wanted her out of the way while I dealt with things. "I think you should speak to Ben about that. He was awake when I left him—still groggy, but able to talk." A little white lie, but I needed her off the estate. "I'd appreciate it if you'd pay him a visit."

She nodded sharply. "I'll do that." She strode over to the door, and I jumped to my feet quickly to follow her. Once Shondra's made a decision, she doesn't hesitate.

She did pause, though, one hand on the doorknob, and gave me a curious look. "Where's your sidekick this morning? Usually he sticks closer than your shadow."

"Even shadows have to pee," I said, which was untrue for both shadows and ghost dogs. "He's smart—when he wants in he barks at the back door."

Once Shondra was gone, I went to my own office and got ready.

My weapon of choice was a cell phone. I used it to call Rustam Gorshkov, first.

"Hello, Mr. Gorshkov? It's Foxtrot. Some of the guests were talking about Kaci and wondered if you could demonstrate what she could do. I was hoping you could do it out by the pool, say in half an hour or so? I can have a nice buffet set up in the cabana for afterward. You could? That's terrific. We just got some excellent caviar in, I know you'll appreciate it. Okay, thanks. Bye."

I called Fimsby next, and then Keene. Both of them agreed that a chance to see Mr. Gorshkov's painting canine wasn't to be passed up, and a nice brunch would go very well with the event.

Then I called Teresa Firstcharger.

"Hello, Foxtrot. I missed you at dinner, last night. But my conversation with your boyfriend more than made up for it."

"Yes, he's fascinating to listen to, isn't he? It's too bad your talk was cut short."

She chuckled. "I thought you might have had something

to do with that. Well, Ben and I can always chat later. I didn't see him this morning, though—did you keep the poor dear up late?"

"It's his day off. But you and I should really talk."

"Isn't that what we're doing?"

"Face-to-face would be better. Do you know where the library is?"

"I think I can find it. When?"

"Five minutes?"

"See you then." She hung up.

Whiskey was waiting for me when I got there. "Everything ready?" I asked.

[Affirmative.]

I took a deep breath, then sat down in an overstuffed chair facing the window. "Then we're good to go."

I was calmer than I expected. I can do confrontation—in my kind of job it's a requirement—but I don't have that much experience in ones where my life is actually in danger. Okay, yes, I have been threatened with all sorts of things by all sorts of people, but none of them has actually tried to carry those threats out.

Teresa Firstcharger was different. She might actually kill me.

Not that she looked like a killer when she strode through the door. She looked like a million bucks, back when a million bucks was a lot of money: elegantly styled long black hair, spilling down the back of a clingy crimson dress so fashionable it had probably time-traveled a few weeks from the future. The smile on her face made me want to throw something at her.

I smiled back. "Hi. I hope you slept well."

She stopped a few steps into the room and glanced around. Nothing to see but walls of books and sunlight streaming through the windows. She had good instincts, though. What a surprise.

"I always sleep well," she said. "How about you?"

"Not really. I don't respond all that well when someone tries to kill my boyfriend."

Teresa's smile widened. "Please. A little snow never hurt anyone. Or was he driving at the time? I suppose I do tend to be something of a distraction, especially for men—"

"Someone shot him. Right in the middle of your little 'distraction.'"

That stopped her. Total, screeching, come-to-a-halt stop. All the playfulness went out of her eyes, leaving only cold calculation. "It wasn't me."

"Why should I believe you?"

"Because you said 'tried.' I wouldn't have screwed it up."

I deliberately looked away from her, focusing on the view out the window. "Nobody's perfect. Maybe you chose an accomplice with bad aim."

If there was one thing an egotist like Teresa couldn't stand, it was being ignored. She stalked forward a few more paces, putting her right into the middle of my field of vision once more.

Perfect—almost.

"I'm telling you, it wasn't me," she said. "Yes, I was trying to get Ben's attention. But not to—"

Whiskey? She needs to back off a little, wouldn't you say?

[I would. And I'd say it like *this*.]

Whiskey sprang to his feet. His ears went back and his lips curled up. He snarled at Teresa and lunged forward.

I don't care how cool you are, having an enraged Australian cattle dog charge at you will make you step back. That's exactly what Firstcharger did, putting her hands up defensively and yelling, "No!" as she stumbled backward.

Now, I thought.

A thick black tentacle of pure shadow shot through

the bookshelf, snaking around Firstcharger's waist. It tightened, yanking her back against the shelves and knocking a few books to the ground.

She gasped, looking down at what had grabbed her. Then her eyes narrowed and she snarled, "*Big* mistake, Fox."

Lightning crackled over her entire body, sparking from her eyes, her fingertips, her teeth. It played along the length of the shadowy cable that had her ensnared, channeling who-knows-how-much voltage into her captor.

To absolutely no effect.

"Yeah, that's not going to work," I said. "And before you think about trying it on me, you should know that Topsy can crush your rib cage to powder in the blink of an eye. Which is exactly what she'll do if you toss a thunderbolt anywhere near me."

From the gasp Firstcharger made, Topsy had just demonstrated that with a little squeeze.

"In case you're wondering, Topsy's an elephant. A dead elephant, executed by none other than Thomas Edison himself, over a hundred years ago. The method he chose—electrocution—means Topsy is now pretty much immune to the stuff. But she can definitely affect *you*."

Firstcharger glared at me, pure murder in her eyes. I stared back, impassively.

"You're making a mistake, Foxtrot. I didn't shoot at Ben."

"Somebody did."

"I don't even own a gun! And I was here, on the estate, all evening!"

Interesting that she thought it was a gun—but a clever killer would have said that to throw me off the trail. "Doesn't matter. As I said, you could have an accomplice."

"Look, this is exactly what the killer *wants:* us at each other's throats. That's what I wanted to talk to you about last night." She was still angry, but had herself under control. Like me, she seemed to do well under pressure.

I leaned forward in my chair, and rested my forearms on my knees. "Okay. I've arranged for us to have some privacy for at least the next half hour—so *talk*."

"Let me go, first."

"Sure. But remember who's watching you, and what she can do."

[And that she's not alone,] Whiskey growled.

Let her go.

Topsy's trunk slithered away from her waist, disappearing into the wall like a phantom anaconda. Teresa put a hand to her stomach, her breathing a little harsh, but she didn't bolt away from the wall like I expected to. Instead, she took one, slow step, not glancing behind her at all. She kept her eyes fixed on mine.

"That was well played," she said. "You're a more skilled opponent than I realized. You have my respect."

"Why are you here? What do you want?"

"I want my people to return. But something out there wants exactly the opposite—it's trying to end us, to destroy the Thunderbirds once and for all."

"Who?"

"Those who have tried before. What do you know of our stories, our legends?"

"Not much," I admitted. "I've read a few online. You people really like fish."

She chuckled darkly. "The Thunderbird and the Killer Whale, yes; many First Nation tribes have a version of that one. But the tale I'm about to relate isn't nearly as well known, because few survived to tell it. It's the story of how and why the Thunderbirds vanished.

"We had many duties in the old days. We brought the rains, and the wind, and even the snow, but that was not all we did. We were the messengers of the gods, and traveled their realms as easily as a salmon swims downstream." She smiled. "Or as a taxi changes lanes, if you prefer a more modern metaphor. However you looked at it, we were important. Valued members of a powerful society, doing a vital job."

"That much I know," I said. "Ben recently brokered a peace treaty between two feline deities."

"Tabby and Calico?"

"Lion and Tigress."

Her eyebrows went up. "Obviously Ben is growing into his heritage better than Anna. It took me a long time to find her, and when I did she was as about as dangerous as a baby deer. I needed to fire up her blood."

I frowned. "So you slept with her husband?"

Teresa waved her hand contemptuously. "He was little more than a possession to her—a kept man in a money-lined cage. I didn't want him—I wanted her. Her *fury*."

"But why? Why did you want her angry?"

"Because of what's coming for us. Because of the Unktehila."

"I don't know what that is."

She made an impatient noise. "Of course not. Why would you? Well, listen up and I'll enlighten you."

She stalked across the room and perched on a chair across from mine. Whiskey eyed her warily but didn't object. "The Unktehila were monsters. They came from the depths of the ocean and were the natural enemies of the Thunderbirds. Human beings were their prey of choice—until the Thunderbirds put a stop to it. Permanently."

"You wiped them out?"

She shrugged. "So the story goes. But really, we just laid down the law. No more eating people—stick to deer or antelope or buffalo or even beaver, but human beings are definitely off the menu. They didn't like the new rules, and there was a war. The Thunderbirds won."

"And the Unktehila?"

"They retreated, to the deepest parts of the sea. Not a place a Thunderbird usually goes."

"I'm guessing they didn't stay there."

Her smile was cold. "But they did. They waited, and they planned, and they very carefully worked out the perfect revenge. What's the one thing that's absolutely necessary to the job of a messenger?"

I thought about it. "Reliability."

"Exactly. Look at the Internet; no matter how fast your connection is, it doesn't matter if you can't trust the information that's coming through. The Unktehila didn't go after the Thunderbirds directly; they poisoned our reputation, instead."

"How?"

She grimaced, and leaned back in her chair. "It's a long story, and one I'd rather not tell twice. Besides, it's not safe to speak certain names aloud, not without precautions in place."

"I know what you mean. You've already met *my* precautions."

Her eyes flickered involuntarily toward the bookshelf that Topsy's trunk had appeared from. "Yes. But this is a story that both you *and* Ben need to hear. We should continue this conversation someplace safe."

"And where would that be, exactly?"

"The Thunderbirds' place of power. Ben knows where it is—or he should."

I knew where she was talking about. But any place of power for Ben was also a place of power for her, and Ben was injured. This sounded suspiciously like a ploy to simply get Ben and me somewhere isolated—someplace my backup couldn't go. "I don't think so. Ben's not going anywhere until he's in better shape, and I'm sure as hell not jumping into another dimension with *you*. You want someplace safe to talk, we can take a little walk over to the graveyard. It's protected." Mostly by me, but I didn't see any reason to add that.

She studied me for a second. "There's one more thing you should know. Thunderbirds heal faster when they're home; if you want Ben out of a hospital bed and back on his feet, all he has to do is take a little trip. So here's what's going to happen: You can tell Ben what I'm suggesting and what the benefits are, and he can decide for himself. If he says no, then we can meet in the graveyard. Work for you?"

Not really. Even without the inducement of a quick recovery, she was gambling that Ben's sense of stubborn male pride was stronger than my ability to convince him otherwise, and I honestly wasn't sure which way that would go. But I could see I wasn't going to get a better offer. "All right, I'll talk to him about it. But don't count on him agreeing."

"I'm not," she said, getting to her feet. "Not with you, anyway."

And then she turned around and swept out of the room as elegantly as she'd entered it.

Thanks, Topsy. You can go now.

<*She already left, Toots. Said the confrontation was over and you didn't need her anymore. Apparently elephants have terrific hearing.*> I couldn't see Tango, but I knew she was just outside the window, on the other side of the wall Topsy had manifested through.

[While we're stating the obvious, I'd like to mention that an elephant's excellent hearing probably has something to do with the size of their ears, and also that Ms. Firstcharger's proposal sounds like a trap.]

I frowned. "I'm not so sure. Technically, if she wanted

to attack Ben, she could do so right now while he's doped to the gills and can't fight back."

<Maybe she doesn't know where he is.>

"She didn't seem to have any trouble pinpointing him last night. Though it might be hard to get at him in a large building like a hospital."

<I'm not quite following this—my ears aren't pachyderm-sized. What did Firstcharger propose?>

"A meeting in Thunderspace." That was what Ben called it; it was some kind of mystical dimension that seemed to be made solely of sky and clouds. Ben had taken me there once, and claimed the place was completely deserted. Being somewhere without solid ground to stand on didn't exactly put me at ease.

Which, of course, was exactly what Teresa Firstcharger intended.

"Whiskey, you're with me," I said. "Tango, stay here and keep an eye on Ms. Firstcharger. We're going to see Ben about setting up a meeting."

CHAPTER TEN

A meeting.

Meetings have become a universal metaphor for boredom. It's where people talk about things you don't care about and they go on forever and there's a very real chance you'll expire from sheer tedium. And it's true, many meetings do fall into that precise category. (By the way, if you're in a meeting and somebody uses the phrase *precise category,* that's the category of meeting you're in. Precisely.)

But not all of them.

I've been in meetings where both people and guns were fired. I've been in meetings that would have shamed Roman bacchanals. I was in one meeting where someone was thrown out a window—twice. (Different windows, though.) It all depends on who you're meeting with, and what you happen to be discussing.

Meeting with two Thunderbirds in a supernatural dimension to discuss the murder of a third was unlikely to be boring. I wondered if I should bring snacks.

[Are you sure this is wise?] Whiskey asked as we left the library. [Ben isn't really in shape to make this sort of decision.]

"Which is why I'm going to convince him to turn her down."

But first I was going to have to negotiate the obstacle course that was my working life. I'd already dealt with the temporary loss of our chef, and now it was time to move on to my other responsibilities—one of which was waiting for me at the base of the stairs.

"Foxtrot!" said Theodora Bonkle. "I'm so glad I ran into you, dear. Really, I have to thank you for introducing me to Mr. Cooper. He and I have been having the most intriguing time."

I smiled and said, "I'm not surprised. Mr. Cooper has led a most interesting life."

Theodora beamed at me, which was a bit like being grinned at by a bulldog wearing makeup. "Ah, but it's the afterlife that's of interest now, my dear Foxtrot. Specifically, that of cats."

Well, she had been chasing after a herd of spectral felines earlier, even if she couldn't actually see them herself. "And what have you found out?"

"I think that's best discussed over a cup of tea. If you have a moment?"

Do you have a moment is the question I get asked more often than any other. Regardless of its accuracy, my answer is always yes; after all, giving my moments to other people is what I get paid for. So, no matter how busy I am, I've perfected the art of looking like I have endless amounts of time to toss around like confetti. I grinned back at her and said, "Of course. How about the sitting room? I'll ring a maid to bring us something freshly brewed and a little to nibble on, too."

When we were properly seated, Theodora straightened her skirt over her knees and announced, "Our investigation is proceeding apace. We have cataloged the gravestones upon which marbles have been placed, to the best of our abilities. There are a total of twenty-three so far, though some of the marbles may have been misplaced over time. There seems to be little correlation among any of the dates; they range over a period covering sixty years, from 1950 to 2010. The marbles are all the same size, but differ in color. The names of the cats have no apparent connection to one another."

"Doesn't sound like a lot to go on."

[Doesn't sound terribly rational, either,] Whiskey added. [But then, she is discussing cats.]

"Now," continued Theodora, "as Cooper said, this marbling activity has been going on for approximately the last year. He's never seen the agency responsible, but estimates a new marble turns up approximately every fortnight. Fortunately for our investigation, he can even narrow this down to the middle of the week; he never finds a new one on the weekend, or even on a Monday. So we can surmise a biweekly visit to the graveyard, sometime between Tuesday and Friday."

I nodded. "Do you have any theories as to why?"

"Well, I—what?" She glanced down, toward my feet. "No, Very British Bear, I haven't forgotten your theory." She paused, obviously listening to a reply. "It doesn't have enough what? Plaws? I don't—oh, I see. No, *plausible* means 'believable.'"

She listened some more, then sighed. "Oh, very well. Foxtrot, Very British Bear thinks you might find it easier to believe his theory than I do. According to him, your believer is in much better shape."

I smiled despite myself. My believer had been pumping some heavy concepts lately, and had the muscles to show for it. "I'll take that as a compliment. What's his theory?"

"Um. Very, would you care to explain? I'll relay it, verbatim." She listened, then scowled. "No, Very. *Verbatim* is not a naughty word in German. Please begin."

[I can't believe we're going to listen to the theory of an imaginary bear instead of dealing with an actual threat.]

Quiet. This is part of my job, too. It won't take long.

Theodora's face was intent, her head cocked to one side. Then she began, pausing occasionally to listen again to the words of her invisible companion. "Cats, as everyone knows, love to play with marbles. But perhaps it is also true that marbles love to play with cats. And seeing as these are Ghostly Cats, perhaps they are Ghostly Marbles; and instead of a Mysterious Person placing the marbles on graves, it may be that the marbles—being Ghostly, as well—are playing a Ghostly Game with the cats."

"I see," I said. "Well, there's just one small problem with that, isn't there? I mean, the marbles aren't Ghostly, are they?"

"*Not,* says Very British Bear, *as such.* But other than that, he thinks it's a very fine theory and absolutely full of plaws."

[It's certainly full of something.]

"What about you, Theodora?" I asked. "What's your theory?"

Before she could answer, Consuela showed up with the tea. I thanked her and busied myself with all the little rituals that go along with, as the British say, a nice cuppa. When that was all sorted and both of us had steaming cups of Earl Grey in front of us, I asked Theodora again.

"Well," she said, "my own thoughts on the matter are not *quite* as fanciful as Very's. I believe the marbles are being placed by a human agency, but as to their purpose I remain baffled. There's a registry of which animals are buried here and who buried them, which Mr. Cooper and I are going to peruse this evening. A connection of some sort may make itself evident, though I suspect the truth will prove elusive."

Theodora started and jerked back in her seat, her tea sloshing over the lip of her cup. Her eyes widened in surprise, then narrowed into a glare.

"What's wrong?" I said. I put down my own cup quickly. "Are you all right?"

"Fine. Other than the fact I have a rather excitable talking jackrabbit in my lap. Doc, you know I don't like it when you do that." She appeared to be talking to something mere inches from her face, her gaze focused downward. Her slightly exasperated but resigned attitude was exactly that of a parent talking to a misbehaving child. "You almost made me spill my tea."

Again, she listened before replying. "No, I wasn't going to forget, I just hadn't gotten to that part yet. And don't call me that, it's highly inaccurate and not a little insulting."

"Tell me what?"

"About the snake."

Whiskey's ears grew points. [The snake? She saw the snake?]

"You saw a snake?" I said. "Cooper's snake?"

"Well, I'd hardly say it belonged to Mr. Cooper, though he was the one who first reported its existence. But yes, apparently there was one; quite an enormous thing, and just as brightly colored as Mr. Cooper described."

"Where did you see it?"

"Slithering between the graves, according to Doc. Very was busy admiring some dandelions, so he didn't notice."

"You didn't see it yourself?"

She shook her head. "I'm afraid not. Doc tried to call me over, but it was gone by the time I got there. He was rather overwrought by that time, what with the bulging eyes and the hopping up and down and the inarticulate cries of horror."

She glanced down, then snorted. "Oh, you weren't frightened? I see. What I took for overwhelming terror was simply excitement at the prospect of facing a worthy foe. Yes, yes, I'm sure you would. But don't use the word *murderize*; it's vulgar. Besides, you're pronouncing it incorrectly."

Doc Wabbit then bounded off her lap and back onto the floor—or at least that's what I assumed by watching Theodora's eyes. She turned her gaze back to me and sighed. "Doc's always running off and sticking his nose into everything. Useful as an investigative tool, but he tends to exaggerate details. Sometimes he even makes things up."

[Imagine that. No, wait, you already are.]

I smiled and took a sip of tea. "Well, this time he might be telling the truth. I've been getting reports that other people have seen this snake, too. Though I have no idea how it might relate to your marble mystery."

"Really? Others have seen it, too? Tell me more."

So I did, though I didn't really have that much to relate. In the end, I told her to go see Caroline, who could provide her with details. She said she would, thanked me, and hurried off.

[So now we have a sighting by a figment of someone's imagination,] Whiskey said.

I took a last sip of my tea and put the cup down. "Which means our snake could be a ghost."

[Or as non-existent as the one who claims to have seen it.]

"It's a mystery, all right. But I don't think it's the one we need to worry about now. Unless . . ."

[Unless what?]

"Those monsters Teresa Firstcharger mentioned. The Unktehila. She said they came from the depths of the sea."

[So?]

"So not all giant snakes are land dwellers. In fact, the bigger the snake, the more likely it is to be at least semi-aquatic—like the anaconda."

[Wonderful. Not only do we have to catch a killer and deal with a rogue Thunderbird, now we have to factor in a sea serpent, as well . . .]

I smuggled Whiskey into the hospital in a gym bag; sometimes it's extremely useful to have a shape-shifting partner, especially one who can keep quiet and doesn't need to breathe.

But when I got to Ben's room, he wasn't there.

I called Shondra. "I'm at the hospital," I told her. "But Ben isn't."

"He was there twenty minutes ago," she said. "Not conscious, though. I stayed for a while, talked to hospital security, and then went back to the house. Not much for me to do until he wakes up."

"There is one thing. Can you take a look at the footage of the security cameras and tell me if any of the guests left the estate last night?"

"You think one of them is responsible?"

"Not necessarily. Just checking out a hunch."

"Okay, I'll call you back."

The nurse down the hall told me Ben had gone for some fresh air—they had a balcony on the next level down where patients could step outside without going all the way to the ground floor. I found an old man in a tattered bathrobe there, tethered to an IV pole by a plastic tube in his arm, sitting on a plastic chair and looking morose. From the collection of soggy cigarette butts on the concrete floor, I could tell that most of the patients who came out here were after air that was not so much fresh as smoked.

"Uh, excuse me," I said. "Have you seen a man out here

in the last little while? Sandy-blond hair, kind of rugged looking, bandaged shoulder? Might have been a little spacey."

The old man gave me a sour look. "Nah, ain't been nobody out here but me. I only been here a little while, though—was too windy, before."

I squinted up at the sunny sky. "Seems nice now."

He shrugged. "Sure. But you shoulda seen it fifteen minutes ago—blowin' like a mother. No way to get a smoke lit, that's for sure."

I glanced down at the discarded butts on the floor. There was something strange about them—they were arranged in a pattern. A *circular* pattern. As if they'd been put there on purpose . . .

Or blown there.

"Oh, no," I said. "He wouldn't have. Why would he? Unless . . ."

The old man saw the look on my face and how I was staring at the butts on the floor. He chuckled. "Hey, don't take it so hard. Everyone sneaks out here for a smoke, no matter how bad off they are. I seen people with cancer puffing away like chimneys. Can't say I blame them—it ain't like quittin' is gonna do 'em any good now."

I barely heard him—I was already on my way back to Ben's hospital room. I'd stashed his cell phone in the drawer beside the bed, and I hoped he hadn't taken it with him. It wouldn't do me any good if he had; I doubted his phone plan covered other dimensions.

But it would tell me who the last person who'd called him was.

When Ben traveled to Thunderspace, he did it via a mystic vortex, one that looked like a whirlwind to an outside observer. It left little circular drifts of detritus in its wake, just like a real whirlwind—just like the circular pattern of butts on the smoking balcony. If Teresa Firstcharger had learned Ben's cell number, she might have tried to side-step me by pitching her idea to Ben directly. And from the looks of things, he'd taken her up on it.

But when I got to Ben's room and found his phone, the last call on it was from me. A trip to the nurses' station and a few questions determined that Ben hadn't gotten a call from one of the hospital's landlines, either, or received any visitors other than Shondra. And then Shondra herself called back. "Okay. Teresa Firstcharger, Efram Fimsby, Hayden Metcalfe, and Keene all went out for a few hours in the evening. I'm texting you the exact times; you'll note that none of them was accounted for when Ben was shot."

"Thanks, Shondra. I'll talk to you later." I hung up.

Ben wasn't here. He'd gone to Thunderspace on his own. Why?

Instinct, maybe. If what Firstcharger told me about a Thunderbird healing faster on their own turf—or rather, above it—was true, then Ben might have gone there without understanding why. He'd had enough presence of mind to step outside first, though I didn't know how conscious he'd been at the time; I had visions of him staggering down the hospital hallway, his wound reopening under the strain, blood staining the fresh bandages . . .

I shook my head. That hadn't happened—the nurses wouldn't have let it. He must have walked out there under his own steam and reasonably alert, and without hearing from Firstcharger.

I was pondering it when Ben walked through the door, still in his hospital gown. Physically, he looked a lot better than the last time I'd seen him; he carried himself without wincing, his back straight and his eyes clear. Clear—but very, very troubled.

"Ben? Are you all right? What happened?"

He closed the door behind him, then came over and sat down on the bed. "I went home," he said. "To the

Thunderbird dimension. Feels funny, calling a place that strange home, but that's what it feels like. And I was sure. So sure."

I put my hand on his injured shoulder, gently. He didn't wince. "How's the injury?"

"What? Oh, the shoulder. Fine. I can barely feel it. Guess it wasn't as bad as we thought."

"You had a steel-tipped rod embedded in your body. Kind of hard to exaggerate that."

He turned toward me, and the pain on his face had nothing to do with his shoulder. "She wasn't there, Foxtrot. Why wasn't she there? I don't understand."

"What, Firstcharger? Did she contact you, after all?"

"Not Firstcharger. *Anna.*"

"Your sister? But she's . . ."

And then I got it.

Sure, Anna was dead. But she was also a powerful entity with supernatural abilities, descended from a tribe that communed with gods. Beings that could travel from one afterlife to another, and had a whole dimension all to themselves that they called home. Where else would her spirit go?

"Oh, Ben," I said. "I'm sorry. I didn't think—that just didn't occur to me—"

"I couldn't find her. It's such a big place, though—like the whole world if there was nothing but sky. Nothing but wind and clouds and sun during the day, and the moon and stars at night. I flew around the whole thing, Trot. Faster and higher than I've ever gone. And when I couldn't find her up there, I dove down. I really thought I'd just go right through to the other side, like crossing through the middle of an empty bubble, but I was wrong. There *is* something, right in the middle."

"Ground, you mean? Actual land?"

He shook his head. "Not exactly. It's more like a forest,

except up and down are all mixed up. The trees grow out of big jagged splinters of rock, and none of them seems to pay attention to gravity, either—they just hang there in space. It's sort of like someone took a few thousand acres of woods and a mountain range and jumbled them all together. It's on a really large scale, too—all the trees are massive, but there's lot of room between them to fly. I didn't go in, just flew around the outside—it looked like a giant maze in there and I was afraid I'd get lost. Do you think I should have gone in? Is that where she is?"

"Take it easy. I don't know exactly how all the afterlife stuff works—but if that's where dead Thunderbirds go, wouldn't the place be a little more populated?"

"I don't know. Maybe they were hiding. Maybe there's something about being a Thunderbird I haven't learned yet. Maybe . . ." He stopped himself and clenched both his fists. "I wish Anna were here," he said quietly. "She was always the one with all the answers."

I didn't know what to say. If I told him about Teresa Firstcharger's proposal, he'd be back in Thunderspace before I could blink. But I couldn't keep it from him, either. "Listen to me, okay? I have learned a few things since I started this gig, and the most important one is that nobody's gone forever. If cats and dogs and parakeets and turtles and fish and birds live on, then so do people. And Anna most definitely was a person."

"Then where is she, Foxtrot?" His eyes were brimming with tears, and his voice was breaking. "Where's my *sister*?"

I took him in my arms and held him as he cried. "It's okay," I whispered. "It's going to be okay." Outside, rain began to spatter against the window.

As I held him, I realized that there was only one way to get the answers he needed, and that was to talk to someone who knew more than we did: Teresa Firstcharger.

Eventually he pulled himself away, wiping his nose against his sleeve in that way men do when they're trying to shift from heavy-duty emotional release back to being manly men. He smiled at me and said, "Got a Kleenex?"

"Of course. We're in a hospital room, after all." I plucked a few from the box on the bedside table and handed them over. He blew his nose and wiped his eyes.

"I have something to tell you," I said. "But you have to promise me two things first. One, that you'll think hard about the possible consequences; and two, that you'll take me with you."

He studied me for a second, then said, "Okay. Where are we going, and why?"

I told him about the conversation I'd had with First-charger, and where she wanted to meet. "When she said 'the Thunderbirds' place of power,' I thought she was just referring to Thunderspace. But considering the scarcity of landmarks, she must have meant that floating rock-and-tree area you found."

Ben got to his feet, looked around, and found the closet his clothes were stored in. He walked over, shucking off his hospital gown along the way, yanked open the door, and started getting dressed.

"I'm guessing you don't want to wait," I said with a sigh.

"Nope. Somebody killed Anna and they tried to kill me. If Teresa's behind it, I want to know now. If not, she might be able to tell us what's going on."

"Ben, she clearly has a lot more experience than you. Thunderspace is a perfect place for an ambush. This is just not a good idea—we should wait and force her to meet in the graveyard."

He shook his head as he pulled on his shirt. "Sorry. I know what the facts say, but there's one thing you don't have and I do."

"Which is?"

"My instincts. And when it comes to Thunderbird business, I gotta go with them."

I got off the bed and walked over to him. "They're saying we should trust her?"

"Hell, no. But they are saying we need to talk to her. *I* need to talk to her."

"Instinct is a powerful force," I said, and tried to keep the insecurity out of my voice. Instinct often led to a lot more than just talking. "If that's how you feel, we should go. But like I said—I'm coming with you."

"Wouldn't have it any other way." He flashed me that heartbreaking smile he did so well, and I felt something give a little crack, just behind my rib cage.

"Then let's go," I said, and did my best to smile back.

We checked out of the hospital first, despite the protests of the staff, and went down to my car. If we were going to disappear in a swirling magical vortex, then I preferred we do it someplace a little more private and secure than a hospital balcony.

So we drove down to the Great Crossroads.

Whiskey spent the whole trip haranguing Ben. [This is an extremely unwise decision. Ill advised, tactically unsound, and altogether feline.]

"Feline?" Ben asked.

[It's a dog's greatest insult. You may substitute any of these words and retain the meaning: stupid, impulsive, idiotic, moronic, irrational, cat-brained, witless, unintelligent, foolish—]

"Okay, I get the idea."

[—ignorant, dense, simpleminded, brain-dead, vapid, thick, lunkheaded, dim, vacuous, obtuse, dopy—]

"I thought Tango was the wordy one."

[My command of the English language is utilitarian.

She's the one who insists on making it jump through flaming hoops.]

Despite Whiskey's stern disapproval, Ben wouldn't change his mind. When we parked in the graveyard's small lot, Ben said, "You know, you could come with us. Or is that against the rules?"

[Not at all. But Thunderspace, as I understand it, is a realm suited to those who can fly. Dogs—even those with imaginary biplanes—do not fly well. Or at all.]

We got out of the car, and made our way into the graveyard. I picked a spot we'd used before, away from the heavy traffic of animal spirits and shielded from most eyes by the gently rolling terrain. I told Whiskey to stay alert in case we had to come back in a hurry, and he promised he would.

Then Ben raised his arms and the air began to dance around us. Even though I'd done this before, it still made all the hairs on my skin stand up. The winds whirled faster and everything outside them seemed to get farther away.

Then we were someplace else.

CHAPTER ELEVEN

I hung in midair, suspended by some sort of natural law that had never been entered into the books of my reality. Below me was a vanilla ice cream landscape of wind-scooped clouds as big as countries; above me was sky the shade of blue that rainbows and musicians dream about. The sun-warmed air was the perfect temperature. It was like lying on a beach, minus the gravity. And the ocean. And the beach.

Ben was floating in the air beside me. Except *floating* wasn't really the right word; when Ben was in Thunderspace, he always gave the impression that he was hovering, the way a gull can stay virtually motionless in one spot by using the wind to generate exactly the amount of lift to keep from plummeting. Not moving in any direction but still somehow flying, body charged with the potential to swoop or soar in an instant.

Unlike me, who always felt a little like a leaf drifting on the breeze. I started to slowly rotate, as I usually did, and said, "Uh, Ben?"

"Oh. Sorry." And just like that, I straightened out, pushed

gently into alignment by a nudge from the air itself. He reached out and took my hand.

"You ready?" he asked.

"I think so—"

And then we were falling.

No, that's not right. Diving headlong is more accurate. If somebody who'd jumped out of a passing plane without a parachute were a hundred feet below us, we would have passed them like a Lamborghini blowing by a tractor.

So, being a mere passenger in said Lamborghini, I politely cleared my throat and said, "AAAAAAAAAA AAHHHHHH!"

We slowed down before stopping, which I was grateful for; if we'd come to an abrupt halt, I think my breakfast would have continued on without me.

"What's wrong?" Ben asked. He sounded genuinely confused.

"Me. Speed. Too much fast," I gasped. "Geez for God's sake give me a little *warning*!"

He blinked. "Oh. Sorry. When I get here, I kind of forget."

"Forget what? How to talk?"

Now he looked embarrassed. "No. I forget . . . it's hard to explain. It just feels so natural to me, being here. It's like all my assumptions about how things work change, without feeling like anything's changed at all. It's more like remembering than realizing."

"Okay. Let's just take it a little slower to start, all right? You can kick in the afterburners once I'm used to it."

We headed down again—*down* being a relative term in the absence of gravity, of course—at a more leisurely pace. This time, I did much better.

But I was a little worried now for a different reason. I thought I understood what Ben had been trying to articulate.

He'd forgotten, just for a second, what it was like to be human.

Because he wasn't, not really. He was a supernatural being, descended from a race of supernatural beings, able to travel between dimensions and control the weather. He might look like a homegrown farm boy, but there was something deeply different in his very essence, something usually hidden from the rest of the world.

But not here. Here, his true nature was free to come out.

I glanced over at him. His face was intent, his gaze steady. Like a hawk, focused on its prey. Both his arms were outstretched as if they were wings, his left hand holding mine and his right palm-down and flat, the fingers spread as wide as they could go. They reminded me of a crow's wingtip feathers in flight.

I think our speed gradually increased, but it was hard to tell. The clouds streaming past weren't much use as a guide, and Ben was doing something to the atmosphere around us to make it easier to breathe; I could see it sometimes as we shot through the mist, a bubble of still air enveloping us.

When our destination finally appeared, my first thought was of a circular, ruined castle, seen from above: the craggy rocks and angular branches suggested broken turrets and ramparts overgrown with redwoods and oaks over a hundred centuries. As we got closer, though, it resolved into more of a globe shape, and the contours of the imaginary castle broke up into a random maze of stone and timber—but the impression of something ancient and abandoned remained.

We slowed, then changed direction to glide above the treetops fifty or so feet away. "Where to now?" I asked.

"I'm not sure. But this feels familiar, somehow. I think . . ."

We veered off to the left. The terrain below, if you could call it that, all looked the same to me.

"Yes," Ben muttered. "*This* way."

I wondered exactly what was going on. Ancestral memories, coded into supernatural DNA? Guiding magic, emanating from the trees and rocks themselves? Or some kind of signal only Thunderbirds could hear?

Whatever it was, Ben seemed to know exactly where he was headed. "We're going in," he announced, and then we were swooping into the tangle of stone and branches.

It cooled off as soon as we were through the canopy. We dove past cliffs of granite dappled with sunlight from above, through deepening shadows and rustling reefs of leaf, the air heavy with the smell of pine and moss. Other than the leaves, the air was silent; no birds sang, no insects buzzed or chirped.

As we flew deeper and deeper, I started to see a kind of path before us, an irregular passageway without rock or branch. Nothing had been cleared away, not that I could tell—it was more like a natural feature, an invisible riverbed in the air. We followed it down to the heart of the floating forest, and though it got dimmer, the light never faded completely away; when I looked upward, I could always still see a flicker of sunlight far, far above, as if every leaf between here and there were cooperating to usher a tiny bit of illumination along with us.

Magical. In every sense of the word.

We must have flown for miles. But at last Ben said, "Here," and we touched down on the mossy surface of an immense branch.

Before us was a vast, spherical space. If you've ever been in a forest of really, really big trees, you know how it feels to stand at the foot of one of them and look up; it's like being in a living cathedral, a tiny living speck next to ancient, silent giants. This was like that, but times a thousand: immense trunks radiated like spokes in every direction, their roots gripping boulders at their bases like huge gnarled hands, the rocks forming the inner boundary of the sphere. A loose network of crooked, thinner roots joined the rocks together, but there were plenty of gaps wide enough to fly through.

It should have been dark as a tomb, this far from the sun, but I could see just fine; it was shadowy and dim, but not gloomy. And very, very still.

"Welcome to the Aerie," a familiar voice said.

Teresa Firstcharger stepped out from behind a craggy outcropping. She stood on a boulder on the other side of the empty space, now dressed in loose denim shorts and a bright red T-shirt with a winged logo on it. Her long black hair hung free and her feet were bare.

Ben stared at her with the same kind of intensity he'd shown while flying. It was a little unnerving, so I said, "Nice place. Very . . . airy."

She smiled. She had the kind of full, red lips people stab their mouths with bee venom for. "Hello, Ben. I see you brought a plus one. What, you were afraid to come on your own? Or did she insist?"

Ben didn't take the bait. "You called this place the Aerie. What is it?"

"If we're going to talk, let's not shout at each other across an empty divide. Shall we meet in the middle?" She stepped out into space as elegantly as a diva onto a red carpet, holding her arms as if offering a hug, and glided to the center of the sphere.

Ben stayed where he was. "I'm fine where I am, thanks. Great acoustics in here—wherever here is. Are you going to answer my question, or do I have to ask it again?"

I thought she might come closer, but she stayed where she was, her toes pointed downward, her arms moving slightly like she was treading water. "Oh, you know exactly where you are. This is the Aerie, the meeting place of the Thunderbirds. Where those who soar alone come to meet and talk, to share news and pass along messages. And sometimes, to discuss more important things."

"Like the Unktehila," I said. I was pretty sure First-charger would completely ignore me if I let her, but ignoring me is a skill set most people never acquire. "You said you wanted us here to tell us about them. So tell."

"You're not the one setting the agenda here, Foxtrot," she said. "This is a discussion between Thunderbirds, which you definitely are not. Unless you have something significant to add to the conversation, you'd be better off listening than talking."

I smiled. My condescension shields are top-notch, too. "Oh, I have information you'll be interested in. When you're done sharing yours, I might even tell you some of it."

We smiled at each other for a second. No teeth were bared, but we both knew they were there—though in Teresa's case, a razor-sharp beak seemed more appropriate.

"The Unktehila," she said. "The ancient enemies of not just the Thunderbirds, but everything that lived. Like us, they were shape-changers; unlike us, they preferred the water to the air, and scales to feathers. They lived in the deep ocean, and ate just about anything that moved. But a seafood diet wasn't enough for them. They moved onto dry land, growing legs when they had to. But mostly they stuck with a serpentine form, good for moving through just about any environment. And swallowing buffalo whole."

Ben glanced at me. "Sounds like some pretty big snakes."

"Big and hungry," Teresa said. "An invasive species with no natural enemies, leading to ecological disaster. They ate all the game and then moved on to eating the people. Which is when the sea serpents discovered that snakes on dry land *do* have a natural enemy: us."

"So there was a war? We intervened on the side of humanity?"

She shrugged, an elegant gesture that seemed to ripple through her entire suspended body and was more than a little sexual. I've always hated women who defy gravity, unless they happen to be Sandra Bullock. Teresa wasn't.

"We intervened—exactly who asked us for help is a little unclear. And we were successful. We blasted them with lightning, and when they tried to hide in rivers or lakes we boiled them alive. Water makes an excellent conductor—or so I've been told." She stared straight at Ben.

Ben stared back, his face impassive. "We both know Anna didn't die by electrocution. But she *did* die in water—are you trying to say the Unktehila are responsible?"

"They have good reason to hate us," Teresa answered. "After we drove them back to the sea, they hid and plotted. As I said, they're shape-shifters—but they're not limited the way we are. One of their forms is a horned serpent with a glowing crystal in its forehead, and that form has powerful psychic abilities—specifically, it sends out a kind of mental lure, one that attracts its prey."

"Like a deep-sea anglerfish," I said. "Sounds like they picked up a few tricks in the depths."

"Well, they taught themselves a few more," she said. "They learned how to do more than just send out a *Come here I'm a friend* signal. They fine-tuned the ability down to just *I'm a friend*. And then they worked on mimicking the human form. Some of their efforts have become legendary."

"Mermaids?" I said.

"And sirens. Practicing their trust-me mojo until they got it just right. Mind-control so subtle that the one being manipulated doesn't even realize it. Perfect for infiltration and sabotage."

Ben took a step closer to the edge of the branch. "And then what?" he asked. I could see from his body language that he wanted to launch himself off it and into space.

Teresa tucked her legs up, crossing them beneath her as casually as I'd cross my arms. Crimson nail polish gleamed on her toes. "That part of the story is less clear. They started by spreading rumors about the Thunderbirds among the animals. They insinuated that we favored certain animals over others, that we looked down on those who couldn't fly. That some of the messages we passed from one animal deity to another were delivered more slowly, or even altered. The Unktehila's abilities lent the rumors weight, made people believe them. When the Unktehila used their shape-changing and persuasive powers to create a full-blown incident, the supernatural community was ready to lay blame at our doorstep. Which was right here."

"Hold on," I said. "That's awfully vague. What exactly was this incident? Who was involved? What were the Thunderbirds accused of?"

She gave me an indulgent smile. "Oh, Foxtrot. So mired in the details of your busy little mortal life. This is the stuff of myth, of legend. It happened a very long time ago, and the story has been passed down through an oral tradition. That means that extraneous details *change:* dates, names, even events. But the central essence of the story, the truth at its heart, that remains pure. And the truth at the heart of this story is that we were betrayed—betrayed by evil— and were forced to hide ourselves among humankind to survive."

I stared at her. She was very, very good. In one concise statement she'd relegated me to the status of a lower being, blithely dismissed little things like facts as irrelevant cultural artifacts, and cast both herself and my boyfriend as romantic refugees who needed to stick together in the fight against Evil. Wow.

"Let's assume you're telling the truth," Ben said. "Thunderbirds went into hiding because of the Unktehila. But according to you, that all happened a long time ago. Why are we being targeted now? What changed?"

"We did. After many generations of remaining hidden, the Thunderbirds are returning to the world. Our true selves are reasserting themselves. Our heritage—our legacy—is coming alive once more. Look around you!"

Suddenly she was in motion, her legs straight and her arms outstretched, soaring and swooping through the air. "This is our ancestral home!" she shouted as she flew. She was skimming the inner surface of the sphere, like a marble rolling around inside a glass globe. "It's been waiting for us all this time, a deserted castle longing for its owners. And that's *us*!"

I glanced over at Ben. He was practically twitching with the urge to leap out there and join her.

"Yeah, sure," I said. "Your ancient enemies, who can apparently look like anything and control people's minds, are out for blood once more. Now's the perfect time to stage a big, public comeback. Your entire race must have decided to abandon their most prized stronghold on a whim—and even if this place is a target, there are *two* of you. More than enough to defend this entire, massive structure."

Ben frowned at me. "Can we have a little less sarcasm, please?" he said softly. "We came here for answers, not to argue."

I shook my head. "And so far, we haven't gotten any. All she's done is rehash what she already told me. We need some hard facts, not—not *legends*."

It was the wrong thing to say. I could see the frustration in his face before he turned away from me. "Well, that's the problem, Foxtrot. People like us, we don't have the luxury of history. We have myths and stories and yes, legends. I don't like it any more than you do, but it's what I've got. And I have to learn as much as I can."

He looked back and said, "I'm sorry."

And then he leapt into the air. "Teresa!" he called out. "Hang on!"

She grinned, more at me than at him, and dove into the tangle of branches. He followed her, as she knew he would.

I sighed, and sank down on the mossy branch to wait. My boyfriend had just flown away with another woman, who might be luring him to his death. Leaving me stranded in the middle of an other-dimensional floating forest. Without the power of flight, or even cab fare.

I scowled. If she didn't kill him, I might.

They were gone just long enough for me to start worrying about whether or not Ben was coming back, which was exactly what Teresa Firstcharger wanted me to worry about. When he did return, he was alone, and not looking nearly sorry enough.

"Well," I said. "Did you get what you wanted?"

He studied me for a second before he answered. Trying to figure out just how angry I was, I suppose. "Not really, no. Mainly, she wanted to play hide-and-seek. I spent most of my time chasing her, and when I finally caught her she was more interested in flirting than talking. That's when I left."

"I can't believe you flew off and left me here. What if this was all a trap?"

"Then I guess I did something stupid. But I told you, I had to follow my instincts."

"Had to follow *her*, you mean."

"Nothing happened. Don't you trust me?"

"You didn't give me a choice! You flew off without even discussing it!"

I knew that look on his face. It was his stubborn, I-don't-give-a-damn look. "I didn't have time for an argument. I just wanted to talk to her."

"Without me around, you mean."

"Well, you weren't exactly helping!"

"What, you mean by using logic and reason instead of my *instincts*?"

He threw his hands wide in exasperation. "What, exactly, about any of this seems logical or reasonable? We're in another dimension, in the middle of a big floating ball of trees and rocks!"

He had a point, but I was too angry to care. "A big floating ball of trees and rocks that you *abandoned* me in. Now, if you don't mind, I think I'd like to go home."

"Fine." He thrust his hand out at me and I took it.

I didn't think it was possible to fly hand-in-hand with your lover through a beautiful, sun-dappled forest and be angry, but I was. In fact, all the beauty around me just made it worse, like I didn't have the right to be angry in a magical place like this.

But I was. I was angry at him for leaving me, and angry at myself for not trusting him, and really, *really* angry at Teresa Firstcharger. For, you know, being young and gorgeous and superpowered and not me.

We flew out of the woods and straight into a whirlwind, which scared me until I realized Ben had summoned it before we got there. We slowed to a hover in the middle of it, stray leaves from the forest below tumbling around us, and then we were back in the graveyard on solid ground.

He tried to hold on to my hand, but I pulled it away. "Foxtrot, please."

"Please what? Do you have any idea what could have happened in there when you flew off? We'd just been told that big, scary, shape-changing monsters with a taste for human flesh are targeting us. What if one of *them* had shown up?"

I hate being powerless, and I'm not crazy about thoughtless boyfriends, either. Ben picked that moment to say just about the worst thing he could have: "The Aerie is safe—the Unktehila can't come there. Teresa told me that much."

I glared at him. "Fine. Tell you what—since I wasn't there, why don't you write down all the nuggets of wisdom she imparted to you in a nice, thick book. I'm sure your *instincts* will tell you what to do with it when you're finished."

And then I turned and stomped away. I'm not really much of a stomper, but I put some effort into it. I stomped right through a stream of gold and white ghostly guinea pigs, and they scattered like I'd kicked them. Ghosts are sensitive to extremes of emotion.

I stopped at the gate connecting the graveyard to the mansion's grounds and used the Crossroads' psychic-amplifying effects to braincast a message to both Whiskey and Tango: *Meet me by my car.* Then I left the graveyard and walked up to the house. By the time I got there I had myself under control, and the stomping had turned into striding. *Self* and *control* were two of my middle names.

Then I pulled out my phone. I called ZZ.

And I took the rest of the day off.

CHAPTER TWELVE

I am not a quitter. I do not quit.

I do, however, sometimes need a break. And while I normally schedule those in five-minute increments—of which four may be spent crying—sometimes I require a little longer.

Which is not to say I just walk away from a job undone. In fact, I made six more phone calls immediately after I talked to ZZ, making sure I wasn't leaving anyone in the lurch. No lurch-leaving, that's always the rule.

I wished a certain reckless cook felt the same way.

You can't always burn the candle at both ends. Juggling all my normal duties plus taking care of the graveyard was a lot, but throw in a hidden, mind-controlling people-eating monster? I needed to regroup.

So I put the least urgent stuff on temporary hold and decided to concentrate on the more immediate, life-threatening stuff. Because that gigantic, rainbow-colored snake slithering through Cooper's dreams and the vision of Bonkle's imaginary friends had to be what Teresa Firstcharger had described.

The Unktehila. A supernatural carnivore that would

probably love to gobble up not only my boyfriend, but a
certain kitty and pooch whom I cared very much about.

Both of them were waiting patiently by my car when I
walked up. Well, Whiskey was waiting patiently. Tango
was on the hood, pacing back and forth and putting dusty
little paw prints all over the paint job.

<What's up, Toots? You sounded agitated.>

I unlocked the doors and opened the rear one. "Both of
you, get in."

They just stared at me.

<Why?>

"Because there's a threat to all of us and we need to go
someplace safe to discuss it and we might be overheard.
So just get in the car, please."

[A threat? We're running away from a threat? That
hardly seems proper.]

"It's not proper, it's prudent. Get in."

Tango sat down. And yawned. <Uh-huh. Calm down
and tell us what's going on.>

"I will. As soon as you get in the damn car!"

Whiskey glanced at Tango. [She's upset.]

<Oh, you noticed that, did you?>

[Hard not to. More angry than scared, though.]

<Mmmm. I'd say it's about fifty–fifty. But she is
swearing.>

[Not a good sign. She must have had a fight with Ben.]

I groaned. "Look, I'll tell you both all about it if you'll
just get in the car!"

[No.]

<Yeah, what he said.>

I glared at both of them, then slammed the door shut.
"Fine. You want to know what's going on? That snake we're
hunting is probably hunting us. Or at least Ben and Teresa
Firstcharger, because it's something called an Unktehila
that just happens to be the ancient, sworn enemy of the

Thunderbirds. Oh, and it can look like anything and persuade anyone to trust it."

My partners considered this, Whiskey's eyebrows going up in worry while Tango took a more relaxed approach and licked one paw.

[You're overreacting,] Whiskey finally said.

<Pretty much.>

"How can you say that? Tango, you were the one all worked up about a giant snake lurking in the shadows—"

<I'm over it. Big snake, big whoop.> She looked at me blandly, reminding me once again that cats are 50 percent stubborn and 50 percent contrary. And 150 percent independent.

[First of all, Foxtrot, you're overstating the situation. Speaking as a shape-shifter myself, there's no being that can look like anything at all. There are always limitations. Second, there's no such thing as universal persuasion, either. Once you're on guard for it, attempts at mental coercion are easily recognized and can be deflected.]

<Third, we don't run from fights. We might back up a little, we might decide we're not in the mood to fight right now, but we don't run away. So, giant shape-changing psychic snakes or not, we're sticking around. Got it?>

I gave up. "Got it," I said. "Okay, we're not running away. But we need a plan. We need to stop bouncing from one event to another. We need to *strategize.*"

[Then by all means, let us do so. It's what you excel at, is it not?]

I smiled. "When I'm not freaking out because my boyfriend and I just had a fight, yeah. I'm actually much better at handling other people's problems."

Tango gave her head a very feline shake. *<Yes, you are. But it's a process I just don't get.>*

[Of course you don't. It requires caring about the problems of a person other than yourself.]

<Oh, please. I care about many people other than me.>

[Any that don't feed you?]

<There's no such thing. Only people who haven't yet realized that one day they will feed me. Or give me cat-nip. Or skritches.>

[It's astonishing how you can transform selfish ignorance into blind optimism in the space of a single sentence.]

<You wanna talk about blind optimism? Any idea what dogs look like when watching their owners eat a steak dinner? It makes me embarrassed that we're both mammals.>

"Guys. Strategy. Us. Now?"

[Well, obviously we need to find this Unktehila creature and deal with it. If it's a shape-shifter, it's probably hiding in plain sight, disguised as something else."

<Something innocent.>

[Something harmless.]

<Something cute, even—hold on. You're talking about me, aren't you?>

[Of all the adjectives that come to mind, *harmless* isn't high on the list.]

I put a hand up. "Stop. Let's recognize the potential for extreme paranoia here. Mind *and* appearance tweaking? That's the stuff of nightmares. So right off, let's just assume that the three of us are, well, the three of us. Because, honestly—I don't think there's anyone, alive or dead, who could imitate the relationship you two have."

<That's exactly what a shape-shifting mind controller would say.>

[Unless they were smart. Then they'd be the first one to point that out.]

I sighed. "Really? We're going to go that way?"

<Nah. I know it's you, Toots. And Muttley's particular flavor of dog-headedness is awful hard to copy, for which

I'm extremely grateful. So we're good—unless Kibble-Breath is still harboring any suspicions?>

[Not as such. It's one thing to fool the eye, quite another to fool the nose—especially my nose. While I might not be able to detect an Unktehila on its own—that scent isn't in my olfactory library—an imposter posing as something they're not is another matter.]

I thought about that. "So if the Unktehila tried to pass itself off as someone you already know, you'd spot it. What about someone you'd never encountered before?"

[That could be a problem. I wouldn't know the difference between an Unktehila's natural scent and the natural scent of a human I was meeting for the first time.]

<You gotta be kidding me. How many humans are going to give off the same reek a disguised sea serpent is?>

[You'd be surprised. Every organism is a complex symphony of olfactory nuance, affected by everything from their diet to their environment. Should we assume our killer is one of the guests because they had sardines for lunch?]

"So it could be one of the guests and we wouldn't know. It could even be Kaci."

[I strongly doubt that.]

<Right, what with you being so objective about her.>

"Let's face it, we don't know who or what the Unktehila is hiding as. But we have to make finding out priority number one."

Tango jumped down from the hood. *<Yeah. So where do we start?>*

"By eliminating suspects. If it's not someone we already know, it might be a guest. It can't be Keene. That leaves Teresa Firstcharger, Theodora Bonkle, Efram Fimsby, and Rustam Gorshkov or his dog."

[Firstcharger is also unlikely. She's the one who alerted us in the first place.]

<I'm not so sure. Snakes are devious. Maybe this is just a way to get us chasing our own tails.>

I shook my head. "If she's an Unktehila posing as a Thunderbird, she's doing an awfully good job. I think we have to assume she's the real thing, which still leaves us with four possibles."

[Fimsby would be my guess. He's been manipulating us from the start.]

<No, no, no. It's the dog. Perfect cover. And that whole psychic thing is clearly Unktehilic.>

"Both good points, but what about Theodora Bonkle? She's so unlikely it would be a stroke of genius. Hiding in plain sight by sticking out as much as possible."

<This is getting us nowhere. We need to do something.> Tango stalked back and forth, her tail high and twitching.

[For once, we agree. Foxtrot?]

I took a deep breath. I felt a lot better than I had a few minutes ago; funny how deciding to act instead of react will do that for you. "Okay. Tango, I'd like you to shadow Fimsby and see if you can learn anything. I'll talk to Theodora, and Whiskey will pay Kaci a visit. We'll rendezvous in the gardens afterward." I paused. "Uh, there's just one problem. I kind of took the day off."

Both of them gave me an extremely skeptical look.

"No, really. I did."

Then they glanced at each other. I felt like a teenager trying to explain something to my parents and they just weren't buying it.

[She *was* upset.]

<Still hasn't told us about the fight with Ben, either.>

I chose to ignore that. "It doesn't matter. I can talk to Theodora in the graveyard—she's probably still hanging out with Cooper. We'll rendezvous by Davy's Grave, instead."

<Workplace romances. Always tricky.>

"I'll see both of you later. Let's get to work."

As I strode away, I heard Whiskey say, [That's why I tend to avoid them.]

But I didn't run into Theodora at the graveyard. I ran into Keene instead.

He sat on a headstone, strumming a guitar, dressed in old black jeans, white sneakers, and a faded TRAVELING WILBURYS T-shirt. I heard him before I saw him, the music starting and stopping as he tried to work out the melody.

"Hello, Trot," he said with a grin as I walked up. "I see you're wearing That Look today."

"What look?" I said pleasantly.

"That one with the bright smile and the carefree voice and the eyes full of murder. You're dead brilliant at it, but you can't fool me."

I blinked. "I don't know what you're talking about."

"Sure you do. You always know *exactly* what people are talking about, and what's really going on, and how to fix things. Only some things can't be fixed, and some people will always talk crap, and usually you're impervious and indefatigable and altogether unbeatable, except when you're not. And on those days, you wear That Look." He frowned down at the guitar and tried a different chord. "No, no, that's not it."

Which is when I noticed he wasn't alone. There was a ghost perched on his back, peeking over his right shoulder. It looked like a monkey, with large, bat-like ears and huge, golden-brown eyes. I knew what it was immediately, though I was surprised to see it on Keene. Ghosts rarely interacted physically with the living.

I glanced down at the grave. It was a tiny plot, much smaller than the headstone itself, which was made of white marble and looked expensive. Chiseled into it was the name

JEEPERS and the inscription BUSH BABY BY NAME, MY BABY BY HEART.

"I've seen you sitting here before," I said. "What's so special about this spot?"

"This? This is my muse. Good old Jeepers, never lets me down. When I'm really stuck on a tune, I play it for him. Or her, I'm not really sure. Did you know he's the only bush baby interred here? Not that surprising, I suppose, considering they're native to Africa."

I tried not to stare at his phantom hitchhiker. Jeepers did, in fact, seem to be listening to something, his head cocked in that universal way. "And how exactly did an African monkey become your muse?"

"Galagos aren't monkeys, though they are primates. And I didn't so much pick him as he picked me—that's the way it often is, with a muse. Just felt drawn to this spot one night, a few years back. Sat right here and did what I'm doing now, and the whole song just fixed itself. Which makes perfect sense, if you think about it."

"How's that?"

He tried a different key and seemed more satisfied with it. "That's better. Galagos are very vocal. They make a lot of different sounds, and their ears are extremely sensitive: They can even hear the sound an owl makes when it glides through the air. Plus, they're both social and nocturnal— much like me. So, it makes sense that they could appreciate a decent melody, don't you think?"

"I would have thought something with feathers would be more appropriate as your muse."

"A bird? Nah. Lead singers are too hard to work with— massive egos, the lot of 'em. I need something with digits, something that can appreciate what I'm trying to do. Galagos even have rounded fingernails, just like us."

"Wait. Aren't you a lead singer?"

"Like I said." He looked up at me and smiled again. He

really did have a very nice smile. "But at least I know it. And so do you, which is how you got me talking about myself instead of you, and right about now is when you're going to ask if there's anything you can do for me, and by the time you've done that and skipped merrily away I'll have forgotten all about the fact that we were talking about *your* problems, which are non-existent in nature and you don't have any, anyway. Right?"

"Absolutely. Ben and I had a fight."

And then my eyes got about three sizes bigger because I couldn't believe what I just said. Or whom I'd said it to.

Keene stopped playing. He put the guitar down, propping it against the back of the headstone. Jeepers leapt off his shoulder—a really amazing leap that covered a good twenty feet, it was a shame Keene couldn't see it—landed on top of a mausoleum, and scampered out of sight. Keene scooted over, patted the top of the headstone, and said, "Sit."

I did. He studied me, a very odd expression on his face, and said, "Talk."

Worry. That was it. He was worried, which on Keene was like seeing a tuxedo on a duck. Just didn't look right.

So I talked. I couldn't tell him everything, of course, but the details didn't matter. What mattered was that my boyfriend and I had a fight, and I was feeling frustrated and alone and not at all appreciated, and he was a sympathetic ear.

Yes, Keene was a rock star. And a flirt, and a party animal, and an overgrown man-child with responsibility issues. But he had a big heart, and I'd never seen him be mean to anyone.

Sometimes, all you want is for someone to listen.

"Ah," he said. "Teresa Firstcharger. Yeah, better watch out for that one. Real man-eater."

I raised an eyebrow. "You know that firsthand, huh?"

"Me? Nah. I like my women a little less predatory—that one starts to salivate at the sight of blood. Saw her hit on Brad Pitt once at a charity bash. Thought Angelina was gonna go all Lara Croft on her, but credit where credit's due; she just smiled and ignored her. Lots of practice doing that, I'm guessing. Plus, being one of the world's biggest movie stars tends to bolster the old confidence."

I sighed. "Yeah, well, I don't exactly have a lot of practice in either of those. I barely have any practice in the boyfriend area, period."

He mock-punched me in the arm. "And whose fault is that? You're the one who decided to be all responsible and jobby every single day. I swear, you wouldn't know a weekend if it threw up on you. Which, granted, is not exactly a ringing endorsement of the process and far too accurate in my own case and I really should stop talking, shouldn't I?"

I laughed. "It's okay. You're right, I've always focused so much on work that I don't leave enough time for myself. But I love what I do, even when it's crazy and intense and overwhelming."

"You love it *because* it's crazy and intense and overwhelming. Same with what I do."

I gave him a skeptical look. "Right. What I do is like being a rock star."

"Bloody right it is. See, you and me are two of the lucky ones, Trot. We get to do what we love for a living—that's something most people don't have. They work to pay the bills, and they use whatever time and money left over on what *they* love. Family or hobbies or sports or friends or whatever gives them joy. But us, our joy and work are all mixed up together. That's a huge thing, a great thing, a thing I always try to keep in mind, just how lucky people like us are. But like the late, great Elvis Presley once said, 'It doesn't matter how rich or famous you are. There's trouble at every level of life.' And the kind of trouble that us lucky, lucky folks have is the inability to separate what we do from who we are. We don't get to put a bad day at work behind us when we go home at five o'clock on Friday night. When something bad happens at our work, it happens to our whole lives."

I thought about that. Didn't I have my own life? Wasn't I more than ZZ's assistant? More than the Guardian of the Great Crossroads?

Of course I was. But Keene was right, I didn't give that part of my life enough attention. I needed to make more space for just being me, instead of spending twenty-four seven worrying about other's problems. I could do that, right?

Right?

"So," I said. "How do *you* cope? Or is the answer the obvious one?"

He grinned. "What, you mean the drugs and the drink and the philandering? Nah, that's just part of the job description. What *I* do is come here."

I sighed. "Perfect. Your escape is my prison. You think maybe I could go on tour with you for my next vacation?"

He shook his head. "Never. You'd lose that last little shred of respect for me that I know, deep down, you still harbor. It's small, it's fragile, and it needs to be tended. So don't ever knock on the door of a hotel room you know I'm in—promise me."

"Sorry, no can do. Gotta give you *some* incentive to be better. In fact, the next time you're on the road I'm going to use my amazing organizational superpowers to track you down and do exactly that. Shall we say nine minutes after one o'clock in the AM, Mr. Keene?"

He stared at me with horror in his eyes. "You wouldn't."

"I would. From now on, wherever you are—Bangkok

or Amsterdam or New York—you better be fully dressed, sober, and alone at one oh nine. Or the shred gets it."

He shook his head in sorrow. "You are a hard, hard woman, Foxtrot Lancaster. Ah, well. I'll probably get more sleep this way."

"No, you'll start every party at one ten."

"One eleven, actually. You're good, but two minutes leeway is only polite."

"Aren't you going to ask why I picked one oh nine?"

"No. I like our relationship to have a little mystery."

I got to my feet. "Thanks for the talk, Keene. I still have no idea what I'm going to do, but I feel a little better."

"Glad to be of help. Now be off with you. Jeepers and I have work to do."

He picked up his guitar, positioned it on his lap, then frowned. "Ah, but he's gone. Bit shy, galagos. Nothing like the legends."

Keene had demonstrated his affinity with living animals many times before, so a connection with a dead one didn't surprise me—he wasn't kidding, he really did know that Jeepers wasn't there anymore. It was the *last* thing he said that caught my attention. "What legends?"

"Has to do with their vocalizations. Some people think they sound like a crying infant—ergo the *bush baby* name—but others hear something a bit scarier. Never made much sense to me, though. Snakes are a quiet lot, for the most part."

"Snakes?"

He looked down and strummed his guitar softly, once. "Yeah. African tribespeople heard galagos screaming in the jungle in the middle of the night and for some reason attributed the noise to a giant, rainbow-colored snake. Said if you ever actually saw the thing, it would drill a hole right into your skull." He poked a finger between his own eyes. "Kill you stone-dead . . ."

I forced a smile onto my face. "Wow. The things some people believe, huh?"

And then I turned around and walked quickly away.

Was that really Keene I was talking to?

It took all my willpower not to look back as I walked away. My heart was hammering and my head felt light. No. No, it had to have been. Even without Whiskey's nose to verify it, I knew Keene. Knew him well enough to spot an imposter, I was sure. Even if the imposter had the psychic ability to get anyone to trust them . . .

I'd confided in him awfully quick.

It really hit me, right then, just how terrible a power an Unktehila had. Posing as anyone was bad enough, but it was the trust thing that was really terrifying. Betrayal waited behind every smiling face.

But didn't it always?

No. It didn't. But the fact that I was even asking the question proved how evil the ability was. Just knowing it existed made me question the trustworthiness of every ally I had, and then question my own ability to judge. What I really wanted to do at the moment was to run and get Whiskey, drag him back to the graveyard, and have him verify that Keene was Keene. But first I'd have to interrogate Whiskey to make sure he wasn't an imposter, either . . .

No. I wasn't going to let this thing get any farther into my head than it already was. I could be obsessive about details, I was a worrier, I worshipped reliability; all characteristics that would make an Unktehila howl with delight—or scream like a milk-deprived infant in the depths of an African jungle.

Keene. Why had I spilled my guts to him?

Because he was my friend. Because he cared about me. Because, under the playful flirting and the outrageous antics, he was actually a gentle soul who just loved life and lived it with glee. He had seen that I was in pain and did whatever he could to make it stop. Well, other than offering me large quantities of pharmaceutical-quality narcotics, which he knew I'd turn down.

Nothing had manipulated me into doing that. I trusted him, because—

I stopped. I stood very still, searching my thoughts, trying with every ounce of self-awareness I had to feel the presence of something alien in my head or heart.

Nope. Just me. And I knew that, really knew that, because if the Unktehila had been posing as Keene and influencing my emotions it would have tried to make me love it. But that wasn't how I felt.

It was how Keene felt, though.

About me.

I found Theodora Bonkle at Cooper's bungalow, him drinking coffee, her drinking tea, both of them hunched over a huge, hand-drawn map of the graveyard that spilled over the edges of Cooper's kitchen table.

"Ah, Foxtrot!" Theodora beamed up at me. "Good to see you. But where is your canine companion?"

"Off doing doggy things. He has his own social calendar."

I sat down next to her. "Find out anything new? Any further sightings of cats, marbles, or rainbow snakes?" I tried to keep my tone light.

Theodora took a sip from a teacup entirely too small for her hand. "In a manner of speaking, yes. Cooper and I have been politely approaching other people visiting grave sites, to see if any of them have crossed paths with our mysterious marbler. After several fruitless attempts, we met with success when we talked to a teenage girl. Lovely thing, shaved head, wearing a leather jacket several sizes too large. She was quite upset over the death of her pet ferret, and came to the graveyard on a regular basis to visit his final resting place."

"See her Sundays, mostly," Cooper said. "Always on her own. Listens to headphones and cries."

"When we approached her, she was wary at first. But no one can resist the charm of Very British Bear and Doc Wabbit when they're on their best behavior."

"She . . . talked to them?"

"Well, not as such. But I've become quite adept at relaying their antics."

Cooper caught my eye. "She usually smokes a little something while she's there, too. I think we showed up just afterward."

I nodded. "So you caught her in an open-minded state as opposed to paranoid." Okay, that might make the idea of Theodora and her imaginary retinue more entertaining than threatening. "What did she tell you?"

Theodora put down her teacup and tapped the map. "Her ferret—Sparky—is buried here. Two of the sites where marbles were found are here, and here." She pointed to two spots on the map on either sides of Sparky's grave. "When we asked if she'd seen anyone placing a marble on either of these graves, she said she had. And gave us a description."

I was less interested in the marble case than the lurking giant serpent, but you never know what piece of information might turn out to be vital later on. "And?"

"Our marble placer," said Theodora, "is a woman in black. Head-to-toe, including a veil and gloves. Age unknown, but probably a senior."

"Not a lot to go on," I said.

"Ah, but there's more to our tale. We have three more pieces of evidence, all of them valuable. The first is her given name: Mary. We know this because it's the name used by her companion."

"She had a companion?"

"Piece number two: her companion. Younger, stout, possibly Latino or Asian. Only seen from a distance, calling for her friend. I believe she's a caregiver of some sort, maybe a nurse."

"Not sure if I agree with that one or not," Cooper said.

Theodora shrugged. "It's only a hypothesis. But the girl in the leather jacket said the woman sounded annoyed when she called for Mary, and made some reference to Mary 'always running off.' That sounds to me less like a family member and more like someone tasked with keeping track of her."

Cooper shook his head. "Could be her daughter. Nothing like family to get you frustrated."

"Granted, but a daughter would be more likely to follow her than call from a distance. A small difference, but a telling one. Family does what it must; employees do what they have to. Which leads us to piece of evidence number three: that our marble placer may be suffering mental confusion."

"Why?" I asked.

"Several reasons. Her manner of dress suggests she's older; nobody wears a veil anymore. That, plus a caregiver who accompanies her on outings, gives weight to the theory that she requires monitoring. The fact that she can outpace her companion means her disability is more likely to be mental than physical."

"So you think it could be as simple as memory loss? She's visiting the grave of her cat but she can't remember the right name?"

"Perhaps. But there has to be more to it than that. She remembers to visit on a regular basis, she remembers the graveyard, she remembers to bring the marbles, she even dresses appropriately; why should something as simple as the location of the grave or the name upon it confuse her?"

"I don't know," I admitted. "Memory's a funny thing. Sometimes I can't recall a name I'm intimately familiar with—it's not like I don't know it, more like something's physically blocking it from traveling from one part of my brain to another."

"Sure," said Cooper, leaning back in his chair and resting one arm on the back. "Everybody gets that. What I really hate is when you're trying to think of a snack food and all that comes up are old Rolling Stone album covers."

Theodora and I shared a glance.

"Or maybe that's just me," Cooper said.

"Sounds like you're making good progress," I said. "Though I still don't understand how the rainbow snake fits in." I did, of course, but I needed to know if they—or Bonkle's imaginary sidekicks—had encountered it again.

"My current hypothesis is that the snake is a hallucinatory feature of the woman's mental state. The fact that it can be seen by others is unusual, but both Mr. Cooper and I perceived it through the filter of an altered psyche. *Why a rainbow snake?* you ask. Ah, that's the *real* mystery, the inner workings of the mind. There's only one solution I can see: track this woman down and ask her."

I realized Theodora hadn't commented on the activities of Doc or Very since I sat down. "What about your partners in detection? Have they come up with anything?"

Theodora sighed. "Not really. Doc finds all this research boring and Very keeps leaving to listen to that musician in the graveyard with his new friend."

"New friend?" I asked.

"Yes, some sort of big-eyed monkey, according to Very. But he's not terribly good at describing things—oh, hello, Doc." Theodora glanced over at the doorway. "What do you have in that sack? Oh, I see. Well, let him out of there."

"Guess Doc missed his friend," Cooper said with a grin.

"Very's always wandering off, and Doc has to go get

him. Thick as thieves, the two of them, but you'll never get Doc to admit it . . . hello, Very. Enjoy the music?"

She listened intently, then chuckled. "He says the songs were very short, but at least they all sounded the same, except when they didn't."

"He was just practicing," I said, then realized I was defending Keene to a figment of somebody else's imagination. He'd get a kick out of that when I told him.

"Hmm? What's that, Doc? At least it's better than the noises you heard coming from Keene's room the other night? Now what would that—oh, that's terrible. You shouldn't eavesdrop on private things like that, it's—"

And then Theodora's mouth opened wide in an expression of utter surprise.

"What?" I asked.

"Doc—this is no time for one of your jokes," Theodora hissed, staring fixedly at a point on the floor. "Never mind the noises, say that last part again."

She listened, then gave me a worried look. "Oh, dear."

"What is it?" asked Cooper. "What did he hear?"

"Some extremely personal sounds, that I won't attempt to duplicate. But there were words, too."

Theodora met my eyes and said, "Anna. Oh, Anna, Oh, *Anna . . .*"

CHAPTER THIRTEEN

I stared at Theodora Bonkle, speechless. I mean, what do you say when somebody's imaginary friend implicates a real friend in a murder?

"Perhaps he misheard," Theodora said. "Or he could be making it up. Doc's *such* a troublemaker."

"Theodora, this is *important*," I said. "Are you saying that Anna was in Keene's room the other night? That he and Anna had *sex*?"

"I'm not saying anything of the sort," Theodora snapped. "*Doc's* saying it. And he's hardly a reliable witness."

I blinked. Theodora's room was beneath Keene's. Even though the mansion is sturdy, it's hardly soundproof—a noisy sexual encounter could conceivably be overheard. Or heard in your sleep and processed through a hallucination of a talking bunny. There was no way to know.

"This raises all sorts of questions," Theodora said. "Anna Metcalfe was a married woman who had a public spat with her husband the night before her death. That's tragic enough for the poor man, but to learn she was having an affair, as well? We must tread carefully, my dear—this is just the sort of mischief Doc thinks is *hilarious*."

And even though Hayden Metcalfe wasn't exactly innocent, there was nothing to prove he'd killed his wife—
and learning that she'd been unfaithful to him in her last
hours was maybe more punishment than he deserved. Especially if the information wasn't trustworthy—which was
exactly what Theodora was insisting.

Trust. While I was feeling sorry for myself because I
couldn't trust those around me, Theodora couldn't trust
parts of her own personality. Maybe I wasn't as bad off as
I thought.

But I needed to know whether or not it was true, whether
Keene and Anna had been together on the night she died.
And I knew just where to start.

"You're probably right," I said to Theodora. "That Doc
is a tricky rascal, isn't he? He really got us."

Theodora nodded, looking relieved; she wanted to believe it was just a joke, no doubt one of many Doc had
played on her. Coop looked less certain, but he didn't say
anything.

"Well," I said, getting to my feet, "I've got to run. Never
enough time, you know?"

"Yes, yes, of course," said Theodora. She pushed her
tortoiseshell glasses up the bridge of her blocky nose with
one large finger. "Please carry on with your day. We'll keep
you apprised of any new developments."

"Thank you. Good luck." I let myself out, and went in
search of Whiskey.

I tried paging him telepathically first, since the graveyard acted as a psychic amplifier. I got an immediate response: [I'm over by Davy's Grave, watching Kaci and
Gorshkov.]

When I headed over that way, I saw the Russian and his
dog, but not Whiskey.

Where are you? I thought.

[Downwind. Behind the tree.]

I glanced in that direction as I got closer, trying not to be obvious, and saw what might have been a nose peeking out of a clump of grass. *Good disguise. What are you, a miniature toy dwarf Pygmanese?*

[Longhaired Chihuahua. Only four inches tall, ideal for surveillance.]

As long as you stay downwind.

Kaci seemed to be painting a picture of a tree, but I wasn't interested in art appreciation at the moment. Their backs were to me, so I stayed out of sight and told Whiskey to come over. I saw some rustling in the grass, and a moment later a tiny, black-and-white dust mop scurried up.

"I think I've seen bigger cheeseburgers," I said.

[It's not the size of your bite, it's the sharpness of your teeth.]

"Very profound. Come on, we need to check something out." I explained to him what Theodora had told me.

We paused at the gate leading to the grounds of the mansion to let him shift into his customary canine form. [So where are we off to? If you want to confront Keene, I saw him earlier in the graveyard.]

"Not my plan. I need your nose to confirm what Doc Wabbit claims he overheard in Keene's room."

[Ah. Well, as long as the maids haven't been too efficient, some olfactory evidence should remain.]

The tricky part wasn't getting into Keene's room—I had a master key to every door in the mansion. No, the tricky part was getting into the mansion itself without anyone seeing me. Even if I was technically off duty, that probably wouldn't stop either staff or guests from asking me to solve their problems; that was my role, after all, and everyone around me was so used to it they'd probably go into shock if I claimed I wasn't working. And it wasn't that I minded people asking for my help; more like I wouldn't be able to say no. Before I knew it, I'd be caught up in a dozen minor details that needed fixing and my own agenda would be completely derailed.

Maybe I really should rethink a few things.

Whiskey and I got as far as halfway up the staircase in the main hall before a maid got me. Consuela called my name from below; I sighed mentally and turned around physically. "Yes?"

"Ms. Foxtrot, you have to do something about the paintings."

"The paintings?"

"The paintings. They are everywhere!"

For a second, my current state of mind conjured up the image of a flock of flying canvases, harassing Consuela like crazed seagulls. Half of them were portraits of Teresa Firstcharger done in oils, the other half watercolor sketches of a rainbow-hued snake. "What do you mean, they're everywhere?"

Consuela gestured with a hand. "Everywhere. In the bedrooms, in the dining room, in the hall. Did you not see?"

I hadn't. I walked back down the steps and saw what I had hurried past a minute ago: that paintings were propped against the walls in the foyer, and down both hallways that led away from it. They were large, at least five feet high, and each one was only a few brushstrokes in bright, primary colors. They seemed to portray either bushes, flowers, or trees—all except one.

Whiskey and I stared at it. Whiskey cocked his head to one side. "Well," I said. "I guess you made an impression on her. Impressionist."

[Is my head really that lopsided?]

Not most days. I frowned. I should have known; when the cat's away, the rats will play. In this case, the rat was Oscar, and he'd wasted no time in taking advantage of my supposed absence to create a little havoc.

"I see," I said to Consuela. "It appears that under Oscar's patronage, Kaci's output has greatly increased."

"Indeed it has," said Oscar, strolling out of the sitting room. "I believe it has something to do with the convivial environment here. Her technique over the last few days has shown such a change. It's become more . . ."

"Economical?"

He smiled, and raised his everpresent glass to me. "Just so. Quick, but focused. It's quite exciting."

"It's quite inconvenient, Oscar. Why are these works of art all in the house?"

"They're drying, of course. Can't be outside—bugs, you know. How would it look if a future masterpiece turned out to have a mayfly embedded in it?"

"Like an opportunity to sell it as one-of-a-kind?"

He looked thoughtful. "I hadn't thought of that . . ."

"Well, now you have. Move the canvases, please—there's plenty of room outside and it's not going to rain."

He nodded graciously. "Ah, of course. I heard you'd taken the day off, but clearly I was misinformed. You were merely busy expanding your realm of control to the weather—I knew it was only a matter of time."

I blinked. "I have to go."

I turned and charged back up the stairs, Whiskey at my heels.

[We should have a word with Mr. Gorshkov. Obviously, he's working Kaci much too hard.]

"She's a working dog, remember? Used to chasing sheep twelve hours a day. I don't think a few brushstrokes are going to wear her out."

We got to Keene's room. I pulled out my master key and took a deep breath. I didn't like snooping on the guests, and I liked snooping on my friends even less, but this was serious. If Anna and Keene had been together, I needed to know.

I unlocked the door and we stepped inside.

Keene didn't have a particular room he preferred over the others; in fact, it was his stated intention to eventually stay in all of them. When I asked him why, he told me, "Because I love this place and want to know all of it, inside and out. Besides, if *every* room is my favorite, then I'll never be disappointed, will I?"

He had, of course, made the room he was currently staying in his own. He never actually broke anything—well, nothing he didn't profusely apologize and pay for—but he did tend to unpack rather explosively. Clothing shrapnel covered a great deal of the room, as well as a number of guitars, a violin on a stand, a large red cylinder attached to a gas mask with a hose, and a great deal of Lego. The top of one table was dominated by a sprawling, free-form sculpture made of the stuff; it managed to be both playful and vaguely pornographic at the same time.

Whiskey was already over by the bed, which the maids clearly hadn't gotten to yet—cleaning Keene's room was always problematic, due to his habit of sleeping at odd hours and behaving oddly the rest of the time. We'd had to let one maid go after she walked in on him, a supermodel, a pair of hip waders, several gallons of vanilla custard, and an industrial paint mixer. Don't ask.

Whiskey sniffed at the sheets. He sniffed at the carpet. He sniffed at the bedside table. He sniffed at several items on the bedside table that I won't describe. And finally, he stopped sniffing, sat down, and looked steadily at me.

[I'm sorry, Foxtrot. Anna was here, with Keene. And they were . . . busy.]

Dammit.

I sat down on the edge of the bed. I shouldn't have been surprised. Keene slept with plenty of women, some of whom he brought with him, some of whom he met here. There was that Nobel Prize winner a while back—nobody saw that one coming except me. Anna was angry at her husband, Keene was sexy and funny and available . . . I found myself more disappointed in him than angry. A woman in Anna's state—he should have known better.

But that was all secondary. Anna was dead, and Keene had lied about sleeping with her. Was he trying to spare her husband the knowledge that her last act had been to cheat on him, or was he covering up something more sinister?

I looked around the room. I'd seen this mess plenty of times before, and even though it was always different it was always the same. There was his favorite silk shirt. There were the leather pants—a blue pair and a red pair this time. Lots of T-shirts, some new, some not. Enough makeup on the vanity to make a model drool.

But something was missing.

I stood up and went over to the vanity. It was the most organized part of the entire room, with all the accessories laid out in a very systematic manner. Eyeliner, moisturizer, hair products . . .

"No hair dryer," I said. "Keene never travels without one. And it's always right there, next to the gel." But not this time.

I searched the room. I found many interesting things, some of which required batteries, but no hair dryer. I was pretty sure I knew where it was, though: in a police evidence locker.

"This is bad," I said.

[There might be an innocent explanation.]

"Sure. Maybe he forgot it. Maybe he took it with him for some bizarre reason. Maybe Anna borrowed it after they had sex and liked it so much it wound up in the pool with her."

[None of those seems very likely.]

No, they didn't. A more likely explanation was that Anna hadn't been alone in that pool. Keene did love a naked, late-night dip, and he preferred his dipping to be done with others. He was vain enough to have taken his hair dryer with him, too.

The hair dryer hadn't killed Anna, though. It must have been thrown in to make us think her death was an accident, by someone who didn't know she was a Thunderbird. Possibly by the person who actually killed her.

But why? Keene had no reason to kill Anna. An accident, maybe?

I just didn't have enough information. I needed to learn what actually killed Anna, which meant talking to somebody official. Fortunately, I knew somebody better than someone official—I knew who did their paperwork.

We left Keene's room. A quick call to the coroner's office put me in touch with Harriet Tilford, who was the coroner's version of me. Harriet couldn't divulge details of an ongoing investigation, except for little insignificant things that might affect the person filling out all the insurance forms, a person she could really identify with and feel sorry for and you never heard this from me, right?

Usually Harriet was extremely helpful, but in this case she didn't have much to offer because the autopsy hadn't been done yet. So I thanked her and asked her to give me a call when she could because we really should catch up. Which I meant, because Harriet is a lovely person and we really do have a lot in common—mostly that neither of us has any time for catching up with friends.

I wondered how Tango was doing with Fimsby. I tried paging her telepathically, but got no response; she must have been out of range. I made a mental note to myself to someday test what the practical limit of that range was, in and out of the graveyard, then pulled out my phone and e-mailed myself a reminder.

"Whiskey, see if you can track down Tango for me and get an update. I'll meet you out by the pool."

[Very well.] He trotted back the direction we'd just come from.

I ducked down the back stairs. Those let out kind of close to the kitchen, and I really hoped I wouldn't run into Ben. I wasn't ready to talk to him yet. But I heard a tremendous racket start up when I was only halfway down, and guess where it was coming from? I had to check it out.

I opened the kitchen door on a blizzard.

I staggered back, blinded by a torrent of swirling, clattering white. It took my senses a moment to register that the temperature hadn't dropped, and a second after that to realize that the whiteness whipping through the air was far too fine to be snow; it was much more like dust.

I licked my lips. Flour. That was a culinary tempest I was looking at, not a seasonal one. Right about then a silver pot clanged loudly off the door frame and I knew why it was so noisy, too.

"Hey!" I yelled into the storm. "CUT IT OUT!"

The wind slowed. I heard the last of the cookware crash to the floor and stepped into a murky, swirling fog of finely ground whole wheat.

I could see two figures, facing each other in the middle of the kitchen. One was Ben. The other was Teresa First-charger.

The good news was, I hadn't interrupted some sort of frenzied Thunderbird mating ritual. The bad news was that they looked like they were ready to kill each other.

Ben was dusted in flour from head to toe, but Teresa looked like she'd just stepped out of a salon; somehow, she'd prevented any of the flour from actually touching her skin. The level of control that implied was terrifying. So was the look on her face. She was smiling. It was the kind of smile you'd wear if you'd learned how by studying pictures of serial killers.

Ben looked a lot angrier, but then it was his kitchen that had just been trashed. His hands were down at his sides, just like hers, but his fists were clenched. Firstcharger's were open, palms up and fingers spread wide.

"Your girlfriend's here to rescue you," she said. "What excellent timing."

"I don't need rescuing," Ben growled. He didn't look at me.

"What the hell is going on?" I demanded.

"A challenge," Teresa said.

"To what, see who's better at redecorating using pastry ingredients? Fine, you win. Now *stop*."

"Foxtrot, stay out of this," Ben said. His eyes were still locked on Teresa's.

"What, so you two can start tossing thunderbolts around? Don't make me call for Topsy, Teresa."

She laughed, a low, throaty sound. "You see what I mean? She likes her possessions on a short leash. Cats, dogs, elephants . . . Thunderbirds."

"This house is my responsibility," I said. "I'm not going to let anything happen to it, and you can't goad either of us into overreacting."

"Now she's telling you what you can and can't do."

"Back off, lady," Ben said. "Nobody messes with my kitchen. *Nobody*."

"Then stop me."

This was getting out of hand. *Whiskey*! I yelled in my head. *I need reinforcements in the kitchen, and fast!*

No answer. He must be out of range.

But the tornado I was expecting didn't happen. Ben's brow furrowed and the winds died down to almost nothing. Teresa's smile changed to something a little less aggressive and more admiring. "Not bad, fledgling, not bad. But you have a long way to go if you're ever going to earn your wings. You need to learn your place."

"My place is here," Ben snarled.

"Here? As a domestic servant to a rich old white woman? You can do better—or at least I hope you can. We'll see."

"What's *that* supposed to mean?" I snapped.

"It means that I'm formally challenging him to a duel. At the Aerie, dawn tomorrow. Under Thunderbird law, you must accept or forfeit your status."

"The only status I have is head chef. You going to confiscate my apron?"

She shook her head slowly, her eyes still on his. "No. I'm going to confiscate your ability to influence the weather. People like us are too powerful to roam around without the proper training, and yours is nonexistent."

"She's bluffing," I said.

"I don't think she is," Ben said. "But it doesn't matter. I accept. Dawn tomorrow it is. Where do you want to meet?"

Teresa looked away from him and at me, an amused and expectant look on her face. "At the graveyard, of course. If that's all right with its custodian?"

"Fine by me," I said.

"Not going to tell your pet to heel, Foxtrot?" Teresa said.

"He's my boyfriend, not my pet." I paused. "And he's going to kick your tail feathers tomorrow. At dawn."

She nodded in an oddly formal way, turned, and left the kitchen without saying another word.

I looked at Ben. He looked at me.

"Well," I said.

"Yeah," he said.

Then neither of us said anything.

"This is nuts," Ben finally said.

"That it is. Nutty as a squirrel café."

"I have to do this."

I took a deep breath. Before I could use it for anything, he said, "I *do*. She's telling the truth about me forfeiting my abilities. Don't ask me how I know, I just do. And there's no way I'm letting her do that, not without a fight."

"I was going to ask what I could do to help."

<Help?> said a raspy feline voice in my head. *<Help with what?>*

Tango strolled into the kitchen through the back door, the one Ben had installed a cat flap on. *<Hey, Toots. Whiskey said you wanted to see me?>*

In a minute, okay? I'm having a discussion with Ben and it's kind of important.

<A discussion? About what?>

"About my status," Ben said. "Seems some people don't have a lot of respect for it."

<Oh, I get it. If there's one thing cats understand, it's pride.>

I sighed. "Tango, this is a little more complicated than that."

<How complicated can it be? Look, Ben, it doesn't matter if ZZ hired you as a favor to your family or not—you're a terrific cook. Everything you give me is delicious, anyway. You have every right to be proud.>

"What?" Ben said.

CHAPTER FOURTEEN

I've never actually seen someone lob a grenade, but I'm guessing that the silence between when it lands and when it goes off was a lot like the silence in the kitchen after that little exchange. Seemed to last forever, but I knew there was going to be a big explosion and a huge mess to clean up any second.

"What?" Ben said again.

Tango looked up at Ben. She looked over at me. She looked back at Ben.

<Whoops. There's no way I can blame this on the dog, is there?>

"My family?" Ben said. "My *family* told ZZ to hire me?"

Sometimes, trying to explain just makes things worse. "Yes," I said.

"And you knew about this?"

"I just found out. ZZ asked me not to tell you."

His eyes narrowed. "Uh-huh. Just doing what our boss says, right?"

"That's not fair—"

"Oh, I'm sorry. I meant to say *your* boss. Apparently

she's not so much *my* employer as the head of the charity dedicated to looking after me."

"I was going to tell you."

"Sure you were. At a time and place of your choosing, right? Funny how everybody but me gets to make all the decisions."

That's the kind of statement there's no good response to—it's 90 percent emotion and 10 percent logic. Pointing out that he couldn't make a decision about something he didn't know about would just get me another angry response, so I kept my mouth shut and gave Tango an irritated look instead. She did that cat thing of crouching down really low and then zooming away like a cruise missile hugging the ground.

Ben untied his apron and yanked it off. "You know what? Teresa's right. I don't belong here. I'm obviously not the chef I thought I was, or even the man. I'm a freak of nature, half weatherman and half goddamn bird. Maybe it's time I faced the truth."

He threw his apron on the floor at my feet. "Tell ZZ she can find another charity to contribute to. *I quit.*"

And then he turned and stomped off through the back door.

Putting out fires is what I do; I do it so often I should have one of those sliding poles in my bedroom. No, wait, that makes me sound like a stripper.

Anyway, Ben's resignation didn't throw me into the kind of panic it might other people. Okay, it meant I was now short one chef, possibly one boyfriend, and maybe even my job—but I could deal. I went out to the pool where I said I'd meet Whiskey, pulled out my cell phone, and started to make calls. It wouldn't do Ben's bruised ego any good, but I had guests to feed and a boss to answer to.

Whiskey didn't show up. Odd. Well, I couldn't wait around for him; I had things to do.

I called the cook who had subbed for Ben this morning and got him to come back. Then I went looking for ZZ and found her in her office, immersed in the Internet as usual. "Oh, hello, dear. Couldn't stay away even for one day, could you? I just won a bet with Consuela."

I sat down in the chair opposite her desk and said, "Officially, I'm still not here. But there's something you need to know: Ben found out."

She stopped what she was doing and looked over at me. "Oh, dear. You mean you—"

"I didn't tell him. He found out on his own." That was about as close as I could come to the truth. "He was pretty upset—in fact, he tendered his resignation."

Her face fell. "Do you think he means it?"

"I don't know. I've lined up a temporary replacement for tonight, and once he's cooled down a little we'll talk. But I really think you need to be part of that conversation, too."

"Of course. I feel terrible about this, Foxtrot. I was only trying to help."

"I know, ZZ. Once he's had time to think about it, Ben will, too."

I told her I had a lot to do—always true—and left. So far, today wasn't going so great.

But you know what they say: Things could always be worse. And for some people, they already were . . .

I heard her crying behind the door as I walked down the hall. Heavy, choked sobs, full of misery. Being the caring-yet-nosy person I am, I stopped outside the door, then knocked gently. "Theodora? Are you all right?"

The crying stopped. I hear her getting off the bed and walking over. The door opened to show me a very tearful Theodora Bonkle, her overly made-up face now a streaky ruin. "Foxtrot," she sniffed. "I'm sorry, dear, I'm a bit of a mess. Do come in."

I stepped inside. From the small mountain of crumpled tissues on the bed, it seemed she'd been weeping for some time. I hoped she wasn't having some sort of breakdown; I couldn't help but think of poor Damon Inferno, sobbing under his bed.

Theodora sat back down beside the white mound. Her shoes were off and her feet seemed huge—I did my best not to stare. "What's wrong?" I asked.

"My investigations have borne fruit," she said. "Bitter fruit, I'm afraid."

Uh-oh. "What happened?"

"Mr. Cooper and I were on, for lack of a better word, a stakeout. According to the pattern the marble placer has established for herself, it was likely she would make an appearance today. The graveyard, as you know, is quite sizable, so Mr. Cooper and I were patrolling it separately. I was the one who chanced to encounter her first, in the company of a woman who was no doubt her caregiver. I approached them cautiously but with a friendly demeanor, and the caregiver—a Mrs. Gonzales—was willing to talk to me. She told me a tale that quite broke my heart.

"Mary, Mrs. Gonzales's charge, is suffering from Alzheimer's. Mary's recall is erratic at best, but there is one thing she seems able to hold on to: the memory of a cat she once owned. She named her Marbles, after her love of playing with them.

"Mary's life has not been an easy one. Both her parents are dead. She has no siblings. She has never had a job or known romance. Mary, you see, was born with Down's syndrome—and while it's entirely possible to enjoy a full and happy life with that condition, it's very hard to do so without help."

Theodora took another tissue and wiped her eyes

daintily, then blew her nose with less aplomb. "Excuse me. I'm sure it comes as no surprise that children can be cruel, especially when it comes to those worse off or different; some sort of barbaric genetic response intended to prune the species of weakness is my theory, though that's hardly an excuse. In any case, the children in Mary's neighborhood were less than kind to her, deriving the usual pleasures of bullies through name-calling and pranks. But the cruelest torment of all was when her cat disappeared."

"Oh, no."

She shook her head. "Oh, yes. You see the crude elegance of their evil, do you not? A chance to panic a victim and inflict what they thought was a clever taunt at the same time? 'You've lost your Marbles,' they jeered at her."

Theodora stared at me with red-rimmed, mascara-smeared eyes. "And she never saw her again . . ."

She collapsed onto my shoulder, sobbing. She wasn't the only one with tears running down her face.

How could people be so . . . so *inhuman*? To not just be indifferent to someone else's pain but actively enjoy it? Even now, decades later, just hearing the story reduced two people who didn't know Mary to tears. I couldn't even imagine the sort of sick mind that would take pleasure in causing that sort of torment.

Eventually we broke our hug—which I was grateful for, because Theodora wasn't exactly a lightweight—and both of us grabbed some tissues.

"That's absolutely horrible," I said.

"It gets worse," she said. "Marbles is supposedly buried here, but Mary can't remember where the grave is. According to Mrs. Gonzales, they've searched the entire cemetery and haven't been able to find it. Cooper and I checked the records, and there's no trace. Either Mary got it wrong and Marbles isn't buried here, or somebody lied to her."

I nodded. "Sure. Tell her a comforting fib and assume she'll never know any different. But she does, doesn't she?"

"Yes. Her world has never been very large, and now it's shrinking every day. Marbles seems to be the one thing in her life she refuses to give up, and all she wants to do is to find where she's buried. I've done my best to help . . . but I've failed."

"I'm so sorry, Theodora." I was, but I was also thinking this didn't have to be the end of the story. Maybe Mary couldn't find Marbles's grave . . . but I knew someone who probably could. "I'll have Consuela bring up some tea and those cookies you like. I know this hurts, but you did your best."

She sniffled. "Not quite. There's still something I can do."

"What?"

Her face hardened. On Theodora, that was scary. "A crime was committed, Foxtrot. The perpetrators were never brought to justice. I can do *that*."

"But—that took place *decades* ago. How could you possibly—"

"I can because I must. And I will, Foxtrot. I *will*."

I didn't try to argue with her. "You know, I believe you. Good luck—and let me know if I can help in any way."

"I shall."

I told her I had to go, and she thanked me and told me she'd be all right.

It wasn't until I was out the door and halfway down the hall that I realized she hadn't mentioned her imaginary friends once.

Then I went looking for my partners.

Neither of them seemed to be in the house, and I couldn't find them on the grounds. That left the graveyard, which I didn't have to search; I just stepped through the gate and yelled *Tango! Whiskey!* in my head nice and loud.

I waited. After a few seconds, I heard a cautious <*Hey, Toots. Still mad?*>

"I'll get over it. Can we talk?"

<*I'm listening.*>

"Did you learn anything when you were spying on Fimsby?"

<*He's a boring old guy who likes to read. In his favor, though, he's fond of tuna fish.*>

"That's all he does? Read and eat tuna fish?"

<*That and—ugh—swim.*>

"Really? I didn't think anyone had used the pool since Anna died."

<*Oh, this would have been before that. I didn't actually see him swimming, but I could tell from the smell.*>

"What smell?"

<*The swimming smell. You gotta know what I'm talking about—the pool reeks of it. And so do those little scraps of cloth most of you wear when you do it.*>

"Chlorine, you mean. And bathing suits."

<*Yeah. There was one in Fimsby's bathroom. Still damp—he must have used it recently.*>

Swimming. Fimsby had been in the pool—and from the timing, he must have done so the night Anna died.

"Thanks, kitty. You can come out now, okay? I'm not going to punish you."

<*The thought never crossed my mind.*> She stepped out of the bushes, still looking a little wary. <*I just felt the need for some alone time, that's all.*>

"Well, apparently so did Ben. He quit."

She sat down and licked one of her paws. <*He'll be back.*>

"What makes you so sure?"

<*I'm a cat. We're always sure.*>

"I hope you're right. Teresa Firstcharger challenged him

to some sort of Thunderbird duel in their home dimension. He, of course, accepted."

<Can't back down from a challenge.>

"Sure you can. Well, maybe you can't. And I guess he can't. Me, I have more important things to do. Like, Whiskey and I found out that Anna slept with Keene the night she died."

Her ears perked up. *<Now, that's interesting. Not really surprising, though.>*

"Not really, no. So Fimsby and Keene are now on the top of our list of suspects."

<You want to tackle Keene first or last? Considering your unrequited crush on him and all.>

I glared down at her. "I do not have a crush on Keene, unrequited or otherwise. And I think we should start with Fimsby, because he's the one who's been all mysterious and behind-the-scenesy."

<Sure, sure. Stealthy or head-on?>

"Head-on, I think."

<What a surprise.>

"What's that supposed to mean?"

She yawned. *<It means you're agitated and need to take it out on someone else. Hey, I'm all for that—as long as it isn't me.>*

Cats. You gotta love 'em—because if you don't, they'll leave and find someone who will.

"Have you seen Whiskey, by the way? I sent him to find you and now I can't find him."

<Nope. But we both know where he probably is.>

"Oh. Guess I should go find our current artist-in-residence, then."

<Oh, leave him alone. Everyone needs a little nookie now and then.>

"But Whiskey's—you know . . ."

<Dead?>

"Well, yeah."

<So what? I've been dead six times already, and I don't let it interfere with my *love life.>*

That was true enough. Tango's last crush had outweighed her by half a ton and expired shortly after they met, but she didn't let little details like *that* stop her.

I sighed. "Fine. Let's go look for the meteorologist, instead."

We found Fimsby on the front lawn, playing croquet with Oscar. I was a little surprised to see Oscar spending time away from his current scheme, but then I remembered how adept he was at separating our guests from their pocket money. I strolled up to Fimsby and said, "How much are you playing for?"

Fimsby, dressed in khaki shorts and a ragged plaid sweater, said, "Mmm? No, no, we're not wagering—strictly for fun."

"Ah, he must be losing, then. Wait for the rematch—he'll offer to make it 'interesting.'"

Oscar approached, his mallet over one shoulder. "Don't fill the man's head full of nonsense, Foxtrot. We're just passing the time."

I gave him a skeptical look. "Sure. That's what you said when you fleeced George Clooney."

"He was the one who insisted on playing for money. I was happy just to be outside, getting a little exercise."

I looked back at Fimsby. "Oscar gets most of his exercise from lifting other people's wallets. Metaphorically speaking."

Fimsby grinned. "I see. I'll be careful."

Oscar wandered back toward his own ball. I studied Fimsby for a moment before replying. "Yes, you're very careful, aren't you? As a scientist should be. But sometimes you have to take risks whether you want to or not."

Fimsby looked down, and carefully lined up his shot. "Very true, especially out in the field. I have a friend who chases tornadoes for a living—you don't get much riskier than that. Personally, I like to mull my data over inside, next to a warm fire and a cold drink."

"You're not inside now," I said softly. "You're out in the field. Anything could happen—you might even get struck by lightning."

He smiled, ever so slightly, before drawing his arm back and taking his shot. His ball rolled a good twenty feet, straight through a hoop.

"Well done," Oscar called out.

Fimsby straightened up and regarded me. "That seems rather unlikely," he said calmly. "Unless one were able to call such a thing out of the clear blue sky."

"Let's stop fencing. I know what Ben is and Anna was, and so do you. If you want me to say the word out loud, I will. *Thunderbird.*"

He seemed to come to a decision. "Very well. No more fencing; we shall put our swords down and our cards on the table, so to speak. Anna could manipulate weather patterns, by a means I was unable to quantify. She came to me for advice and assistance in controlling these abilities, as she was afraid she might lose control and cause some sort of massive disaster. Though I was skeptical at first, she quickly proved her claims. After that, I did my best to help her in any way I could."

"Which was doing what, exactly/"

He met my gaze squarely. "I tried to measure the extent of what she could do, without endangering her or anyone else. That was fairly straightforward. Then we devised a series of exercises designed to refine and direct her control. I'm happy to say we were quite successful, and Anna was eager to share her discoveries with her brother. But then—there was a problem. A *threat.* Convinced her brother was in danger, Anna insisted we meet here, and that we do so without revealing our true purpose."

"And I know why," I said. "Thunderbirds are powerful entities, and as such have powerful enemies. Like the Unktehila."

He looked away, then back at me. "So you know."

"Yes. A shape-shifting monster that can psychically manipulate people into trusting them? I understand now why you were being so cautious—but you still haven't given me much reason to trust *you*."

He hefted the croquet mallet in his hand, as if testing its balance as a weapon. "I understand. Shape-shifting and mind control . . . hard to trust anyone under those circumstances, isn't it? Still, you're here talking to me; I assume that means you've granted me at least temporary human status."

I squinted at him in his baggy shorts and ragged sweater. "For now. But there are still a few things I'd like to clear up before I share any more information with you."

"Such as?"

"Such as why you lied about sharing the swimming pool with Anna Metcalfe on the night she died."

I couldn't prove that, of course, but I suspected it was true. He hesitated, then shook his head. "Ah. Yes, it's true. The conversation I mentioned having with Anna that night took place down at the pool, not in the hallway as I claimed. She insisted on meeting there, though she wouldn't say why."

"Why did you lie about it?"

"Because it looked suspicious, of course. As you said, you don't have much reason to trust me—and becoming a murder suspect certainly wasn't going to help my cause. I apologize; it was an error in judgment."

"Your shot, old boy," Oscar called out.

I considered what Fimsby had just told me while he took his turn. *What do you think, kitty?*

Tango had been stalking a yellow croquet ball nearby, and now she pounced, leaping on it and batting it away with one paw. Then she sat down and stared at it, tail twitching like she expected it to counterattack any second. *<I think I prefer tennis balls. Softer and furrier. I just wish they were easier to disembowel.>*

That's my cat. Utterly focused and easily distracted at the same time—not to mention cute as the Dickens and bloodthirsty as Jack the Ripper.

Fimsby lined up his shot and tapped his ball. It rolled a short distance toward the next hoop and then stopped. Fimsby rested the head of his mallet against the ground and stared down at it. When he spoke, his voice was low and measured. "I realize you have little reason to trust me, Foxtrot. A woman is dead and I was most likely the last person—other than the killer—to see her. You don't know me, and I'm sure recent events have left you as bewildered as I. But please, listen to what I have to say."

I crossed my arms. "I'm listening."

"Though I only knew her briefly, Anna impressed and astounded me. Confronted with the onset of vast and mysterious powers, her first instinct was to go somewhere she wouldn't hurt anyone else. Power may corrupt some, but not her. Once she was certain she was no danger to others, her second instinct was to seek out someone who could help her understand her situation. That was me, and I'm both honored and terrified by her choice. I'm a scientist, you see; I live—or did, until recently—in an ordered world, one bounded by rules I understand. Meeting Anna has upended that world, emptying out the rules to shatter on the unforgiving terrain of a strange and unknowable realm. My initial reaction was one of horror—but the scientist in me soon prevailed. Information, no matter how disturbing, is always a good thing."

"Is it?" I asked. "Some people don't take well to that kind of change. They even react violently."

He shook his head, a sad smile on his face. "That's the kind of emotion a true scientist can't afford. The truth is what it is, regardless of how it makes us feel, and those of us in my profession have a responsibility to that truth and the world at large. I've always taken that responsibility very seriously—so I swore to Anna I would help her in any way I could."

He took a step closer to me, tossing the mallet aside. "Thunderbirds and shape-shifters and murder—it's all a bit much, isn't it? But in such an uncertain world, allies are *vital*. I can help, Foxtrot—I can help Ben understand and control his abilities, just as I did for Anna. Please—let me."

I studied him, and considered how I felt about his offer. Hesitant and unsure, mostly, with some trepidation sprinkled on top. I smiled. "Tell you what, Mr. Fimsby. I'll talk to Ben about this and see what he says. But right now, I'm leaning toward trusting you. Know why?"

"Because I'm telling the truth?"

"Nope. Because I don't *know* whether or not you're telling the truth, and that means you probably are. Probably."

He looked a little confused, but I didn't feel the need to explain any further. "Thank you," he said. "I suppose I should finish this game."

"Go right ahead," I said. "I'll talk to you later."

I turned and walked away. After a few moments, Tango scampered after me in a way that suggested we both just happened to be going in the same general direction and she wasn't even aware of my presence.

<So you trust him?> Tango asked.

"Still not sure," I murmured. "But I get the feeling he genuinely wants to help."

<Me, too.>

So that was two votes for. If Whiskey gave him the okay, we might actually have found a friend.

Or made a horrible, horrible mistake.

CHAPTER FIFTEEN

Whiskey finally turned up, in my office. I didn't notice at first, because I couldn't see him; my first clue he was in the room was a faint, almost imperceptible whine in my head. "Whiskey?" I said. "Where are you?"

[Under the couch.]

I have a dark-brown leather couch against one wall, long enough for me to stretch out on if I really need to. No way there was enough room underneath it for a blue heeler, which meant Whiskey had assumed a different, much smaller form. "What are you doing under the couch?"

[Meditating on the absurdity of existence.]

"Ah. Well, hanging out with dust bunnies always makes me go all Zen, too. Contemplative little buggers, aren't they?"

[I assume that was a rhetorical question.]

"Assume away. Would you care to do your assuming face-to-face, or are you really grooving on the whole furniture underworld vibe?"

[I'm fine down here.]

"Haven't seen you all afternoon. What's up?"

[Nothing. Where's the cat?]

"Using her litter box. Anything you need to tell me, Whiskey?"

There was a long pause. [Perhaps.]

"I'm all ears, doggy."

When he crawled out from under the couch, I knew I wasn't going to like what he had to tell me. He was wearing his Chihuahua form, all big eyes and tiny, quivering body. He looked up at me with that universal look all dogs mastered long ago, the one that says *I know I'm bad but don't hate me.*

I groaned. "Okay, okay. What did you do?"

[I suppose you could say I went on a date.]

"Mmm. I don't have to ask who with, do I? And yes, that *was* a rhetorical question. What did you—"

And that's when the smell hit me.

I bolted up from my chair and leapt for the window. Actually, after getting the window open I considered leaping *through* it, just to escape the stench. No, it wasn't the aroma of skunk—though it might have been a *former* skunk.

"Gaaaahh," I said. I'm pretty sure it was the first time I'd ever said that particular word. "Oh, that is *ripe*. What *is* that?"

[Badger,] he said miserably. [I'm sorry, Foxtrot, I truly am. Things sort of . . . got out of hand.]

I kept my head out the window and breathed through my mouth. "Well, that can happen on a date. I've never been on one where I wound up smelling like a zombie locker room, but obviously I've led a sheltered life. Care to explain how this delightful condition came to pass?"

[I went to see Kaci. Her owner was taking her for a walk, and he didn't care for my presence. Kaci disagreed, and bolted. She ripped the leash right from his hand.]

"Very romantic," I said, trying to breathe as shallowly as I could. "So you two ran off together?"

[I suppose. I intended to bring her back, really I did—but it was just so enjoyable, running alongside her . . .]

"I get it. The thrill of a new relationship, the flirting, the feeling that anything is possible . . . and then, of course, the inevitable rotting corpse."

[It was at the side of the road. Its owner didn't seem to have any further use for it.]

I turned to look back at him accusingly, and immediately regretted it. "Oh, he didn't, did he? Maybe we should stroll on down to the graveyard, find the badger afterlife, and ask him? Excuse me, Mr. Dead Badger, sir, do you mind terribly that my canine associate here writhed around on your discarded, decomposing flesh? See, he was on a first date and really trying to impress her."

[I couldn't help it. My instincts just took over.]

"Your instincts? You talk like a nineteenth-century butler, you can control your own size and shape, you have no problem conversing telepathically—but one whiff of road-kill and you go all junkyard dog on me?"

He lay down and put his head on his paws. [I know, I know. I'm terribly ashamed of myself. But you have to understand why dogs find that particular experience so . . . irresistible.]

"Then explain it to me, please. Because you're right, that's something I've never understood."

[You do understand, though, that a dog's primary sense is that of smell? Our noses are thousands of times stronger than that of a human being. What is completely undetectable to you is blatantly obvious to us. We live in a very, very different world than yours.]

I thought I was getting used to the reek, but the breeze shifted and I got a fresh whiff. I gagged, spun around, and stuck my head out the window again. "Yes, you certainly do. But that still makes no sense. If what you experience is a thousand times stronger than what I'm experiencing now, how is your *head* not exploding?"

[It . . . sort of is.]

"What?"

[Foxtrot, how much time, effort, and study do human beings put into preparing food?]

"Speaking from a personal point of view, none whatsoever. I've just decided I'm never eating anything again."

[It's a huge part of your culture. Elaborate rituals and endless variations, all for what is essentially a very simple process. Why?]

"Well . . . enjoyment, basically."

[Yes. Which is entirely understandable. But what about the extremes people go to? Creations made almost entirely from sugar, or spiced so severely they cause actual pain, or even foods that are technically poisonous? What is the reasoning behind consuming such things?]

I was starting to see where he was going with this. "Human beings go to extremes like that because human beings are drawn to extremes. Sports, sex, food, drink, art, toys: If there's any way to amp an experience up to eleven, human beings will do so within five minutes of that experience being discovered or created. It's what we do."

[Rolling around on things that smell really, really strongly is what dogs do. For someone with a nose like mine, it is the most extreme sensory experience possible. About the only other thing that compares is sticking my head out the window of a moving vehicle—but that one's more about variety than intensity.]

That actually made sense. There's something about a really, really intense sensation that just trips the circuit breakers in your brain and shouts *more*. "So the stink is actually . . . intoxicating?"

[Only in the moment. The feeling wears off all too soon, leaving only guilt and shame behind.]

Talk about morning-after regret. "All right, quit it with the pathetic act. I worked for a CEO once who liked to do a shot of pureed ghost pepper—which is approximately four hundred times as hot as Tabasco sauce—before board-room meetings. Claimed the pain kept him sharp, but I think he was just addicted to the endorphin rush. I may not approve, but I do understand."

[I will endeavor to maintain control in the future.]

"Fine. Now let's get you cleaned up—I like my sub-stance abusers clean and shiny."

Kaci, Whiskey informed me while I gave him a bath, was back safe and sound with her owner. Needless to say, he wasn't exactly overjoyed at the condition she arrived in; I expected to get a very angry phone call from Rustam at any minute. In fact, it was rather strange that it hadn't hap-pened already.

While I soaped and scrubbed Whiskey, I gave him the lowdown on what had happened while he was off gallivant-ing with his new lady love.

[I see,] he said. He'd switched back to his usual Austra-lian cattle dog form, and his face now wore the long-suffering look most dogs use while being bathed. [I leave for a few minutes and everything falls apart. It's all Tango's fault, of course.]

"Some of it, anyway. But Ben was going to find out sooner or later—in fact, I was going to tell him. But the timing was awful." I scooped up some water with a small pail and poured it over Whiskey's back.

[So Keene slept with Anna, Fimsby claims he's on our side though he lied about where he talked to Anna, Theo-dora Bonkle is set on avenging a dead cat, and Ben and Teresa are dueling at dawn. Have I covered all the major events?]

"I think that's it. Oh, the Four Horsemen of the Apocalypse rode through about an hour ago, but they just needed directions. Apparently they aren't supposed to show up *here* until next week."

[You show a definite tendency toward sarcasm when under pressure.]

"Nice guys, actually. We got to chatting—you know, as you do—and they told me most people aren't all that happy to see them. Not us, I said. We're used to that sort of thing. Why, we can even put you up if you need a place to stay, and I'm sure our stables can accommodate a few more horses, even if one is entirely skeletal and another seems to be on fire. Then I offered to get Famine a snack and everybody laughed. Pestilence has an *extremely* infectious giggle."

[Have you been drinking?]

"Contact high, I think. Damn telepathy."

[I assure you, I'm entirely sober at this point.]

"And yet you still smell really, really bad. I'm gonna keep scrubbing."

My phone rang. I dried my hands, checked the display, and groaned. "Rustam Gorshkov, of course. Stay in there while I try to save your bushy tail. Hi, Mr. Gorshkov! I am *so,* so sorry—"

"Ms. Lancaster. It seems we have a problem." His voice held no anger, only weary resignation and a touch of wry amusement. That was a lot better than I'd hoped for. "Kaci and your dog—Whiskey, correct?—had themselves a little adventure, yes?"

"It seems so. I have him in the tub right now, and he is *not* enjoying it." I glared at Whiskey as I said that, and he whined and looked away. "Is Kaci all right?"

He chuckled. "Yes, yes. Very smelly, of course, but otherwise unharmed."

"Good, good. Listen, there's a great little dog spa in town. I will personally drive Kaci down there and get her all cleaned up at no expense to you. She'll come back cleaned, groomed, and happy."

"No, no, that's fine. I have washed her in bathroom already. But I think, maybe, you and I should have talk face-to-face, maybe set some, what is the words, ground rules? To keep from more incidents in future."

"Sure, absolutely. Whenever's good for you."

"I think sooner is better, yes? I am in my room."

"Okay, then. I'll get Whiskey dried off and be right up."

"*Da*, thank you." He hung up.

I pocketed my phone and grabbed a big towel. "Okay, you. Out of the water."

Thankfully, *eau de ex-badger* washed off easier than skunk juice, and I pronounced Whiskey stink-free as I dried him off—other than the aroma of wet dog, of course. "All right. I'm going to smooth things over with Gorshkov, who thankfully seems understanding. Then I'll come back and we'll discuss how you're going to act around Ms. Kaci from now on."

[I assure you, from here on in my intentions will be strictly honorable.]

"It's not your intentions I'm worried about. It's your actions."

"Come in, please," Gorshkov said when I knocked on the door to his room.

I went in. He was seated by the window, with the drapes closed, his hands resting on the cane between his legs. A single lamp beside him lit the room. Kaci was nowhere in sight.

"Come in, sit," said Gorshkov. His tone was neutral.

I closed the door behind me, then sat in the large chair opposite him. The room was large and furnished in ZZ's eclectic style; Picasso and Dalí prints hung on the walls, the bedspread was a huge splash of Jackson Pollock colors, the carpet underfoot was a deep black inlaid with a pattern of faithfully reproduced star constellations, while the ceiling was painted with a hyperrealistic undersea scene featuring a tropical reef. The overall effect was a bit unsettling, but the room was popular and often requested by repeat guests.

"Where's Kaci?" I asked, glancing around.

"In the bathroom, drying off. I thought it best we talk alone."

"Not afraid she'll overhear us telepathically?" I said, trying for a little humor.

"That is not how it works," he answered. "It is very much a conscious decision between both of us, to share our thoughts."

That seemed to be how it worked for Whiskey, Tango, and me, too—though sometimes the occasional stray thought slipped out from me to them. "You don't have anything to worry about, Mr. Gorshkov. I promise, Whiskey will be on a short leash as long as you're here."

"But I do have to worry, Ms. Lancaster. You see, my bond with Kaci is unique. Should something happen to her, I could not simply replace her. It would devastate me."

"I understand—"

"No. You do not." His voice was soft, but there was something very sharp beneath the words. He got out of his chair, not using the cane for support at all, and stared down at me. "The life of an artist is always a hard one. Emotionally, creatively, financially. Kaci does not experience this, of course—I ensure her happiness in all things."

Not all *things,* I thought.

"*I* am the one who endures the hardships so that Kaci can create. I feed her, shelter her, nurture her. I *protect* her."

"Yes, I know—"

He cut me off again. "I do not believe you do." He took several deliberate steps toward the door, but when he reached it he stopped and turned back toward me. He held the cane in one hand like a club, his fist clenched around the middle. "Belief, Ms. Lancaster, is tricky thing. Like a ghost it can be, appearing to some but not others. Some people believe only what they experience themselves. Kaci's paintings are real, so people believe she can do what I say she can. It is not a claim, it is true thing."

"Nobody's claiming otherwise, Mr. Gorshkov."

He continued as if I hadn't spoken. "Now, should you claim that during our conversation something unusual occurred, and I insisted it did not, then it would all come down to a matter of belief. Some would believe you, some me. There would be no proof—it would be *hearsay*, correct?"

"*My word against yours* is another way to say it."

"Yes. And words, like beliefs, are tricky things. They can mean more than one thing, they can be made to twist and jump and even dance. Sometimes, the perambulations they perform are so intricate as to be almost unbelievable."

My eyebrows went up, just a fraction. That was some pretty good wordplay from a guy who struggled with *hearsay*.

But my eyebrows hadn't heard anything yet.

"It seems as though your companion, a canine like *mine*," said Gorshkov, "has taken my dog's affection as some sort of *sign*."

That part of my brain that keeps track of puns, alliteration, and rhymes noted what he'd just said, and the part of me that worked my mouth kept it shut.

"This is not wise. This will not do. Your dog with mine must not screw," Gorshkov said.

No, he didn't, my brain silently replied. *That's ridiculous.*

"Rolling around in dead things that stink? That's not proper canine behavior, I think. Maybe for a schnauzer, an Alsation or hound, but not for a dog that's celebrity-bound. A husky or poodle could frolic that way, but my Border collie must not go astray. She's destined for much better things, as you know, so gallivanting with roadkill is not apropos. She's not an Airedale, a basenji or pug, she's not a sheepdog with a coat like a rug. She doesn't scare folks like a snarling rottweiler; her art sparks ideas, she's a real thought-riler. Her health and well-being are all I desire . . . so stay away or I'll kill you. And set the body on fire."

I stared at him. He stared back, calmly. And then he spun around, opened the door, and left.

My brain was totally stalled. I tried to get it going, but it just sputtered a few times and refused to do anything else. My eyelids still worked, so I blinked them a few times to reestablish a feeling of control. My eyebrows were stuck at the highest possible setting.

"What. The. Farfegnugen," I said at last. "That was . . . that was . . ."

<Seussian,> said Tango. *<Yeah, that's really the only word that applies.>*

I'd gone back to my office to regroup. Not much surprises me and even less rattles me, but having my life threatened by a poem had accomplished both. Which was, I realized, exactly what it was supposed to do.

Whiskey was gone but Tango was there when I came back. "It's kind of brilliant," I said, stroking Tango's glossy fur. She was curled up in my lap while I tapped away at my laptop's keyboard.

<Not really. Derivative in style and devoid of imagery, for the most part. Though it did have at least two clever rhymes.> I have a rather impressive memory—in my job, you have to—and I'd just finished reciting the whole ditty for Tango as I typed it up.

"Not the poem itself—the fact that he used it to deliver a threat."

<Okay, so he's got style. Threats are supposed to inspire fear, not admiration.>

"No, threats are supposed to make you back off—the fear is only a means to an end. What Gorshkov did was twofold: He made me doubt his sanity—guaranteed to provoke caution in somebody as order-oriented as I am—and provided himself with plausible deniability. Who's going to believe he threatened me in rhyme? It just makes me look like a flake—so much so that I probably won't tell anyone, which isolates me and increases my fear. Oh, he's *good*."

<Or, you know, just crazy.>

"Okay, also a possibility," I admitted. "Which means he just might be serious about the whole post-murder arson thing. I should really make sure Whiskey's up to speed— did he say where he was going?"

<Someplace far, far from me was my suggestion. Because of the smell.>

"Does he still stink? I did my best to scrub the dead badger off."

<Dead badger would be an improvement. I was talking about the aroma of wet dog, one of the cornerstones of feline philosophy.>

I gave her a look. Specifically, Foxtrot Look #7, the *My Animal Companions Are Pulling on One of My Lower Appendages for Their Amusement.* "The aroma of wet dog is—no, no, I'm not going to repeat that statement. But I would like an explanation. Well, maybe *like* isn't the right word."

<Cats know immersing yourself in water is deeply wrong, and the smell emitted by wet dog fur proves we're right. We're always right, of course, but it's nice to have the principle demonstrated.>

"So your belief system is buttressed by an offensive odor?"

<*It's not a belief system, it's science. Belief is a lot more personal—you want to kick off a serious feline debate, bring up the significance of the Little Red Dot.*>

"I wouldn't dare."

<*I know, right? I mean, everyone agrees that the Laser Pointer is the one True Bringer of the LRD, but what is its true purpose? Is it there to inspire us to never give up, or to teach us patience? Will we all catch it at once, or will there be one lucky cat who is Chosen?*>

"Um . . . I know I shouldn't ask this, but—what if it's never caught?"

She glared up at me from my lap, then bolted with that sudden burst of speed cats can summon at will. She bounded over to the open crack of the door and stopped, looking back at me. <*I expect that kind of blasphemy from a dog, but you? You should know better. The Little Red Dot will be caught one day. Oh, yes, it will.*>

And then she slunk through the doorway and disappeared. I shook my head and wondered what cats had worshipped before the invention of Laser Pointers. Flashlights, maybe? And what about before that?

Whiskey interrupted my thoughts by sticking his nose through the space Tango had just occupied. [I caught the tail end of that. Are you deliberately trying to antagonize her or just unlucky?]

"I think I just attract abuse, frankly." I told him what had transpired in Gorshkov's room.

When I was done, Whiskey growled—both in my head and aloud. [A threat conveyed through rhyme is still a threat. Perhaps we should threaten him in return.]

"With what? Iambic pentameter?"

[I was thinking along more direct lines.]

"I think rolling around on rotting flesh has riled up a few too many of your primal instincts, pal. How about we ignore the overblown threats and stick to catching an actual killer, okay?"

[Hmmph. I suppose. What avenue of investigation should we pursue next?]

I sighed. I'd been putting it off, but I knew I had to face it sooner or later. "I was thinking it's about time we had a little talk with Keene about his late-night activities. And his hair dryer."

CHAPTER SIXTEEN

"Hullo, Foxtrot," Keene said. He was in the billiards room, playing against Oscar. "Care for a game?"

"Not right now, thanks. But I would like a word."

"Mamihlapinatapei," said Oscar. He leaned over the table, lining up his shot carefully. "A wordless yet meaningful look shared between two people who desire each other but are both reluctant to initiate proceedings."

Keene looked at me. I looked at him. Both of us grinned and looked away again.

"I meant a word with Keene," I clarified. "Though, as far as words go, that one's pretty good. Kind of hard to pronounce, though."

Oscar sighed and put his cue down on the table. "Very well, Foxtrot. I shall leave you two alone, to do . . . whatever it is you two do. If only there were a word for it . . ." He strolled out of the room, humming something I couldn't quite identify.

"So what can I do for you?" Keene asked, leaning against the billiards table. "Got a dragon needs slaying?"

That was uncomfortably close to the truth—but I was

about to yank him a whole lot closer to an even less comfortable one.

"I know you slept with Anna," I said.

He stared at me with those big, long-lashed puppy eyes, then looked away. "Ah. Well, I won't insult your intelligence by denying it. Yes, I did. Though I'm not sure why you would care."

"I care because she died, Keene. And because I know what your hair dryer looks like."

"My what?" Now he looked confused. "You mean you've seen it? Excellent. I can't find the bloody thing anywhere."

"I'm not the one who found it. The police did—in the swimming pool."

"But—oh. You mean *that's*—I thought she drowned."

"She did," I said. "The police think it was something called electric shock drowning, which happens when an electric current in water paralyzes a swimmer."

He shook his head vehemently. "What, from *my* missing appliance? I suppose Anna could have nicked it on her way out the door—I was, sad to say, just a wee bit unconscious at that point. But what does that mean? Was it an accident? Or did she—you know . . . top herself?"

"We don't know exactly what happened," I said truthfully. "But I'm doing my best to find out."

He nodded. "If anyone can, you can, Trot. I mean that." He hesitated. "But there's something you should know. About me and Anna, I mean."

"You don't have to justify yourself to me, Keene."

He smiled. "Wouldn't dream of it. No, I'm just a big old man-slut with poor impulse control—that's pretty much a given. I'm talking about Anna, and why she decided to . . . you know. With me."

"Let's see. Because she'd just learned her husband had cheated on her, and you're a great big man-slut?"

"No. It was because of a song I wrote. 'Midnight Melody.' It was their song, you see. Now she can't hear it without her heart breaking. I know what that's like—everybody does, I think. I told her I was sorry, and asked if there was anything I could do. She told me she wanted to change what that song meant to her, and there was only one way she could think of to do that."

He crossed his arms, looking more like he was hugging himself than anything else. His eyes were sad.

"Wow," I said. "That has to be one of the best pickup lines I have ever heard."

"I know," he said. "I've heard them all, and that one is clearly on the top of the heap. What could I do? I let her drag me off to bed and did my best to be . . ."

"Memorable?"

"That's it. So don't think too badly of me, okay? She knew what she needed right then, and I've always found it hard to turn away someone in pain. So I didn't."

"Good for you," I said, and I meant it.

"Electric shock drowning, huh? I notice you said the police think that, not you. What do you think really happened?"

"Like I said, I don't know. But by now, I bet the coroner does."

Harriet Tilford's work voice mail told me she wasn't in today. However, something I heard in the background of her message gave me an idea, and I decided to drive into town to the coroner's office, her place of employment, anyway. And I took Tango with me.

"Now remember," I told her as we pulled into the parking lot. "We need a cooperative ally, not a terrified prisoner, okay?"

She gave me a relaxed glance from where she sprawled on the passenger seat. *<Yeah, yeah. I'll be friendly. Don't I look friendly?>*

"You look like a cat," I muttered as I turned off the engine.

<What's that supposed to mean?>

"It means you're in the habit of ignoring what I tell you and doing whatever you want."

<I fail to see your point.>

"Exactly."

The building the Hartville coroner's office was in was also the town hall, which wasn't surprising considering Hartville's size. It was a three-story brick structure that tried for stately but barely managed county. We went up the worn stone steps, through the front door, and into a lobby with a signboard and a marble staircase to one side. There was a short hallway to the left, which from prior experience I knew held the restrooms, a storage closet, and the coroner's office at the very end.

When Tango and I got there I tried the door: locked. I tried knocking, but nobody answered—well, nobody human, anyway.

Squawk!

Tango lowered her head in that way cats have when they spot a bird. *<Hmm. Lineolated parakeet—from Venezuela, by the accent. Great mimics, but they have a tendency to mumble.>*

"Well, we'll just have to listen really closely. I need to find out if the autopsy found anything unusual about Anna's death, and I can't wait for Harriet. Besides, she'll clam up on me if the coroner found anything that points to murder. She's helpful, but she's not stupid."

<Sadly, her bird is probably the other way around.>

"Don't be so negative," I whispered. "Birds have great memories, especially for sounds. Now go on, get her attention."

<His. Male parakeets are the talkers. In the bird world, flamboyance is more important than testosterone—the

guys are all bright colors and loud voices and hey, look at me.>

I thought about Ben and how upset he was to learn he'd gotten his job through his father's influence. "Yeah, birds have definite ego issues. So this is how I want to handle this . . ."

I told Tango what I had in mind, and she agreed it was probably the best approach to take. She cleared her throat, then warbled in Parakeet the words I whispered to her telepathically:

<Hey there, good-looking!>

"Hey there yourself, beautiful," Tango translated. "Where are you and why aren't you in here with me? Also, what do you look like?"

Perfect.

<I'm a lonely female parakeet who just moved in down the hall. Tell me about yourself.>

"Me? My name is Rudolfo, and I'm a full-blooded barred parakeet from Caracas, baby. My plumage makes sunsets weep and my voice brings the stars out at night. I have the wingspan of an airplane and the talons of an eagle. But enough about me—what about you?"

<I'm told I'm a very pretty bird. Sometimes it's phrased as a question, though, so I'm not sure. Maybe they're actually talking about you.>

"That could be—though the same question has been asked of me, many times. I think sometimes the woman who takes care of me may have something wrong with her brain."

<Listen, I could use your help.>

"What would you have me do? Fly up to the sun to pluck its brilliance from the sky? Steal the feathers of a condor to line our nest? Anything for you."

<Oh, it's nothing that difficult. It's just that the man who takes care of me is sort of in trouble, and it's my fault.>

"What? Never! Such a thing simply could not be so. Tell me who made such terrible false accusations and I shall rend him limb from limb!"

<No, it's true. I knocked over his coffee and it spilled all over his laptop and now there's this report he can't deliver. He needs to get the information from the woman who takes care of you, but he's afraid to ask.>

"Ah, I see. You need me to ask her for him. I shall do my best, though I fear my command of her language is rudimentary. It is my only failing."

I was starting to warm up to Rudolfo. He might be an avian Lothario, but I sensed some genuine loneliness beneath his bluster.

<I was hoping we could avoid her finding out at all. You see, the report my caregiver lost was about something called an autopsy. I'm sure you've heard the term before.>

"Yes, of course. Many times."

<Then maybe you've heard a few other things, too.>

"I hear many things, *señorita*. Many, *many* things."

<Yes, I'm sure you do. This particular autopsy would be very recent; it was done on a woman named Anna Metcalfe.>

"Ah. You are hoping, perhaps, to glean any information on this Anna Metcalfe autopsy that you can, in order to relay it to your caregiver, salvage his reputation, and thus redeem yourself in his eyes. A noble endeavor, indeed. *But.*"

<But?> Uh-oh. This was the part where he wanted his paramour to promise something she couldn't deliver.

But Rudolfo surprised me.

"My memory, sadly, is not the equivalent of my other attributes. It pales, for instance, beside my abilities at lovemaking. It is as nothing when compared with my skill as a nest builder, and no more than a joke when viewed next to my magnificent plumage. I apologize deeply for this."

I sighed under my breath. *<I get it. But I'd appreciate it if you'd try, anyway.>*

"Try? Try? You misunderstand me, madame. I will not just try, I will succeed. I am merely apologizing in advance for not living up to my own exacting standards."

There was a pause, which I supposed was Rudolfo concentrating. And then:

"Dr. Kaufman? I've finished typing up the forms for the Metcalfe autopsy. Thank you, Harriet. How about the tox screen? Yeah, that's done, too. You want me to send it right over to Forrester? No, I'll do that in person. He's going to have questions about the results and I'll probably have to walk him through it. Suxamethonium chloride isn't going to be something he's familiar with. Is that unusual? It is in a drowning victim. In fact, it pretty much proves this was no accident. Hey, Rudolfo. Who's a pretty bird? Who's a pretty bird?"

Rudolfo paused. "There is more in that vein, but I believe we have already covered that. Do you wish me to continue?"

<No, no, that's really all I need. Thank you so much.>

"It was my pleasure. And now . . . it is time you told *me* the truth, my sweet."

<Um, what? No, don't translate that.>

"Aha! You are revealed! It all makes sense, now: the long pauses, the hesitation, that maddeningly alluring accent. You are not what you claim to be, are you?"

<I don't know what you mean. I have to go.> I motioned for Tango to follow me, but she stayed right where she was, listening intently at the door and continuing to translate.

"You do not dwell in an office down the hall. You are not a domesticated parakeet at all."

"Tango!" I hissed. "Let's go!"

<Not yet,> she told me. *<This is interesting. What am I then?>*

"You are . . . a pigeon! Drawn inside by your inescapable attraction to me!"

<I'm going now.>

"Not a pigeon, then. A robin?"

<Good-bye, Rudolfo.>

"A sparrow? A blue jay? A grackle? You have the insouciance of a grackle."

Tango shook her head, then got to her feet and padded down the hall after me.

"You just couldn't tear yourself away from his adoration, huh?" I asked.

<Hey, love is love. I'll take it where I can get it . . .>

When we got back to the mansion I looked up suxamethonium chloride online. It was a depolarizing neuromuscular blocker, commonly used to help intubate patients through muscle relaxation and short-term paralysis. It acted quickly and was metabolized just as fast. Most important, though, it mimicked the effects of electric shock drowning, making it impossible for the subject to move while still retaining consciousness. Under certain conditions—like drowning—the drug could also lead to hyperkalemia, a massive release of potassium in the body that often induced cardiac arrest.

"So that's how she was killed," I murmured. Tango was napping on my office couch while Whiskey was sitting next to me, staring at the screen attentively. "But how was it administered—and by whom?"

[Someone with medical credentials, perhaps?]

"Or access to hospital-grade drugs. Theodora Bonkle is no stranger to that environment."

[Being a patient is hardly qualification for administering drugs.]

"Granted. I mean, Fimsby has a doctorate, but that

doesn't make him a doctor. But maybe we're not asking the right question, either."

[Which would be?]

"If the big bad guy is a shape-changing, psychic snake, why would it kill Anna with a drug?"

[Misdirection? The Unktehila seems to be a creature that thrives on deception. That would color its entire approach to life—and death.]

That did make sense, in a very primal way. Big powerful people often favored the charging-headlong strategy, smart people preferred to negotiate, charismatic people were inclined toward seduction. Go with your strengths, right?

The problem was, the Unktehila seemed to possess all three of those traits in addition to a talent for fooling people. It could be posing as any of the guests, really. Couldn't it?

"Let's try to break this down," I said. "Unless the Unktehila can mimic a Thunderbird, it can't be Teresa First-charger. I think we can cross her off the list. That leaves Gorshkov, Bonkle, Fimsby, and Kaci."

[It can't be Kaci.]

"Why not?"

[It just can't. My instincts tell me so.]

I shook my head. "Instincts can be fooled, Whiskey. But let's leave Kaci out for now. That leaves three other prime suspects. Fimsby seems desperate to help, Gorshkov wants to protect his investment, Bonkle is wrapped up in another case. Any of them could be creating an elaborate smokescreen and none of them has an alibi."

We stared at each other in frustration for a moment. Whiskey actually whined.

"Let's take this step by step. How did this all start? What was the very first thing that happened?"

[Chronologically? That would be Anna realizing she had Thunderbird abilities.]

"Right. She comes here, drops a few hints to Ben, then freaks out and runs when her powers come on even stronger. Lands in Australia, looks up the local expert, uses him to run a few tests, and gets herself under control. Then—according to Fimsby—they discover the Unktehila threat, realize they can't trust anyone, and arrange to get together with Ben to warn him in person. Does that seem right?"

[No. They could have warned him from afar.]

"Especially with something as ominous as a shape-shifting, mind-warping monster. Then again, maybe that's why it had to be face-to-face; it's too easy to dismiss a phone call, especially one as crazy sounding as that one would have been."

[True. But it tells us one important thing: They learned of the Unktehila while still in Australia.]

That was something I hadn't considered. I'd been thinking of the Unktehila as a North American beastie . . . but then I remembered what Keene had told me about bush babies and how their cries had been attributed to a rainbow-hued serpent that bored into your skull. Could it be that the Unktehila were global in scope?

[I know that scent. You're about to do research, aren't you?]

I frowned at him. "I smell a particular way when I'm about to do research?"

[Yes. I call it *eau de Google*.]

"That's the aroma of curiosity and intellectual pursuit, my friend. *Tally ho!*"

I bent over my keyboard and started tapping keys. *Rainbow* plus *snake* plus *Australia*. Just for good measure I added *mythic,* then hit search.

Hmmm. Interesting, and not what I expected. There was an aboriginal myth about something called the Rainbow

Serpent, but it wasn't nearly as nasty as the Unktehila was supposed to be. In fact, it was more like a god than a monster, one often associated with water and creation rather than death and destruction. It was a myth found the length and breadth of the Australian continent, rearing its scaly head in every tribe, and though the story always had a few constants—association with deep water holes and rainbows—local variants connected the serpent to many other things: land, life, the moon, social relationships, weather, menstruation, falling stars, coming-of-age rituals, geological formations, fertility, rivers, and floods. "Well, that narrows it down," I muttered.

There was a knock at the door. I looked up to see ZZ standing there, a large, brightly colored woven bag slung over her shoulder. "Hello, dear. I'm running into town to pick up a few things and I just wanted to see how things were going with you."

"Going? With me? Smooth and steady, as always."

ZZ sighed. "And with Ben?"

"Ah. I haven't talked to him since . . . you know."

"Don't leave it too long, dear. I know you're busy, but keep your priorities straight."

"Plus, you want your chef back."

"That, too." She took a step into the room and glanced at the screen of my laptop. "Snakes? Whatever are you studying now?"

"Oh, it's nothing, really. Caroline's been getting reports of a large snake on the grounds, and I'm trying to figure out what species it might be. *Imaginary* is high on list, so you don't have to worry."

She peered down at the screen intently. "Oh, I'm not worried. I like snakes, especially the larger ones. I used to own a few, many years ago. Had to leave them behind, sadly."

"Leave them behind? Where?"

"Peru. The Zoransky family lived there for a while when I was a child, and I took an interest in the local wildlife; I suppose that's where my interests in animal conservation started. I had a couple of lovely *Epicrates cenchria* I got locally, and a few more from Colombia. My father didn't know about them until we moved back to the States; then he wouldn't let me bring them along. Against the law, he claimed—though I later learned snakes of that type were common in the pet trade and were imported to the US all the time. I suspect he just wanted an excuse to get rid of them."

"*Epicrates cenchria*? What kind of snakes were those, exactly?"

ZZ smiled. "Rainbow boas, dear. Different coloration from species to species, but they all had the same lovely iridescent sheen when the light struck them. Beautiful creatures; I hope they lived long and happy lives after their time with me."

And then, with a wave of her hand, she was off. Leaving me with a dumbfounded expression on my face and way too many questions.

<It's obvious, Toots. It's a ghost.>

I'd been having this argument with Tango ever since she woke up. She'd caught the last part of my conversation with ZZ and had, with maddening feline logic, abruptly, completely, and stubbornly changed her opinion on what it was we were chasing.

"Look, I agree it's something of a coincidence that ZZ used to own snakes—"

<Snakes with rainbow right in their name.>

"Yes, all right, but this is ZZ we're talking about. She's owned practically every kind of animal at one time or another, and rainbow is her favorite color."

<The woman does like a bright palette, I'll give her that. But let's look at the facts, okay? The only witnesses who have verifiably seen this snake are Cooper, the Bonkle woman, and a dead shark.>

[Hardly the most reliable of witnesses,] Whiskey pointed out.

<True, but all of 'em have already proven they can see ghosts. Bonkle saw the ghost cats—sort of—Two-Notch is a ghost herself, and ghosts often show up in dreams— like the one Cooper had.>

"That still doesn't *prove*—"

<Fimsby didn't claim he actually saw one, did he?>

I thought back to our conversation. "No," I admitted.

<And we don't trust Teresa Firstcharger's word on anything, do we?>

"Not . . . as such."

Tango has the annoying habit of grooming when she thinks she's winning an argument. Which is to say, constantly. *<So there you have it. Birds are paranoid at the best of times—I think Firstcharger's got her feathers in a knot over nothing. This whole brouhaha is over a prowler, plain and simple. Dead snake drawn to its former owner, case closed.>*

[You have the singular ability to trivialize the most momentous events.]

<Aw, thanks.>

[That wasn't—]

"Guys. A woman was killed. Now, I know I'm a little unclear on the rules, but I'm pretty sure deceased, limbless pets don't go around murdering people with paralytic anesthetics." I paused, then dug out a notepad I'd crammed in my hip pocket earlier.

[What are you doing?]

I scrawled a note on a page and then stuck the book back

in my pocket. "I decided to keep track of how many ludicrous yet factual comments I actually speak aloud from day to day."

<How's that going?>

"I'm gonna need a bigger book."

<As I was saying—you're looking at this all wrong. Simple case of overreaction. Ghost python equals panic, which leads to murder.>

[Let me enumerate all the ways in which your theory is unsound. First, this began in Australia. The python in question would have originated in South America.]

<So it got lost. Everybody knows snakes have a lousy sense of direction.>

[For over fifty years?]

<Hey, it had to crawl from Peru to Perth. That could take a while.>

[And yet, it presumably followed Anna from Australia to here in a remarkably quick fashion.]

<Shortcut.>

Whiskey looked at her in that way dogs have, like they're simultaneously intrigued and confused by something. [None of your lives were terribly long, were they?]

<Don't change the subject. I'm telling you, we're chasing our tails here. All this talk about a scary, shape-changing, mind-bending monster—well, if it's so scary, why is it hiding? And more important, why is it hiding so badly?>

I stared at her. Whiskey stared at her. She ignored both of us and cleaned the tip of her tail.

After a moment, I said, "You know, you might actually have a point."

[I reluctantly concur.]

<No, you're a reluctantly conned cur. Nobody likes being fooled—it's just that you're so good at it.>

"Okay, you can quit showing off how smart you actually are. You're right—for a creature that should be a master of concealment, it's been awfully obvious. Maybe it had no control over Cooper's dreams, but Caroline's been getting phone calls from people in the neighborhood who've actually seen it. That sounds more like it *wants* to be seen."

[Or doesn't care.]

<Or like those phone calls are being faked by First-charger to make everyone nervous so she can swoop in and save the day.>

"I thought you said Firstcharger was being paranoid. That sounds more like she's playing us."

<One doesn't cancel out the other. She's an opportunist—you can see that, right? Amping up everybody else's fear then bravely saving the day? Makes perfect sense. In fact, she and the snake are probably in cahoots.>

I leaned back in my chair and shook my head. "Oh, man. That's *almost* a coherent theory. I mean, it would explain how the snake got here from Australia so fast—"

[Foxtrot. I cannot believe you're seriously considering this. If Firstcharger and the rainbow snake are, as Tango says, "in cahoots," then it logically follows that Firstcharger must have manipulated virtually every event that has occurred. She would have needed to locate an appropriate ghost snake to play the role of the Unktehila, transport it to Australia to intimidate Anna, then transport it back to America to haunt the local environment. And even if she managed to do this, how did she know ZZ once had a pet snake, let alone locate its spirit?]

"Those are all good questions," I said. "But just because we don't have the answers doesn't mean there aren't any to be had. Firstcharger as the mastermind behind all of this is just barely plausible. And there's one more factor that tips the scale, too."

[Motive.]

"Yeah. If she's going to these kinds of lengths to scare us, then Tango's probably right—she wants to play the heroine and rescue everyone. That would position her as the top bird on the totem pole."

<*Exactly. Which is why Firstcharger killed Anna—from everything we've heard about Ben's sister, she wasn't the kind to take orders from anyone.*>

"Maybe. It's still pretty far-fetched as a theory . . . but then, what about this isn't?" I sighed. "About all we've accomplished is to eliminate a single suspect—then put her right back on the list twenty minutes later. And that very same suspect is the one who's challenged my boyfriend to a supernatural duel tomorrow . . ."

Tango, now convinced she was on the right trail, announced that she was going to track down this ghost python once and for all, and bounded off before I could stop her. Whiskey stared after her in dismay, then gave a low grunt of annoyance and lay down with his head on his paws. [Hmmph. I will never comprehend what passes for rational thought in that animal's head.]

"I think I do, at least a little. Tango hates to admit she's scared of anything, and she is afraid of snakes—live ones, anyway. Gigantic superpowered ones, too. So she came up with an explanation that eliminated both those possibilities, relegating the perpetrator to a scaly phantom that can't hurt her."

[Ah. Of course. Mere reality is no match for the stubbornness of a cat.]

"Of course not. Ignorance may be bliss, but willful denial of the facts is—well . . ."

[Feline.]

"I just hope she doesn't find more trouble than she's looking for."

[If she does, we'll just have to rescue her.]

I beamed at him, then scratched behind his ears. "Aw, that's sweet. You look out for her, no matter how irritating she can sometimes be—"

[It's sheer self-interest, I assure you. If she dies, we'll have to wait for her to reincarnate—and as annoying as cats can be, they're not nearly as unendurable as kittens.]

"Oh, please. Even you aren't immune to that amount of cute."

[*You've* never had one decide your nose is a rodent. Or that it's going to be the first thing they ever kill.]

I glanced at the time. "Okay, enough investigating for now. I have to meet with the chef who's filling in for Ben and go over tonight's dinner."

The chef's name was François. He wasn't our usual substitute, but he was the one who'd stepped in after Ben was injured, and had done a perfectly acceptable job. For some reason I couldn't get hold of our regular stand-in; I'd left several messages on his voice mail but he still hadn't gotten back to me.

I was going over the evening's menu with him when Whiskey stuck his nose through the kitchen's swinging door. "The soup looks good," I said. "Now, about the mains—"

"No!" François abruptly snapped—not at me, but at Whiskey. "No dogs in the kitchen! Shoo! Away!"

Whiskey gave me a long-suffering look. [Will you please tell this interloper that I'm allowed in here?]

"Sorry, Whiskey," I said, "chef's kitchen, chef's rules. Even if he's not permanent."

[Hmmmph.] He shot me a reproachful glance and withdrew.

"I'm sorry," François said. "The only place for animals in my kitchen is on the plate." He glared suspiciously at the door as if he expected Whiskey to make another attempt. "Also, I am very allergic."

I raised my eyebrows, then glanced at Tango's bowl in the corner. He followed my eyes, then shrugged. "Also, I was bitten by a dog once, as a child. Keep him out, please."

"Not a problem."

After the menu was finalized, I did some paperwork and made half a dozen phone calls and talked to Consuela about vacation days and arranged for the stables to be painted next week. You know, all the stuff I actually get paid for.

Then it was time for dinner.

ZZ's dinners are, quite rightly, legendary. They've been attended by Nobel Prize winners, sports legends, movie stars, and royalty. The food is always excellent and the discussions tend to be lively, which is just how ZZ likes it. I decided that tonight I'd take my boss up on her standing invitation to attend; I needed to keep an eye on my suspects and see how they were behaving.

Especially Teresa Firstcharger.

I changed into something a little more formal: higher heels, a shorter skirt, a pearl necklace. Simple, elegant, and no dry cleaning required. I went downstairs and took my customary place at the table, which meant any spot that wasn't taken and looked like it needed to be filled; in this case, it was between Teresa Firstcharger and Theodora Bonkle. Oscar was directly across from me, Rustam Gorshkov was next to him, and Hayden Metcalfe was at the end of the table.

Hayden looked even worse than the last time I'd talked to him. According to the staff, he'd spent most of his time sleeping or drinking in his room. He'd ventured out once— the night Ben was shot—and came back almost sober. That hadn't lasted.

Gorshkov glanced at me with a neutral look on his face when I came in, but said nothing. Whiskey sprawled in the corner, where he wouldn't be underfoot but could still keep an eye on everyone. Mostly, though, he seemed to be staring at Gorshkov.

"Ah, Foxtrot," said Oscar. "I was wondering if you would put in an appearance. In fact, I was on the verge of *Iktsuarpok*."

"Yes," said Keene. "As was I. But only if that word means 'about to have a large amount of drinks.'"

"Already there, my good man," Hayden muttered.

Oscar raised his own glass in salute to Keene. "While I applaud the sentiment, the actual translation is 'the frustration felt while awaiting someone's arrival.'"

"I see," said Keene, nodding vigorously. "Klingon, is it? It sounds Klingon. They're notoriously impatient. Like to set fire to waiting rooms is what I hear."

"Inuit, actually," said Oscar.

"Well, of course *you* knew it," said Keene, pressing the button for the drinks trolley repeatedly. "You said it, didn't you? Unless this is Foxtrot practicing her ventriloquism again."

"I keep telling you," I said. "I'm not a ventriloquist."

"Then why is your voice coming from that potted plant?" Keene demanded.

"A question you should really ask your psychiatrist," Oscar said. "Or possibly your pharmacist."

"But not your lawyer," Hayden interjected. His voice was slurred. "Lawyers only give you *bad news*."

We all more or less ignored this non sequitur, except for Theodora. She was watching with the fascination of a cat studying a badminton match. "Oddly enough, this is a conversation I feel qualified to join. Law, psychiatry, pharmacology, and voices coming from strange places— all subjects I'm intimately familiar with."

Keene grinned at her. "Ah, an expert! Just what we need. However, if you didn't just say that and Foxtrot is having me on, I apologize."

Theodora chuckled. "No, I'm fairly certain that was me. I—" She stopped in mid-sentence, a surprised look on her face. She stared accusingly at the floral centerpiece on the table and said, "Very! What do you think you're doing? Doc, I expect that sort of behavior from, but you?"

"This should be interesting," Oscar murmured.

Theodora listened attentively to something the rest of us couldn't hear, then glanced down at the floor. "Oh, I see. Doc, that is *not* the proper use of a catapult. You're just lucky poor Very landed in the flowers."

"Are they here?" asked Keene eagerly. "Doc Wabbit and Very British Bear? Oh, this is bloody exciting."

"That's one word for it," said Teresa Firstcharger. She looked amused but tolerant.

"Could you introduce me?" Keene asked. "Asking for an autograph is obviously out of the question, but I would consider meeting them a huge honor."

"Of course," said Theodora. She gestured with one hand toward the floor. "The little barbarian with the siege engine is Doc. Doc, say hello to Mr. Keene."

"Just Keene. Mr. Keene's my willie. I'm sorry, I didn't mean to say that out loud."

"And the somewhat bashful creature peering out from behind the centerpiece is Very British Bear."

"Hullo, Bear," said Keene. "I'm a big fan of yours, you know."

Theodora paused, listening, then said, "He says he didn't know. And that you don't look much like a large fan at all. A bit like a toothbrush, though."

Keene laughed. "Well, I've been called worse. A pleasure to meet you."

Efram Fimsby walked in and took a seat next to Teresa Firstcharger. "Good evening, everyone," he said. "Looks like we're all here but our host."

"She'll be along soon," I said. "ZZ never misses a dinner."

"Sadly," said Fimsby, patting his belly, "neither do I."

"Ah, here she is now," I said. ZZ swept in—she's great at sweeping—in a long, elegant turquoise gown, a brilliant abalone-shell comb holding her orange hair in an elaborate pile on her head. She took her place at the head of the table, greeting everyone by name, and the dinner began.

The new chef did fairly well: smoked lobster bisque; a salad of mixed organic greens, mandarin orange slices, and candied pecans; then a poached salmon for the main course. I was a little disheartened by how good everything was—it seemed to underscore what Ben had said about him being a charity case. Not that I believed that for a moment, but none of us is quite as irreplaceable as we like to think. Even me.

"This certainly is wonderful, ZZ," said Teresa, gesturing with a fork full of salmon. "My compliments to your chef."

"Thank you," ZZ said. "He's new, actually."

"Oh? Well, he certainly gets my vote. It's nice when someone finds their niche, don't you think?" She glanced ever-so-casually in my direction.

"I don't believe in niches," said ZZ. "It's just another word for 'rut,' as far as I'm concerned. People should stretch their wings whenever they can, and there just isn't enough room in a rut."

"Well put," said Teresa. "Niches are comfortable, but boring. It's nice to have a nest to return to, but there's a whole sky out there to explore."

"Yes, indeed," said Fimsby. "A sky full of increasingly chaotic weather, unfortunately. Civilization generates heat, and heat is simply energy; pour enough energy into any enclosed system and it will generate violent results."

"A shame we can't find a way to control such things," said Gorshkov.

"Tame them, you mean?" said Teresa. "I'm glad we can't. Some things are meant to be wild and free. We need to adapt to the world, not adapt it to us."

"And what an odd world it can be," said Theodora. "Still, no odder than human beings, eh? You have to go pretty far to outstrip *our* strangeness."

"Hear, hear!" said Keene. "And by that, I mean *here, here.*" He pointed two thumbs at himself.

"What happened to your old chef?" Teresa asked ZZ.

"He needed some time off to take care of a few personal matters," ZZ said.

Teresa dabbed at her perfect lips with a linen napkin. "We all need that, from time to time. I hope things work out for him."

She looked directly at me, and smiled. It may have been a trick of the light, but something seemed to flash, deep in her black eyes.

"Yes, by all means," Hayden said, raising his glass and sloshing half of it onto the table. "Let's hear it for good old Ben Montain. Stood up for himself. Found out the truth and it set him *free.*"

"That's enough, Mr. Metcalfe," said ZZ. "I understand that you're in pain—"

"You don't understand a damn thing," he snarled at her. "In pain? I'm more than in pain. I'm destitute." Despite his inebriation, he pronounced the last word perfectly (if somewhat carefully).

"She didn't leave me a thing," Hayden continued. "Turns out she knew about me and *you* all along." He pointed an accusatory finger at Teresa. "That was the last thing she said to me, you know. She told me she was leaving me and that she'd already cut me out of her will."

"You said you wanted to be free of her," Teresa said calmly. "Now you are."

"Free. Sure, I'm free as a bird. A bird with no place to live and nothing to eat. Sooner or later ZZ is going to throw me out on my ear, and then I'll be a . . . homeless bird. With a busted ear."

"Then I advise you learn how to walk," said Teresa. She rose from her chair. "Time to turn in. I have quite the day ahead of me tomorrow . . ."

I stared after her as she left. Hayden killing Anna made far less sense if he didn't stand to profit from it. Unless . . .

Unless the news itself had been enough to drive him to murder.

CHAPTER SEVENTEEN

I went home after dinner, but I didn't sleep much. Mostly, I lay awake wishing Ben were with me. I got up, dressed, and slipped out of the house when the sky was just starting to lighten. Whiskey hopped in the car with me and we drove out to the graveyard in silence.

They didn't have to meet on this plane at all, of course. They could have just whirlwinded themselves right to Thunderspace and done the whole thing there—but they didn't. Dueling is always ritualized, and part of that ritual is meeting your opponent face-to-face beforehand. I'm pretty sure that part was invented to give both parties an excuse to reconsider and maybe even settle things peacefully.

I parked at my regular spot beside the mansion and entered the graveyard via the same wooden gate I always used. Tango darted out from beneath a bush and joined us without a word as we marched along. It felt a bit like going to meet a firing squad, only it wasn't us that was about to be shot at.

"Any luck on the ghost python front?" I asked.

<Yes and no. No, I didn't find it, and yes, I'm still right. Because of the marbles.>

"Theodora's case? How do you figure?"

<You told me a cat was murdered and her former owner is still around. Where's the cat's ghost?>

[Reincarnated, I would guess.]

<And guessing is all you can do, because you don't know how feline reincarnation works—and no, I'm not going to enlighten you, either. But then it hit me: The ghost cat must have been eaten.*>*

[By the ghost python, of course. A brilliant theory, except for the fact that we both know that's impossible.]

<It's a work in progress. So, how's this duel going to work?>

[They're going to *fight,* Tango. Surely you've grasped that much?]

<But how *are they going to fight? Toss lightning bolts at each other? They're both immune to electricity.>*

"Good point," I said. The grass was cold and wet with dew. "Maybe they'll throw hailstones at each other. Or blizzards."

"Not quite." Teresa Firstcharger stepped out from behind a tree, something she was apparently quite good at. She wore a loose-fitting track outfit and sneakers, looking more like she was dressed for jogging than a battle. "Thunderbirds are as immune to cold as they are to lightning. Both are only by-products of what *really* creates weather."

"Weathermen?" I said.

"Air," said Ben's voice behind me. He walked up, dressed in jeans and a plain white T-shirt. I guess this duel wasn't as formal as I thought. "Hurricanes, tornadoes, snowstorms, cloudbursts . . . they're all just the result of air moving around. Wet air, warm air, cold air, whirling air. It's all air."

"Air and energy," replied Teresa. "Fimsby had that much correct. He simply failed to acknowledge there are other kinds of energy at work in the world that aren't quite as predictable as heat."

"Whatever," said Ben. "I didn't come here for a lecture on metaphysics. We gonna do this or stand around talking?"

Teresa smiled. "My, how alpha male of you. Let's see just how hot that air of yours is, shall we?"

"That," I said, "is possibly the weirdest, most self-referential compliment/put-down/come-on I have ever heard. And I have a telepathic cat."

<*I think you just one-upped her, actually. Thank you/ go to hell/not interested.*>

[Excuse me,] Whiskey said. [Will the duelists require persons to fulfill the role of seconds?]

Strangely enough, nobody was confused about Whiskey's use of the term *seconds,* which in this context meant someone to provide assistance or support to the people doing the actual dueling. I've never been all that clear on what a "second" was supposed to do, other than open the wooden, velvet-lined box that contained two pistols and offer them to the combatants. Help clean up the blood afterward, I guess.

"You may have one if you wish," Teresa said to Ben. "The traditional role of a second is to ensure that the conditions of the battlefield and the weaponry are fair to both parties. I'm already satisfied that this is so."

"Well, I'm not," I said. "You're clearly more experienced with your abilities, and more familiar with the terrain. Plus, as the challenged, Ben should be the one to choose the battlefield."

Ben shook his head. "Experience is never equal. What matters is that we both *have* the same abilities, and the venue is fine by me. I don't want our scrap starting tornadoes in downtown Manhattan."

"Well, then," I said. "The other traditional role of a second is to bear witness. And that's exactly what I intend to do."

Both Whiskey and Tango stared at me like I'd gone crazy.

[<NO,>] they said simultaneously.

"Fine by me," said Teresa. "You can watch from the Aerie. But I can't promise you'll be able to see everything that happens, or that it'll be safe."

"Absolutely not," said Ben flatly. "Are you insane? Do you have any idea how dangerous this is going to be?"

"Do you?" I countered. "Look, I still don't trust her. The role of a second is to keep the duel honest, and that's just what I'm going to do."

"No, you're not. You're going to get yourself killed, because while you're busy looking out for me you don't have anybody looking out for you. The only way I'd allow you along is if you had a second yourself—and they'd have to have wings."

<Technically, I think you'd call that a third,> said Tango.

[A flying third. Lets me out, I'm afraid. Four paws, no wings.]

<Me, too. I don't mind the flying, but cats hate being third at anything.>

"Lucky for me," croaked a familiar voice. "Three's my favorite number."

A white shape flashed through the predawn light and landed on a nearby headstone. Eli, my ghost crow boss, had decided to put in an appearance.

For the first time, Teresa didn't look quite as sure of herself. When she spoke, there was genuine deference in her voice as opposed to amusement. "Ah. I see we've attracted the attention of the local authorities. Greetings, Venerated One."

If a crow could snort, that's the sound Eli made. "Me?

I'm just an old bird that's too stubborn to quit flying. Foxtrot here is the closest thing the Great Crossroads has to an authority figure."

It was my turn to smile. "Thank you, Eli. I do my best to maintain some semblance of order." That was a blatant overstatement, but when your boss shows up to back your play, you're allowed a little leeway.

"Yes, you do. Replacing you, should you come to harm, would be a lot of work. And I *hate* work. In fact, I'd probably take up a new hobby just to have an excuse to avoid doing said work. Any guesses what that hobby might be?" He fixed a beady eye on Teresa as he said this, but of course it was Tango and Whiskey who chimed in with suggestions.

[Cooking, perhaps? With a focus on poultry-based dishes?]

<*Nah. Taxidermy. Displaying dead birds who've died horrible deaths due to bad decisions.*>

[Or there's always quilting.]

<*Sure, quilting. Wait, what?*>

[Who doesn't like a nice quilt? Especially one stuffed with feathers.]

<*Oh, I see what you did there. Nice.*>

[Thank you.]

"If you two are quite done," Eli said, "I think my point has been made. Don't you, Miss Firstcharger?"

"It's Ms. And yes, I understand perfectly. No harm will come to Foxtrot at my hand."

"Hold on," interjected Ben. "Don't I get a say in this?"

"I doubt it," said Eli. He launched himself into the air and flapped away.

Ben gave me an exasperated look, then threw his hands in the air in defeat. "Fine. Who am I to argue with a magic albino crow? As long as it's safe."

"Nothing's safe, Ben," said Teresa. Stray bits of grass and leaves began to gently swirl around her feet, rising higher and higher as the air moved faster. "Time for you to find that out, firsthand."

I took a step closer to Ben, and he took my hand. He looked into my eyes as the winds began to spin around us. "I hope you know what you're doing," he muttered.

"Me, too," I muttered back, and squeezed his hand.

The world I knew got farther away, and a new one took its place. The ancestral home of the Thunderbird race, a realm of mostly sky. Teresa Firstcharger was nowhere in sight, which worried me. "Keep your eyes open," I said. "I don't trust—*whoop!*"

Without warning, he dove straight down, me hanging on to his hand for dear life. I don't think he was happy with me.

Too bad. If it would save his life, he could stay mad at me as long as he wanted. Forever, if it came to that.

We plunged into gray clouds heavy with rain, and the combination of rushing air and humidity had me drenched and shivering within seconds. I didn't complain, though; it takes more than a little physical discomfort to make me give in. I grit my teeth and did my best to pretend this was just a ride at an amusement park. *Whee! Look at all the fun I'm having!*

I didn't think Teresa would outright attack us, not while Ben and I were together. She may have been arrogant, but she wasn't dumb—and I saw the wary respect on her face when Eli showed up. She probably had a better idea what he really was than I did.

It didn't take long to get to the Aerie. The clouds broke a few hundred feet shy of it, a vast, curving green-and-gray sphere. I looked around nervously as Ben came to rest on a large, flat-topped rock gripped by the thick, gnarled fingers of a dozen tree roots.

Before he could say anything, I grabbed him and kissed

him, quick and hard. "Go kick her tail feathers," I said. "Don't worry about me."

"I'll do my best," he growled, and took off like a rocket. In a few seconds he'd disappeared into the clouds.

"Hey," I said. "Wait a minute. How the heck am I supposed to observe anything like this?" For some reason it had never occurred to me that he might simply fly away; it wasn't like I could chase him, after all. No wonder he didn't put up more of a fight.

I was alone. Just like last time . . . except this time he might not come back. Or he might return minus his Thunderbird powers.

I sat down on the rock and thought about it. Was that really such a bad outcome? He could go back to being a chef, which was something he loved. Hopefully, a chef that would still be working for ZZ—but I'd settle for a chef that I was still dating. And one that was, you know, still breathing.

Then someone set off the biggest flashbulb in the universe.

KRAKKOOOOOOOOOOOOOOOOOM!

I nearly jumped right off the rock. That was, without a doubt, both the loudest sound and the brightest light I'd ever experienced. My ears rang like car alarms and my vision was full of jiggling black spots. The air smelled like burning ozone—okay, maybe that isn't scientifically accurate, but that's what my nose was insisting—and I swear I felt an actual shockwave ripple through the air an instant after the sound hit. I found myself gripping two tree roots and wishing I'd thought to at least bring along a rope to lash myself to something.

The wind picked up, going from a gentle breeze to a blustery gust in seconds. Maybe I wasn't going to get to eyeball the action itself, but I had a ringside seat to the consequences. I scuttled farther back on the rock and tried to find a more secure place to wedge myself into, which turned out to be easier than I thought; there was a natural little cave at the base of the tree, hollowed out by nature. I ducked inside and found that I still had a pretty good view of the sky out the entrance.

And what a sky it was.

The gray clouds were retreating, churning as they went like some kind of upside-down landslide in reverse. When they got high enough, they tore themselves in two and the sun blazed out of a blue rift in the middle.

The clouds piled themselves up on either side, two huge tidal waves of dirty gray poised to crash into each other. I expected the thunderbolts to start crackling between them any moment—but that's not what happened.

The cloud fronts surged together instead, two sumos made of smoke trying to outbelly each other. They met, merged, and began to spin. A storm cell was forming right above me, the eye of a developing hurricane. The wind howled outside my little shelter like a crazed animal. *Then* the lightning started crackling. And the eye, instead of expanding, got smaller and tighter and turned into a tornado. Which was then attacked by another tornado, except the second one seemed to be full of hailstones, and then it started raining really hard. Sideways.

I was starting to get the picture. This duel wasn't so much about inflicting personal harm on the other guy as it was about demonstrating who was better at flinging weather around.

I sat back and sighed in relief. "Okay. This isn't a fight, it's a *dance-off.*"

One that still had dire consequences for losing, but at least I could be reasonably sure Ben would survive it. And hey, it was pretty amazing to watch.

Ever seen snow flurries with a rainbow in the background? Me neither. Or sheet lightning flashing through hailstones, turning them into a skyscape of brilliant, falling diamonds?

But it wasn't all about flashy moves. Some of it was about power, pure and simple, and when I saw one of the storm fronts abruptly recede across the sky, pulling back all the way to the horizon, I thought I might be seeing a surrender.

I was wrong.

Something was forming, out there beyond the curve of the Aerie. Something big and black and circular. It almost looked like a gigantic mouth.

Opposite this was a wall of white, an endless expanse of cloud that reached from the surface of the Aerie to the top of the sky, a huge blank piece of paper.

I could see the shape of the thing on the horizon now, a long, writhing tube of black and white that looked very much like a gigantic serpent. It was a tornado traveling lengthwise, a whirling tunnel of wind and hailstones carrying a terrifying amount of kinetic energy. It charged forward, lightning spitting from the depths of that dark maw, and in the instant before it slammed into the wall of white I saw the silhouette of a large winged shape above it.

And I knew, in my heart, who that winged shape had to be.

The tornado ripped the wall of white apart. Shredded it, consumed it, made it part of the tornado itself, until there was nothing left but a huge, whirling funnel cloud writhing overhead. It withdrew, back toward the horizon, and a second later I saw an almost identical tornado appear on the other side of the sky and get closer. A retaliation?

No. It drew closer and merged seamlessly with the first tornado, forming an unbroken loop of whirling wind encircling the entire Aerie, an orbiting vortex of air. And a declaration of victory.

The winged shape had been hidden on the other side of the tornado ring, but now it swooped around into sight, one wing tip almost grazing the tornado's edge. It made a few lazy circuits around the funnel cloud, then dove into the rushing winds like an osprey hunting a salmon.

When it emerged, it held a still figure in its enormous talons.

Ben.

CHAPTER EIGHTEEN

The Thunderbird—what else could it be?—swooped down
to the flat rock Ben had deposited me on and dropped Ben
on it. She was fairly gentle, but I rushed out of my hiding
place and over to him immediately. "Ben! Ben, are you all
right?"

"He's fine," Teresa said. I looked up into the face of the
giant bird of prey a few feet from me and did my best not
to glare. Up close, she looked a lot like a bald eagle, except
her head was more of a silver color than white, and her
beak was black as night. Part of my brain was marveling at
the fact that only a few short months ago this would have
boggled my mind, and now it seemed almost ordinary.
Almost.

"What did you do to him?" I demanded.

Teresa cocked her head at me and blinked. "Sucked
all the oxygen out of his lungs through rapid depressur-
ization," she said. "He's unconscious, but he'll recover
quickly. You don't have to worry."

"No? You just used a tornado to beat the crap out of my
boyfriend and now you're looking at me like I'm a fish

dinner. In a world, I should mention, that seems remarkably devoid of fish."

She chuckled. "Is this form bothering you? My apologies." Her beak began to shrink, her feathers became skin and hair, and her body shifted from avian to humanoid. In less than a minute there was a naked woman standing in front of me instead of an oversized falcon. It didn't really make me any more comfortable.

"So now what?" I said. "Did you suck all of Ben's abilities out of him along with the air? Or is that some whole other ritual?"

Teresa shook her head. "Foxtrot, do you know what *counting coup* means?"

"I do, actually. The Plains Indians used it to commemorate acts of bravery—usually touching an enemy with a hand or coup stick, then escaping without injury."

"That's right. The idea, as my first husband explained it to me, was that it took more daring to not harm your enemy, while proving that you could have. By choosing not to hurt them when you could, you demonstrate not only that you have power over them but that they have none over you; by giving them their lives you assert your superiority. It's a strategy I have a great deal of respect for."

I cradled Ben's head in my lap. He coughed a few times, and his eyelids fluttered.

"So that's what this is?" I asked. "You're counting coup on another Thunderbird? Why? Who, exactly, are you demonstrating your bravery for?"

She shook her head. "This isn't about bravery. It's about me asserting my power over another member of my tribe. It was never my intention to steal Ben's powers, Foxtrot, but it was vital that I demonstrate exactly where he and I stood in relation to each other, and that I do it in a formal, ritual manner. He was raised in a culture very different from that of his ancestors, and I needed to remind him of his roots."

"What?" Ben moaned. "Ahh. Make the world stop spinning . . ."

"Many Native American tribes are matriarchal," Teresa said. "So are Thunderbirds. I'm not Ben's enemy, Foxtrot. I'm his *teacher*."

Ben sat up. He looked at me first, a little groggily, and said, "I don't want to go to school today, I'm sick."

"It's okay," I said. "You can stay home, drink ginger ale, and watch cartoons."

He put one hand to his head. "Oww. Did I win?"

"Not so much. But you did come in second, and that's still pretty good."

He mustered enough energy for a glare. "I'm not finished." He tried to stand up, failed completely, and wound up rolling away from me. He made it to his knees, then lurched over to the edge of the rock and retched.

"No," said Teresa, "you're not. You're just getting started. Meet me here tomorrow, same time, and I'll show you how to do that ice tornado trick."

Ben turned around, stared at her, and blinked. "You're not going to de-thunder me?"

"Not if you show up on time and pay attention in class."

"Uh . . . okay?"

"Good. I'll see you tomorrow." She rose into the air, a whirlwind forming around her, and vanished.

Ben and I looked at each other. "Why was she naked?" Ben asked.

I grinned. "After what just happened, *that's* your first question?"

"It seemed like a good place to start."

"I'm guessing she ditched her clothes when she changed shape."

"She changed shape? Into what?"

I sighed. "A gigantic marshmallow man. Into a bird, doofus. Any guesses what kind?"

He rubbed his forehead with both hands. "No, that one seems pretty obvious. Sorry, my brain's still in neutral. What just happened?"

"A giant supernatural bird just kicked your butt with an electric hail vortex. But you put up enough of a fight that she doesn't consider you totally hopeless, so instead of taking your powers away she's going to train you how to use them. Got it?"

"I think I'm going to throw up again."

But he didn't. He just took a few deep breaths, stared out at the sky—which was now a pretty, cloudless blue—and said, "She's not the enemy."

"Doesn't look like it. We had a talk before you woke up, and she informs me that Thunderbirds are a matriarchy. She just felt she needed to make that clear in a way you would understand."

"Huh. She could have just told me." He didn't sound resentful, and I thought that was probably a good thing.

"Like you would have listened."

"I'm not completely thick-skulled."

"No, just mostly." I walked over to where he stood and took his hand. "You need to learn when to let people help you. Nobody can do it all on their own."

"Says the woman who does everything for everyone."

"Yes, but not by myself. I have partners. I have friends. I have people I trust to look out for me when I can't look out for myself."

He met my eyes, then looked away. "Okay, okay," he sighed. "I may have a problem when it comes to letting others give me a hand. It's just that I always felt I needed to *prove* myself, you know? You might think suddenly being able to control the weather would make you feel powerful, but mostly I feel like I'm a kid again. Not knowing exactly what I'm supposed to do, just knowing I can't screw it up."

"That's not how kids are supposed to feel," I said softly.

"Maybe not. But that's what it was like in my family. 'You're responsible for your own success and your own mistakes,' my father always said. I guess that's why I always fought so hard to win on my own terms—if I was going to take all the blame for my failures, then I was sure as hell going to take all the credit for my accomplishments."

"No one's trying to take anything away from you. Especially not me."

He looked back at me, his dark eyes serious. "I know that. You're good at giving—I'm just not so good at receiving. Some part of me needs to *earn* what I get, and another part feels that I've haven't earned *anything* in my life. I didn't earn these powers, I inherited them. I didn't earn my job, it was given to me."

"No. Opportunities are what you were given. It's what you do with them that earns you the right to keep them. That's how it works for everyone. And you do a damn fine job of earning that, every day."

"Well, I haven't given anybody food poisoning, yet. Or flooded a town."

"True," I said. "And as much as you hate to accept gifts, you've just been given another opportunity—the chance to learn how to really use your powers. Which, considering your stance on responsibility, I really think you should take advantage of."

"So you trust her now?"

"Hell, no. But I trust you. And I don't believe she means you any harm. She may not be a stellar human being, but she seems to be on our side. Or your side, anyway."

"And how about you?" He took my other hand in his. "Are you still on my side?"

"Always," I said. Then, being no fool, I kissed him. On the cheek, because he'd just thrown up.

Did I mention that times passes differently in the Thunderbird realm? You can stay there for an hour or two and only minutes go by back in the default world. Why, you could spend a whole morning in the Aerie—even sunbathing in the nude if you wanted, because who would see you?—before going back to plain old reality. Yep, you could totally do that.

But it would help if you came prepared.

"Next time?" I said as the winds spiraled up and Thunderspace faded away, "I'm coming prepared. A blanket, some sunscreen, and definitely some food. I am *starving*."

He wrapped an arm around me and pulled me closer. "Well, we did burn off more than a few calories . . ."

[Ahem.]

<*What he said.*>

"Oh, hello," I said to my two partners. "We're, um, back."

Whiskey discreetly sniffed the air. [Indeed. May I conclude from the post-coital pheromones you're both exuding that the duel went successfully and this is a celebratory occasion? Or is it more in the nature of a reconciliation in the aftermath of crushing defeat?]

<*Since they arrived under their own power, I'm gonna go with victory nookie. What did you do with the body? Hers, I mean, not yours.*>

I looked around, stretched, and yawned. "Not as simple as all that, kitty. Ben lost the duel, but won . . . a scholarship, I guess."

[Intriguing. She's taking you under her wing, then?]

<*Hey, that was* my *line!*>

[No, your line was going to be about dismembering and eating a Thunderbird, and speculations about its flavor.]

<Well, yeah. But stealing my thunder was still rude. You know, considering the circumstances.>

[Quite right. I apologize for inadvertently invoking a metaphor that was situationally awkward, and follow that with congratulations to Mr. Montain on retaining said weather phenomena for himself. Does this mean you're departing for some sort of extradimensional college, or will we have the pleasure of once more enjoying your daily cuisine?]

Ben laughed. "I'm coming back to the kitchen, Whiskey. Foxtrot convinced me to stick around for a while, anyway. But yeah, looks like I'll be studying with Professor Firstcharger, too."

Tango gave an annoyed flick of her head. <Great. More unscheduled rainstorms. I can hardly wait.>

Ben bent down and stroked Tango's back. "It won't be like that, kitty. I think we'll do most of it in Thunderspace. What do you say we celebrate with some of those CatYummi treats you like so much?"

<You can't bribe me with food. Let's go.>

"Where to?"

<The kitchen, of course. You're going to feed me CatYummis and I'm going to eat them and refuse to be bribed. Have you forgotten how this works?>

Ben grinned. He has one helluva grin. "Right."

<Also, there will be skritches. Which will fail to work, too, despite the enormous amount of time and effort you will dedicate to them.>

"Got it." Tango trotted away, then stopped and looked back. Ben surrendered to the inevitable and followed her. "Guess I know what I'm doing for the foreseeable future."

"Don't be too hard on François," I called after him. "He knows he's only temporary."

"He better not have rearranged my pots . . ."

Whiskey and I watched them go. [Well. That seems to have worked out.]

"One crisis down. Well, two, actually; three if you count my love life. A good morning."

[One that's barely started. The sun just came up.]

"Oh, right, the time difference thing. Hey, if we hurry we can still make breakfast. I am *starving*."

But then I heard the sirens.

As I realized they were getting closer, I broke into a run, Whiskey at my heels. Oh, well—three solutions forward, one problem back. That's a dance step I'm all too familiar with: the Catastrophe Foxtrot, named after its creator and most experienced practitioner.

I just hoped nobody else had died.

The sirens, it turned out, were those of a police vehicle as opposed to fire or ambulance. It seemed Sheriff Brower had decided to make a spectacular entrance—either that or he'd forgotten how to work the on/off switch for the siren, which was also entirely plausible. The amount of respect I have for Brower is equivalent to the admiration Tango has for swimming dogs, which is zero. She likes to watch them, though; when I asked why, she made an optimistic reference to sharks and drowning.

I sighed as I walked into the house via the back door, and wondered if Brower ever went to the beach. Maybe I could send him a surfboard anonymously. And a one-way ticket to Australia.

I found him in the foyer, talking to ZZ. Brower's in his sixties, with thinning white hair and a protruding belly; ZZ's around the same age, but she carries her years with a great deal more grace and style. Today's style was an art-print T-shirt of Godzilla stomping on Rush Limbaugh, with black yoga pants and gladiator sandals. Brower was dressed like a sheriff, or at least someone who liked to pretend he was one.

"And I'm telling you, ZZ," Brower fumed, "I have a warrant for her arrest. I know she's staying here, so tell me where she is!"

"If you have a warrant, show it to me," ZZ said pleasantly. She had this trick where she would match her politeness and cordiality to the other person's belligerence, becoming nicer and nicer as her victim got more and more upset. Brower always seemed to fall for it.

"It's just a figure of speech," said Brower. "It means I have a good reason to arrest her and that's what I'm going to do."

Brower seems to have gleaned most of his legal knowledge from watching cop shows and action movies. "It's not just a figure of speech," I said. "It's an actual, real document. You don't need one to arrest her, of course—but you do need to have some kind of reason. Who are we talking about?"

I was secretly hoping it was Teresa Firstcharger, but Brower surprised me by saying, "Theodora Bonkle. I know she's here, so you'd best give her up."

I knew Brower wasn't going to give me any more information than he had to, but I had to ask. "On what charges?"

"I don't have to answer that unless you're her lawyer. Are you?"

"No. But I am the one that can probably locate her."

"Then do it. I'll wait."

I looked to ZZ for guidance, since it was her call. She nodded and said, "Go ahead, dear. Give her a call and see if you can find her, anyway."

I pulled out my phone, got Theodora's number and hit call. She answered right away. "Hello?"

"Hi, Theodora, it's Foxtrot. How's your day going?"

"Oh, fine, fine. Last night was somewhat eventful, but a good night's rest has put it all in perspective. And you?"

"Oh, you know—same old same old. Listen, there's a police officer here who would like to talk to you. Do you have any idea why?"

"Yes, I'm reasonably certain I do. I expect he wants to arrest me."

"Why?"

"Well, that's a bit of a tale. Is there any chance I could regale you with it over a hot cup of tea?"

"Fine by me. Just hold on a second." As I talked I used one thumb to turn the sound all the way down, then took the phone from my ear and looked at it in irritation. "Damn. I got cut off. Sorry, Sheriff. ZZ, can I try yours?"

ZZ has the same model of phone as I do. I took hers and pretended to call Theodora back. "Can't get a connection. Oh, well, I'm sure she'll call back." I casually pretended to hand ZZ's phone to her, but palmed it at the last second while surreptitiously slipping my own phone into my pocket. Now that I had both phones I breezily said, "Well, I was just on my way to grab some breakfast. I'll let you know if she calls back—"

Brower held up one beefy hand. "Foxtrot. Give me your phone, please."

"Why?"

"So you can't call Miss Bonkle back and warn her. You think I was born yesterday? Now give it here or I'll charge you with obstruction of justice."

I resisted the urge to make any sort of reply, and instead handed him ZZ's phone with a resentful frown. ZZ herself didn't say a word, just smiled at me in a *Good job, dear,* sort of way. Then I turned around, marched resentfully away, and once I was out of sight in the kitchen I put my own phone up to my ear and turned the volume back up. "Sorry about that. Earl Grey okay?"

"Splendid."

"And where am I bringing it to?"

"Ah. Well, that's a bit unusual, I'm afraid. I'm in an animal pen of some sort. In the menagerie."

"Um. Which one?"

"I'm not sure, honestly. I was following Doc and Very; it was their idea, you see. In hindsight that may not have been the wisest course of action, but I was feeling a bit anxious."

Anxious enough to follow your hallucinatory friends into a wild animal pen, I thought. I just hoped it wasn't the jaguar or that boar with the enormous tusks. "Look around you, Theodora. Tell me what you see."

"I'm in a small, shed-like enclosure. There's some straw on the floor, which I'm reclining on. I had thought I was alone, but I see now there's something in the corner under the straw. Not terribly large, perhaps the size of a beaver. White fur, with darkish bits. Can't see it terribly well."

"White fur with darkish—wait, like white on top and dark on the bottom?"

"Ah, it's shifting a bit. Yes, that seems to be accurate. Looks a bit like an oversized skunk, really, though it doesn't smell like one."

I swallowed. "I'll be right there, Theodora. Whatever you do, don't antagonize it."

And then I was running, the phone still to my ear, calling out mentally for Tango to meet me *immediately*.

At the honey badger pen.

Honey badgers, for those of you who aren't familiar, are native to South Africa. In terms of durability, attitude, and behavior, they make a wolverine look like a field mouse. Their skin is so tough it can deflect arrows, they will eat *anything*—including hooves and horns—and seem to be incapable of fear. A honey badger is like a small, stubborn, hungry tank, one that considers lions a minor annoyance and cobras a tasty snack. Their totem animal is Chuck Norris.

And now Theodora had invaded a honey badger's home. Well, not its actual home—it was staying in a temporary pen while Caroline made some modifications to its old one. Honey badgers are also smart, and if you aren't very, very careful, they'll escape.

And this honey badger, unfortunately, I knew all too well.

I heard Tango in my head before I saw her. *<Hey, what's the big rush? I was right in the middle of some serious skritches.>*

Theodora's in the pen with the honey badger.

<I see. Well, my hostage negotiator skills are a little rusty, but I'll see what I can do. Hope Owduttf is in a good mood.>

Owduttf was an acronym for what the honey badger claimed was its name: "One Who Does Unspeakable Things To Foxtrot." That was the short, paraphrased version, as the real thing went on for a while, making it hard to pronounce.

Also, it was horrifying. And extremely personal.

I got there at the same time as Tango. "Okay, Theodora, I'm here," I said into my phone. "What's the honey badger doing?"

"Snuffling, mainly. He knows I'm here but hasn't approached. Doesn't seem all that bothered, really."

Which meant nothing. Honey badgers didn't really get bothered, they just wreaked destruction. "Just stay still for a moment, okay?"

"I shall, certainly. But I'm afraid I can't say the same for Doc or Very."

"Just—just let them do their own thing. I don't think the badger will notice."

<What do you want me to say, Toots?>

Let's start by getting his attention. Fortunately, Tango spoke fluent Honey Badger. *Hey, Owduttf!* I thought. *Long time no see!*

Tango listened to my thoughts, then translated them into a series of grunts, snorts, and chuffing. After a moment, a reply in the same vein issued from inside the enclosure, and the conversation was on.

<He says: Hi there, Foxtrot. Are you here for breakfast?>

Possibly. I'm not breakfast itself, *if that's what you're asking.*

"The beast," said Theodora in my ear, "is making an awful lot of noise. Very says it's having a conversation with another badger outside. Also, he's disappointed that there doesn't seem to be any actual honey about."

"Just stay put and keep quiet for a minute, okay? I'm trying to convince your roommate of your good intentions."

<He says: That's not what I meant at all. Would you like some breakfast? I have a large supply of fresh meat inside.>

Um. No. No, definitely not. In fact, I'd kind of appreciate it if you'd let that meat go.

<He says. Go? Go where?>

Outside. Where I am.

<I thought you said you didn't want any.>

I don't. But the meat is—well, not meat.

<You're not making any sense. Maybe you should eat some meat.>

"It's uh, coming toward me."

No! Look, just come outside and talk. Don't bring the— don't bring anything.

<Well, all right. But I'm really going to need some breakfast soon.>

The honey badger shuffled out into the bright morning

sunshine, bits of straw stuck to it, and yawned with a mouth full of short, pointy teeth. *<Hello, Foxtrot. Hello, small-morsel-that-talks-for-Foxtrot.>*

"I'm surprised you translated that," I said out loud.

"Surprised I translated what?"

I suppose I deserve that. This was starting to get confusing, so I told Theodora to stay where she was until she heard from me and hung up my phone. Then I turned back to Owduttf and concentrated on just talking to him. "Okay. There's a friend of mine in your house. Please let them leave without harming them in any way."

Owduttf stayed exactly where he was, half in and half out of the entrance, blocking the doorway with his short, squat body. *<Oh, a friend of yours? Why didn't you say so? Friends cost extra.>*

Tango turned an accusatory glare on me. Right, admitting the hostage meant a lot to you probably wasn't the best tactic. Too late now.

"Okay, I'll pay. What do you want?"

He launched into a long, expressive series of grunts and chortles. Tango started to translate, then quit with a disgusted look on her face. *<I want . . . oh, forget it. I'm not saying that.>*

"Is he asking for *anything* that doesn't concern my vital organs, bones, or flesh?"

<Depends on what you consider vital. Do you really need all your hair? Or toenails?>

"That detailed, huh?"

<I think he must have made a list and memorized it.>
Interrupt him, please. Hey, Owduttf!

The badger stopped making noises and looked at me quizzically.

That's not an option. How about something more reasonable?

<He says: I will consider giving the meat-woman to you

in return for two things. First, I want to be moved back to my old enclosure. This one has a very hard floor that I can't dig through.>

Well, that was easy enough, since Caroline was about to move him back, anyway. *What's the second thing?*

<Honey. A large vat of it, full of tasty grasshoppers, sheep eyeballs, and carrots. The crunchy ones, not all soft and bendy.>

Will you settle for crickets? Grasshoppers are out of season.

<I suppose.> He shuffled out of the doorway and onto the concrete floor of the pen, then looked back expectedly. I called out, "Theodora? You can come out now."

Theodora Bonkle stuck her head through the entrance, then crawled out on her hands and knees. She looked somewhat disheveled, her dress rumpled and straw stuck in her hair. She straightened up, peered curiously at Owdutff for a moment, then marched over to the bars. "I may need some assistance getting out," she said. "I used a ladder to gain access to the roof, then jumped from the eaves into the pen."

The door to the pen, not surprisingly, was locked. "I'll be right back," I said.

It didn't take long to locate the ladder she'd used and reverse the process, lowering it into the pen so she could climb out. There was a nerve-racking minute when I thought Owdutff might make a break for it, but apparently he decided that climbing a ladder wasn't on his agenda today. He went back inside the shed instead.

When I had Theodora safely outside and the ladder stowed away, I said, "Okay. Now, would you mind sharing the series of events that led to you taking refuge in the pen of an animal known to attack Cape buffalo?"

Theodora picked a piece of straw out of her hair. "Not at all. But I would still like that tea, if I may."

I sighed. "Come on. Caroline always has a stash of orange pekoe in her office."

I led Theodora to the clinic that functioned as the HQ of our resident vet. She wasn't there yet, but I used my key to get us inside, sat Theodora down, then dug out two mugs. I filled them with water, stuck them in the microwave, and found the tea and some sugar while they were heating. Tango, who'd come inside with us, immediately jumped into Theodora's lap and began purring; she's good like that. I placed the mugs on the table, sat down across from Theodora, and said, "I'm listening."

"Well. The last time we talked, I told you about what I'd uncovered concerning Marbles the cat and her unhappy disappearance. I was rather distraught."

"Yes, I remember."

<Wait, who?>

Shush. I'll tell you later.

"Well, my resolve to find the perpetrator was undimmed. Fortunately, I was able to talk further to Mary's caregiver, and even look through some old books of photos. Mary's lived on the same street her whole life, and even though many of the properties in the neighborhood have changed hands over the years, it's still a matter of public record who owned them when she was a child. That gave me a list of names, and it was a logical step from there to court documents. Anyone who hurts animals as a child has a much higher chance of breaking the law as an adult. From there it was a matter of matching last names and ages to get a suspect pool, which was quite small. I asked Mary herself if she could remember the names of any of those who bullied her, and she supplied me with only one: a boy named Herman."

She stopped, stirred her tea, and fished out the bag before taking a sip. "Herman Klomm was arrested for arson when he was twenty-two, and for assault several times after that. He was an only child, and the Klomm family lived on Mary's street for many years. They eventually moved away, but bought another property nearby. Herman Klomm inherited the title to that house some years ago, and has been living there alone ever since. I went to visit him, under the guise of a reporter doing a story on retirees and their hobbies. The interview . . . did not go well."

I winced. "Theodora. What did you *do*?"

She stared at me defiantly. "It was quite unplanned, I assure you. I simply meant to talk to the man, to see if I could get a sense of who he was. It's not as if I expected to find a cat's head preserved in formaldehyde on his mantelpiece."

"You . . . didn't, did you?"

"No, of course not. He was short and fat and smelled of cigar smoke, but he was pleasant enough. His house was rather messy, but some people find little incentive to clean when they live alone. In any case, the entire incident was Very British Bear's fault. Oh, don't look at me like that, Very; you know what you did."

I involuntarily glanced down at the spot on the floor Theodora was glaring at. Nothing there, of course. "Very British Bear? I thought Doc Wabbit was the troublemaker."

"He is. But in this case, Very was the instigator. What's that, Doc? No, that isn't a type of instant alligator. Anyway, I was asking Mr. Klomm a few initial questions when Very said *Do you think it hurt?*"

"Did what hurt?"

"That's what I wondered, but I couldn't just ask him, not with Mr. Klomm right there chatting about his interest in old baseball cards. But Very didn't give up. He said . . ."

Theodora broke off and looked away. She blinked a few times, clearly upset, then said, "He said, *When Mr. Klomm killed Marbles. Do you think it hurt?*"

"Oh."

<Saw that one coming.>

Theodora set her mug of tea down on the table and regarded it as if she'd never seen such a thing before. "It's not like Very to say things like that. Doc, yes, but he'd make a joke. But Very knew, you see; he knew that Mr. Klomm, for all his smiles and friendliness, was not a good person."

"What . . . what did you do?"

"I sneezed. Quite loudly. Then I complained about the severity of my allergy to cats, and asked if Mr. Klomm had one. When he replied in the negative, I congratulated him on his good judgment and—" Theodora looked down at Tango, and stroked her fur gently. "I apologize in advance, Tango. I had to tell a most horrendous lie in order to draw the man out."

<You're forgiven. We cats have heard them all, any­way.>

"I said," continued Theodora, "that they were vile creatures, and if I had my way they would all be put down. It had the desired effect."

"Which was?"

"His eyes flickered, ever so slightly, to an old baseball bat he had mounted on the wall, next to a framed picture of himself wearing some sort of sports uniform. "I don't know about putting them down," he said, "but I do know they'll go up, if you hit them just right.""

She stopped then, and just stared at her tea. I felt a little sick. Tango stopped purring.

"Well," Theodora said at last. "I no longer had the stomach to talk to that monster, so I directed my next remarks to Very. *I expect it did hurt,* I told him, *but only for a second. Now go in the other room, please; I don't want you to see this. Doc, would you be so kind as to hand me that bat? Yes, you can have a turn, too.*"

And that was why the police were here. Too bad; I would have given her an award. "Did you leave him alive?"

She picked up her mug and took a long sip before answering. "Oh, my, yes. I'm no killer, my dear. But his injuries, I'm afraid, were fairly extensive. I meant to stop after breaking his jaw, but—"

"Doc Wabbit kept encouraging you?"

"He can be most convincing when he puts his mind to it. Inventive, too."

I sighed. "Okay. I applaud your motives, but the authorities have taken a decidedly different view. You're going to have to turn yourself in. But I'm pretty sure ZZ will find you the best representation possible, and probably pay for it, too."

Theodora nodded. "Yes, that's the outcome I expected. But don't worry yourself, dear; I have plenty of money, and Doc assures me that he's willing to 'take the rap' as he puts it. I'll be fine."

Considering her fame as a writer and her well-documented schizophrenia, she could be right—while a stay in a medical environment was likely, I doubted Theodora would spend any time in prison.

But one consequence was almost certain. "You realize that you're going to have to start taking your medication again," I said gently.

Her face fell. "I know. Previously, when I've tried to explain that to Doc and Very, they've reacted badly. They don't like being sent away, you see; they miss me. But this time they're being very brave. Very has promised to write every day, and save up all the letters to bring to me when they come back. Doc says he'll take care of Very, and not to get into too much trouble. It will be hard, not seeing them, but I expect I will manage."

We sat in silence for a moment, sipping our tea. And when we were done, we got up and went out to deal with Brower.

CHAPTER NINETEEN

Tango wasn't satisfied.

We stared after the police car driving away with Theodora in the backseat, Whiskey, Tango, ZZ, and me, and Tango said, *<This doesn't make sense.>*

[Which part? The mentally unstable author beating an animal abuser with a baseball bat, or the fact that it's illegal?]

<No, that all worked out pretty much the way I thought it would. It's Marbles *that I still can't figure out.>*

[It's a game involving small, shiny balls that roll around. Much too complex for the feline mind, I know.]

<That's not what I meant, and you know it.>

[You mean you can't figure out why Marbles is absent.]

<Exactly. Someone who loves her is dropping by a great big portal into the animal afterlives, and Marbles is a no-show? Where the heck is she? Certain factors dictate how long each cat's life is, how much time they spend in the afterlife between incarnations, and where they go from life to life. Considering how Marbles died—and that her former person is a regular visitor to the Great

Crossroads—Marbles should be somewhere in the vicinity. But she's not.>

[Indeed. A cat doing something they're not supposed to. How terribly, terribly unusual and noteworthy. Perhaps I should inform the press.]

<I think I was right in the first place. Ghost python with a hunger for ghost cats.>

ZZ looked at me with a sad smile. "This is unfortunate, Foxtrot, but not as bad as it looks. Call the lawyers, will you? We'll foot the bill on this—I may not approve of her actions, but her heart was in the right place. While you're at it, make sure she's getting proper psychiatric care, too; I don't want her stuck in some state-run horror show of an asylum."

"Will do," I said. I hesitated, then asked, "ZZ? Theodora's story was kind of . . . odd, but you seem to be accepting it at face value. And even Theodora admits she's delusional, at least about certain things. I'm not sure I understand."

ZZ sighed. "I'm not sure I do, either. But that woman, for all her flaws, writes one hell of a detective story. Maybe this is just me being a fan—but if she says a crime was committed and she's found the perpetrator, then I tend to believe her. Even if the crime happened fifty years ago and she has no hard evidence, her story had the ring of truth. It's a matter of instinct, I suppose."

I nodded. "Yeah. I know what you mean." And I did; despite my telepathic, supernatural companions, I didn't really have any more to go on than ZZ when it came to Theodora's conclusions. But I believed she was right, all the same.

<This isn't over yet,> Tango said. *<Not until I find Marbles—or the snake that ate her.>* And with that, she darted away.

ZZ watched her go. "Cats," she said. "Tango hasn't been

here that long, but she's already part of the family. I can't imagine someone doing to her what happened to poor Marbles."

[I can.]

Oh, shut up. If anything actually happened to her, you'd make what Theodora did to Klomm look like a tickle-fight.

[You don't expect me to admit that, do you?]

Not out loud, no.

[Then we understand each other.]

Theodora was in jail. Teresa had revealed herself not as a giant shape-changing snake, but a giant shape-shifting teacher. Assuming neither development was some sort of clever ruse, I was down to three suspects: Fimsby, Rustam, and Kaci. Fimsby claimed to be an ally, Rustam claimed to be psychic, and Kaci had claimed Whiskey's heart.

And Rustam had threatened me, in a bizarre and hard-to-prove fashion. Would a metamorphic, mind-warping snake do that? Or would it just try to get me to trust it . . . like Fimsby was?

If he was, it wasn't working. Which, if you thought about it, was the perfect cover. Also a terrific way to drive someone as analytical as me completely crazy, because after the fourth time you had second thoughts about triple-guessing yourself, you were about ready to just give up and stop thinking. Which is just what they wanted you to do—and off we go on the crazy train again, no stops in sight. Some days, I really hate my brain.

The problem was that I was just reacting, bouncing around in a never-ending hall of mirrors. I needed to take control, smash through the glass and out into the daylight. But how?

Stop trying to figure out who the Unktehila was, and *make* them tell me. Force them out into the open. And then . . . well, then I had two Thunderbirds, an ectoplasmic dog, a telepathic cat, and a graveyard full of animal spirits backing me up. As soon as the cat got back from her investigation, anyway.

I thought about it as I made the calls ZZ had requested, the back of my mind gnawing away at the problem while I talked and took notes and dealt with the mundane realities of lawyers and doctors and bureaucracy. When I'd ascertained that Theodora's interests were being looked after by highly paid professionals—and confirmed tonight's menu with Ben—Whiskey and I went for a walk in the graveyard. I found Cooper, working on an old lawn mower in the shade of his bungalow, and told him about Theodora; he was saddened but not surprised, and asked me if I could find a way to relay messages to her. "If there's one thing you look forward to in stir," Coop told me, "it's mail from the outside. Reminds you of what's waiting for you, keeps you connected. I'd like to do that for her, if I could."

I said I'd make it happen, then asked him if he'd had any more dreams featuring giant snakes.

"Not as such," he answered. "Did have one with Very British Bear and Doc Wabbit, though. Funny thing, they looked different from how I always imagined them; never thought of Doc as wearing a fedora, though it did look good on him."

"What did they have to say?"

Coop scratched his cheek with a grimy fingernail. "Well, Very told me they'd be going away for a while but they'd take good care of Theodora. Doc just pulled out a bazooka and used it to blow up a hot dog stand. No idea what that was about."

"Sounds like she knew she was going to get in trouble."

Cooper shrugged and wiped his hands on an oily rag. "Could be. Or they did."

I nodded. "Hard to tell what's real and what isn't, sometimes."

"Oh, that's easy." He leaned down and started tinkering with the mower's engine again, prying at something with a wrench.

"Yeah? How so?"

"If it hurts, it's real. If somebody thinks it's gonna make them rich overnight without any work, it probably ain't."

I grinned. "Thanks, Coop. I'll let Theodora know you're going to write her."

As Whiskey and I strolled away, I thought about Coop's homily. It was basically a folksy version of *Life is pain; anyone that says otherwise is trying to sell you something.* Pretty cynical, but all too often the truth. That got me thinking about Rustam and Kaci, and Oscar's scheme to turn a sizable profit from canine paintings—and that made me realize that I'd completely forgotten something I'd asked Whiskey to do.

"Whiskey, you told me you didn't get any sense of telepathy from Kaci, right?"

[That is correct.]

"But you were going to ask her directly—dog-to-dog, as it were—if she and Rustam talked to each other mentally. Did you?"

Whiskey flattened his ears and looked away in shame. [I apologize, Foxtrot. I meant to, but I got swept up in the heat of the moment.]

"And the ecstasy of expired badger, I know. Well, maybe we should follow up on that now. *If* you think you can keep yourself under control."

His ears perked right up. [Certainly. But how, when I've been barred from her presence?]

I reached down and ruffled his fur behind his ears. "Don't worry. There's always a way for a determined Romeo to see his Juliet. How are you at climbing ladders?"

* * *

The ladder, it turned out, wasn't necessary. All that was required was my phone, Whiskey's shape-shifting ability, and a little deception on both our parts.

"Hello, Mr. Gorshkov? Foxtrot here. We need to talk. Where are you now? Painting, I see. Well, Whiskey's on the loose and he had a wild look in his eye when he bolted. I think you should put Kaci safely in your room until I round him up. No, not a problem. You're very welcome. Buh-bye."

And then, before he could get up there, I used my master key to let Whiskey into Gorshkov's room, where he hid under the bed. "Are you sure this will work?" I said.

[Not to worry. The form I'm taking is Kaci's own, right down to her scent. Then, once Gorshkov has left, I'll shift back and reveal myself. A few questions later and you can come back and let me out. Stay nearby and we can continue to converse telepathically.]

It sounded simple enough. But that's what I'd thought last time.

I let myself out and found an unoccupied guest room across the hall. I sat down on the bed and thought, *Whiskey?*

[Present and accounted for.]

Good. This shouldn't take too long.

Soon I heard footsteps in the hall, then a key turning in a lock.

[They're here.]

A few seconds later, the door closed again. [Gorshkov has left. I will wait until he's out of earshot in case Kaci's reaction is overly enthusiastic.]

This turned out to be a good idea, as Whiskey's sudden appearance produced a volley of overjoyed barking. I held my breath, but Gorshkov didn't come back.

I couldn't understand what they were saying to each other, but Whiskey relayed the content of their conversation. We learned some very interesting things, and when I'd heard enough I went downstairs to find Mr. Gorshkov

and discuss them. I didn't bother letting Whiskey out,
since I knew he could do that himself. And hey, he and
Kaci deserved a little alone time together.

Especially since Mr. Gorshkov would be leaving soon.

I found him in the gardens, cleaning some brushes next
to Kaci's easel. It looked as though he'd had a productive
morning, with several canvases propped up against a
nearby hedge. Oscar would be pleased.

Oh, no, wait. He wouldn't.

"Hello, Rustam," I said. My voice was light and cheerful, because that's the kind of mood I was in. "Doing a little
cleanup? Good idea."

He glanced at me, the look on his face as welcome and
friendly as mine. "Hello, Foxtrot. Yes, it's always a good
idea to treat your equipment well." We were out in the open,
and he was too smart to say or do anything threatening now.
In fact, if I was to bring up his little poem, I knew exactly
what his reaction would be: puzzlement, followed by confused denial. He would do his best to make it seem to
anyone eavesdropping—electronically or otherwise—
that he was being confronted by a lunatic.

Too bad for him I had no intention of doing that.

"Yes, especially when it's so specialized," I said.
"Like the bone phone implanted in Kaci's chew toy that
you've strapped to that brush. Looks like it's just there to
give her a better grip, but what it really does is transmit
prerecorded verbal commands via bone conduction right
through her teeth, along her jawbone, and into her ears.
Where's the transmitter, in the cane?"

Okay, so maybe I rushed it. I could have drawwwwwwn
it out, played with him for a while, got him to think I
was going one way and then slap him down when he
least expected it. But I had a lot going on, I still hadn't
caught the killer, and frankly I just didn't have the patience. Sometimes you toy with the mouse, sometimes

you go for the kill. Also, without Whiskey or Tango here, it just wasn't as much fun.

I did get to enjoy the look on Rustam's face, though. Like a mannequin with a painted-on smile, frozen in an expression that seemed more and more like a grimace the longer you stared at it.

"That was a rhetorical question, by the way," I said. "About the cane, I mean. But the whole idea is very clever. Originally I thought maybe you were using ultrasonics that human ears couldn't hear, but that wouldn't work with other dogs around, would it? Don't answer that. Bone conduction means nobody can hear your instructions except Kaci, and Border collies are really good at memorizing cues. Not that you'd need that many, for painting: up, down, left, right, maybe a few simple shapes. After all, it doesn't have to be good, just good *enough*. Right?"

The expression on his face slowly collapsed, like a snowman melting. I thought I'd enjoy it, but I actually felt kind of bad. Sure, he'd threatened me, but I'd been threatened with far worse by far scarier people. All he'd really done was try to fleece a greedy man, one who wasn't exactly a model of honesty himself.

Gorshkov lowered himself onto a bench. "It was not as easy as all that. Many, many months spent teaching her. And she is quite talented, as far as technique goes. Sometimes I think she has a style all her own."

He chuckled. "But she does not understand what we are trying to accomplish. If I do not give her commands, she will sit and wait, patiently. She wants so badly to please."

I sat down beside him. "Look on the bright side. You trained a dog to paint. That's pretty awesome, in and of itself. In fact, I'm pretty sure that if you came clean and confessed what you've been doing, you could not only sell your paintings honestly, you could probably avoid going to jail. Probably."

He sighed heavily. "I suppose. The public adores the unique, but there is a vast difference between a dog who is an actual *artiste* and one who is simply well trained. Perhaps I can make a few dollars peddling them as novelties."

"I think you'll do all right—though Oscar isn't going to be thrilled."

He nodded. "You require me to return his money, of course."

"Oh, I don't know. I'm a big fan of poetic consequences—and Oscar paying a lot of money for dog paintings that aren't quite as valuable as he thought seems like a perfect example of that. Besides, it'll give me something to poke him with for *years*."

"I see. Then I am free to go?"

"Not just yet. We're going to work out a few details concerning when and how you're going to make a public admission of what you've been doing, and I want you to know I keep a very close eye on certain communities. If you try to pull something like this again, I'll know—and I'll talk."

"Certain communities, eh? Are you talking of the art world, or the criminal one?"

"Neither. I was referring to the animal kingdom." I got to my feet. "Just remember, Rustam—I'll be watching."

Rustam wasn't the Unktehila, and neither was his dog. If a monster who could make anyone trust him disguised himself as a con artist, the con would be a lot less elaborate; you could just walk up to people and convince them to give you their money. And while pretending to be the hapless canine accomplice would be a pretty good cover, it would require undergoing months of training in order to fool your owner. Again, there were far easier ways to insinuate yourself into the situation.

That left two possibilities: Fimsby, or a massive mistake on my part. Technically, the only people I'd completely ruled out were Ben and Teresa, because they'd both demonstrated their Thunderbird abilities in my presence and I was pretty sure that wasn't on the long, scary list of what an Unktehila was capable of. Still, I was mostly going on assumptions and instinct; the Unktehila could still turn out to be one of the household staff, or even one of the animals in the menagerie.

I really, really didn't want it to be the honey badger.

So. Back to the problem at hand, which was trying to figure out a way to get the Big U to expose itself. I needed bait, a plausible way to dangle it, and a way to deal with the thing once I caught or cornered it. Not impossible hurdles, but not insignificant, either.

How had the Thunderbirds dealt with them in the first place? Teresa Firstcharger had said they zapped them from above, or boiled them alive in their pools. But how had they found them in the first place?

Maybe I should just ask her.

I pulled out my phone, took a deep breath, and punched in her number. *We're allies now,* I reminded myself. *Sure. Absolutely.*

She answered on the third ring. "Foxtrot. What can I do for you?"

"Tell me more about the Unktehila."

She laughed. "Oh, so you're taking the threat seriously, now?"

"I never said I wasn't. I just wasn't sure how accurate the information you were giving us was."

"I see. And now you want *more* of my inaccurate information?"

She wasn't going to make this easy. "Look, believe it or not, we seem to have wound up on the same side. We don't have to like each other, but can we concentrate on fighting the big bad supernatural threat first?"

"You have a point. What would you like to know, exactly?"

"How your people located them. What their habits are. If they have any weaknesses we can exploit. What their favorite flavor of ice cream is."

She hesitated. "The legends don't go into detail about how we located them—I think it was largely by instinct." I was really learning to hate that word. "As far as habits go, they lurk in deep pools and use the crystal on their foreheads to attract game. They have a very particular spot, seven rings down from the head, that's vulnerable—that's where the heart is. Favorite flavors? They really seem to like human. Anything else?"

"Let me get back to you on that." I rang off.

So they hung out in pools (presumably with large amounts of suxamethonium chloride for killing any Thunderbirds that dropped by). Pretty risky, considering how Thunderbirds liked to use lightning to boil the snake's living quarters—but the method of murder did make a gruesome, poetic sort of sense now.

Still, there was no way I was going to be able to lure a wary Unktehila into a swimming pool with two Thunderbirds around. No, I had to present our serpent with an irresistible target that also looked safe.

Like maybe two birds with one stone. Two birds that didn't suspect a thing, because they were really, really busy . . .

Did I mention how much I hate my brain, sometimes?

<Hey, Toots. You seem a little upset.> Tango strolled into view. *<In fact, the noise you just made in your head reminded me a little of what I sound like when I cough up a hairball.>*

"Just contemplating the unthinkable, Tango. And ways to implement it, as usual."

She yawned. *<Uh-huh. Well, let me know if you need any help. My abilities are fearsome, you know.>*

"Oh, I know."

<No, you don't. Go ahead, ask me.>

"Uh—are your abilities fearsome?"

<No, no. Ask me how fearsome they are.>

"They're extremely fearsome, I'm sure."

<Why, thank you for asking. They're so fearsome I've solved the case.>

"I didn't ask—wait, *what*?"

<Yep. Just little old me, all by my lonesome. Fearsome and lonesome, that's what I am.>

"You forgot annoysome. Now, are you going to share this astounding discovery or keep it to yourself?"

She sat down and started grooming in that self-satisfied way cats have. *<Okay, okay. The murder victim is . . . not dead.>*

I stared down at her in bafflement. "Tango, we saw them take the body out of the swimming pool. And if she wasn't dead *before* the autopsy, she sure as heck was afterward."

<Not that case—the Marbles murder.>

"So Marbles wasn't murdered?"

<Of course she was. Didn't you just hear me call it the Marbles murder? Pay attention.>

"Just tell me what you found out."

She flopped down on her side and looked up at me expectedly. I sighed, knelt down, and rubbed the point of her chin with my index finger. *<Yeaaahhh, that's the spot . . .>* As she started to purr, I wondered how many other sleuths had to provide skritches in order to solve a case. Probably more than were willing to admit it.

<So, I went to the graveyard to do a little snooping.

Took a stroll down the alleys of cat heaven, asked a few questions. Some mook tried to give me a hard time, so I flashed the claws to let him know I was a bad *kitty.>*

"Wait. Cat heaven is based on film noir?"

<Maybe. Maybe I'm not allowed to let you know what it's really like, so I'm disguising the facts with an entertaining story.>

"Okay, tough guy. Continue."

<I hit all the regular dives and catnip dens, but nobody'd seen hide nor hair of my suspect. Either she was hiding, or she had no hair. I hit the Abyssinian quarter just to make sure, but nobody down there had seen her, either.>

"Abyssinians are short-haired, not hairless. You're thinking of the Sphynx or maybe the Peterbald."

She glared up at me. *<Look, Google Junkie, who's telling this story, you, me, or Wikipedia?>*

"Sorry. Carry on."

<Ruining a perfectly good yarn with facts . . . where was I? Oh, yeah. Cats are good at not being found, but nobody's that good. I called in a few favors and dug up a little dirt. Amazing what you can find when you start to scratch, and some of it doesn't smell too nice.

<She wasn't in, so she had to be out. The world's a big place, but I knew where to start. I hit the bricks and made my way to the scene of the crime. The trail was cold, but so was the killer's blood. And that's when I saw her.

<She was an old cat, a blue-point Siamese with cream-colored fur and a dark, wise face, lying in a sunbeam on the front stoop. We stared at each other, our eyes saying more than words ever could, and after a few minutes of that she acknowledged my presence with a flick of one tall, well-shaped ear.

<"Haven't seen you around here before," she said.

<I sat down to put her at ease. "Just passing through."

<"*Aren't we all?*"

<"*I guess. But some of us stick around longer than others.*"

<*Her eyes narrowed. She knew what I was talking about. "You a cop?"*

<"*Strictly freelance,*" *I told her.* Glorified security guard was closer to the truth, but I didn't think her laughing in my face was a good way to start the conversation.

<"*You seem to know a lot for someone who isn't a cop.*"

<"*I have friends. Seems like you do, too.*"

<"*Is that what you think happened?*"

<"*I don't know what happened. Why don't you tell me?*"

<*She glanced away, pretending to be interested by a passing fly. "Why should I?"*

<"*Because of your friend. The one you stuck around for.*"

<*That got her attention. She got to her feet and stared me down. "What about her?"*

<"*Take it easy. I'm not here to make threats, just pass on a little good news.*"

<"*Yeah? Like what?*"

<"*Like a certain someone who once introduced you to a nasty individual by the name of B. Bat has now made the acquaintance of said individual himself. Numerous times.*"

<*She didn't react for a long moment, just staring off into space. Then, very softly, she said, "Well. That is good news. Thank you."*

<"*You're welcome. How about you return the favor and tell me a story.*"

<"*About Mr. Bat? I'd rather not.*"

<"*I'm more interested in what happened afterward.*"

<"*I died.*"

<"*Been there. Done that. Own the squeaky toy.*"

<"How many times?"

<"Six and counting. How about you?" I already knew the answer, but I wanted to hear her say it.

<"This is my last turn at the scratching post. Eight down and one to go."

<"Hope they were good ones."

<"Oh, they were. Didn't like how some of them ended, but then, who does?"

<"How'd you do it?"

She knew exactly what I was asking, but she wasn't just going to come out and admit it. "Do what, exactly?"

<"A cat has nine lives for a reason. It lets us live places, experience things that otherwise we'd never get to do. But you found a way around that. Your very first life started right here . . . and so did every other.">

"Wait," I said. "Marbles didn't just spend her first life with Mary—she spent *all* of them?"

Tango rolled over and got to her feet. <*Make a lap, please.*> I sat down on the grass and did so, and Tango jumped into it and made herself comfortable. <*Thank you. As I was saying . . . yes, that's exactly what Marbles did. Mary was her first caregiver—and her second, and her third, and so on. Completely against the rules, but cats look at rules the same way we look at mice: fun to play with until you get bored.*>

"There must have been consequences."

<*Oh, sure. Considering when she started, Marbles could have been only halfway through her allotment of lives by now. I'm guessing she made some kind of major trade-off to be able to keep getting reincarnated in the same place over and over.*>

I thought about that. Nine lives, stretching over as long as 180 years, spread out over the whole globe. And Marbles gave up most of that to spend her lives with one lonely, disadvantaged woman.

"So she's there now?" I said. My eyes were a little blurry for some reason, but I was smiling. "With Mary?"

<*Yeah. What's so funny?*>

I laughed as I dug in my pocket for a tissue. "Turns out the joke is on Klomm. Mary *didn't* lose her Marbles. She had them—one after another—the whole time."

And then we just sat there in the sunshine, Tango purring in my lap, and I stroked my sweet kitty's head and thought about the fact that I would always—*always*—have her around, no matter where *around* might turn out to be.

Love, after all, beats Death.

Every time.

Chapter Twenty

Now that my suspect pool had dwindled—probably—down to one, I decided the best course of action was to concentrate on Fimsby. If he *was* the Unktehila, maybe I could force his hand, trick him into revealing himself. The two most likely adjectives I could attach to this plan were *dangerous* and *difficult,* but at least it didn't require me picturing Teresa and Ben in a compromising position. Or positions, dammit—throw the ability to ignore gravity into the equation and everything gets so much worse.

Anyway.

Whiskey, Tango, and I were having a war council to discuss our options.

<*Attack,*> Tango said, and yawned. <*All-out assault. Claws and fangs and that weird hitting thing that people do. He'll be forced to defend himself.*>

Whiskey gave her a disapproving look. [That's a terrible idea. If he *is* the Unktehila, he'll retaliate with power we can't match. If he isn't, we'll have attacked an innocent man.]

<*So? At least we'll know. And we'll have two Thunderbirds to back us up.*>

I leaned back in my office chair and took a long sip of tea. "Tango, we are not mugging a guest. For one thing, do you have any idea how difficult it is to get a ski mask in your size? No, we're going to have to be sneakier than that."

[Setting a trap, perhaps, with irresistible bait?]

"Only as a last option," I said quickly. "No, we just need to prove he has supernatural abilities. Shape-shifting would be good. Whiskey, you're the expert—under what conditions would you be forced to take another form?"

[One rather obvious situation does come to mind: making myself smaller in order to fit into an available space.]

<Oh, is that what you were doing up in that room? Fitting into an available space?>

[That is unworthy of a reply.]

"Yeah, Tango, try and focus, okay? I think Whiskey's on to something."

<Or he was, not too long ago.>

[You're simply envious, because canine procreation does not require the assistance of barbed genitalia.]

I thought about taking out my notebook to jot that one down, but realized I hadn't actually said it myself and decided not to. It's important to have standards.

<Right. You just get stuck, like a giraffe trying to use a revolving door.>

[While an entertaining image, your metaphor is hardly accurate. It's more akin to a monkey attempting to grab a banana inside a jug with a narrow mouth, and discovering that his fist wrapped around the fruit is now too bulky to remove.]

<Stupid monkey. A cat could get that banana.>

[It's just a metaphor. The banana in question fulfills the same role as the giraffe in yours.]

<Why would a giraffe want a banana?>

"Valid point," I said. "In the sense that *valid* means 'completely loopy.'"

<*A cat would just reach in, sink her claws into that banana, and yank the sucker out.*>

Ever seen a dog wince? I have.

<*It might damage the banana a little, but so what? It's just a banana. It's not like it's gonna start bleeding or anything—*>

"And that's enough of that," I interrupted. "Getting back to the question at hand—can we put our alleged Unktehila in a situation where he's forced to get smaller? Present him with an opening he needs to get through, maybe, one that's too small for a human being?"

[That part should be simple. The question is, what can we put on the other side that he'll desperately want to acquire?]

And then I had an idea . . .

"I'm afraid Rustam won't be joining us for dinner tonight," Oscar said, taking his usual place at the table. "He's been called away on urgent business. Promises to return as soon as possible, but isn't sure when. Kaci, of course, has gone with him."

"We'll just have to manage without him," ZZ said with a bright smile. I'd told her what I'd found out about Gorshkov, and she'd approved of how I handled the situation. "And at least we won't have wet paintings propped against every available surface. Though you must be feeling a bit cramped at the moment."

Oscar took a long sip of his sherry. "Not at all," he said, trying to sound chipper. "I hardly ever use my living room, anyway."

Teresa Firstcharger, Efram Fimsby, and Keene were also in attendance. Keene was his usual ebullient self, while

Teresa Firstcharger seemed on edge. Fimsby appeared to be enjoying himself, chatting with ZZ about a hurricane that had once trapped him in a coal mine. Me, I was keeping an eye on everyone while trying to look casual.

Ben had decided to signal his return with an epic feast; I was currently enjoying lobster in a lemon cream sauce, with a wild mushroom risotto on the side.

Whiskey and Tango were not present.

"So," I said around a mouthful of heaven, "what exactly have you been doing, Keene? I haven't seen you around all that much."

"Communing with my muse," Keene said. "Me and old Jeepers have really hit a groove lately. Been spending a lot of time writing it down."

"Can we expect a new album, then?" Teresa said. "Sometime soon?" The look on her face told me she was hoping for more than just music from him.

"Can't rush genius, love," Keene replied. "It'll be done when it's done. Or when my producer pries it from my unconscious fingers, whichever comes first."

"Speaking of communing," I said, "I recently spent a little time at the lake, communing with nature."

"Oh, is that what you did on your day off?" ZZ asked. "Because I was getting reports you were still here, even when you were off duty."

I shook my head and tried to look embarrassed. "This was on my *last* day off, actually. Ben and I went together."

"There are several lakes nearby," said Oscar. "Which one did you go to?"

I laughed. "Believe it or not, I can't tell you."

"Why on earth not?" Oscar said, sounding annoyed.

"Because I don't know. Ben took me there, and made me wear a blindfold on the drive. Said he knew this great little spot for a getaway, but wanted it to be a surprise. I thought he was being romantic, but then he spent the whole afternoon fishing. Apparently the lake is really, really deep, which supposedly guarantees really big fish. Not that he caught any while we were there, though we did see a lot of deer. Really *big* deer, too."

"Maybe they thought they were fish," said Keene.

"Well, they came right down to the water to drink. Amazing to see, though it made me kind of nervous."

"Nature can do that," said Teresa. She smiled at me innocently.

"Yes, it can," said Fimsby. He dabbed at this mouth with a napkin. "It can be both beautiful and downright terrifying, often at the same time."

"Well, the joke's on Ben," I said. "He may think his secluded little fishing hole is still a secret, but I've got a GPS tracker built into my tablet. I haven't bothered, but I could find my way back there if I had to."

ZZ shook her head. "You took your tablet along? No wonder he went fishing—you were probably working the whole time."

"Not true," I said. "I have a very firm rule about that tablet—it's only for work. In fact, I lock that tablet in my office every night. It's there right now; I refuse to bring work home with me."

"No, of course you don't," Oscar said drily. "Just to the beach."

"Well, I hope you enjoyed yourself, dear," said ZZ. "Even if Ben didn't catch any fish, he certainly found some delicious lobster."

That was a sentiment everyone agreed with. Fimsby even asked for seconds, which helped explain his paunch.

Or maybe he was secretly thinking about all those big, fat deer at that deep, secluded watering hole . . .

<This is not *going to work.>*

[Quiet. We're dealing with a psychic creature, and we

don't know the extent of its capabilities. It might be able to overhear our telepathic communication.]

Our trap had been set. The bait—my tablet—was in plain sight on my desk. The door was locked and the window was open a few inches and locked in that position. A shape-shifting burglar looking for quick directions to an all-you-can-eat venison buffet wouldn't find it difficult to gain entry, but they'd need to squeeze through a narrow gap, first: either through the window or under the door. Tango was outside in a tree, Whiskey was hidden under my desk, and I was across the hall in a storage closet, peering through a keyhole. If anyone tried to get in, one of us would know.

Unless, of course, all the mental chatter alerted said shape-changer and scared them off.

<Doesn't matter. The big snake ain't coming.>

Neither Whiskey or I responded, but that didn't stop Tango. *<See, this thing is an ambush predator. Lies in wait and then springs out. Okay, it uses its mind-whammy to lure prey in, but that's the kind of strategy other ambush predators use, too. My point is, it doesn't go out hunting. Doesn't matter how good our bait is, the Unktehila isn't going to bother with heading all the way out to some supposedly well-stocked lake for a midnight snack. That's not how it thinks.>*

I sighed. *Look, we agreed to give it a try. Old habits die hard, and from all accounts these creatures had big appetites and liked deep water. The combination might prove irresistible.*

<Hey, I've got no problem with waiting. Cats invented waiting. But you're forgetting two things: one, that snakes can go a long time without food; and two, that if it were really that hungry, it has a whole animal smorgasbord right next door.>

I know that. But if a zebra or something disappears, it'll look suspicious. It's too sneaky for that.

<Is it? Because it doesn't seem to be hiding itself all that well, what with the reports of ordinary people spotting it.>

[You said Firstcharger was faking that.]

<She wasn't. Try to keep up.>

You couldn't have pointed this out earlier?

<I was waiting for the right time. Right now, with both of you bored but reluctant to interrupt? This seemed about perfect.>

Her logic was impeccable. Highly irritating, but impeccable. I scowled and tried to think of a way to gracefully admit she was right. *Tango? I hate to say it, but—*

<IT'S HERE.>

[What? *Where?*]

<Outside! Under the tree!> She sounded terrified. *<It's huge!>*

[Stay calm. Is it approaching the house?]

<No. It's heading toward the menagerie!>

[Maybe you were right about its choice of cuisine.]

I stepped out of the closet, darted across the hall, and opened the door. Whiskey burst out and sprinted down the hall, with me right behind him.

[Can you still see it?]

<Just barely.> She sounded a little calmer now. *<It's slithering past the hippo pool. Moves pretty fast for something that big.>*

Are you chasing it?

<Well, someone has to, and you guys weren't here.>

[We're right behind you. Don't get too close.]

<Don't worry, I won't.>

We were sprinting across the lawn now, but I still couldn't see Tango. Time to call in the reinforcements.

Cell phone. Speed dial. Two Thunderbirds waiting on the second-floor balcony of the east wing, ready to take flight and bring the lightning.

No service.

I stared down at my phone in disbelief. It stubbornly refused to change its mind and start working. I felt like I'd been betrayed by one of my own organs, like my pancreas had suddenly decided to go on strike for better working conditions and more bile.

I didn't have time for a Plan B. I kept running.

I caught up to Whiskey at Oswald's enclosure—the large fenced pen that housed our resident ostrich. Oswald's something of an escape artist, so the fence was high and the gate locked. Despite that, something had managed to get in.

Something really, really big.

Tango was on top of a nearby post, while Whiskey had shifted form to his true shape, the one he'd been born with: a three-hundred-pound brute with a pedigree that included English mastiff, Great Dane, St. Bernard, and Alaskan timber wolf. He was growling, deep in his broad chest, at the thing that rose up in the pen before us.

The serpent was big enough to swallow a Volkswagen, long enough to block six lanes of traffic, and as brightly colored as a bag full of Skittles. It should have left ditch-deep tracks, but I couldn't see any trail at all. Nor had it smashed through the fence; it must have gone over the top without crushing it.

We stared at the giant snake coiled around the shed Oswald slept in. It looked as though the Unktehila was in the mood for some chicken—or maybe it just preferred the taste of bird.

And then it noticed us.

It stared down. We stared up. I had this horrible feeling in the pit of my stomach. It's my least favorite feeling in the world, and it's worse than just fear. It's how I feel when I'm *unprepared;* it feels like falling, deaf and blind and naked, and having absolutely no idea how far away the ground is. Somehow, I'd managed to get not only myself but both my partners into that particular situation, and any second now we were all going to hit the planet with a great big *splat*.

Or, you know, get eaten by a giant mythological snake . . .

CHAPTER TWENTY-ONE

I'm a detail-oriented person. I notice the little things, even when big things are happening all around me. I once had to use a fire extinguisher on a bass guitarist who'd managed to set himself afire during a solo, and even while I was literally putting out a fire I still noticed that one of the buttons on his shirt had popped off and would need to be replaced before the next show. Custom-tailored, bone buttons shaped like little *T. rex* skulls, handmade in Portland, Oregon. It's just how I'm wired.

So, as I was contemplating being devoured by an immense, supernatural serpent, I couldn't help but notice it was the wrong one.

A tongue like a two-pronged pitchfork made of bubble gum popped out of its mouth, flapped at us, and popped back in again. It was tasting our scent, seeing if we were gobble-worthy or not. It considered the information it had just gathered, then reared up like a subway train thinking about a sudden career switch to rocket.

No, not rocket. Rainbow.

It arced through the sky in a long, graceful curve, more like an inchworm than a snake. That arc went right over the far side of the fence, the serpent's whole body flowing in a gravity-defying wave that made it look as if it were moving through water instead of air. In a matter of seconds it was gone.

We just stood there.

I was the first one to finally speak. "No horns," I said. [No large crystal on its head.]

<No idea what you two are talking about. DID YOU SEE THE SIZE OF THAT SUCKER?>

I winced. "No need to yell. Something isn't right, Tango. An Unktehila is supposed to have horns and a big, mystic crystal on its forehead. That had *neither.*"

<So? It was a gigantic, multicolored snake! What are we supposed to do, ask to see its driver's license?>

[A gigantic snake that could have easily consumed us. Yet it did not.]

<Haven't you ever heard the old saying, Don't look a gift hearse in the mouth? *The hearse that just took off had more than enough room for all three of us, and you're worried about whether or not it had the right hood ornament?>*

"That hood ornament is a central part of the myth," I said. "It's how it controls minds. Why wasn't it—hey. *Look.*"

I pointed at the ground inside Oswald's enclosure. It was mostly hard-packed earth, with some patchy grass and a few bushes, but that was changing before our eyes. Spots of green were springing up, in a line between us and Oswald's shed, as well as in a ring around it. Grass, growing in the path the snake had traveled.

<Okay, that's pretty weird,> Tango admitted. *<Any theories?>*

"Well, well, well," said a familiar voice behind me. I turned around to see Keene strolling toward us, a grin on his face and a drink in his hand. "Late-night walkies? I thought you went home ages ago, Trot."

"I came back to get something I forgot," I said. I wasn't looking at him, though; I was looking at who was walking beside him.

Fimsby.

"Ever so glad you're here," said Keene. "I've been attempting to educate Efram here on the finer points of snooker for the last hour, to no avail. Care to join us?"

"He's been with you the whole time?"

"And Teresa. She took off about twenty minutes ago, though. Said she had something to attend to."

"Thanks for the offer," I said, "but I've got to get home."

"Suit yourself. Ta."

I watched him and Fimsby go back to the house. "I think," I said softly, "that it's time to reconsider some of our assumptions."

But first I had to go reassure Ben and Teresa that we were still on the outside of any neighborhood reptilian esophagus. I found them on the balcony, deep in conversation about rain.

"Foxtrot," Ben said. "Everything all right? I thought you were going to call."

"So did I," I said. "But my cell phone abruptly stopped working. No idea why, unless the presence of massive, brightly scaled monsters makes technology malfunction." I told them what had—and hadn't—happened.

"No horns or crystal? You're sure?" Teresa asked. "That makes no sense."

"Neither does the new lawn in Oswald's pen, but it's easy to verify. In fact, you could take a little stroll down there right now." I smiled sweetly at her, and she took the hint more gracefully than I thought she would.

"I'll see you in the morning, Ben," she said. "First class is promptly at ten o'clock. Don't be late." She sauntered away without wishing me a good night.

"Ten?" I said to him. "That seems kind of late. What happened to dueling at dawn?"

He slipped an arm around me. "I have to serve up breakfast first, remember? And this isn't going to be a duel. It's instruction."

"Just remember there's no teacher's petting in this class."

"I promise. You know you have nothing to worry about, right?"

I looked him in the eye. "Of course not. Just because you and a gorgeous woman with superpowers are going to be spending a lot of time together in another dimension where no times passes and nobody can see what you're doing and you'll probably both be drenched to the skin within minutes and okay, maybe I'm a little worried. I mean, this is not exactly an ordinary level of trust you're asking for, here. For all I know she's going to tell you that the only way you'll ever learn how to master your abilities is to have wild, mind-blowing eagle sex."

He frowned. "What's eagle sex?"

"It's where two eagles lock talons while flying and go into a cartwheeling dive, pulling apart at the last second before they hit the ground."

"Sounds next to impossible. For one thing, I'm pretty sure I don't have talons. And even if I did, I doubt that's where my sex organs are located."

"It *is* impossible. It's a myth. Which is exactly my point—if she told you something like that, how would you know if she was telling the truth? Everything *about* this is mythical. Thunderbirds, Unktehilas, ghosts, and gateways to other dimensions—she could tell just about any lie and get away with it."

He reached down and took my hand. "Not everything is a myth, Foxtrot. The real world is still here, ticking away like it always does. And there are real things in it, too. Like me and you."

He kissed me. It was a nice moment, a verging-on-momentous moment, because he was coming awfully close to saying that particular phrase, the one that's so hard to say the first time and eventually turns into something you say so often it loses all meaning.

Which is when, in a flash of clarity, my brain made a connection it hadn't before.

I broke the kiss and pulled back, leaving Ben staring at me with a puzzled look on his face.

"The real and the unreal," I said. "I've been trying to make them fit together the whole time, because that's what *my* life has become. But what if they *don't* go together? What if this two *different* kinds of weirdness that both showed up at the same time?"

"I'm . . . not following. But I know that look."

"I need to go do some research, right now."

"Yeah, that's the look I meant." He shrugged. "Okay, go. I'll see you at breakfast?"

"Absolutely."

And then I sprinted to my office and hit the Internet. Whiskey looked up, heaved a doggy sigh, and put his head back down on his paws. Tango, curled up on the couch, only twitched her tail.

It was dawn before I'd gathered enough information to formulate a solid theory. I'd had to make some long-distance calls to firm it up, but the murder finally made sense to me. I'd figured out who'd done it, and why. The how was a little trickier, but only the actual method the suxamethonium was delivered by; I already knew that Anna's death by drowning was caused by chemical paralysis.

I talked things over with my partners. We made some plans.

And then we called a meeting.

I held it in the study, just before breakfast. I was already seated, Tango in my lap, when the first attendee showed up: Ben. He was dressed in his chef's whites and looked a little distracted. "What's up, Trot? I have eggs to Benny."

"Have a seat, chef. This won't take long, but it will be instructive."

He shrugged and sat down next to me on the divan.

The next to arrive was Teresa Firstcharger.

I already knew she was an early riser, but she'd still sounded a little annoyed on the phone at being summoned at this hour. She was dressed casually, in track pants and a tight neon-orange jogging top, her long black hair tied back in a ponytail. "I'm here, Foxtrot. What's so important it couldn't wait?"

"Answers, Teresa. Answers to some very important questions. For instance, the Unktehila: What is it, really?"

She regarded me coolly. "The ancient enemy of the Thunderbird race. I already told you that."

"That's one answer, sure. But some questions have more than one answer, don't they? Don't answer that, it was rhetorical. I seem to be asking a lot of those lately."

On my lap, Tango stretched and yawned. *<I wouldn't worry about it, Toots. It's just a phrase you're going through.>*

I ignored that and continued. "Another answer to that particular question is: 'a big scary monster that can control minds and look like anyone.' Right?"

"That's one way to put it."

"No, that's how *you* put it. Because answer number three is, the Unktehila is the bogeyman. Kind of the ultimate paranoia inducer, isn't he? Not just the monster under the bed, but a monster that can disguise itself as a dust bunny *and* make you doubt your own judgment."

Teresa crossed her arms. "Are you trying to tell me the Unktehila doesn't exist?"

I leaned forward and picked up my mug of Irish breakfast tea from the coffee table. "Existent, non-existent—those are such narrow definitions, aren't they? Like you said, this is the stuff of myth, of legend. Extraneous details *change,* right? Facts are just window dressing. Which is awfully convenient for someone trying to inspire fear in a potential follower."

"Not a follower," Teresa said. "A student."

"Uh-huh. My point," I continued, "is that for a teacher, you don't seem to, a lot of regard for hard data. And the reason for that is simple: You don't know as much as you pretend to."

"I see," said Teresa. The smile on her face was dangerously close to a smirk. "Are you feeling a little threatened, Foxtrot? Information is supposedly your domain, but now someone's come along who knows more than you?"

I smiled right back. "Oh, I have no problem with that. Lots of people know more than I do; I spend much of my time figuring out which ones they are, so I can pay attention and learn from them. As a side benefit, I also wind up figuring out which ones are trying to snow me. Whoops, sorry, little weather joke there."

"I don't have time for this," Teresa sighed. She pulled a pair of earbuds out of her pocket and plugged them into the music player strapped to her upper arm. "I'm going for a run—"

Which is when Kaci walked into the room.

Ben frowned. "I thought Gorshkov left—"

"He did," Teresa said. She took a step backward, away from the dog. "I saw him get into a cab yesterday."

Kaci sat down. She stared at Teresa intently.

"The Unktehila could be anyone, right?" I said. "Anyone at all."

"That's just a dog," Teresa said. "I don't know what you're trying to pull, but—"

Kaci changed shape, flowing into something that looked like a pit bull covered in scraps of dirty cloth. (Trust me,) she said. (I'm a lot more than that.)

Teresa shrieked, holding her hands in front of her to fend off any possible attack—and then twin lightning bolts crackled from them.

Kaci, though, was too fast. She shrank down to Chihuahua size in the blink of an eye, the bolts passing over her head.

"Stop!" I yelled. "That's not the Unktehila!"

Teresa glanced at me, her eyes wide with fear, then looked back at the dog—who shifted into a much more familiar form: Whiskey's.

"What?" she said. "Your dog is—"

"Not a giant mind-controlling snake," I said. "But yeah, he is a shape-shifter. See, you *don't* know everything."

[I apologize for the deception, madame. But it does illustrate Foxtrot's point rather well, don't you agree?]

"*I* don't agree," said Ben. "Exactly what *is* your point, Foxtrot?"

"Exactly what I just said—that Teresa doesn't know everything. In fact, there's a whole *bunch* of things she doesn't know, and the first and most important one is this: that giant snake we've been chasing? Not an Unktehila. It doesn't have horns or a mystic crystal embedded in its forehead, and I'm not sure it's even hostile. What it is, is *Australian*."

Ben and Teresa both replied at the same time: *"Australian?"*

"Yeah. See, the Rainbow Serpent myth pops up in more than one culture, and means more than one thing. In Australia, it's a god of creation, associated with all sorts of life-positive things: watering holes, menstruation, healing."

Teresa looked skeptical. "If this Rainbow Serpent is so life-positive, why did it kill Anna?"

"It didn't. It's not an Unktehila; it doesn't take on any form it wants, nor does it control minds. It brings life, for the most part—though it can also have quite the temper. Want to know how it demonstrates anger?"

"Eating people?" Ben ventured.

"No. It causes storms—thunder and lightning and flash floods. See, the Rainbow Serpent is also a *weather spirit*." I paused for a moment to let that sink in. "Anna went into the outback to test her abilities. She must have attracted the attention of the resident weather manipulator—who then followed her all the way here."

"For what purpose?" Teresa demanded.

I shrugged. "I don't know. But I do know one thing: It wasn't to inject Anna with a paralytic that caused her to drown in a swimming pool. That kind of thing was just barely plausible for a shape-shifting bogeyman, but we're talking a whole other level of power here; the Rainbow Serpent is closer to a god than a monster, the kind of being that puts the *super* in supernatural."

"That—that actually explains quite a bit," Teresa muttered. "The vision I had never showed me the serpent's head, just the body. And the power I felt flowing to this place—I thought it was just three Thunderbirds coming together, but it wasn't."

"Nope. Three Thunderbirds, two turtledoves, and an Australian Rainbow Serpent. In a tree."

Ben gave me a look, which Teresa seconded.

"Okay, there's no tree. But *ostrich enclosure* didn't scan and anyway, you just admitted you got most of your information in a peyote-induced haze."

Teresa glared at me. "I never said anything about peyote."

"No, you didn't. You also didn't say anything about

trying to manipulate Ben into accepting you as his teacher by scaring him with monster stories. But that's exactly what you did."

"It wasn't manipulation. I honestly thought he was at risk—that we all were. But even if it wasn't an Unktehila that killed Anna, she's still dead. So who's responsible?"

And then, with utterly perfect timing, the last person I'd invited to the meeting walked in.

"What's this all about?" said Efram Fimsby.

CHAPTER TWENTY-TWO

"Dr. Fimsby," I said. "Thank you for joining us. I've been thinking hard about your offer, and I've decided to take you up on it. Please sit down; we need your help."

He glanced at me and Ben, then looked more intently at Teresa. She looked back neutrally. Fimsby chose an overstuffed chair and sat. "Well, I'm overjoyed to hear it. I take it we're all . . . *informed* as to the situation?"

"Not quite," I said. "That's one of the reasons I called this meeting. There's been a lot of secrecy and paranoia about the 'situation' as you call it, and that has to stop. We're going to share our information, and hopefully arrive at some conclusions.

"First of all, as you may have guessed, Teresa Firstcharger is also a Thunderbird." I paused, mainly to enjoy the uncomfortable look on Teresa's face. "Yes, that's right," I continued. "Teresa, Dr. Fimsby here not only is aware of the existence of Thunderbirds, but also assisted Anna when she first discovered her powers and fled to Australia. Though he took a very different approach, he was trying to do for Anna the same thing you're trying to do for Ben:

teach a fledgling weather spirit how to spread their wings. A noble goal."

Fimsby gave Teresa a warm smile. "It seems we have something in common. I do hope we can stand united against a common threat."

"Perhaps," Teresa said. "Though Foxtrot seems unclear on exactly what that threat is."

"Oh, I know exactly what it is," I said. "It's somebody who's targeting Thunderbirds. Somebody who killed a Thunderbird in such a way that only another Thunderbird would know it wasn't what it appeared to be. Well, another Thunderbird or somebody familiar with their abilities, anyway."

"Why?" asked Ben. "If it wasn't an Unktehila, then what was the motive?"

"Twofold. The secondary reason was to attract the attention of other Thunderbirds, so they could be targeted as well. The primary reason was fear."

"Fear?" asked Fimsby. "Of what?"

"Of a race of supernatural beings that could control the most powerful force on the planet—the weather. To the killer, this was like handing the trigger of an atomic bomb to a toddler. They were so afraid of the possible consequences that they decided the only course of action left to them was to kill each and every Thunderbird they could locate. I imagine they thought they were saving the human race."

I looked Fimsby in the eye. He looked back calmly, but after a moment, he blinked, then looked shocked. "What? Surely you don't think *I'm* the guilty party!"

"You've insisted on secrecy from the beginning, implying there's some sort of threat. When I mentioned the Unktehila, you acted as if I knew what I was talking about, though actually you were just playing along—because, as it turns out, there is no Unktehila. You admitted to being in the pool the night Anna died . . . because you were the one who killed her."

Fimsby said nothing for a long moment. When he spoke at last, his voice was soft but urgent. "Nonsense. I've done nothing but offer my help. You have only the vaguest circumstantial evidence—"

"You're not just a meteorologist," I said. "You have a medical degree, as well. Not only a smart person, but a compassionate one. Is that why you quit medicine to concentrate on exotic weather patterns? You thought you could do more good on a grand scale than a personal one?"

Fimsby got to his feet. "I don't have to sit here and listen to these groundless accusations—"

"Doctor," Teresa said. "Sit down, or I'll electrocute you on the spot."

Fimsby froze. And then, very slowly, he sank back into his seat.

"I haven't known Foxtrot for very long," said Teresa, "but I do know this about her: She doesn't jump to conclusions without knowing all the facts, and she is very good at collecting facts. If she says you murdered Anna Metcalfe, then you need to explain why she's wrong—and it better be an *extremely* good explanation."

Ben still hadn't said a word, but the look he was giving Fimsby said it all. I hoped we weren't about to have an indoor hurricane.

"Anna must have told you about Ben," I said. "That's probably what tipped you over the edge—the idea that Anna wasn't just an isolated case, there were others like her. You convinced her that you could help Ben the same way you helped her, but insisted on secrecy. Once she was dead, it was easy to suggest someone was out to murder Thunderbirds—because there was. You.

"On your second attempt," I continued, "you tried to

frame Teresa by shooting Ben with a crossbow. Native Americans didn't use crossbows, but that's a minor detail, easily glossed over. Lots of people miss little details like that—and it's usually up to someone like me to catch them. The details, I mean. Like the fact that an old-school buddy of yours back in Oz fondly recalled going hunting with you and your Barnett Ghost 410. Which is a crossbow. One that's probably in a Dumpster miles away from here by now."

Fimsby's face hardened. "Fine. In the end, it doesn't matter what I say, does it? I'm only human. I can't generate terajoules of energy with a wave of my hand, or drop the ambient temperature a hundred degrees on a whim. You're going to do whatever you want to anyway, and to hell with insignificant human customs like the police or courts. If you can ignore natural laws, why should you pay any attention to ours?"

And there it was. The Unktehila in the room, so to speak. When it comes to deception, violence, and manipulation, you don't have to go looking for mythological monsters; the human race makes its own all the time.

Ben leaned forward. Suddenly I could smell ozone in the air. "You did it. You really did it. *You killed my sister.*"

"You have no idea what you *are*," Fimsby hissed. "It's not just your potential for destruction, which God knows is immense. No, it's the very fact of your *existence*. You invalidate the idea of science itself. You should be impossible, yet here you sit; mocking everything I know to be true, revealing that the world as I know it is an illusion, an ill-fitting suit of rational clothing hung on a ravening beast of chaos. There is nothing you can do to me worse than you have already done."

"You're wrong," Ben said. "About everything. No, the universe isn't the clockwork mechanism you thought it was. It's big and messy and confusing and contradictory.

So what? People—and yeah, I count myself among them—are made to deal with messy and confusing and contradictory. We try, we screw up, we figure things out and move on. It's not reliable or predictable or even consistent, but there's this terrific concept built in. It's a term engineers like to use, but it's popular with chefs, too: *forgiveness.* You'd probably call it chaos, but I like to think of it as freedom. It's what lets you make mistakes. Making mistakes is how you learn, and learning is how you stop making mistakes and get it right. That's what Anna was trying to do, and that's what she thought you were helping her with."

Fimsby shook his head. "When somebody like you makes a mistake, people die. Maybe by the *thousands.*"

"Or maybe they don't," Ben said. "Maybe they get saved by the thousands. Maybe somebody like me pushes a hurricane away from landfall, or convinces a tornado to go around that trailer park. That must have crossed your mind."

Fimsby's voice was unrepentant. "I couldn't take the chance."

"No? Well, life *is* chance, Doctor. Just because you don't know the outcome doesn't mean you refuse to roll the dice. And even if they aren't as reliable as mathematics or chemistry or physics, there are still some things worth gambling on."

Ben looked over at me. I blushed. I never blush.

"Thunderbirds are a lot more human than you seem to think," Ben said. "You assume we're just going to pass judgment on you because we can. Because we think we're above you. Well, I don't feel entitled to pass judgment on anyone except maybe another chef, and even then I'll give them a lot of leeway. I may have a supernatural heritage, but I have a human one, too. You might be a murderer, but I'm not. I'm nobody's executioner."

"Speak for yourself," Teresa said coldly. And I do mean

coldly; the temperature was dropping like umbrella prices in a drought. "You've as much as admitted your guilt, which is all the proof I need. But Ben's right: We're not the monsters here. So I'm going to give you more than you gave Anna: a choice."

"Which is?" he asked.

"Turn yourself in to the authorities and confess."

"And if I don't?"

Teresa smiled. It was a very wintry smile. "Then I'd advise you to spend the rest of your life in a submarine at the bottom of the ocean, because that's about the only place I won't be able to find you."

Fimsby just sat there, his shoulders slumped. And—eventually—he nodded.

I pulled out my phone. I already had officer Forrester on speed-dial.

CHAPTER TWENTY-THREE

Fimsby had used a gas-powered needleless syringe to inject the drug into Anna when they were both in the water. He'd concealed the injector inside a pool noodle, one of those floating Styrofoam tubes people use as flotation devices. A playful poke with the end of a fluorescent orange toy had been easy to get away with, and the injector used an orifice only 0.18 millimeter in diameter to deliver the paralytic to her subcutaneous tissue in a fraction of a second. Once the drug went to work he just had to make sure she was facedown, then toss the hair dryer in.

To his credit, Fimsby didn't make any outrageous claims about supernatural beings to the police. He knew how that would sound, and there was no way for him to prove his allegations—Ben and Teresa certainly weren't going to help him. He told Forrester he'd killed Anna over a lovers' quarrel—believable, considering the public fight the Metcalfes had that night—and in a way, it was even true. All scholars have a deep love of the subjects they study, and Fimsby had studied weather. He'd stared deep into the eyes of storms, admired the elegance of snowfall and the passionate fury of lightning. In his mind, Anna had taken all that away from him—so he'd taken her life in return. As is often the case in love gone wrong, at least one of the parties involved did nothing other than exist, and wound up being punished for it.

Love beats death. But death usually gets a few nasty punches in first.

"I'm proud of you," I told Ben. We were curled up together on the couch in my office, Whiskey at our feet. Tango was prowling around somewhere outside. "You proved him wrong, you know. You didn't just talk the talk, you walked the walk. You are one talking walker."

"Thanks. You have no idea how hard that was—really, I just wanted to toss him into the sky and drop him from about a thousand feet. Maybe hit with a few thunderbolts on the way down."

I snuggled into his shoulder. "But you didn't. You did the right thing, and he'll still pay. Not a lot of weather in prison."

"Oh, I don't know." Ben's voice was hard. "I have the feeling every single hour he gets in the yard will be subject to sudden, unseasonable downpours."

I didn't answer that. He was still angry, and had every right to be. He'd let it go in his own time.

"It's been a rough morning," I said. "Still planning on going to school?"

"Yeah, I think so. Feels like the right thing to do, you know? Anna did her best to learn about her abilities, and I should do the same. She just picked the wrong person to confide in."

I nodded. "And you're sure Teresa is the right one?"

"Hell, no. Like you said, she doesn't know nearly as much as she claims. But she *does* know more than me, and she's willing to share. There's more to it than that, though." He shifted position so he could look me in the eye. "She's right about us Thunderbirds having enemies, she just got the details wrong. If our people are coming back to the world, we're going to need to band together. That means leadership, that means planning—or the next Fimsby that comes along might take out more of us. Might even be working for some three-letter government agency."

"Okay, valid concern. If, you know, anyone can actually convince a bureaucrat of the existence of the supernatural."

He shrugged. "I don't know. But better to be united and informed than alone and ignorant. The next Thunderbird that suddenly wakes up to what they can do might not be as responsible with their powers as Anna was, and all it takes is one confused newbie to make all of us seem like monsters. We're going to have to do something about that."

"So that's the new career you're training for? Finding and training fledgling Thunderbirds?"

"Something like that. We'll see how it goes. For now, I'm happy to spend my days cooking, my nights with you, and getting in touch with my roots when I have the time. Which, when you think about how time works in Thunderspace, is pretty much unlimited."

"I think you mean feathers, not roots."

"I think I mean I'm going to be too exhausted to come up with proper metaphors."

I grinned and snuggled back under his arm. "Then that'll be my job. You whip up thunderstorms, I'll come up with clever ways to describe them."

"I can't wait."

"Metaphor Girl! With her lightning-quick wit, her thunderous vocabulary, and her whirlwind of meteorological references!"

Whiskey lifted his head. [You might want to add deluge of verbosity. In the interest of accuracy, you understand.]

I squinted at him. "Are you saying I talk too much?"

[Not at all. I'm saying that compared to you, a babbling brook only mutters sporadically.]

Ben laughed. "You're not exactly the speechless type yourself, Fido. And by the way, what the hell was that thing you turned yourself into that freaked Firstcharger out so badly?"

[It's a Hungarian breed called a komondor. Thickest, heaviest coat of fur of any canine breed.]

"Looked kind of like a four-legged, albino Rastafarian," Ben said.

[They're sometimes called mop dogs because of their appearance. Those long cords are a kind of natural armor, protecting them from attackers like wolves. They can take up to two and a half days to dry after a bath.]

"Well, you definitely got a reaction out of her. Which was the plan, right?"

I shrugged. "Why would you think that? That would be mean and petty and pretty much impossible to prove."

He laughed again. "Uh-huh. I think I should get going. I've got a little time between now and lunch, and I plan on packing a full day of instruction into it."

I sighed and moved over to let him up. "Okay, okay. But if she works you too hard she'll have to answer to me."

"Walk me to class?"

"Ooh. Only if I get to carry your books, too."

Ben called Teresa on the way out the front door to let her know he was on his way. "Yeah, I'll meet you in the graveyard. What? Over by the statue of the bear. No, the *bear.* I can barely hear you, either. No, *barely,* not—never mind." He disconnected with a grimace. "Damn phone isn't working. Lots of static, and now I'm not getting a signal at all."

I frowned. "Weird. That's what happened last night, when I tried to call you about the serpent. I wonder if it caused it, somehow."

[Entirely possible,] Whiskey said as we walked past th swimming pool. [Powerful spiritual entities have bee known to interfere with electronic devices.]

"By accident or on purpose?" I asked.

[Both. But let's be alert; we're still uncertain what th Rainbow Serpent's intentions are.]

We entered the graveyard and almost immediately sa Eli, who flapped his way over to us and landed on hi customary perch, a nearby headstone. "Well, it's abou time. I thought I was going to have to wait all morning."

"Had this little matter of sending a killer to jail," I sai "What's up?"

"What's up," Eli rasped, "is your cat. And what she' up *to* is making trouble. In *my* Crossroads."

I've noticed that when there's a problem he wants me solve, Eli usually refers to the Crossroads as the respons bility of yours truly. When he's genuinely annoyed, thoug ownership reverts to him.

"*My* sweet little kitty?" I said. "Getting up to *no good* Heavens to Betsy."

"Heaven's not where she's headed if she keeps actin like this," Eli growled.

"It can't be that bad," Ben said. "What's she been do ing, using a grave as a litter box?"

"No. She's laying siege to a portal. It's more psycholog ical warfare than anything else, but she needs to stop."

"Which portal?" I asked.

"The one to the snake afterlife."

I frowned. "I'll take care of it."

I pretty much had most of the major portals and thei locations memorized. The one that led to the serpentin paradise was over by the north fence, an unassuming littl brass plaque set flat into the ground. Tango was crouche directly in front of the grave, staring intently into empty air as if she were watching a mouse hole.

The hole she was so focused on only came into existence when someone—a skinny, scaly, legless someone—wanted to use it. Then a white oval opened in the earth, looking a lot like an eye, and a bright orange snake slithered out.

Well, attempted to, anyway. I'm pretty sure it wasn't expecting the black-and-white streak that pounced on its head with both paws. Those paws passed harmlessly through its immaterial body, true, but the experience still must have been disconcerting. The snake reacted by wriggling violently away, which led to a prolonged pouncing attack by Tango, who looked just about exactly like a cat trying to catch the little red dot of a laser pointer.

<Ha! Gotcha! Gotcha! Gotcha again! And again! Where'd you—there! Gotcha! There's no escape! Gotcha again! You can't get—gotcha! Okay, you can go.> She stopped and abruptly began licking her paw. The snake had already disappeared into a clump of grass, no doubt extremely confused and more than a little traumatized. *What, I left heaven for this? I could be digesting a woodchuck right now!*

"Tango," I said. "What in the world do you think you're doing?"

<Confronting my fears. And seeing if I could get a certain oversized reptile to notice me.>

[How terribly feline. When in doubt, terrorize something.]

I shook my head. "Tango, you can't just scare the crap out of a bunch of dead snakes as a form of therapy, or to attract the attention of a gigantic, weather-controlling Australian—wait, did I remember to bring my notebook with me? No, I left it in the office."

"She's right," said Ben. "As usual. Fear isn't a great tool. Has a tendency to backfire on you, for one thing."

<Please. I'm not trying to inspire *fear, I'm trying to fight*

it. Successfully, I might add—did you see how I took o *that boa? Wham, pow, wham again!>*

[Yes, truly courageous. Perhaps you could work you way up to battling dead iguanas, or possibly live worms.

<You're just envious of my superior strategy. Soone or later, one of those snakes is gonna go running to Daddy and when he shows up—>

"Yes?" I said. "When he shows up, what then?"

<Then we'll take care of it. Come on, this is our home turf; nobody pushes us around in here.>

Whiskey made a gruff little noise that I knew from prio experience was the equivalent of him clearing his throat [If I may? There are two major flaws with your "strategy," as you refer to it. First, snakes are not known for thei strong family ties, so it's unlikely any of them will "go run ning to Daddy." Second . . .]

<Yeah? Go on, spit it out.>

[I can't. I thought it was possible to sum up the many many problems involved with luring an immensely pow erful supernatural entity via unprovoked assault on othe members of its species in a single, pithy statement, but find the task is beyond me. I shall be forced to wait unti the disastrous aftermath of the inevitable apocalypse, and then say: "My second point? *This*."]

<Oh, please. I'm not doing any real harm to the little reptiles, so there's no reason for Snakezilla to get too up set. They get a scare, the Big Slither shows up, we take care of business. It's all good.>

[It is not "all good." Very few parts are even somewha good—]

KRAKKABOOOOM!

Thunder. Very close, very loud. Ben's head snapped in the direction of the explosion, and then he was sprinting toward it. Whiskey, Tango, and I were right behind him.

We crested a rise and skidded to a stop. Below us, in a

shallow valley between two gentle, grave-studded hills, were Teresa Firstcharger and the Rainbow Serpent. It was rearing up like a cobra, and she was standing her ground and hurling lightning bolts at it.

The lightning didn't seem to be doing much more than bouncing off the thing's brilliantly colored scales. In fact, the snake didn't seem to be all that upset, though it's hard (unless said snake comes with a rattle on its tail or a spreadable hood) to read a snake's emotional state.

Mostly it was just staring down at Teresa, its tongue flickering out of its mouth in her direction. Maybe it was trying to figure out how tasty she'd be.

I glanced over at Ben, who looked like he was about to leap into the fray but had no idea what to do. "Lightning's not working," I said. "Cold might be a better approach."

He grinned at me. "Cold-blooded opponent, right. Let's just turn down the thermostat . . ."

He reached toward the sky with one hand, his fingers outstretched like he was trying to grab on to something, and a frigid wind blew in from nowhere. The clouds overhead turned slate gray, and within seconds heavy white flakes were tumbling through the air.

I looked around. Where was Eli? One misbehaving kitty and he's on my back, but a huge carnivorous snake appears and he's nowhere to be found? I really hoped the serpent hadn't started with a little crow appetizer before the main course . . .

The snow seemed to be confusing it, at least. It lowered its head and studied Teresa face-to-face. It was close enough now that one swift strike would put her down its gullet, and that combined with the complete ineffectiveness of her lightning was enough to unnerve her.

She transformed.

I've seen Whiskey shift into other forms and even seen Teresa change from bird to human, so I should have been

prepared—but there's something very different abou
watching someone go from human to not. It was deeply
disturbing, bothering me on some atavistic level; as feath
ers sprouted from her skin and her face reshaped itself into
a huge, cruel beak, I wasn't so much fascinated as trans
fixed. *That's what your boyfriend can do,* a part of my
brain was yelling at me. *That! Right there!*

Except he couldn't, not yet. Maybe that was one of
the very first lessons she'd planned to teach him—
Metamorphosis 101—but since he hadn't actually attended
any classes yet and the teacher was in danger of being
eaten, it was sort of up in the air as to whether or not Ben
would ever get to be—well, up in the air.

She launched herself skyward with a tremendous beat of
her enormous wings. The serpent had more than enough
time to snatch her in mid-flight.

But it didn't. In seconds she was out of its reach, and it
barely seemed to notice. Its head swiveled around as it
tasted the air, looking almost like a kid trying to catch
snowflakes on its flickering tongue.

When it spotted Ben, it froze.

But only for an instant. It lunged in his direction, and
all I had time to do was scream. (I didn't, though. Not really much of a screamer.)

It stopped directly in front of him, face-to-face like it
had with Teresa, its tongue flicking in and out even faster.
Oh, this wasn't good—

And then something large and hairy launched itself past
Ben and at the serpent: Whiskey, in his natural (well, pre-
death, anyway) form. It looked a bit like a cross between a
bear, a wolf, and a wolverine, weighed in the neighborhood
of three hundred pounds, and had jaws that would make
a hydraulic press weep with envy. Those jaws fastened themselves on the snake's throat—to be fair, a snake is mostly
throat—and held on while Whiskey emitted a combination

snarl-and-growl that reminded me of a chain saw having a hissy fit.

It provoked a reaction, anyway: The snake reared up, its mouth opening in surprise or anger, while Whiskey hung on grimly and tried to worry it like a rat.

His attempt fell far short of worrying though, barely reaching mild concern. Whiskey himself fell considerably farther, as the creature whipped its body around and sent him flying through the air at a height of thirty feet off the ground. He disappeared over the crest of the hill, one of the snake's iridescent scales still clamped in his jaws.

Ben took advantage of the respite to whip the freezing wind into a frenzy—a spinning, funnel-cloud frenzy. I didn't know if even a tornado would be strong enough to stop this thing, but it was probably his best idea so far—

And that's when it ate him.

No, you didn't read that wrong.

It ate Ben. Whole.

That massive, rainbow-hued head darted down, jaws wide open, and snapped shut around Ben's body. The head tilted skyward again, Ben's feet sticking out from between its scaly lips, and then the snake gulped them inside its maw, too. It reminded me of a duck eating a grasshopper. It was probably my imagination, but I thought I saw the serpent's throat bulge as it swallowed.

I didn't just see that. That didn't happen. It's a trick. Any second now Ben's going to blast his way free from the thing's gullet with a lightning bolt, and—

And lightning didn't work on the Rainbow Serpent.

—and then he'll use a blizzard to freeze it into a giant ice sculpture and we'll zoom down it like one of those twisty slides and—

The wind died down. The air began to warm noticeably, creeping back toward a more seasonal temperature.

—and we'll celebrate with omelets, his omelets are se
good, and I'll make bad jokes about snake eggs and Whis
key will be droll and Tango will be snarky—

<*Foxtrot. We have to get out of here. NOW.*>

The snake lowered its head. It was looking at me now
but I wasn't worried. Snakes can go a long time withou
eating after a big meal, so I doubted it was very hungry
Because, you know, it had just eaten my boyfriend.

A bird of prey screamed somewhere above me, and I
saw the shadow of huge wings pass along the ground and
over the snake's body. Teresa, circling overhead, just as
helpless as I was.

Normally, in a crisis situation, I become incredibly efficient. I can make snap decisions on almost no information, I can multitask, I can be analytical and objective and
maintain my concentration even while others are running
around on fire. But not this time; this time was different.
Part of me was in shock, locked in some kind of denial
fantasy, while another part seemed completely removed
from what had just happened. It's called compartmental-
ization, and until now I'd always been able to make it work
for me.

What finally got me unstuck was that neither of those
parts seemed inclined to *do* anything, and immobility is
just completely contrary to who I am.

So I spoke up.

"Hey," I said. "You. Technicolor-prehistoric-anaconda-
monster. I don't know exactly what you are or what you
want, but you can't just roam around *eating* people."

<*Foxtrot, this isn't going to solve anything. We have to
go, before it—*>

"Do you have any idea what you've done? He wasn't a
snack, he was a person. His name was Ben Montain, and
he was an incredible chef and an amazing kisser, and he

was stubborn and generous and proud and kind *and I loved him!*"

I'm not much of a screamer, but I'm a terrific shouter. I don't do it very often, because I consider it to be a failure on my part to stay in control. I was shouting now. And weeping.

"He was a *good* man! He laughed at my jokes! He *listened* to me! I don't care if he could call up hurricanes or make it rain toads or any of that! *You give him back, goddammit!*"

The snake looked at me quizzically. You know how I could tell? It tilted its head to one side, ever so slightly. According to Tango, that's pretty much universal body language for "Huh?"

A greyhound came tearing over the hill. Whiskey, of course. I hadn't even been worried about him; I knew he would have shifted into a much smaller form to minimize impact before he hit the ground, and that his ectoplasmic body would be able to take the shock. [Foxtrot! Where's— oh, no.]

Funny thing about how my mind works. It pretty much never stops; I make plans while I'm showering, think about options while I'm on the toilet, make lists in my dreams. And even now, shattered by grief and rage and despair, I was still thinking. Not only about what just happened, but what *wasn't* happening.

"Why are you still *here*?" I demanded. "You've gotten what you came for, haven't you? And it was *Ben* you came for—you didn't eat me when you had the chance, or even Teresa. If you followed Anna all the way here, you probably could have eaten her, too—but you didn't. Why not?"

I didn't really expect an answer. It hadn't replied to any of my questions yet, so why should it now? But when I heard a dry, sibilant chuckle inside my skull, there was no doubt where it came from.

{No need. Femalesss ripen on their own. Malessss need sssome help.}

Help?

A distant part of my brain was tugging at my medulla oblongata, trying to get my attention. I'd uncovered a lot of material on giant mythical snakes when I was doing my research, but I'd focused on horned serpents because I thought we were dealing with a monster. But while the Unktehila was basically a predator, the Rainbow Serpent was much, much more. It could be angry and vengeful, but it was mostly a symbol of life. And on the long list of things it was supposed to have created and events it was responsible for, there'd been something about men. Young men. And some sort of . . . ritual?

No. Not ritual. *Rite.* Rite of passage.

Please. Please, please please let me be right—

The Rainbow Serpent reared up once more. It looked down at me. It opened its mouth, revealing fangs that were shorter than I thought they'd be.

And then it threw up.

What landed at my feet wasn't human. It was a big brown ball of slime-covered fur.

<Snakes hack up hairballs?>

[That's not hair, Tango.]

"No," I said. "Those are *feathers.*"

Teresa Firstcharger came in for a landing, large wings flapping like bedsheets in the wind. She took a step closer on talons that look like they could rend steel, and tilted her head curiously at the quivering bundle of gooey feathers on the ground.

The bundle stirred, then unfolded itself into another Thunderbird. It looked a little dazed, blinking its large yellow eyes like it was unaccustomed to light.

"Ben," I breathed.

"Foxtrot?" The voice coming out of his beak sounded exactly like Ben's normal one. "I've—I've got feathers. I'm covered in feathers."

<*And snake vomit,*> Tango added helpfully.

"Yeah. You know that transforming thing that Teresa does that you hadn't figured out yet? Well, turns out the Rainbow Serpent decided to give you a little assistance."

"Assistance? It *ate* me!"

"Remember all those things I listed off that are associated with the Rainbow Serpent? Fertility was one of them. You might think that a snake would obviously be some sort of phallic metaphor, but not Down Under—they see it as more of a feminine thing. Being swallowed and then regurgitated is a symbol for rebirth, something young aboriginal males undergo as a rite of passage into manhood."

[The passage in this case being the snake's esophagus,] Whiskey said helpfully.

"Congratulations," I said. "You're a man! I mean bird. Bird-man. Man Bird?"

Ben extended one wing and looked at it in amazement. The slime on his feathers was evaporating in the sun, leaving a glossy shine behind.

Teresa Firstcharger studied him. "It's true," she said. "You have matured. I can feel it."

Ben extended both his wings and gave them an experimental flap. "I can, too! This—this feels perfectly natural. In fact—"

And then he launched himself into the air.

"Waaaaahoooo!" he yelled. He soared up to around thirty feet, then went into a long, lazy circle around us and the serpent, which was watching this whole spectacle with a smug grin on its face. Okay, maybe that was projection on my part.

I looked over at Teresa. "Well? Why aren't you up there with him? I thought you were his instructor."

She looked at me for a moment with those large, yellow eyes, and then she transformed back into her human shape. Naked, of course. "Then I have your blessing?"

I shrugged. "I have no problem with letting professionals do what they do best. He may have learned the shape-shifting trick, but I'm sure there's still a few things you could teach him. Just try to keep the naked thing to a minimum, all right?"

She nodded. "Thank you, Foxtrot. I promise you, I will impart to him as much wisdom as I can." She paused. "With my clothes on."

And then she shifted back to avian form and took off after him. They soared into the sky, got smaller and smaller, and then disappeared entirely. Off to Thunder-space, I guess.

I turned to the giant snake. "He's going to be able to change back, right?"

{Yessss.}

"Okay, just checking. I mean, I like birds and all, but that's not what I want to snuggle up to while watching a romcom and snarfing back popcorn. Plus, he's going to have a heck of a time making waffles like that."

That was the total extent of the words I exchanged with the Rainbowed One. Twelve in all. Despite how they're often portrayed in popular media, snakes aren't all that talkative. Maybe things would have been different if I'd been hanging around an apple tree.

He didn't even say good-bye, just slithered off into the sunset. And by sunset I mean sort of northeast, toward the statue of the horse, but more to the left, kinda.

Eli flapped up and landed on a headstone. I wondered if I should knit him some sort of grave-cozy, so his little white crow-claws wouldn't be cold on the stone. Too bad I didn't knit.

"Well," said Eli.

"Sideways it's a tunnel," I replied absently. I was still staring after the disappearing giant snake.

"What?"

<*A well. Turn it sideways and—*>

"Is that supposed to be relevant?" Eli sounded a little peeved.

"Just an observation," I said. "Like, *Hey, you didn't get eaten by a huge snake.*"

"So you're just stating the obvious?"

"Is that a rhetorical question?"

"Obviously."

There was no reply to that, so I didn't make one. After a moment, Eli cleared his throat and said, "So."

"A needle pulling thread."

"What's—will you please stop doing that?"

"Eventually. When I get tired of tormenting you."

He flapped his way from one headstone to another. "Why would you want to torment me? And no, that isn't a rhetorical question."

"Ask Whiskey."

Whiskey and Tango had been observing this exchange mostly in silence.

"Well, Whiskey?" asked Eli. "And try not to reference tunnels or embroidery in your reply."

[She was worried about you. Her initial thought when the serpent appeared and you were absent was that it had devoured you. Now that she knows it did not, she assumes that not only were you never in any danger, but you deliberately stayed away in order to let events progress to their inevitable conclusion.]

<*You forgot to mention how pissed she is for you letting*

her think her boyfriend was on a one-way trip through a
snake's digestive system.>

[I thought we were done with stating the obvious.]

"I'm sorry," said Eli, "but I couldn't interfere. These things have certain protocols."

"A simple heads-up would have been nice."

"You might have warned him. And if we're going to have a Thunderbird on our side, I prefer one at the height of his abilities. So to speak."

I sighed. "Yeah, fine. I get it, I do. So where's the Big S off to? Are we adding him to the roster of entities that like to hang around the Great Crossroads?"

"No, she's strictly a tourist. On her way back to Australia via the Dreamtime, I expect. Or maybe she'll take the scenic route and swim the Atlantic. I doubt she's in any hurry."

I stretched and yawned. Only halfway through the day, and already I was exhausted. Time for more Irish breakfast tea, and possibly an intravenous drip to deliver it. "Okay, I guess that about wraps things up. Shame about Anna, but things more or less turned out all right. The Big Bad even turned out to be a good guy—er, gal—instead of a shape-shifting mind-controlling monster."

Tango gave her furry head a shake. *<Yeah, thank Bast. Snakes still give me the creeps, but an Unktehila sounded way worse.>*

"They are," said Eli. "Why do you think I wanted Ben in full control of his powers?"

Whiskey, Tango, and I stared at him. He didn't say anything else, just took to the air and flew off.

<Was that a rhetorical question?> asked Tango.

[I don't think so,] said Whiskey. [Remember that heads-up Foxtrot said would be nice? I think we just got one . . .]

I shrugged. "Or maybe it's just payback for me tormenting him. Either way, it doesn't matter. We're here, we're together, Ben is fine, the killer's in jail and it's a sunny, sunny day. Let's try to enjoy it, all right?"

But there was one last thing to take care of. Well, two, actually, but in a way they were kind of the same thing. It happened a few days later, after Ben had survived his first few lessons with Teresa and the guests had finally said their good-byes and the estate was back to what passes for normal around here.

Ben still hadn't spoken to ZZ.

He'd made her breakfast, lunch, and dinner, and she'd eaten it. It had all been up to his usual standards, and she seemed perfectly satisfied.

But.

The atmosphere was different. There were things that needed to be said, on both sides, and neither one seemed to know how to say them. So I decided to take matters into my own hands.

"Okay, this is ridiculous," Ben said as he took another slow, careful step forward—slow and careful because he was blindfolded and I was leading him. "I know I did this to you on our first date, but—"

"No buts, mister. All right, you can take the blindfold off."

He did so, saying, "What's the big surprise? I really hope you're naked—"

"Hello, Ben," ZZ said.

Ben stared at his boss. She looked back with eyes full of regret.

"Hello," Ben said. "Um." He looked around and saw where he was for the first time: in the graveyard, beside a brand-new headstone and the freshly turned earth of a new plot. "Well, this isn't what I expected. Why are we—oh." He'd finally noticed the name on the headstone: MARBLES.

"It's never too late to do the right thing," ZZ said. "That's what I believe, anyway. It was Cooper's idea to put this headstone up, even though the grave is empty. Foxtrot got in touch with Marbles's former owner and told her we'd finally located the grave she'd been looking for. Do you know what she said?"

"I have no idea," Ben said.

"She told me," I said, "that she already knew that. She had a dream with a white crow in it, and he told her she was finally going to be able to say good-bye. In fact, I think I see them now." I pointed. Two women came slowly over the hill, one dressed all in black. Mary and her caretaker.

Mary walked right up to the grave, more or less ignoring us. She reached into the black purse she carried and pulled out a small, very worn bag made of scraps of cloth sewn together.

A large white crow flapped its way over to a nearby gravestone. ZZ didn't see it, of course, and the rest of us pretended not to.

Mary carefully opened the drawstring of the bag. Then she upended it on the grave, spilling out dozens of brightly colored, highly polished marbles. They glinted in the bright sunshine like precious jewels.

"There," Mary said. "Now you can play with these in heaven. I miss you, but the crow said you are happy. I'm not so sad now. Good-bye."

Then she looked up, her face composed and serene, and looked directly at Eli. "Thank you," she said.

"You're welcome," Eli said.

At my feet, Whiskey whined, very softly. Tango, a few feet away and sitting on another grave, meowed once. They didn't say anything else, and they didn't have to.

Mary turned and walked away, her head held high. Her caretaker, after giving us a smile and a nod, walked after her.

"I'm sorry I hurt you," ZZ said to Ben. "But I'm not sorry I hired you. You're the best damn chef I've ever encountered, and if and when you decide to move on, I will trumpet that fact to anyone who asks and many who don't."

"Apology accepted," Ben said. "Sometimes life just pushes us into corners and we have to do our best. Can't fault you for that."

<Sure you could,> Tango pointed out. *<But I wouldn't.>*

[Yes, you would.]

<Okay, so I would. But I'm a cat.>

[Must you remind me? I'd almost convinced myself you were some kind of horrible hallucination on my part.]

I looked around at them my crazy, extended, dysfunctional family: ZZ, Ben, Tango, Whiskey, even Eli. I'd love them till the end.

And even after that.

Don't miss these other novels in
Dixie Lyle's Whiskey, Tango & Foxtrot series!

"Blends pet cemeteries, animal spirits, and
a cast of zany human characters . . . those who read
paranormal mysteries will enjoy."
—*RT Book Reviews*

A TASTE FUR MURDER

TO DIE FUR

Available from St. Martin's Paperbacks